THE MAR

Anne Herries was ... up in Hastings and Ely. At eighteen she married, and ran her own business before moving to Cambridge, where she began to write. She now does so full time, and is the author of many successful novels and short stories. Anne Herries and her husband divide their time between Spain and their home in Cambridge.

ANNE HERRIES

The Marriage Chests

HarperCollins*Publishers*

HarperCollins*Publishers*
77–85 Fulham Palace Road,
Hammersmith, London W6 8JB

A Paperback Original 1993
1   3   5   7   9   8   6   4   2

A catalogue record for this book is
available from the British Library

ISBN 0 00 647283 4

Set in Meridien

Printed in England by Clays Ltd, St Ives plc

For my friend Judith Murdoch,
who has helped me so much

PROLOGUE

There were moments when Adam Blackwell thought of taking a violent revenge, moments when the rage inside made him want to strike out in anger. Sometimes the bitterness was so thick in his throat that he almost choked. A younger Adam might have acted instinctively and thrown caution to the winds, but the man was wiser. His turn would come, for now he had work to do: a commission that held a special meaning for him.

Adam laid out his design on the layers of different coloured woods, cutting skilfully so that the pattern would be delicate and pretty, exactly what was required for a marriage chest. When the pieces of wood were cut and ready, they would be glued to a sheet of paper and then applied to the drawer fronts of the travelling cabinet he was making for Miss Susanna Warwick. There were to be two matching chests, one for Miss Warwick herself and the other for the man she was to marry.

Adam's face was grim as he worked and his body was stiff and sore from the beating he had been given, a beating he would never forget. Sweat stood out on his brow as he bent over his bench, and he knew that his mother was right: he ought to have stayed in bed for a few more days. Only Adam's pride and stubbornness were keeping him on his feet. The bitterness stirred in him, eating at his insides. He was going to finish this damned chest if it was the last thing he did! He was going to show the Warwicks he was a man to be reckoned with, and that his talent as a cabinet-maker could not be denied. Ambition burned brightly in his heart. One day he was going to be as rich and famous as the best cabinet-maker in London

1

and then ... Adam's thoughts were interrupted as his father spoke.

'I'll be back in a moment,' Thomas Blackwell said. 'I want a word with your mother.'

As his father went through to the back kitchen, Adam took a scrap of paper from inside his shirt, folded it very small and popped it into the secret compartment he had concealed behind one of the marquetry drawers. It might be that Susanna Warwick would never find it, but if she did she would know why he had chosen to add a tiny broken heart to his design. It would ensure that every time she looked at her marriage chest, she would remember the man who had made it for her ...

CHAPTER ONE

It was the summer of 1766, and Susanna was fourteen years old. Half woman, half child, she was a complete innocent that day she set out to search for her dog, Sultan, her head full of childish stories and dreams. Four years younger than her brother Stephen and two years older than her sister Beatrice, she avoided their company whenever possible. She would not have dreamt of asking either of them to help her in her search. Stephen would probably have done his best to thwart her escape and Beatrice would certainly have gone running to their mother.

It was very warm, with only the droning of bees and the song of the blackbird to disturb the soft, hazy stillness of the morning as the girl slipped quietly away from her home, her one thought at that moment to find her beloved pet. The dog was a huge grey wolfhound that usually followed Susanna wherever she went, but for three days now it had been missing. She had cried herself to sleep every night, needing the comfort of her faithful companion at the foot of her bed. Then, that very morning, she had happened to overhear a conversation between her mother and father.

"The dog has probably been taken by gipsies," Lady Patricia Warwick observed, unaware of Susanna listening wide-eyed in the hall outside her mother's dressing-room. "And good riddance as far as I'm concerned. It was a nasty, smelly brute and the maids were all terrified of it."

"Nay, Patricia, it wasn't that bad," Sir William replied in a softer tone. "And the girl does love it so."

"Well, don't look at me like that," Lady Patricia snapped. "I have not had the wretched creature put down, so don't imply it."

"I've been thinking it may have wandered off to the woods," her husband replied reflectively. "It could have been caught in a trap. Beech said that the poachers had been at work again recently."

"Then you had better find it and put the poor creature out of its misery," Patricia Warwick said. "If its leg has been broken it will be savage by now and fit for nothing else."

"Yes, exactly what I was thinking," Sir William replied. "If it is badly injured the kindest thing may be to shoot it."

Susanna drew back, clapping a hand over her mouth to stop herself crying out. They were going to kill Sultan! They were going to murder her dog! She was filled with a terrible rage. How could her mother talk about Sultan like that? How could her father agree that he should be put out of his misery?

Without stopping to think, Susanna ran from the house. If it had been anything else, she would have wept and pleaded with her father, knowing that he would more than likely give in to her rather than see her miserable. Susanna was aware that her father spoilt her. She was his favourite child, though he tried not to show it, and she could usually twist him around her dainty little finger. But Sultan's fate was too important to be risked. She knew that she must find the dog and rescue him herself, before anyone else could kill him.

The woods were at the edge of the Warwick estate, lying between the park and the village of Chorley Hale, which was itself some twenty or thirty miles distant as the crow flies from Norwich, the city that had flourished from the Middle Ages because of its thriving wool trade. Chorley Hale had belonged to the Warwick family from the time of the Conqueror and had in its time been a prosperous area, with many rich farms and large houses in the district. In later years some of its prosperity had faded away, and now it was a sleepy little place with a church, blacksmith and one inn instead of the three that had flourished when the wool trade was at its height. The woods had been planted by some long dead Warwick and were vast, stretching away as far as the eye could see.

4

Susanna had been forbidden to go there alone. It was too dangerous, her mother said. Gipsies camped there sometimes, and there was no love lost between them and the Squire, whose bailiff often drove them away with shots and curses. The bailiff had also set cruel man-traps in the undergrowth to frighten away the poachers who preyed on Sir William's game. Lady Patricia said the gipsies would kidnap Susanna and take her away to make pegs and tell fortunes. Sometimes Susanna thought it might be exciting to be carried off by the gipsies, imagining she would enjoy travelling all over the country, telling fortunes and sleeping under the stars.

She was dressed that morning in a gown of dark green wool, with a collar of satin and lace, and her pale yellow hair was curled into long ringlets that bounced on her shoulders as she ran. The gardeners at work in the formal borders hardly lifted their eyes as she hurried by. Mistress Susanna was still a tomboy despite the blossoming of her lovely young body, forever escaping her nurse's regime to be off riding her pony or playing hide and seek in the grounds with her sister Beatrice. No one took any notice as she slipped away through the park, nor would she be missed until it began to grow dark.

"Sultan . . . Where are you, boy? Can't you hear me calling you?" Susanna's voice was growing hoarse. She had been searching all day and she was close to tears. "Oh, Sultan, where are you?"

At first it had seemed a great adventure. It was fun to be in the woods, especially as it was her first time alone. When she went to the village, she always took the short cut, riding across the meadows with her groom. Only once before had she been in the woods with her father and brother, when they were shooting rabbits, and that had upset her. She had hated to see the way the poor things twitched before they died. It had made her cry, and Stephen laughed, calling her a baby. After that, she hadn't really wanted to visit the woods. Now, however, she discovered she liked the smell

5

of the bracken and the silence that seemed to enfold her. She could hear noises . . . the piping of a little blue bird as it fluttered in the branches above her head . . . the sound of a squirrel searching amongst the leaves for fallen cones or seeds . . . the grunting of some animal in the undergrowth. An animal too shy or nervous to show itself.

But there was no sign of Sultan. Susanna had walked and walked all day, until her feet hurt inside her black, laced boots, and now she was hungry and tired. The tears were pricking behind her eyes, but she was determined not to cry. She wasn't a child. Her mother was always telling her that she was a young lady now, and it was time she grew up. Besides, it had been her idea to come.

The fact that she was lost had been gradually dawning on her for a while, but she would not admit it. The woods couldn't go on forever; they had to end somewhere. All she had to do was find her dog and then they could both go home.

"Oh, Sultan," she whispered chokily. "It's getting dark and I'm afraid of the dark . . . Sultan, where are you?"

Susanna ran towards the sound of barking. That was Sultan, she would know his bark anywhere! Her pulses raced as she saw that she had come upon a large clearing, in which several caravans were gathered. The gipsies had tethered their horses and dogs near the brightly coloured covered waggons, where there were small cooking fires with women tending the heavy iron black pots. Several children were playing in the clearing, and an old man was sitting on the steps of his waggon, smoking a clay pipe.

Suddenly, Susanna saw the huge dog tied up behind one of the waggons and let out a scream of delight. It was her dog! Without thinking, she ran towards him, oblivious of the startled looks of the gipsies as she appeared out of nowhere.

"Sultan . . . oh, Sultan darling!" she cried. "I've found you. I've found you at last."

"'Ere – wot do you think you're doing?"

A young gipsy boy of fifteen or sixteen had moved to block her path as she tried to reach the dog. Susanna stared up at him imperiously, her eyes flashing with temper.

"Pray stand aside," she said. "I want to untie my dog."

"Your dog?" The gipsy boy looked at her angrily, his dark eyes as defiant as hers. "He's mine. You jest leave him be."

His hand shot out, catching her wrist, his dirty, clawlike fingers digging into her flesh and hurting her. His dark face was full of menace, as if he meant to harm her. Unused to such rough handling, Susanna felt a ripple of fear, remembering all the warnings her mother had given her.

"Let me go, you dirty gipsy," she yelled, anger almost overcoming the fear. "Don't you dare try to stop me getting my dog."

She struggled wildly, biting and scratching in a sudden fury, her screams echoing in the clearing and bringing the other gipsies out of their waggons.

At eighteen, Adam Blackwell was exceptionally tall and well-formed. Stronger than most of his contemporaries, he was the champion of many a wrestling match at the midsummer fair. Black-haired, he had serious grey eyes set beneath a determined brow, a face that was pleasant rather than handsome, and long, capable fingers that were often stained with dyes or polish from working at his trade as an apprentice carpenter. He had spent the day engaged in coppice work, gathering small timber that sprouted from the cut-down trunks of larger trees. These poles were used by chair bodgers and the task was specialized and time-consuming. Adam had worked hard and was ready for his supper as he drove his waggon along the well-worn woodland path.

Hearing the terrified screams, he pulled sharply on the reins, listening intently. They had come from somewhere to his right. Now he could hear a dog barking wildly and loud voices. It was probably the gipsies he had glimpsed earlier that day when he passed their encampment, he thought, and was about to drive on when he heard the screaming start again.

That seemed like more than just a normal quarrel. It was a young woman by the sound of it. Knowing that he was a fool to interfere in something that did not concern him, he tethered his horse to a low-hanging branch and went in search of whoever was making that appalling noise.

The scene that met his eyes as he entered the clearing was one of utter confusion. A small cluster of gipsy caravans had gathered around a patch of open ground, and several old men, women and children had gathered to watch what was going on. In the middle of the clearing a gipsy youth was attempting to subdue a very angry young woman, who by the look of her clothes was obviously the daughter of gentry.

"He belongs to me!" the girl yelled, kicking and beating with her fists at the youth who was stronger and older than her. Despite his size, he was having difficulty in holding her off and he yelped as several of her blows struck home.

"Sez you," he taunted. "I found 'im caught in a trap, so I did. Look at where he nipped me when I got 'im free." The gipsy boy showed her the teeth marks on his dirty hand. "Died he would 'ave, if I hadn't a found 'im – so that makes 'im mine."

"He's mine," Susanna cried, pointing at the dog who was tied up behind one of the brightly painted caravans and furiously straining at his leash in an attempt to get to her. "Look at him. You can see he wants to come to me. Sultan . . . here, boy!"

"He's mine, I tell you," the gipsy boy said, ducking as she hit out at him again. "You little hellcat. I'm going to teach you not to poke your nose in where 'tain't wanted." He seized a handful of her hair, pulling it hard so that the tears came to her eyes. "You'll get a hidin' if you kick me again."

"I'll tell my father," Susanna cried. "He'll send the bailiff after you."

As Adam watched, a dark-eyed gipsy walked forward. He was perhaps twenty-two or -three, his long hair greasy and tied back off his face with a red handkerchief. He had a scar from the corner of his eye to his mouth, which gave him a villainous appearance. As she saw him, the girl suddenly went still, her face going pale. She was obviously frightened now, even though she still looked defiant and proud.

"And what have we got here?" the man with the scar said, eyeing the girl speculatively. "You've caught a valuable property 'ere, Tam. Squire's daughter, I reckon."

There was a murmur amongst the other gipsies, and a variety of opinions.

"Let her go, Severiano. We don't want no trouble with the Squire."

"Aye, let her go, and the dog."

"Take 'er with us and teach them up at the Hall a lesson. We've got a score or two to settle with Squire and his damned bailiff. She be worth a bit in ransom . . ."

Adam had seen and heard enough. The situation was deteriorating fast. If something wasn't done quickly the girl would be in serious trouble. These gipsies were all right as long as you didn't interfere, but they had nasty tempers and he knew enough of their hatred for the Squire's bailiff to know that his daughter was in danger of being kidnapped and perhaps even of her life. He stepped forward into the clearing so that they were suddenly aware of him.

"That would be most unwise," he said. "Unless you wish to hang for the crime of kidnapping?"

Adam's arrival produced a tense silence. All eyes were turned on him, watchful and resentful. He could see at least three men of about his own age standing on the sidelines and several older men, besides all the women and children. If they attacked him, he would be outnumbered, but he knew that his main opponent was the one they called Severiano. It was at him Adam looked, unafraid.

"And who are you?" Severiano's black eyes glittered in the firelight. "We don't like spies here."

Adam met the challenge of Severiano's gaze with one of his own, daring the gipsy to question his authority. It was something he'd learned in the wrestling ring, a way of out-staring your opponent to establish superiority, and it stood him in good stead now. For several minutes they eyed one another steadily, measuring, assessing, and then Severiano turned away with a curse. He went to where the huge wolfhound was straining at its leash, its teeth bared as it growled and barked savagely. He took a knife from his belt to cut the cord that bound it. Sultan took off like a tornado, hurtling across the clearing to throw himself at his young mistress in an excess of delight.

"I reckon the dog is hers, Tam," Severiano said. He turned his black eyes on Adam. "Take her and go, we don't want no trouble."

Susanna was on her knees, her arms about the dog as she hugged and kissed him, getting her face covered in wet licks in the process. She looked up in surprise as Adam touched her arm.

"Tam rescued your dog," he said. "I think you should say thank you."

Susanna saw the dressing of leaves and moss on the wolfhound's leg. As she looked at the gipsy youth she caught a glimpse of the tears he was struggling to hide, and realized he really loved Sultan, just as she did. She hesitated and then went forward, offering her hand.

"Thank you for rescuing Sultan," she said. "If you hadn't helped him he might have died."

"Ain't no might about it." Tam sniffed, ignoring her outstretched hand and wiping his nose on the sleeve of his ragged shirt.

"You can visit him sometimes," Susanna offered rashly. "I take him for walks in the park every day. You could meet me and make friends with him."

Tam's eyes gleamed, but then he shook his head. "Squire's park ain't no place for us," he muttered. "You take good care of 'im in future. You 'ear me?"

Susanna smiled and placed her hand on the dog's head. "I will, and thank you."

10

"Come on now," Adam said. "Your mother will be worried out of her mind over you. I'd best take you straight up to the Hall."

Susanna looked up, really noticing him for the first time. His eyes looked very serious, almost stern, and she wasn't sure if she liked him or not. Then he smiled and held out his hand to her.

"You can ride with me on the waggon," he said.

"Can Sultan ride too?" Susanna asked. "He's limping."

"So I see." Adam nodded. "Yes, we'll find room for him in the back."

He glanced back towards the gipsy camp. Most of the old men and women had melted away, but Severiano still stood there, his black eyes watching. Adam frowned. He had little doubt of the girl's fate if he had not arrived just when he did. She would not have been the first young girl from the area to disappear when the gipsies went a-wandering . . .

"You wicked girl!" Lady Patricia shrilled, pouncing on her daughter and shaking her. "We have had everyone out searching for you."

"I had to find Sultan," Susanna said. "He had hurt his leg but a gipsy boy looked after him and . . ."

"Haven't I warned you to stay away from the woods? You disobedient girl!" Lady Patricia's hand moved as if she would have hit her daughter, but something about Adam Blackwell stopped her. She looked at him, her thin lips drawing into a hard line. "Go up to your room at once, Susanna."

Susanna stared at her rebelliously. She wasn't a child and she wouldn't be treated as one, she thought, glancing at Adam, as if seeking reassurance. He nodded slightly, which made her feel better. She rather liked the young man who had rescued her from those awful gipsies. Her spirits lifting, she smiled at him and then ran from the room.

"We are grateful to you, Mr Blackwell," Lady Patricia said.

11

"I was glad to be of service, ma'am." Adam did not smile. He had never liked the Squire's wife, thinking her hard-faced and haughty, though Sir William was a decent man and a friend to his own father.

"You should have some reward," Lady Patricia went on. "I shall tell my husband. He will know what is proper."

She frowned in annoyance. The look in his eyes was too proud. He was after all only the son of the local carpenter, but from his manner he appeared to think himself her equal.

Adam felt his cheeks growing warm. She was dismissing him as if he were a servant. The Blackwells might not be rich, but they were freemen from the time of the Conqueror and owned their own house, humble though it might be. Adam's father was a tradesman and they needed no one's charity.

"I need no reward for doing what was right, ma'am."

"Well, you may go now," she said, her manner becoming even more haughty. "Sir William will call to see your father."

Adam inclined his head and walked from the room, his pride ruffled. She was a shrew by all accounts and if rumour were true, no better than she should be. He found himself feeling sorry for her husband – and Susanna.

He left the house and began to walk across the back courtyard to where he had left his waggon. Then, hearing a cry, he turned, waiting as the girl came running towards him, her curls flying.

"Adam," she called breathlessly. "Adam Blackwell!"

"Your mother sent you to your room," he said, frowning at her. "You're not running off again, I hope?"

"No." She smiled shyly up at him. "I came to give you this . . ." She held out her hand.

Adam hesitated, still angry at her mother's dismissive treatment. "What is it?"

Susanna opened her hand. Lying on the palm was a shiny stone that nature had fashioned into a pleasing shape. Oval, smooth and bluish-grey in colour, it looked almost like a duck's egg. It was a child's treasure. Looking at her, Adam realized that she was completely innocent. Almost a woman in form and shape, she was still a child at heart. The realization touched something inside him, and he felt a surge of affection for her. She was like a young kitten, trusting and friendly, nothing like her shrew of a mother.

"I found it once," Susanna said, a touch of anxiety in her voice as she waited for his reaction to her gift. "It's my favourite thing."

A slow, warm smile spread over Adam's face. Unhesitatingly, he took it from her, examined it with proper reverence and then slipped it into his jacket pocket.

"Thank you, Miss Susanna," he said. "I shall keep it always."

Susanna smiled, then turned and ran back towards the house. Laughing, Adam took up the reins and flicked them. His anger had all gone.

"Walk on, boy," he said. "I be fair famished."

"Mama is cross with you," Beatrice taunted as she swung on the bedposts of her sister's bed, her frilly petticoats flying as she twirled. "You could have been kidnapped by the gipsies."

Susanna frowned at her sister, irritated because she knew it was the truth. "Oh, do go away, Bea," she said. "You're only a child. You don't know what you're talking about."

Her pretty young face assumed an expression of superiority, knowing that it would annoy her sister. Beatrice hated being reminded that she was the youngest of the family.

"You had to be rescued by a common carpenter's boy from the village," Bea said, grimacing. "I heard Mama telling Papa. She said it made her feel ashamed to be indebted to a Blackwell."

Susanna looked at her sister uncertainly. She knew that Adam Blackwell was the son of the village carpenter, because she had asked her brother about it. Stephen too had said that the Blackwells were common, but she had liked the young man who'd rescued her. He had a nice smile and he'd treated her as if she were his own age, though there must be at least four years between them.

Susanna's mother was always telling her she should behave like a young lady. Nanny Giles, who had been with the Warwicks for years, scolded her for being a hoyden, but none of them talked to her as if she were a woman. Adam Blackwell had not made the mistake of talking down to her, and his smile had stuck in her mind. Suddenly, Susanna knew that she wanted to see him again. She wanted to discover what he was really like.

"Oh, do go away, Bea," she said again, deliberately taunting. "You belong in the nursery with your nanny. You really are such a baby . . ."

Bea's eyes filled with tears and she glared at her sister angrily. "I hate you," she said, and ran from the room.

Susanna watched her go, feeling a twinge of regret. She really wanted to be friends with her sister, but she was such a jealous little thing and always running to their mother with her tales. It had been necessary to get rid of her before she could carry out her plan . . .

Susanna dismounted from her pony, jumping down with her skirts flying before her groom could assist her. She handed him the reins, and stared at the house in front of her. Situated in the centre of the village, it was a long, low cottage with faded red brick walls and a sloping thatched roof. She could see evidence of a large garden at the back, where hens were clucking. The Blackwells probably had their own small vegetable plot as most of the villagers did, but the house was different from the others in the street. It looked very old, with a welcoming aura, but despite being larger than most of the cottages, it was still rather small by Susanna's standards. Too small, she felt, to house the man who had rescued her from the gipsies. She had imagined him in a house similar to her father's or those of her parents' friends, with rooms for the servants as well as the family. She glanced at her groom, frowning slightly.

"Are you sure this is it?" she asked.

"Yes, Miss Susanna," the groom answered. "I don't know what her ladyship would say about you coming here, though."

Susanna tossed her head. "Oh, she wouldn't mind," she replied blithely.

She stepped up to the door and rapped twice with the black iron knocker. It was two or three minutes before the door was opened and Adam stood there. He stared at her in bewilderment, glancing beyond her to where the groom stood waiting.

"Yes, Miss Warwick?" he asked. "What can I do for you then?"

Susanna smiled beguilingly. "I've come to visit you," she said, her eyes very bright. "Won't you ask me in?"

Adam hesitated. It was a rare honour for the Squire's daughter to come calling, but he doubted that it would please Lady Patricia. He was silent for a moment, then he nodded.

"You'd best come in then," he said, stepping back to let her enter.

Susanna followed him inside, looking round her with interest. They were in the long, low front parlour that Tom Blackwell used as his workshop. It smelt strongly of glue and fresh wood shavings and was littered with the tools of his trade. The only seat was a hard wooden bench by the window.

"You had best come through to the kitchen," Adam said uncertainly. "This is Father's workshop. You would be more comfortable in the back."

"I want to stay here. Please. Please, let me stay."

Her smile was dazzling and the young man blinked. She was certainly a charmer. Even at fourteen she had a way of making your pulses race. Within a year or two she would have every young sprig in the district dancing to her tune,

15

he thought, then told himself not to be a fool. Susanna Warwick was gentry. Between his world and hers was a wide chasm that could not be bridged.

Amused at his own thoughts, Adam nodded. He directed her towards the bench in the window. "Bide you there while I speak with Ma then, and it would be best if you don't touch anything. These tools are sharp; you could cut yourself." He spoke with authority but there was nothing patronizing in his manner.

Susanna nodded meekly, perching obediently on the hard edge of the bench. As soon as Adam had gone through into the back room, she was on her feet again, her curiosity aroused by the tools and half-finished objects around her. Ignoring Adam's instructions not to touch, she picked up anything that took her fancy, turning the wooden spindles of a chairback in her hand to examine the shape of them more closely.

"That be part of a set of chairs for the kitchen up at the Hall," Tom Blackwell said, his voice soft as he entered the workshop from a door at the rear and saw the interest in her pretty young face. In her velvet riding gown and with that pale hair hanging in ringlets down her back, she was a sight for sore eyes, that she was! "Well, now, Miss Susanna, this be a pretty kettle of fish. What happened with that dog of yourn?"

Susanna dimpled, recognizing the indulgent tone of the older man and responding to it with an innocent pleasure. That was just how her father talked to her, when he had a few minutes to spare in her company.

"It was the gipsies," she said, pouting. "They were in the woods and they had poor Sultan tied up behind a caravan. He does so hate to be tied. One of them said that because he had set Sultan free from a trap he belonged to him."

"That be the gipsy way," Tom nodded sagely.

"Dirty, thieving beggars, that be gipsies," Jeanie Blackwell said, bustling in from the kitchen, her square, heavy face flushed from the heat of the oven. "Heaven preserve us

16

from mad dogs and gipsies, for the two go hand in hand, I'll swear to it! 'Tis as well you rescued your dog, miss, or he would have ended up a savage brute."

"Now then, wife," Tom Blackwell said good-humouredly. "The gipsies bain't all bad, and a snarling dog bain't necessarily mad."

"I mind when I was a child, not much older than Miss Susanna," his wife grumbled on, ignoring his comment. "There were an outbreak of biting by mad dogs — bit the baker's wife, they did, and she went round barking and foaming at the mouth until she dropped down dead. I'll be warning our Maggie to stay clear of the woods while gipsies be about."

"Hush, woman, you'll frighten Miss Susanna with your tales."

"I'm not frightened," Susanna said, her eyes bright and wide with curiosity. No one talked to her like this up at the Hall. "Did the baker's wife really bark like a dog?"

"True as I'm standing here," Jeanie Blackwell nodded, her three chins waggling solemnly. "It's as well my Adam was there to save you or you would have been carried off by them gipsies." She looked fondly at her son as he came in from the kitchen, carrying a cup of warm milk sweetened with honey.

"I brought you this," he said, offering it to Susanna. "It's only milk and honey."

Susanna took the thick earthenware mug and retreated to the window seat, perching on the edge and sipping the drink. Tom Blackwell had picked up the wooden spindle she had been looking at earlier and was running it between his fingers.

"What are you doing?" she asked.

"Testing for smoothness," he replied. "These need a mite more shaving, son."

"Yes, Father." Adam nodded, glancing at Susanna, who had just finished her drink. "I'll do it when I've seen Miss Susanna on her way home."

"Do I have to go?" She turned her pretty, pouting face instinctively towards the older man. "Can't I stay, just for a little longer? Please, Mr Blackwell?"

"Don't you want to go home?" He scratched his head, puzzled. He was blowed if he knew what to make of this visit. She had a child's charming manners, but she was almost a woman growed.

"No." Susanna sighed and fluttered her lashes at him artlessly. A born coquette, she had learned how to get her own way with her father long since. "Papa is from home and Mama is always busy with her friends. I've no one to talk to."

It was of course untrue, for Beatrice would have much preferred to be in her sister's company than be sent to the nursery, but Susanna was keen to stay here and talk to these people who amused her with their tales and their funny way of speaking.

"Let her rest here a bit, Adam," Tom said, enchanted by Susanna's smile. The girl had brought the sunshine indoors with her. "She'll come to no harm."

"Provided she doesn't touch anything sharp," Adam remarked gruffly, but no one was listening to him.

Tom Blackwell had picked up a long-handled tool with a heavy metal head that looked rather like a misshapen hoe. His back was bent as he began to work on a piece of solid wood. Susanna moved shyly to his side, standing quietly to watch with an intentness that was rare in her.

"What are you doing?" she asked after a moment or two.

"I'm adzeing the seat of this 'ere chair," Tom replied, not looking up. "This tool be an adze, see, and it gives the seat of the chair a special shape. This 'ere be what folks are pleased to call a Windsor chair."

"You must be very clever," Susanna said admiringly. She had never before seen a craftsman at work and it fascinated her. "The wood is very pretty when you've finished." She ran her hand over the arm of a chair that had been polished to bring out the natural beauty of the wood.

18

Tom nodded, his homely face reflecting his pleasure at her interest. She were a pretty girl, he thought, intelligent and well-mannered. "This be a good bit of elm, Miss Susanna. You see them stretchers there?" He smiled as her eyes turned in the direction he pointed out. "Now they be yew. Some folks use beech, but not Tom Blackwell. Nothing but the best timber will do for my chairs. I make every bit meself. Some folk use a chair bodger for the legs and stretchers, but I were trained to use me own pole lathe as a lad. I can turn a leg with the best of them. Your father, now he's a man of taste, Miss Susanna. He knows a good chair when he sees one."

"A work of art, your chairs, Tom," Jeanie agreed. "Now I'm away to my kitchen, for there's the dumplings to boil and Maggie will be back with the milk at any minute." She smiled at no one in particular and went through the door at the back of the workroom.

After she had gone, Susanna watched Tom Blackwell for a while, then moved to stand by Adam's side. He was using an odd-looking tool that consisted of a shaped wooden back with a straight blade at the front, and he held it in both hands, using a rhythmic motion to smooth slight imperfections in the turned wood of the chair legs. He worked steadily, ignoring her as she shifted from one foot to the other; then after perhaps twenty minutes had passed, he looked up.

"Do you want to go home now?"

Susanna had become aware of hunger. An appetizing aroma was drifting through from the kitchen; her stomach rumbled, reminding her that she had slipped out to go riding without eating her breakfast purposely to cross Nanny Giles. She wondered if she could persuade her new friends to share their meal with her, but the grey eyes were looking at her impatiently and she decided it was time to leave.

"Yes, please," she said meekly, and waited as Adam laid down his cleaning iron and took off the leather apron he was wearing.

19

"I'll see you on your way," Adam said.

"Thank you. You are very kind, Adam Blackwell." Before he could answer, she turned and curtsied gracefully to his father. "Thank you, sir. I have spent an interesting half hour in your workshop. Please – may I visit you again?"

The man looked at her indulgently. Such a dainty miss, and such perfect manners. "Should you wish it, Miss Susanna. You must always be welcome in this house – what say you, Adam?"

"It's your house, Father."

Adam frowned as he led the way outside. He wondered what Lady Patricia Warwick would say to further visits. He shrugged mentally; it was of no real consequence. The girl had been amused for a while, but she would no doubt forget all about the Blackwell family when she returned home.

"Have you seen this, m'dear?" Sir William offered his wife a news-sheet with a scurrilous lampoon of the Earl of Bute and the Princess of Wales. "Amusing, what?"

Sir William's heavily embroidered waistcoat rested precariously on the curve of his generous stomach, topping a pair of mauve breeches that clung a little too tightly to his thick thighs. His powdered hair was curled over his cheeks with a false pig-tail pinned on at the back; his coat had a high collar and large cuffs, braided with gold twist, and his stock was of the finest Brussels lace.

He looked ridiculous standing there before the mantel with that fatuous grin on his face, Lady Patricia thought. He was old before his time, ruined by the pleasures of the table and his passion for fine claret, in which he indulged all too often. She found herself wondering what had induced her to throw away her life by marrying a country squire when she might have done so much better.

Tossing the printed page aside with a frown, she said, "I see little to amuse in John Wilkes's spite. He and that friend of his, Charles Churchill, are dissipated rakes, fit only for

20

company in the Hell-Fire Club or wherever it is men of their stamp meet these days."

"I believe they call themselves the New Franciscans," Sir William murmured. "Their motto is 'Do as you like', as I understand it. Irreverent rogues they may be, m'dear, but Bute is a scoundrel of the first water. There was that iniquitous tax on cider – and now they're saying that he took a bribe for the Peace of Paris." Sir William shook his head. "Pitt would never have given so much away. We had the military advantage, and that fool let his bargaining power slip through his fingers."

"Politics!" Lady Patricia snorted, her thin face contemptuous. "You have been from home more than a month, and all you can talk about is the intrigues of Parliament and the King's favourite. I want to talk to you about Susanna."

"Susanna?" Sir William's bushy brows lifted, his look indulgent. If there were any person other than himself he truly loved, it was his eldest daughter. "Now what has the minx been up to?"

"She has fallen into the habit of visiting the Blackwells." Lady Patricia screwed up her mouth in an expression of distaste. "I have forbidden it, naturally, but I dare say she will disobey me. She pays scant attention to anything either I or Nanny Giles say. You have spoiled her utterly, and she knows she may apply to you for whatever she wants."

"Now, now, m'dear," he muttered uneasily. "The gel is a little high-spirited sometimes to be sure, but . . ."

"I shall not allow my daughter to become intimately acquainted with persons of that order, Warwick!"

Sir William knew that when Patricia called him "Warwick" in that tone, a storm was brewing. He would have to do something about the matter, tiresome as it was.

"Well, you know, Tom Blackwell isn't a bad sort," he began, hurrying on as he saw her eyes flash. "I agree that it won't do to have the gel visiting. Won't do at all, m'dear. I'll ride over in the morning and have a word with Tom."

21

"I suggest you would do more good by taking a strap to your daughter, sir." She saw the horror in his eyes and sighed. "No, I haven't done so, nor shall I – though she tempts me sorely."

Sir William smiled and patted her arm in a friendly gesture. "She's your daughter, ma'am. As I recall, you were a high-stepping filly in your salad days."

Reminded of a foolishness she would rather forget, Lady Patricia blushed and turned aside. William Warwick had been handsome in his youth, and she had been born with an itch between her legs that had led her astray. She recalled the scent of fresh summer grass crushed beneath her as she lay in the meadow, and the passion the young William's kisses had aroused in her loins. For the sake of a few minutes of pleasure, she had squandered her chances of a richer prize – and for what? A husband who snored beside her, while she felt the itch grow ever stronger and was forced to ease it with lovers she would not once have favoured with a second glance.

She would not allow her daughters to make such a fatal mistake. They must marry men of both rank and position. She had decided that they would have everything that had been denied her; real wealth, a substantial house in London besides country estates, important jewels – but most of all, social standing; that was what really mattered to a woman. Love faded, husbands grew fat and tedious, but the power of a renowned hostess remained. William had never lived up to her expectations, but when Susanna married an earl or even – dare she hope for it? – a duke, everything would be different.

Nothing must be allowed to spoil her dream. These visits to the Blackwells were in themselves harmless enough, for Susanna was still very young. Her mother did not fear a foolish romance so much as a genuine attachment to the family as a whole. No one but Lady Patricia must have real influence over the girl. William indulged her, but he was a careless guardian and as time went on his interest would

22

fade. When Susanna no longer threw her arms about him and kissed him, begging to be petted, he would leave her to her mother's care.

Sir William groaned as he dismounted and tethered his horse in the village street. Riding was no longer the pleasure it had once been. He felt a sharp regret for the days of his youth. Had he ever been as strong and fit as Adam Blackwell?

"Good morning, Sir William," Adam said, inclining his head respectfully. "Pa says the chairs will be ready next week as agreed, and Ma asks if you would be pleased to step into the kitchen for a glass of her elderberry wine."

Sir William cleared his throat. This was a deuced awkward business. He was damned if he knew what to say! Patricia made too much of things. If it wasn't for this young man's prompt action, Susanna might have been carried off by those rogues in the wood.

"Tell your mother I shall be pleased to take a glass of wine in the workshop. I want a word with your father."

Adam nodded and led the way inside. He went through to the kitchen at the back, leaving Sir William alone with his father.

"Well, now, Sir William," Tom Blackwell said a little awkwardly. "I should have been pleased to attend on you at the Hall if you'd sent word."

"It suited me purpose to ride this way." Sir William avoided his eyes. It wasn't as if Susanna was of marriageable age – damn Patricia and her scolding tongue! Surely a man could be left in peace in his own home? "How's that son of yours coming along then, Tom?"

"Wonderful well, sir," Tom answered proudly. "You just look at this 'ere apprentice piece he done. Better than I could manage meself."

Sir William examined the miniature chest of drawers, surprised at the exquisite workmanship. Tom Blackwell was a good man for country furniture, and his stick-backed chairs were as fine as you could buy anywhere, but this piece was something more. It was as well executed as something a London cabinet-maker might produce.

"Adam has talent," Sir William said. "Would he make a small chest for me? A piece to fit in an alcove – not more than three feet across."

Tom's face lit up. "It would be an honour for him, Sir William. His first real commission."

"I want quality timber, mind. Something figured with plenty of colour . . ." He broke off, remembering the true reason for his visit. "I was wondering . . . Lady Patricia . . ." He floundered and fell at the first fence. "It's me wife's birthday in two months' time . . ." He couldn't insult the man by refusing to let his daughter visit the house. The Blackwells were a good honest family; Adam had saved the gel's life. Patricia asked too much of him. "I suppose that's too soon to expect . . ."

"Well, it's a tight squeeze," Tom said, frowning. "But if we work on it together, we might have it done."

Sir William nodded, unhappily aware that he had bungled the affair. Patricia would call him a fool, and fool he was, but he'd never been able to ride rough-shod over the feelings of others. He knew that his friends took advantage of his good nature; he was often cheated in business and at the card table, but he could seldom rouse himself to do much about it. He smiled as Jeanie Blackwell brought in a tray with wine and glasses. Fine looking woman, Jeanie. Bit stout now to be sure, but still had that twinkle in her eye. He'd known the time when . . . Giving himself a mental shake, he cleared his throat.

"Your good health, Jeanie. And yours, Tom. How's that gel of yours getting along, then?"

"She's very well, Sir William. Clever too. The vicar's wife has been teaching her to read."

"Excellent." Sir William beamed at Jeanie. "Another glass of your wine, m'dear, and then I must be going."

CHAPTER TWO

Susanna had successfully sneaked away from the watchful eye of Nanny Giles, leaving Beatrice fuming because she had been dragged off to the nursery wing and was even now at work on her sampler, something she hated and avoided whenever she could. Walking across the meadows with the sun on her head, Susanna was feeling very content. She enjoyed visiting her friends the Blackwells, all of whom she had now met.

Maggie was not at all like her brother; a pert, pretty but slightly sulky girl of sixteen, she was the least friendly towards Susanna. Yet even though she sensed something in the older girl's manner, Susanna liked her because she was Adam Blackwell's sister.

Susanna's opinion of Adam had grown higher at each meeting. She liked the way he treated her as a young woman, his serious eyes sparkling with good humour whenever he spoke to his family, and she wished that her brother would be as nice to her. Stephen was quick-tempered like their mother, and dismissive of both his sisters, whom he seemed to consider as nuisances. He would never think of talking to either of them as an equal.

It was as she was nearing the village that Susanna saw the two young men standing together. Her brother and Adam Blackwell. They appeared to be arguing and as she stopped, pausing to watch uncertainly, Stephen pushed Adam as if attempting to start a fight. Adam made no move to retaliate, and in a temper, Stephen turned, mounted the horse he had been holding on its rein and rode off in the opposite direction. Susanna hesitated, but when Adam turned towards the village she called to him to wait. He glanced over his shoulder, seemed undecided, but stood where he was until she caught up with him.

"I was just coming to see you," Susanna said, breathing hard. "Were you arguing with Stephen?"

Adam was silent for a moment, then he nodded. "We had words," he said. "But it's nothing for you to worry your head over."

"Was it about me?" Susanna asked anxiously. "Only if it was, you mustn't take any notice of him. I don't care what he thinks or anyone else. You're my friend . . ." She blushed as Adam's brows lowered. "You saved me from the gipsies and I shall never forget it, Adam Blackwell."

"It was nothing," Adam said, his frown deepening as he looked at her. Her eyes were so clear and open, her smile so genuine. Did she not understand how inviting her manner was? In almost any other girl, he would have thought he was being invited to kiss her. In fact, her mouth was so tempting that it was taking all his strength of will not to do something he knew would be disastrous. "I don't think you should come to visit us so often. It's not wise . . ."

"Adam . . . Adam Blackwell . . ." Susanna caught his arm as he turned to go on. "Please, don't be angry with me because of something Stephen said. Please, I couldn't bear it. I really couldn't . . ."

Her blue eyes were misted with tears. Adam stared at her, something catching at his heart strings. It was wrong of him to take his frustrations out on Susanna. He might hate Stephen Warwick's guts. He might be itching to get the Squire's son in the wrestling ring and show him a thing or two, but the girl had offered him nothing but friendship.

"Please, Adam . . ."

Hearing the note of appeal in her voice, Adam moved towards her, his breath jerky as he tried to control the hammering of his heart. She was so lovely as she stood there looking up at him, her eyes as blue as a summer sky, and he felt an overwhelming desire to hold her and kiss those tears away. She was delicate and precious and he wanted to protect her, to make her mouth curve with laughter and her eyes dance with that hint of mischief he found so tantalizing. She was more woman than child, though in her innocence she was unaware of her power.

"Susanna . . ." he murmured throatily. "Susanna . . ."

For a moment they stared at each other in surprise and awe, aware of some strong feeling between them. Adam had known passion but never this tenderness the young Susanna had aroused in his breast, while Susanna was a stranger to the turmoil she now felt stirring inside her.

"Adam," she whispered, her eyes opening in wonder. "Adam?"

For a moment longer he stared at her, surprised at the force of his own emotions, then he remembered who she was and he drew back, a closed expression coming over his face.

"Excuse me," he said. "I must go. Your father is visiting mine. I came out on an errand of my own . . ."

Susanna watched as Adam strode away across the village green, knowing it would be unwise to follow him when her father was at the Blackwells' house. Besides, she was bewildered and uncertain at the way her heart had begun to pound wildly when he'd looked at her so strangely. What did it mean? Why had she felt so peculiar? Almost as though she wanted . . . She wasn't sure what she had wanted, but she thought it might have been to be held in Adam Blackwell's arms.

Lulled to a feeling of well-being by several glasses of Jeanie's wine, Sir William rode slowly home, relaxing in the warm sunshine. Happening to glance away from the road, across the meadows, he saw two young people. Even from a distance, it was obvious that they were completely unaware of anyone else, with eyes only for each other. For a moment he thought the man was going to embrace the girl and he tensed, knowing that if that happened he would have to do something. But Adam turned and strode off, leaving the girl staring after him.

Sir William realized that his wife had been right. Susanna was becoming too involved with young Blackwell. If nothing was done, it would end in tears, because a match between them was out of the question. Oh, he liked young Blackwell well enough, but even he couldn't accept the idea of his daughter marrying a carpenter's son. His sense of unease returned. He'd done nothing to prevent Susanna's visits to the Blackwell family, and he knew Patricia's sharp tongue would heap scorn on his head the moment he confessed his failure.

Riding home, he mulled over his predicament. It was such an awkward situation. The Blackwells were a pleasant family and he hated the necessity for a rift between them. Why did Susanna have to take it into her head to go looking for that dog? If it hadn't been for the incident with the gipsies, she would never have met Adam.

"Damn it," he muttered as he left his horse to a willing groom and walked a trifle unsteadily towards the front steps. It was all such a nuisance. That little meeting he'd witnessed between Susanna and Adam had been innocent enough. He tried to tell himself no harm would come of it. After all, Susanna was only fourteen. "No harm in the gel visiting Tom. Good man, and Jeanie's a damn fine woman. Fine looking boy . . ."

But Adam Blackwell wasn't a boy, he was a man, and a man with a mind of his own. Susanna might be unawakened as yet, but at fourteen she was on the verge of womanhood, and vulnerable. Sir William knew that he would have to do something – but what? Simply ordering his daughter to stay away from the Blackwells would only make things worse.

It was as he negotiated the steps, which seemed all at once to have grown steeper, that the idea occurred to him. Susanna clearly had some kind of fixation about the young man who had saved her. Natural enough in the circumstances. Remove the object of her admiration and she would soon tire of visiting the Blackwells. Although generally held to be something of a fool, William Warwick was astute enough in his own way, and he understood his daughter's failings. As stubborn as a mule, Susanna was easily bored. Left to herself, she would find other amusements. His idea was in every detail superior to that of his wife, and so much pleasanter all round. Delighted with his own brilliance, he summoned a servant and issued a series of swift commands.

"Have the carriage put to immediately, and tell my valet to pack sufficient for a week or two."

"Yes, sir." The servant turned obediently but was recalled.

"Is your mistress at home?"

"She went out an hour since, sir."

Sir William nodded, relieved at the news. He smiled affably. "You may tell Lady Patricia that I have urgent business in town, Jeffries."

"Yes, sir."

Sir William departed to his library, whistling cheerfully, while Jeffries scurried off to do his bidding and spread the news.

The master off to town when he'd scarcely been in the house a couple of days! Something must be afoot — and the news wouldn't please her ladyship!

Susanna had at last managed to escape the watchful eye of Nanny Giles, who had been especially vigilant for days. Susanna knew it was because her mother didn't want her to visit the Blackwell family, which made her more determined to do so. Since her last meeting with Adam, she had spent many hours thinking about him, wondering what had made her feel so peculiar when he looked at her so oddly. Susanna knew nothing of love or passion, but she had read romantic stories of princesses in towers being rescued by their prince, and had dreamed of the day when her champion would carry her off to a land of dreams.

For the first time, Susanna had begun to think about the reality of love between a man and a woman. In her heart she knew that the stories she loved were just stories. Princes didn't ride around fighting dragons and marrying maidens. They met someone suitable and married according to their position, as she knew she would do one day. Her mother had spoken of it once or twice. Marriage meant looking after a large household, managing servants and . . . and having babies. Yet there must be something more, Susanna thought. Something that made a man look at a woman the way Adam had looked at her.

Was she a woman yet? Susanna wasn't sure. There had been changes in her body recently, some of them pleasant, like the arrival of her small firm breasts, which made her gowns look better, and others that weren't as nice, which one didn't talk about. Susanna wished that there was someone she could ask about such things. She couldn't talk to her mother and Beatrice was younger than her. She longed for an older sister . . . someone like Maggie Blackwell . . .

Maggie was sixteen, just two years older than Susanna. A pretty, lively, intelligent girl, she was forever teasing her brother. Sometimes he cuffed her ear and lectured her for being cheeky, but Susanna had sensed the deep affection between them and she almost envied Maggie. Her own brother was a tormentor who lost no chance to pull her hair or taunt her.

Adam was handsome, tall and strong. Maggie had told Susanna how he could beat every challenger in the wrestling booths that came to Chorley Hale at fair time. Adam blushed and got angry when Maggie told tales, but Susanna loved to hear them. She thought that Adam might be the kind of man she wanted for her husband one day. She was aware that he wasn't rich, but he was clever and brave and she was sure he would make a fortune. If not, she would ask her dear Papa to give him lots of money.

Still wrapped up in her own thoughts, Susanna reached

the village and began to run as Maggie emerged into the street, calling to her to wait.

"I was just coming to visit you," Susanna said. "Is Adam in the workshop?"

"You must have just missed him," Maggie said. "He was sent for up to the Hall."

"Adam was sent for?" Susanna stared at her, wide-eyed. "Who sent for him? Why?"

"It was your father, I expect," Maggie said resentfully. "How should I know? Anyway, that's where he's gone."

"What's wrong?" Susanna asked, sensing her resentment but not understanding it. "Don't you like me, Maggie?"

Susanna stared at her uncertainly, waiting for Maggie to say something, but she didn't answer. Feeling uncomfortable and wondering what she'd done to upset the other girl, she began to run back the way she'd come. If she was lucky, she might meet Adam as he left the Hall.

Maggie stared after her, envying her the pretty blue gown she was wearing. It wasn't fair that the Squire's daughter should have so many dresses, while she had to make do with her old ones. What Maggie wanted more than anything else in the world was a red velvet dress. She wanted it so badly that it was an ache inside her, but she knew that she wasn't likely to get it. Red velvet was very expensive and her father couldn't afford to spend money on luxuries. Besides, he would say that it was a waste. She had nowhere to wear it. Susanna Warwick probably had a dozen pretty dresses to choose from.

Scowling, Maggie turned away. She knew that she'd been unnecessarily rude to the Squire's daughter, but she didn't see why she had to be nice to someone who only came to the house to visit Adam. Before her brother had rescued Susanna Warwick from the gipsies, the girl wouldn't have looked at her twice. So why should she go out of her way to be friendly?

Adam wiped the palms of his hands on the seat of his

breeches. He felt overwarm after his walk and he was nervous. Sir William probably only wanted to talk about that chest of drawers, but still . . . He drew a deep breath and rang the bell at the tradesman's entrance. It was opened by a very grand personage in a black coat and breeches, who peered down his long nose.

"Adam Blackwell to see Sir William. I was sent for."

"Ah yes." Jeffries was disapproving. "The carpenter's boy. Step inside the kitchen while I see if Sir William is at home."

Adam gritted his teeth, realizing that in a battle of words he would be the loser. He clenched his fists and wished passionately that he had Jeffries in the wrestling ring.

"Take no notice of him." A moon-cheeked woman spoke from the washing tub near the scullery fire. "He's in one of his moods."

Adam smiled but said nothing. At home in the workshop he was content with his lot, but at times like these he was vaguely aware of a sense of dissatisfaction.

Jeffries returned, his expression even sourer than before. "Sir William will see you. Please follow me."

His face grim, Adam obeyed. He had always liked the Squire, whose easy manners never varied no matter what his company, but this servant was altogether too proud. He might have been the master for all his airs and graces!

"Blackwell to see you, sir." Jeffries beckoned impatiently as Adam hovered uncertainly on the threshold of a spacious room. "Come along then."

"Come in, Adam."

Sir William's welcoming tones saved Adam from giving vent to his temper. He drew a deep breath and went forward, his boots scraping on the polished floor. He was immediately conscious of the exquisite furniture that stood about the room, and overwhelmed by the desire to touch the surface of a satinwood table. This was the first time he'd been inside the Hall, except for the servants' quarters downstairs, and he was amazed at what he saw. The pictures, the glittering mirrors in their gilt frames, the silver

and porcelain, and the wonderful, wonderful furniture.
Never had Adam realized how exquisite a well made piece
of furniture could be. His father's work was good, but it
didn't compare with the things he could see here. It excited
him and he longed to turn things upside down to examine
the workmanship. He could feel a tingling down his spine
and a desire to know more, but he knew he must be on his
best behaviour. He looked at the Squire, schooling himself
to patience.

"You wanted to see me, sir?"

"You may go, Jeffries." Sir William dismissed the servant.
"Don't stand on ceremony, Adam. Come, take a glass of
madeira with me and tell me what you think of it."

Adam wiped his hands on his breeches before accepting the
delicate glass. He sipped the liquid, finding it strangely bitter
after the sweetness of his mother's homemade wines, but his
expression gave nothing away as he said, "It's very good, sir."

"You would prefer cider I dare say – if Bute hadn't levied
that ridiculous tax." He set his glass down and looked at
Adam. "I've news for you. Important news."

Adam blinked, withdrawing his eyes reluctantly from a
pair of fine cabinets he had spotted at the far end of the
room.

"Beg pardon, sir. You have such wonderful things.
Finer than I've seen anywhere, even in Norwich. Those
cabinets . . ."

The pair of impressive cabinets Adam was so taken with
were tall, made of a richly-polished mahogany with clean,
elegant proportions rising to a magnificent fretworked and
swan-necked pediment.

"Ah, they were made by Mr Thomas Chippendale of St
Martin's Lane in London – have you heard of him?"

"I've seen a copy of his book of designs – *The Gentleman
and Cabinet-Maker's Director* – but I've never seen an example
of his work before. They're magnificent."

Sir William smiled. "Have you never been to London,
Adam?"

"No, sir."

Adam had been to Norwich but three times in his life. London seemed as if it were at the other side of the world. Ashamed of his ignorance, he stood silently, waiting for Sir William to continue.

"How would you like to visit London?"

Adam stared. "I – I don't know. I've never thought of it."

"Just imagine what you could learn if you were apprenticed to a good master – a man who could teach you to make furniture like that you see in this room."

"To Mr Chippendale, sir?"

"Not exactly." Sir William frowned. "To a Mr Robert Carter. A good honest man with a reputation for fine work."

"My father could never stand the expense of it."

Sir William beamed. "Supposing a friend were to pay board and lodging as well as your bond?"

Adam blinked. "But who would lay out so much money on my behalf?"

"It has all been arranged." Sir William thrust his thumbs into the pockets of his silken waistcoat. "Three nights since I rose from Lord Cockleton's card table four thousand pounds richer than I sat down. The whole business has been settled and it hasn't cost me a penny piece."

"You – you have paid Mr Carter for my apprenticeship?"

"Signed and sealed," Sir William crowed, much pleased with his own cleverness. "Don't say a word, Adam. I want no thanks for the deed. I've not forgotten what you did for my Susanna. Do not thank me. Go home and tell your parents."

"But . . ."

Before Adam could continue, the door opened and Lady Patricia swept in, her heavy silk gown making a swishing noise as it brushed the ground. She ignored Adam, walking past him and up to her husband.

"Warwick, I want to speak to you."

"Patricia, my dear," he said awkwardly. "I was just telling Adam the good news."

Her eyes flicked contemptuously towards the young man and then back to her husband. "In private, Warwick. Now!"

Sir William frowned. Sometimes she was a little high-handed but it was easier to comply than argue. "We had finished I suppose. Tell your father I'll ride over in a day or so, Adam."

Realizing he had been dismissed, Adam walked from the room in a daze. He was to go to London, to be apprenticed to a cabinet-maker and all his expenses paid. It couldn't be true. He must have mistaken the Squire, yet the words had been clear enough.

Standing in the hall outside Sir William's library, Adam tried to come to terms with what had happened. He was to go to London, that meant he must leave his home and family. He felt a momentary reluctance, but it was soon followed by elation. He would be leaving everything he knew, but he would learn so much. It was a wonderful opportunity. He suddenly saw how extraordinarily generous Sir William had been – and Adam himself had not spoken one word of gratitude. He had simply been overwhelmed by it all. He turned back to the door, which had not quite closed behind him, but then he heard Lady Patricia's shrill laughter.

"It was a brilliant ploy, Warwick," she cried. "To remove a source of danger so completely. Once the son has gone, Susanna will soon tire of visiting the parents. I've no doubt it's his handsome face she admires so. It can be nothing else. He is a dull-witted oaf. Not I think fit company for Susanna."

"Adam has talent, Patricia . . ."

Sir William's defence was spirited, but Adam was no longer listening. His face was grim as he strode through the house. Lady Patricia's scorn pricked all the more because his honesty forced him to admit that there was some truth in what she said. He could scarcely read, though he was good

35

with figures and could reckon swiftly in his head, but he had had no real education. He knew little or nothing of the world outside his own village.

Anger and shame warred inside him as he walked home through the Squire's park. How dare they conspire to send him away? How dare they order his life, as if he were of no account? He would not go. He would stay here and defy them all! They could not force him to leave his father's house. He was a free man, not a servant. He could do as he pleased, and he would!

Susanna was walking through the park when she saw Adam coming towards her. He seemed preoccupied and she felt her heart jump as she waited for him to reach her, but he looked as if he would pass her by without speaking.

"Adam!" she cried. "Adam, what's wrong?"

For a moment Adam was tempted to ignore her. It was because of her that Lady Patricia had poured scorn on him, condemning him as an ignorant oaf. And yet there was something in Susanna's eyes that made him stop; his tone was harsh as he said, "I'm on my way home, nothing is wrong."

"Are you angry with me?" Susanna stared at him anxiously. He had been so odd the last time they met and now he looked furious. "Have I done something to upset you?"

"You . . ." Some of the anger drained out of him as he looked at her. "No, you haven't done anything. It's . . . it's someone else."

"Is it Stephen?" she asked. "I know you quarrelled."

Adam shook his head. "That was nothing," he said. "An argument over something your brother said to . . .Well, it doesn't matter. No, this is something different."

He frowned as he looked at her. Now that his anger had cooled, he was beginning to understand that he had actually been offered a wonderful opportunity to make something of his life. He knew that he was poorly educated. Until now it hadn't seemed to matter, but Lady Patricia's words had changed everything. The ambition that had lain dormant in Adam's breast suddenly burst into life. Why should he not become rich and famous like Mr Chippendale? Why should he not make his fortune in London and then come back and claim the Warwicks' daughter for his own? That would be a fine revenge on Lady Patricia. He realized that it would also give him great satisfaction. He looked into the anxious eyes of the lovely young woman, for woman she was even if she did not yet know it herself.

"I may be going away," he said slowly. "I may be going to learn how to make fine furniture."

"Going away?" Susanna drew a deep breath as she felt a little pain around her heart. "Why? Don't you like it here?" She blinked rapidly, crying out impetuously, "Oh, I wish you wouldn't go, Adam!"

Her cry made him smile. She was still so innocent. Almost any other man would have taken advantage of such a trusting child but its effect on Adam was to make him feel more protective towards her.

"Don't worry, Susanna," he said, using her given name in the familiar way for the first time. "I shan't forget you . . . and maybe one day I'll come looking for you."

As he walked on past her, Susanna stared after him. What did he mean? Her heart raced wildly and she wanted to call him back. She wanted to ask him what he meant, but she couldn't find the breath to speak.

"And where have you been?" Stephen looked suspiciously at his sister. "Not sneaking out to visit the Blackwells again, I hope? Mama will give you the whipping you deserve if she catches you with that carpenter's boy."

Susanna looked into the sneering face of her brother and shivered. Sometimes she thought that he really hated her. Yet in her heart she knew that it was just because he was so selfish and cared only for himself. Stephen didn't realize how much his careless taunts hurt other people, because he thought only of his own pleasure.

"No, I haven't been to the village," she said, lifting her head proudly. "I've merely been taking Sultan for a walk in the park."

"That smelly brute," Stephen said, looking at her darkly. "The damned thing bit me the other day. It's a pity the gipsies didn't steal it – and you with it."

"Stephen!" Lady Patricia came into the room in time to hear her son's last words. "Don't speak to your sister like that. I won't have it. And where have you been? Your tutor tells me you've been missing your classes again."

Stephen scowled and Susanna felt a flicker of triumph, pleased that he was getting the scolding for once. Stephen was their mother's favourite child, and very rarely could he do any wrong, but obviously he was in trouble now.

"I've outgrown old Tomkins," he said, glaring at his sister because she was giggling behind her mother's back. "I'm not a child anymore, Mama. I don't need a tutor. It's time I was helping Papa run the estate. Goodness knows someone needs to look after things with Father in London half the time."

"Yes." Lady Patricia nodded, in agreement with him now. "At least that might save you spending all your time with those friends of yours, Stephen. Most of them are highly unsuitable and not at all what I want for my son." She frowned at him. "I heard that you took part in a wrestling match at Ludham fair – is that true?"

Stephen looked annoyed. "What of it? It was just a lark."

"Then I suppose it was true that the Blackwells' son beat you and won the purse of ten gold sovereigns?"

Now Stephen's cheeks were on fire. He glared at his sister as he saw the delight dawning in her eyes. "He cheated of course. I had him in a grip and then . . ."

"Spare me the details," Lady Patricia said, curling her lip. "I just wish you hadn't done it, Stephen. It's bad enough that Susanna chooses to spend so much time with them."

Lady Patricia turned to her daughter and frowned. "You can take that smile off your face, miss. I want to talk to you in my dressing-room in five minutes. Now leave me alone with your brother – and no listening in the hall!"

Dismissed, Susanna pulled a face at her brother as she left the room. Yet she was delighted with what she'd just heard. So Adam had beaten Stephen in a wrestling match at Ludham fair. Perhaps that was what the quarrel she'd witnessed was about. She would ask Adam the next time she went to visit his family.

"What do you mean?" Susanna looked at the other girl, sensing her dislike more strongly than ever. "Where has Adam gone?"

"To London," Maggie replied, her eyes red from crying. She glared at the Squire's daughter, jealousy surging. It was all her fault. "Your father arranged for him to be apprenticed to a cabinet-maker there."

"My father?" Susanna stared at her in dismay. "But he only said he might be going, he didn't say it was definite. When did he go? When will he be back?"

"Not for years and years, if ever," Maggie said. She felt a surge of satisfaction as she saw the shock and pain in Susanna's face. Her own feelings were a mixture of loss and sadness at her brother's departure, and envy. Why couldn't it have been her who had been given a chance to go to London? Why couldn't she have been apprenticed to a fashionable gownmaker? "I shouldn't think he'll ever come back. I wouldn't."

"Not come back . . ." Susanna's throat closed with emotion and she felt the sting of tears behind her eyes. "But he didn't come to say goodbye . . ." How could he have gone without saying a proper goodbye to her? She had never imagined that she would not see him again before he left. She had not really believed in her heart that he would go . . .

Maggie stared at her, seeing the pain Susanna was

struggling to control. Maggie knew why her brother had been sent away, but decided to keep it to herself, sensing that it would hurt the other girl more if she believed Adam hadn't cared enough to say goodbye. He had wanted to, but their father had advised against it, telling his son that it would be foolish to arouse the Warwicks' anger. Her eyes glittered as she looked at Susanna.

"Why should he say goodbye to you?" she asked derisively. "You're not his sister or anyone he cares for, are you?"

The spiteful words cut Susanna to the heart. She gazed at Maggie, beginning to understand the jealousy behind those strange looks. Her chest was tight and she felt that she was being crushed to pieces by the awful pain inside her. She had believed that Adam was her friend, that he liked her and enjoyed her company as much as she enjoyed his. She had even dreamed of a day when they might mean even more to each other. Now he had gone, without a word to her. But even though it hurt that Adam hadn't cared enough to say goodbye, she wasn't going to show it in front of this hostile girl. Susanna wouldn't give Maggie the satisfaction of knowing how much she had wounded her.

Susanna walked away without speaking again, her head high. It was only when she had left the village behind her that she began to run. She ran and ran until her breath was gone, and then she threw herself down on the grass to weep.

The next morning, Beatrice came into Susanna's room and was shocked by her sister's red eyes. Susanna seldom cried, unless she was trying to get her own way with Papa, and then they were only crocodile tears. This time she looked as if she had really been sobbing her heart out.

"What's wrong?" Beatrice asked. "What's the matter with you? Do you feel ill?"

"Go away," Susanna said, lifting her head from the pillow. "Why can't you just leave me alone? I don't want to talk to you."

40

Beatrice pouted. "You never want to talk to me. You hate me, don't you? You prefer that common Maggie Blackwell. And so does Stephen."

"What do you mean?" Susanna became alert. "I didn't think Stephen even knew Maggie."

"Well, he does." Beatrice looked at her triumphantly. "I could tell you a secret if I wanted to but you're horrid to me, so I shan't."

"Tell me!" Susanna jumped off the bed, running after her sister as she dodged about the large bedchamber, shrieking with delight. "Come on, Bea, tell me. Please!"

"Why should I? You never let me come with you when you go out these days. You never want me around. Why should I tell you anything?"

"Please," Susanna said coaxingly. "I'll give you my coral beads if you tell me what you know."

Bea looked at her speculatively. The coral beads were very pretty, but not what she wanted. "I'll tell you if you promise to stop running off without me all the time," she said. "I'm your sister. It's not fair that I should be stuck in the nursery while you have adventures."

Susanna smiled and nodded. It was easy to promise now, for she would not want to visit the Blackwells' so often now that Adam had gone. Besides, it was obvious that Maggie didn't like her much.

"I promise," she said. "Now tell me what you know."

"Well . . ." Bea's eyes sparkled. "I saw Stephen talking to Maggie in the park the other day."

"Is that all?" Susanna was disappointed.

"No," Bea looked at her in triumph. "I was up a tree and they didn't see me. I saw Stephen try to grab her and give her a kiss, but she pushed him away and slapped his face. She told him she wasn't going to be one of his whores . . . what's a whore, Susanna?"

"I'm not quite sure," Susanna said, avoiding her sister's bright gaze. "But it's not nice and you mustn't let Mama hear you say it. She would be so angry with you."

41

"Well, I shan't," Bea said. "You know she wouldn't listen to a word against Stephen, but it was rather strange, wasn't it?"

"Yes, it was," Susanna agreed, smiling at her sister. "I'm glad you told me, Bea, We must share all our secrets in future."

"Will you tell me yours?"

"Yes, of course," Susanna said, knowing even as she spoke that there was one she could never share with her sister. "Yes, of course I'll tell you, Bea. From now on we're going to be friends, aren't we?"

"Can we go riding together this morning?"

"Yes," Susanna said. "Go and get ready and I'll dress."

On the threshold, Bea looked at her doubtfully. "You won't change your mind and sneak out without me?"

"No. I promise to wait for you," Susanna said. "Go on now, I want to wash."

As her sister left, Susanna poured water from the porcelain ewer into a matching basin and began to splash her face. She mustn't let her mother see her red eyes or there would be questions, and she didn't want to explain the reason for her tears. In fact she couldn't explain, because she didn't understand it herself. She just knew that her heart felt as if it were broken.

CHAPTER THREE

It was a pleasantly warm spring day, a slight breeze just ruffling the girl's pale gold hair as she strolled through the orchard and across the meadows behind her home. She was dressed in a simple gown of blue dimity with a white apron and a large muslin kerchief draped over her square-necked bodice. A straw hat had slipped from her head and hung on blue satin ribbons down her back, adding to the carefree air of her general appearance. Yet even dressed in this plain attire, no one could have called her less than beautiful.

At eighteen, Susanna Warwick was everything her mother could have wished. Possessed of a sweet singing voice, she could play both the harp and the spinet. Her nimble fingers could sketch a tolerable likeness of any face within seconds of seeing it, and her embroidery was a credit to Nanny Giles's dedication. Together with her pretty face and neat figure, these attributes – in her mother's estimation – made her a fit companion for the highest in the land. There was little visual evidence now of the child who had run away to the woods in search of a dog. No sign of the girl who had cried herself to sleep because a young man had gone to London without saying goodbye.

"Susanna will marry to oblige us," Lady Patricia was fond of telling her husband. "When we take her to London for the Season, we need have no fear that she will be anything but a credit to us."

Perhaps her ladyship might not have been quite as confident if she could have seen her daughter wave excitedly at the man who had come across the meadows to meet her. But fortunately for Susanna, Lady Patricia was not there to witness the meeting.

"Mademoiselle Warwick, you came!" The man's face lit with eagerness.

"I said I would. Did you not believe me, monsieur?"

"I was afraid something would prevent it." Edouard Dubarry gave her a passionate look that said much more than he had thus far dared to put into words.

Susanna dimpled, her thick, surprisingly dark lashes fluttering as she glanced up into his adoring eyes, and then quickly away.

Edouard Dubarry was so handsome, with his lithe, graceful figure and delicate, almost feminine looks. His pale skin and bee-stung red mouth made him look like a poet, and his smile could set her heart racing wildly. She knew that she was risking her mother's censure by meeting the music master alone, for Lady Patricia would not countenance any attachment between them. For years it had been made plain to Susanna that she was expected to marry well, and if she were honest, the girl was looking forward to her Season in London for more than one reason. She wanted all the things that her mother had told her were her due, she intended to marry well, and yet she still hadn't been able to resist meeting Monsieur Dubarry like this. It was so delightful to flirt with a man who obviously worshipped her, even though he had not touched her own heart. How could he, when it had long ago been given to someone else?

"Shall we walk for a while?" he asked. "Perhaps towards the house so that we can say we met by chance and merely walked back together?"

Susanna inclined her head in assent. She kept a little distance between them so that it should not look too obviously an assignation. Her heart was thudding in her breast, but she had been well disciplined to hide her emotions by her mother and she contrived to appear unconcerned as she asked, "What was it you wanted to say to me that could not be said during our lessons?"

Edouard sent an agonized glance her way, longing to

pour out his love and devotion, yet still afraid to speak. She was so far above him that he wondered at his own daring in asking for this meeting. Seeing his expression and interpreting it as correctly as her innocence would allow, Susanna blushed and lowered her gaze.

"You will be going away soon now." Edouard spoke at last in anguished tones. "I suppose you will not think of me when you are in town?"

"I'm sure I shall often think of you." Susanna kept her eyes downcast. "You have taught me so much, Monsieur Dubarry. I must always be grateful to you."

"Is that how you think of me?" he asked, suddenly desperate. If he meant to speak it must be now! "As a teacher only?"

"How else should I think of you?" Her blue eyes sparkled with sudden mischief.

He stopped walking and turned to her, his face working with the force of his emotion. "Surely you know that I ceased to think of you as a pupil long ago?" Ardour bolstering his courage, he took an impulsive step towards her. "I can no longer remain silent. Susanna, I adore you! I worship the very ground your feet touch. I am wretched at the very thought of our parting."

"Oh . . ." Susanna's mouth opened in surprise. She had not expected such a passionate declaration. Dallying flirtatiously with Edouard was deliciously exciting, but his intense tones made her oddly nervous. "Monsieur, I . . ."

Throwing caution to the wind, Edouard decided on action. As she stared in bewilderment, he reached out and took her into his arms, kissing her with an urgency that terrified her, making her recoil at once. Romantic dreams were one thing, but this sudden assault on her virtue was quite another. She struggled, pushing him away in distress.

"No! No, you must not."

Edouard's face fell in almost comic dismay. He stepped back, his manner abject as he saw that he had misjudged her mood. She had seemed to encourage his advances, but he realized now that it was merely a game. She was prepared to accept pretty compliments, but not his kisses.

"Miss Warwick, I beg your pardon. I meant no offence. I was so carried away by your beauty that I forgot myself."

Susanna shook her head, not daring to look at him. She was embarrassed, shocked at what had happened. It had all gone so terribly wrong! She ought not to have come. Backing away, her face suffused with colour, she stared at him in reproach. Surely he understood that there could never be more than dalliance between them?

"I must go," she whispered. "Do not come to the house for a lesson today, I beg you. I could not bear it with Beatrice watching."

"But . . ." He gazed unhappily as she turned and ran towards the house. "Miss Warwick, forgive me . . ."

Susanna didn't look back. Her cheeks were hot and she was mortified. How dared he kiss her like that? To step beyond the line that convention had drawn between them was to presume too much. He was merely a music master. He could not have thought that . . . She might have shown him some kindness, but he should have kept his place.

While admitting in her heart that she was at least partly to blame, Susanna excused her own weakness in encouraging his advances. He must have known that she was only playing a game with him, practising her feminine arts against her imminent introduction into the drawing-rooms of London society. She was just eighteen, while he was a man of eight and twenty. He ought to have understood!

Her head down, cheeks flaming, Susanna failed to notice Beatrice watching her from the branches of a gnarled old apple tree at the edge of the orchard. She ran straight past and on into the kitchen gardens, disappearing from sight under a walled arch.

Perched in her tree, Beatrice had been able to see everything from her vantage point. She glanced towards the disconsolate music master, who was still standing as if turned to stone, gazing after the fleeing girl. Beatrice's green eyes glittered with jealousy. She wouldn't have run away like that if Edouard had kissed her, but of course he hadn't even looked in her direction. She was only sixteen, and with her thin, flat-chested body still a child in his eyes. Besides, he was in love with Susanna . . .

Beatrice knew that she would never be as beautiful as her sister. Her hair was a mousey brown and fell heavily like a thick curtain about her long face. She envied Susanna her pale curls, wishing she had been the favoured child. It was her sister who was to marry a duke or an earl. Susanna was the apple of her mother's eye . . .

A smile of malice touched the girl's mouth. Sometimes apples had worms in them.

Stephen Warwick was bored with his life. He spent much of his time these days attending to estate business, which should rightly have been his father's prerogative had he been at home to see to it, which he seldom was. Sir William preferred to stay at his club in London or visit his friends, attending race meetings and gambling. Stephen would have liked to spend his life that way, too, but his allowance would not stand such an extravagant lifestyle, nor would the estate. The income was stretched to the limits now and could barely cover Sir William's excesses.

Sometimes, Stephen felt like running off to London and finding himself a rich heiress. He had tried courting some of the daughters of wealthy landowners in the county, but found his offer of marriage brusquely refused by the fathers if not their daughters. It was because of his reputation, of course.

Scowling, Stephen regretted that he had indulged so freely in his drinking, brawling and whoring. He should have been more circumspect, at least until he was married. It was a nuisance, but he would have to look further afield for his heiress. In the meantime, he meant to enjoy himself with the village girls, though most of them had already succumbed to his wiles, and once they had he was no longer interested.

He gave a little smile at the thought of the one girl he really wanted who had as yet refused all his advances.

Maggie Blackwell. She was a real beauty and a hot little piece if he was any judge. So far she had given him nothing but smiles or pouts, but one of these days . . . One of these days he was going to have her, willing or not.

"Well, you may think yourself lucky that I do not have you confined to an asylum," Lady Patricia stormed, pacing about Susanna's bedchamber in a fury. "That a daughter of mine should sink so low as to let herself be kissed by a music master!"

Susanna stared at her, white-lipped. Her mother's threats were not as outrageous as they sounded. It would not be the first time that a wayward girl had been locked away for a crime such as hers. She felt a little sick and faint as she looked at her mother, but did her best to hide it.

"I – I didn't intend it to happen, Mama. It was a game, only a game. I didn't expect him to declare himself so – so strongly."

"Then you are a fool, Susanna." Lady Patricia's tones were cold and clipped. "Let it be a lesson to you. A gentleman would have understood your game, but men of Dubarry's class are too base in their natures. If you must take a lover, let it be a man of your own class, someone you can rely on to keep your honour sacred – and wait until you have given your husband an heir. Once the succession is safe, you may do as you please, providing that you act with discretion. Meeting in an open meadow where anyone can see! Foolhardy and careless!"

Susanna stared at her mother, suddenly knowing that the whispers she had dismissed as servants' gossip were all true.

"Is that what you did, Mama? Tell me – am I Sir William's daughter?"

Lady Patricia almost slapped the girl, but changed her mind and laughed harshly. "At least you have spirit. Since you ask – yes, you are William's child. Strange as it may seem, I loved him once. I was faithful to him until after Beatrice was born. And I took care never to carry another man's child. William could not satisfy me – but in every other way, I have been a loyal wife to him. He is well pleased with his bargain."

Susanna nodded, feeling a reluctant sympathy for her mother. Sir William had grown very stout of late, and spent most of his time with friends in London. Even when at home, he seemed to shut himself away from his family and was seldom seen by them.

"Poor Father." Susanna sighed. "He hasn't been the same since he invested in those ships . . ."

Lady Patricia snorted with disgust. "Sunk in mid-ocean with all their cargo aboard and not a penny piece recovered. It has always been thus with your father. It's a wonder he hasn't ruined us before this. If it were not for my father's legacy last year, we should have ended in the workhouse!"

"Surely things are not that bad, Mama?" Susanna looked at her anxiously. "Can we afford to take a house in London this Season?"

"We cannot afford to neglect your marriage prospects," Lady Patricia replied, frowning. "That is why I'm so cross with you for risking everything by allowing that upstart to kiss you in full view of anyone who might have been passing. We were fortunate you were seen only by Beatrice. Promise me now that you will never be as foolish again!"

"I give you my word." Susanna bit her soft underlip. "It went further than I intended, Mama. I hadn't expected him to actually kiss me."

"No doubt you imagined he would kiss your hand or the hem of your gown." Her mother smiled wryly. "Men are creatures of the flesh, Susanna. Remember that and you hold them in the palm of your hand. You have beauty and an intelligent mind. Use both to your own advantage and you may avoid making the mistakes I made."

"Yes, Mama." Susanna looked at her uncertainly. "What is to happen to Monsieur Dubarry?"

"He has a year's salary and a recommendation to his next employer." Lady Patricia's eyes were flinty. "I assure you, he believes himself to have been fairly used. I could have ruined him had I so chosen."

"And with him my reputation."

"Exactly. I see we understand each other, Susanna. Very well, we shall say no more of this. There is no need for your father to know anything."

"Thank you, Mama. I am grateful for your forbearance."

Lady Patricia nodded, hesitated and then went out. The unfortunate incident was perhaps partly her fault for not having instructed the girl sooner in the ways of men. Innocence was desirable but not always practical. Susanna would not make the same mistake again.

Left to herself, Susanna went to stand at the window. She was annoyed with Beatrice for telling tales to her mother, yet there was also a sense of relief that she wouldn't have to meet the music master again. The memory of that kiss had become shameful to her now, especially since her mother had spelled out exactly what might have happened. The realization of what had truly been in his mind sent waves of humiliation flowing over her. How could he have imagined that she would welcome his advances in that way? She wondered if he had heard the whispers about her mother and her cheeks grew warm. Did Monsieur Dubarry think that she held her virtue so cheaply that she would . . . It had been foolish to meet him. Her head full of romantic dreams, she had never really understood the stories about Lady Patricia, though Stephen had told her their mother was being talked about in the village. Now that she knew exactly what he meant, she was ashamed that she had ever agreed to meet the music master. The reality was harsh and sordid. Reputations were lost for less. If she were to marry well, she would have to be more careful in future.

"So you're to go to London after all." Beatrice cast envious eyes over the array of gowns scattered around her sister's bedchamber. "It seems that Mama cannot be displeased with you, no matter what you do."

Susanna laid down the ballgown she had been holding against herself. It was a pink open-robed silk, trimmed with flounces and bunches of flowers made from silver tissue, and was worn over a white petticoat that had been richly embroidered with silver thread and brilliants. The silk for this gown had cost six guineas a yard and there were at least twenty yards in the skirt, and then there was all the expense of the trimmings and the making. Susanna dared not even contemplate the total sum spent on her new clothes. Money she was sure her parents could not afford.

"Don't be jealous, Bea," she said and sighed. "Your turn will come."

"Only if you marry well," Beatrice replied, her mouth drooping at the corners. "I heard Mama and Papa talking. She's pinning all her hopes on you. We shall be ruined unless you find yourself a rich husband."

"Surely things are not that bad," Susanna cried, but her voice lacked conviction. She was well aware that her father had dissipated most of his fortune one way or another. "What else did Mama say?"

"Oh, a lot of stuff about Papa taking a house in a fashionable area. She's had letters from ten of her old friends, and you're to be invited everywhere." Beatrice gave a wail of discontent and threw herself across the bed. "And I'm to be stuck here with Nanny Giles. It's not fair!"

"No, it isn't," Susanna agreed, suddenly bending to stroke her sister's hair. "I wish you could come with us, Bea, but it wouldn't be much fun for you. You couldn't go to any of

51

the dinners or balls. It's much better that you should wait until you're a year or two older, then you can find a rich husband of your own."

"And I shall." Beatrice jumped off the bed, her eyes brilliant. "Mama says you're to marry a duke or an earl, but I don't care about that. I shall be certain that my husband is rich and can buy me all the gowns and jewels I want!" So saying, she flounced out of the room.

Susanna went to the window and looked out at the formal gardens with their neat rose beds and manicured lawns. Beyond was the lake and the summerhouse where she had played as a child and dreamed of a knight in shining armour, who would one day sweep her up on a white, prancing horse and ride away like the wind to a land where she could eat strawberries and cake all day. A knight whose face resembled that of a young man she had once known. Adam Blackwell still haunted her dreams sometimes, and she would wake with her face wet with tears and longing for something she didn't understand. At other times, she was angry with Adam. Angry because he had gone away without saying goodbye, angry because he had never once sent her a message, though she knew that he sent letters to his mother every now and then. Maggie read them to her mother, because Jeanie could not read for herself. Occasionally Maggie would tell Susanna little things, almost as if she wished to torment her, as if she could see into her heart.

Every now and then Susanna met Maggie when she was walking to or from the village. They spoke to one another and smiled but they were not really friends. Susanna knew that the other girl resented her for some reason, and all her friendly advances were met with spiteful words. Maggie's attitude was one of the reasons she seldom went near the Blackwells' cottage these days. But it was time she stopped thinking about Adam or his family.

Susanna's chin lifted and she turned away from the window, putting aside her dreams. As a young girl she had given her heart to her champion, but things were different now. She had grown up. She was a woman who must face reality. She must marry to oblige her family, and she would do so, her mind was made up. In two weeks' time she would be presented at her first ball, but until then she was free to do as she pleased.

Reaching for a fine wool shawl, Susanna threw it around her shoulders and left the room. Soon she was walking in the direction of the summerhouse. In the distance, she could see her brother Stephen riding his horse. She frowned slightly. The years had not improved her brother. If anything he was more selfish and unkind than when they were children, though she knew the village girls found his handsome face and charming smile irresistible.

Susanna grimaced. If they knew Stephen as well as she did, they would not be so anxious to flirt with him.

Stephen Warwick saw the girl walking through the meadow ahead of him and he spurred his horse to a canter. He was sure he recognized her, though he had not yet seen her face, but only Maggie Blackwell walked like that, with her head up and her slim hips swaying in that madly seductive fashion. Maggie was by far the most attractive girl in the village as far as Stephen was concerned. He had been after her for a long time, and he knew that his interest in her had not gone unnoticed. Maggie's eyes were bright and when they looked his way, they seemed to promise much. So far she had resisted him with spirit, but he thought he knew the way to her heart and he was almost ready to put his plan into action. Yet he was in no hurry, the chase was exciting and he intended to enjoy every moment of her seduction.

As he drew level with her, Maggie glanced up, her full, ripe lips curving in a smile. Stephen felt an urgent quickening in his loins. She was a hot wench and no mistake! He doffed his hat to her politely.

"It's a fair day, Mistress Blackwell."

53

"Yes, sir. So it is."

Maggie shaded her eyes as she looked up at him, well aware of the effect she was having on the Squire's son. His hair glinted in the sunshine, revealing a hint of red, and his blue eyes tantalized her with their mockery. He was a devil – but such a handsome one! Stephen Warwick had a reputation with the village girls, many of whom had shared a romp in the long, sweet meadow grass with him. Maggie couldn't help feeling excited when she saw that look in his eyes, but she was already promised to Tom Sutton, a farmer's son from over Ludham way. It was a good match for her, and she had no intention of throwing her future away for a pair of sparkling blue eyes. But a few smiles and a walk in the sunshine couldn't do any harm. So she felt no alarm as Stephen dismounted and began to walk beside her, leading his horse.

"May I walk with you for a while, Maggie?"

Maggie looked at him, shading her eyes from the sun. The girls who had been with Stephen Warwick said that he was generous. She had no intention of giving him her favours cheaply, but Maggie's chief desire in life was still for a red velvet dress. She had been to Norwich market with her father some months back and had seen one that made her almost sick with longing. She would do almost anything for a dress like that. Except what Stephen wanted. She was too sharp to be caught like that. Other girls might sell themselves cheaply, but Maggie was ambitious. She was promised to Tom, but the Squire's son was another matter.

Smiling, she said, "Suit yourself. I'm on my way to the vicarage. You can walk with me if you like."

It was her first large dance in London. Susanna was so excited she could scarcely breathe. Walking into the ballroom on her father's arm, she felt that her life was just beginning. Surely she would find someone who would make her heart beat wildly, someone suitable who would make her forget the young man she had idolized as a child. She wanted to marry well to oblige her parents, but she also wanted her husband to make her feel the way Adam Blackwell had that day in the park.

"Now remember what I've told you," Lady Patricia said as they took their places at the side of the ballroom. "Be charming and obliging – and don't talk too much."

"Yes, Mama," Susanna said meekly. "I remember everything you've told me."

Sitting down on one of the dainty gilt chairs, Susanna let her eyes rove freely round the crowded room. So many people, and all dressed in silks and satins – and the jewels. She had never seen anything so fine. They must all be very rich, but so many of the men looked old, much older than she'd expected. There were young ones, of course; she could see a group of them clustered around another young girl who was simpering and smiling up at them in a way Susanna thought was ridiculous. Surely it was not necessary to behave like that!

"Excuse me, madam, may I ask you to present your daughter to my brother?"

Susanna looked at the woman who had spoken to her mother. She was very tall, richly dressed in a gown of heavy crimson silk embroidered with silver, and she wore a necklace of huge rubies around her thin neck. Her perfume was so overpowering that it made Susanna's head begin to ache.

"Lady Munford," Lady Patricia simpered and smiled. "How delightful to see you again after all these years. I should be delighted to introduce Susanna to Lord Digby."

A very stout man in a puce satin coat and grey breeches was waiting just behind the tall woman. Meeting his eyes, Susanna felt something inside her go cold. She disliked the way he was looking at her, as if he were assessing her like a piece of merchandise.

"Miss Warwick." Lady Munford smiled at her, but Susanna thought that her eyes were hard and calculating.

"May I present you to Lord Percival Digby and beg you to give him the favour of this next dance?"

Susanna glanced at her mother, who was smiling approvingly. Murmuring her assent, Susanna gave her hand to the man, feeling the moistness of his palm at once. He was clearly very warm and uncomfortable.

"Charming," he said as he led her on to the floor. "You are new in town, I believe, Miss Warwick?"

"Yes, yes, I am. This is my first dance, Lord Digby."

"And are you enjoying yourself?"

"It is all very exciting," Susanna replied truthfully. "Everyone looks so wealthy. I had not seen such magnificent jewels before. Mama once took me to an assembly in Norwich, but it was nothing like this."

"This little affair?" Lord Digby looked around him, his brows lifted. "It is very well for the first ball of the Season, but there will be many more much larger than this. My sister is to hold a ball next week, shall you be there?"

"I'm not sure that we've been invited."

"Then I shall make sure you are." Digby squeezed her hand. "I should be so disappointed if you were not."

Susanna was relieved when their dance was over and she was returned to her mother. Lady Patricia, clearly pleased, whispered behind her fan, "To be singled out by Lady Helen Munford and Lord Digby at your first dance is quite a feather in your cap, Susanna. Not that there is any need to be overwhelmed with gratitude. I'm sure you will meet many more eligible gentlemen this evening."

Susanna wasn't at all sure that she wanted to meet more gentlemen if they were all like Lord Digby. However, she had been noticed on the floor and several young men approached her mother after that, asking to be introduced. Susanna danced with all of them; most were pleasant enough, but she did not actually meet anyone who made her heart beat faster. She talked freely, airing her views on various things and completely forgetting what her mother had told her as she became embroiled in a heated discussion over politics with one young man. He seemed quite put out as he led her back to her chair, leaving her with a curt bow.

It was as Susanna fanned herself that she sensed someone watching her. Watching her with more than a casual interest. Glancing up, she found herself looking into the face of a man who sent a shiver down her spine. He was good-looking in a rather heavy, coarse way, with thick lips, a Roman nose and piercing blue eyes. Something about the way he was staring at her made Susanna distinctly uncomfortable and she quickly turned aside, hoping that he would go away.

"Miss Warwick, I believe?"

The deep voice made her quiver inside. She glanced up again, her cheeks hot. "Yes, sir. I do not believe I have the honour of your acquaintance?" She glanced at her mother, who was deep in conversation with a dowager.

"I am the Marquis of Brandon, Miss Warwick," he said. "May I request the favour of this next dance?" He held out his hand almost imperiously. "Come! I assure you, I am generally held to be quite respectable."

Susanna felt herself blushing. She did not have the courage to refuse him, and yet she was most reluctant to accept. Torn between her desire to escape and her embarrassment, she was relieved when her mother turned to her with a frown.

"I am about to go into supper, Susanna," she said. "Excuse me, my lord, I think you must press your suit another time."

Taking Susanna's arm, she bore her away, whispering once they were safely out of earshot. "That is one man I would prefer you not to encourage, Susanna. He is received everywhere, of course, but I have never cared for him. I should avoid him whenever you can."

"I intend to do so," Susanna said, relieved. "Thank you for rescuing me, Mama."

Lady Patricia nodded and smiled. "You have done well

for your first evening, Susanna. I think we shall leave soon. I do not want you to tire yourself too much."

"I am quite ready, Mama."

"At least you made the right impression on Lady Munford," Patricia Warwick said. "She has invited us to her ball next week. It will be one of the grandest of the Season. I had not expected to be asked. It is quite an honour."

Susanna said nothing. She knew that it was Lord Digby who had prevailed upon his sister to make the invitation, but she preferred not to say any more on the matter. This was only her first dance. She had met no one she would even think of marrying as yet, but there was plenty of time.

CHAPTER FOUR

Adam left his lodgings in Swann Alley and walked down the wide thoroughfare of Colbman Street with its busy shops, inns and three-storeyed houses, past Carpenter's Yard and White's Alley, narrow little courts of tenements and indifferent housing. Here and there merchants had built fine houses that stood out from the others, but the only court of any real importance in the immediate area was King's Arms Yard, where Robert Carter had his house and workshop. Adam was on his way there now.

It had been cool all week, but now it was much warmer; the start of a glorious June day, he thought. As the summer wore on the stench from the gutters in the meaner streets would intensify as the rubbish rotted, becoming almost unbearable at times, but he had grown used to it during the four years he had lived in London. When he'd first arrived, it had seemed impossible that anyone could endure the filth and poverty that existed in the warren-like rookeries inhabited by the city's poor. He'd been appalled by the sight of ragged, bare-footed children staring at him from sunken eyes in dirty grey faces as they came to the doors of their hovels to watch in sullen silence as he passed by. He'd missed the fresh air of Norfolk and in the first few weeks he had longed desperately for his home and friends. London had seemed vast and inhospitable then, but now it had become a second home.

For this much of the credit was due to Mary-Ellen Watts, Adam reflected as he made his unhurried way towards his employer's home. Mary-Ellen had been a widow for ten years now; though some years older than Adam, she was an attractive woman with dark, humorous eyes and a wide, ever-smiling mouth. She had a generous nature to go with her ample charms; she had taken her young lodger under her wing within a few days of his arrival in the city, and it was she who had helped and encouraged him with his efforts to better himself. Mary-Ellen could read and she had found her guest willing and eager to learn.

Within weeks of his arrival he had mastered his letters and though at first painfully slow, read newspapers, learned essays by Dr Johnson, Cowper's poetry and works by Pope and Walpole from start to finish, his inquiring mind desperate for the education he had hitherto been denied. He visited places of public interest, admiring great buildings and paintings. His thirst for knowledge was insatiable as he read and studied everything he could lay his hands on, coming to appreciate and love the classical lines of ancient Greece and Rome. His interest in politics grew swiftly as did his ambition to make something of himself, and he found himself confessing his secret desires to his obliging landlady. His entry into Mary-Ellen's bed had followed soon after, and she catered for his carnal needs as cheerfully as she cooked and cleaned for him, asking very little in return.

It was a very satisfactory relationship, Adam thought, remembering the excellent breakfast that had followed a night of comfort rather than of passion. Because of Mary-Ellen's good nature, he had never needed to go in search of the whores who haunted the narrow alleys and dark side streets of the city. Nor had he given much thought to marriage, though he could not help being aware of the unspoken hopes of his employer. Of late Robert Carter had begun to drop more and more hints concerning Adam's future at the workshop.

"Your apprenticeship was completed these two months past," he'd said just a few days previously. "Since then I've come to rely on you, Adam. Your work is excellent, and you know how fond we have all become of you. My wife thinks of you as a part of the family, as I'm sure does Jane."

This last remark was accompanied by such a pointed look that Adam couldn't fail to notice. It had made a deep impression on him, causing him to examine his feelings towards Jane Carter. A child of fifteen when he'd first come to London, Jane was now a young woman of marriageable age. Quietly spoken, she was of medium height and build, neither pretty nor plain, except when she smiled. Her smile had a gentle warmth that lit her dark eyes and made her seem attractive.

Adam liked Jane well enough. She was always pleasant when they met, mild-mannered and softly spoken. He thought her rather a nonentity, neither particularly liking or disliking her. Surely he couldn't have mistaken Robert Carter's meaning? Adam had nothing to bring to the marriage, except the skill in his hands, yet he saw that it would make sense to the older man, a way of making sure that the craftsman he had trained wouldn't desert him for another master. Adam had already had two definite offers to work for other men, but for the moment he was biding his time.

Remembering a conversation he'd had with a group of his contemporaries in one of the popular coffee houses he frequented of an evening, Adam frowned. He had been offered a wage that was almost double what he now received from Robert Carter. He would be a fool to turn it down, and yet it was not what he truly wanted. His dream was to set up in business for himself, and to that end he had saved every penny he could spare from his wages ever since he'd arrived in town. Despite his frugality, it wasn't enough. Not if he wanted to stay in London. The cost of renting a workshop would soon eat into his slender funds, and he would need to invest heavily in quality timber if he were to produce the fine furniture for which he intended to be known.

It seemed he would either have to go back to his own village and join his father, or take up this new offer of employment, which according to the contract he must sign would mean having to pledge himself to a new master for at least another five years. Neither choice would please his present employer, nor, if he were truthful, himself. He enjoyed his life as it was, but he couldn't let things drift on for much longer. A decision would soon have to be made.

A sedan chair had stopped outside a silk mercer's shop just ahead of him, and a servant in green livery hurried to help a young woman alight. Adam paused rather than attempt to push past on the narrow pathway, watching with interest. The woman was wearing an open-robe of dark green silk over a plain petticoat of a lighter shade. Her straw hat was tied with a big satin bow beneath her chin, and pale golden curls tumbled from under the hat to fan out over her shoulders. As Adam hesitated, entranced by this vision of loveliness, she dropped her parasol. He moved quickly to pick it up and hand it to her and for one breathtaking instant, their eyes met and held.

"Thank you, sir," she said, dimpling. "How kind of you."

"My pleasure," he murmured.

She was ravishingly lovely! He caught his breath, stunned by her creamy complexion, perfect bow-shaped lips and wonderful eyes. Never had he seen anything as exquisite as this girl's face. For a moment he stared in wonder, then something stirred deep in his memory and he was reminded of a young girl he had once rescued from the gipsies. Susanna Warwick! Could it possibly be her?

In his own mind, he was certain he was right. Those eyes – he could never forget them. The eyes that had haunted him for weeks after he'd left home. So many times he had remembered that meeting in the meadows when she had looked at him meltingly. He had wanted to take her in his arms and kiss her, but commonsense had held him back. Yet those eyes were ingrained into his memory. This fashionable young woman was very different from

62

the Susanna he'd known, but the eyes were the same. It had to be her!

Even as Adam hesitated, uncertain and struck dumb by her beauty, Susanna turned away and went into the shop, followed by another woman, who looked as if she might be her maid. For a moment longer, Adam stood staring at the empty pavement, still under the spell the girl had cast. Then he shrugged, frowned and glanced at his silver pocket watch. If he didn't hurry he would be late for his appointment with an important customer.

Could it really have been Adam Blackwell? For a moment she had thought so, but it was such a long time ago and she wasn't sure. The shock of seeing him so unexpectedly had made her drop her parasol. When he picked it up, she'd thought that for a moment there was recognition in his eyes. Yet neither of them had said anything. It was as if they had both been robbed of speech, except for those few inane words she had gushed like a silly idiot. This was the chance she had waited for and now she had thrown it away. She ought to have asked if he was Adam. She ought to have asked after his family and how he was getting on.

Susanna found herself unwilling to concentrate on the merchant's wares. She had wanted some silk for a new domino for Lady Munford's masquerade party next month – the second dance she had been asked to by Lord Digby's sister! – but the prospect of a new cloak did not please her any more. The delights of London society had already begun to pall, though she dare not say as much to her mother.

Susanna had been in London for three weeks now and, despite being introduced to so many suitable gentlemen that she was quite unable to remember all their names, she had met no one she wanted to marry.

To her surprise, Susanna had discovered that most of the young men she met at parties seemed a little in awe of her. Although not at first aware of it, she had made the mistake of talking too seriously and had gained the reputation of being a "bluestocking". Immediately attracted by her beauty, the young bloods had lost interest when Miss Warwick was found to have her own opinions on subjects thought more suitable for the coffee houses than fashionable drawing-rooms. Young ladies were not supposed to be able to discuss Grenville's Stamp Act or the sad loss to the nation in 1768 when the Earl of Chatham had been forced to resign from his ministry.

Bored with the polite chatter about clothes, cards and parties, Susanna had been unwise enough to show her impatience too plainly. Lady Patricia had been quick to notice the change in attitude towards her daughter, scolding Susanna for her lapse of good manners, but the damage had already been done.

"If you do not take care, you will waste all your chances of a good match," Lady Patricia had warned the previous evening. "Gentlemen do not want to discuss politics with young ladies. They come to dance and flirt, and look for a comfortable wife."

"But you've always said that an influential hostess should know these things." Susanna's mouth drooped sullenly. "Why did I have to study so hard if I'm not allowed to discuss anything?"

"When you are married you will have your own social circle," her mother said. "As time passes you can build a reputation as a woman of sense and good taste, and then, sometimes, you may give your own opinion. But the role of a good hostess is to listen. You must understand politics so that you know who is important and can manage your gatherings with ease, but to hold forth on the iniquity of one country imposing taxes on another, as you did last night, is the height of folly."

"But all the trouble in America is because of the unfair taxes imposed by successive governments. Mr Pitt said . . ."

"The Earl of Chatham is a great statesman, Susanna." Lady Patricia frowned at her. "What he may say is one thing. It is quite another for you to argue with the wife of one of His Majesty's ministers."

"Well, she was wrong," Susanna said. "She obviously didn't understand the reasons behind the riots in Boston, and I told her so."

"And ruined your chances with her nephew at the same time."

"He has spots – and bad breath!"

"And at least twenty thousand a year."

The argument with her mother had rankled, lingering in Susanna's mind as she tossed restlessly in her bed all night. It was easy for Mama to say she must marry well, but she wouldn't have to live with a man she disliked. At least she had loved Sir William when she married him!

Annoyed with her mother, Susanna had slipped out of the house to go shopping with her maid and a footman as an escort, rather than accompany Lady Patricia to yet another al fresco breakfast, where she would meet all the same people and hear the same gossip about members of the small, exclusive circles who made up the Ton. She was, she knew, privileged to be accepted into the upper echelons of society, but her lively mind had soon begun to seek more interesting company. She would have loved to visit the 'Club', a small society of distinguished men who met regularly to dine and exchange views on the issues of the day. The arguments of Dr Johnson and Sir Joshua Reynolds would, Susanna thought, be of more interest than listening to a lisping Macaroni waffle on about the precise folds of his cravat, but as a woman she could never hope to be admitted to such circles. In her heart, Susanna knew that her mother was perfectly right. She was required only to look pretty and smile, and if she wished to marry well she ought to accompany her mother on every occasion. Her reckless behaviour this morning would probably bring her another lecture, but it was worth the risk to escape for a few hours.

While examining the various qualities of silk, Susanna was recalling the look of admiration in the eyes of the man who had stared at her in the street. Now, he was just the sort of man she had hoped to meet at one of the parties she attended with her mother! Not as outrageously handsome as Edouard Dubarry, but attractive with expressive grey eyes and a pleasant smile. He would have no need of the padding some of the men she met wore in the shoulders of their coats and, to her surprise and disgust, in the calves of their stockings!

Wistfully, Susanna thought that she might have been content to smile prettily at her suitors and say nothing if even one of them had looked like the young tradesman. Was it Adam? Her heart quickened at the idea, though in another moment she had remembered her pain and heartbreak at his desertion four years previously. For a long time she had cried herself to sleep every night, but then made up her mind to forget him, and she had tried. In her heart she knew that she must do as her mother wanted: marry someone who could restore the family fortunes. Yet the man who had picked up her parasol was so different from all the men she had been introduced to in the drawing-rooms of polite society. Why couldn't she meet a man who didn't either bore her or fill her with disgust – like the Marquis of Brandon or that fat, foolish Lord Digby? The brother of Lady Munford had proved a persistent suitor.

It was strange, Susanna reflected, but neither of the two men she so heartily disliked had been in the least deterred by her reputation as a "bluestocking". Lord Digby patted her hand at every opportunity, telling her what a pretty, clever gel she was, and the Marquis simply watched, eyeing her through his quizzing glass.

Merely despising Lord Digby, Susanna instinctively feared and disliked the Marquis. He must have been an extremely handsome man in his youth, and she supposed that some people would still call him attractive. To Susanna's eyes, his heavy jowls and thick lips were repulsive. His eyes glittered beneath drooping lids rather like a lizard's, so fixedly hypnotic that it unnerved her. She could not bear to be touched by him, and having once been unwise enough to accept him as her partner for a country dance, could not escape from his moist clasp too soon. She had taken care never to let him claim her as a partner since that night, something which she knew had annoyed him. Twice, she had deliberately turned to Lord Digby to avoid the Marquis's attentions.

Surely there must be a man in London who would fulfil her mother's ambition and her own very modest requirements! Sighing, Susanna shook her head and left the shop without buying anything. Was it too much to ask that her future husband should be an attractive, intelligent man who would not bore her?

Adam wrote down Lady Chandler's order, thanked her for her valued custom, and accompanied her to the door. She smiled and touched his out-stretched hand with the tips of her gloved fingers, thereby according him a privilege she didn't grant to many tradesmen. Adam smiled to himself as he held the door for her to go out, knowing that his physical attributes had contributed as much as his skill at furniture-making to the recent upsurge in trade. Lady Chandler wasn't the only lady of quality who called at the workshop in person these days.

"So, Adam." Robert Carter looked at him as he came back to the benches. "Her ladyship ordered another bookcase for her husband's library, and a new set of steps. That's the third time she has been here this year."

"Yes." Adam nodded. "She said she's told a friend of hers about us."

"About you, I dare say." Robert took off his little gold-rimmed spectacles and rubbed the bridge of his nose, feeling that odd pain in his chest again. "Can you spare me a few minutes, please, Adam?"

"Of course."

Adam looked at his employer thoughtfully. Robert Carter was a slight, pale man with thinning hair and a pinched nose. He coughed often and of late he seemed to have difficulty in catching his breath.

"Is something wrong, sir?"

Robert hesitated, glanced over his shoulder towards the door leading through to the living quarters, and nodded.

"I begin to wonder if I shall see next spring, Adam."

"You are ill, sir?" Adam had sensed something but not this. "Have you seen a physician?"

"Quacks, the lot of them!" Robert frowned, shaking his head. "I'll waste no more time and money on them, so save your breath. We have more important things to discuss."

Adam felt a surge of excitement. If Robert really believed he was seriously ill, it could mean important changes. He genuinely liked Robert and wished him no harm, but sentiment and business were uneasy bedfellows.

"What did you want to discuss, sir?" Adam managed to keep his tone level, but his pulses quickened and his eyes were bright and watchful as he waited for his employer's reply.

"I cannot have many years left to me," Robert said calmly, showing no distress at the prospect of his own demise. "I don't wish for death, but it waits for us all, and sooner for me than others. My main concern is for my wife – and Jane."

"Yes, of course." It was coming now. "But you are not a poor man. They will be well provided for, after all."

"Money isn't everything, Adam. Lily and Jane are not accustomed to business; they cannot manage their own affairs. They need an honest man to look after them."

Adam nodded, keeping a still tongue as he waited for Robert to come to the point.

Disappointed that Adam had made no comment, Robert cleared his throat. The pain was there again, seeming as if it would crush his lungs. It was worse this time . . . Now it was easing. He took a deep breath and looked the younger man in the eye. What must be, must be.

"If you were to marry Jane, I would make you an equal partner in the business now, and when I die you will have complete control."

Now it was said and Adam was unprepared. He hesitated, knowing that he should seize his chance with both hands. It was an opportunity he could not afford to miss, and yet . . . Ridiculously, he found himself thinking of the beautiful creature outside the silk mercer's that morning.

"Well, Adam?" Robert sounded surprised and a little annoyed. "Have you nothing to say?"

Recalled, Adam met his questing gaze. "I'm honoured by your proposition, sir."

"Honoured be damned! Jane's no beauty, but she's a good girl and she'll make a good wife. What are you waiting for?"

Cursing himself for a fool, Adam realized that he had offended his employer. What had he to do with a young woman of quality? They were worlds apart! He spoke carefully, trying to retrieve the situation. "I respect Miss Carter too much to accept your generous offer without thinking carefully, sir. I have nothing to lose and everything to gain, but I must be certain that this would be in your daughter's interests. If you will permit me, I should like to discover for myself how Miss Carter feels about such a marriage."

"Jane is a sensible girl. She will do as she's bid. Besides, she likes you."

"I should prefer to talk to Miss Carter and then give you my answer, sir."

"Talk to her this evening then."

"Surely there's no rush?" Adam frowned. "Give me a month and I'm sure you will not regret it."

"A month?" Robert knew he had no choice, though he disliked the younger man's hesitation. "I suppose Jane is entitled to be courted – but don't disappoint me, Adam. I've set my heart on this."

"I'm sure you won't regret your forbearance, sir." Adam smiled and took off his coat, rolling up his shirt sleeves. "And now I should begin work – we promised that bachelor's chest to Captain Saunders for next week."

CHAPTER FIVE

"How dared you go out without telling me?" Lady Patricia glared at her daughter. "I have been distracted with worry. Where have you been?"

"I went shopping with my maid." Susanna stared at her mother sulkily, wishing she had not come to London at all. She did not want to be paraded before all those gentlemen as if she were a thoroughbred horse. "I'm so tired of all this fuss. At home I can come and go as I please."

"In London you must take more care. Since you were shopping with Dulcia, no harm has been done. I thought you might . . ." Lady Patricia stopped abruptly and Susanna laughed.

"You thought I had an assignation – oh, Mama! With whom did you believe I had run away? Not one of my suitors has the courage to suggest an elopement – or the imagination!" Her smile faded as she saw her mother's expression. "You couldn't have thought . . ."

"Monsieur Dubarry is in London. I'm sorry, Susanna. I ought to have known that you would not be foolish enough to meet him again."

"Yes, you ought," Susanna said, her face hard. "I may not always do what you wish, Mama, but I am not a fool – and I do have some pride."

"Yes, I see that I have misjudged you." Lady Patricia looked thoughtful, then anxious. "To be truthful, Susanna, I am worried about your father. He has been with his friends at Newmarket for the past fourteen days and not a word from him."

Susanna understood her mother's anxiety. When Sir

William stayed away from home for so long without at least writing a letter to his wife, it could only mean trouble.

Susanna followed her mother dutifully into Lady Maddison's house. They had arrived for yet another tea-party and she knew she was going to be bored. Her mother had strictly forbidden her to mention politics or the situation in America.

"You may talk about the weather, music or fashion," Lady Patricia said, frowning at her daughter. "Possibly the hunting season. Nothing else, do you understand me? I didn't bring you to town at great expense only to stand idly by and watch you throw away all your chances of a good match."

"Yes, Mama," Susanna replied, hiding her surge of rebellion. She knew that it was her duty to do as her mother told her, but could not help remembering her accidental meeting with Adam Blackwell. She had almost convinced herself now that it had been him outside the silk mercer's.

"And don't look so sulky," Lady Patricia snapped. "You'll get lines before your time."

Susanna forced a smile to her face. It was no use, there was no way to get out of another boring afternoon spent gossiping over the teacups in Lady Maddison's elegant salon. She would just have to endure it.

Yet a short time later, Susanna was rescued by Lady Maddison herself, who introduced Susanna to her niece, a girl of the same age, and sent them out to walk round the gardens while she and Lady Patricia put their heads together.

"We can have a nice little gossip, and you two gels can get to know one another," Lady Maddison said with a smile.

The two girls got to their feet with alacrity, relieved to be allowed some freedom at last. They walked together in Lord Maddison's extensive gardens, in perfect harmony.

"And did you enjoy Lady Munford's ball?" Miss Maddison

asked politely. She was a petite girl with reddish-brown hair and green eyes, and Susanna had noticed her at various functions, though they had not been formally introduced. "I saw you dancing with Lord Digby. Such pleasant manners. I believe he is very taken with you, Miss Warwick."

"Do you think so?" Susanna repressed a shudder. "You were with the Earl of Grafton I think? He looks rather attractive, though I have not met him."

Miss Maddison blushed faintly, and looked at her companion. "Can you keep a secret?"

"Yes, certainly." Seeing her blushes, Susanna guessed what she was about to say. "Am I to wish you happy, Miss Maddison?"

"Yes . . . but it is not to be announced until the end of the Season, so you must not breathe a word to anyone."

"Of course I wouldn't dream of it." Susanna felt a prick of envy. The Earl was one of the few men she had seen who were at all attractive. "I'm very happy for you."

"Thank you." Angela Maddison smiled dreamily. "Shall we walk to the summerhouse, Miss Warwick? My uncle has just had it refurbished and I should like to see if they have finished it at last. I'm hoping it will be ready for my engagement party."

Susanna agreed and they strolled across the smooth lawns towards a pretty little building at the other end of the long gardens. It was easy to see that it had been undergoing refurbishment, for there were still workmen's tools on the steps leading up to the door. Just as they arrived, the door opened and a man came out, carrying a chair. Susanna's heart began to beat rapidly. It was Adam Blackwell. This time she was certain. He was dressed informally, his shirt sleeves rolled up to the elbows, and he was wearing a leather apron just as he had in his father's workshop.

As Susanna stood still, her heart beating so fast that she did not know what to do, another man came out, spoke to Adam and then turned to go back inside. At the sight of him, Miss Maddison gave a little cry.

73

"Excuse me for just one moment," she said. "I must speak to my uncle."

As Angela Maddison disappeared inside the summerhouse, Susanna stood unmoving, waiting for the man to reach her. She looked up, meeting his eyes. She could tell by his expression that he too was remembering.

"It is Adam Blackwell, isn't it?" Susanna said, a little breathlessly. "It was you in the street the other day – you picked up my parasol."

"Miss Warwick," Adam said, frowning as he looked at her. "I'm surprised that you remember me."

"Of course I remember you," she replied. "How could I forget the man who rescued me and my dog?"

"And how is your dog, Miss Warwick?"

"Unfortunately he died last year," Susanna said, blinking as she remembered the grief she had felt. "He was quite old, you know."

"I suppose he would be old for a dog," Adam said. "Well, I have work to do. You must excuse me, Miss Warwick. It was nice meeting you. Now I must get on."

Susanna hesitated, wanting to delay him for just a little longer. "How is your family?"

"Well, when I last heard," Adam said gruffly. "And your father?"

"My family are all well."

Susanna could think of nothing more to say. Besides, Miss Maddison had come out of the summerhouse and was walking towards her.

"Goodbye then . . ."

"Miss Warwick." Adam nodded his head and walked on.

Disappointed, Susanna fought to control her feelings as the other girl joined her. Of course Adam Blackwell had never meant any of the things he'd said in the park. The remark he'd made about never forgetting her was something anyone might say.

"I'm sorry to have left you like that," Miss Maddison apologized. "I just wanted to ask my uncle if we could have a look and he says we can, though it isn't quite finished. The cabinet-makers haven't brought the right chairs. There was some misunderstanding about the design, but Mr Blackwell has promised we shall have them in time for my party."

Susanna smiled as the girl led her inside the summer-house, still chattering away. How silly she was to have kept that promise in her head all this time. Obviously Adam Blackwell wasn't in the least interested in her. She must put him out of her head once and for all, and make up her mind to marry well. Angela Maddison had found someone she really liked, and there was no reason why Susanna shouldn't. After all, she had the whole of the Season.

"Well, there it is then." Sir William stuck his thumbs in his waistcoat pockets and tried to brazen it out, but the stricken look in Susanna's eyes made him ashamed. "Don't look so upset," he muttered guiltily. "The man's not so very old and . . ."

"The Marquis is twice Susanna's age," Lady Patricia cut in angrily. "And his reputation is unsavoury to say the least. You should never have entertained his offer for an instant. I shall not allow my daughter to marry that man."

"Thank you, Mama." Susanna was grateful for her mother's intervention. "The Marquis of Brandon frightens me. I just couldn't marry him."

"Nor shall you," her mother said. "There is no hurry for you to decide." Seeing Sir William's expression, she stared at him suspiciously. "What is it, Warwick?"

Her husband quailed visibly. He had been dreading the scene that must follow, but it could be postponed no longer. A gambling debt was a debt of honour.

"The fact is, m'dear, that Susanna must marry the Marquis or we're ruined. I owe him more than I can pay, and a marriage settlement is the only way out of it."

"No!" Susanna looked at her mother wildly. "Oh, Mama, please don't make me do it. I would rather die."

Lady Patricia glared at her husband. "You're a fool, Warwick," she said waspishly. "I always knew your gambling debts would bring us down."

"I won't marry the Marquis," Susanna cried, tears beginning to form. "I won't do it, Mama."

For a moment her mother studied her lovely, mutinous face in silence, then she sighed. "Then you must take Digby," she said. "I'm sorry, Susanna. Lord Digby isn't quite what I wanted for you, but he's wealthy enough to pay your father's debts without noticing it and pliable enough to manage. You could do much worse."

"But Digby hasn't come up to scratch," Sir William objected.

"Don't be more of a fool than you need," his wife snapped. "He's besotted with Susanna. If she had given him the least encouragement she might even now have been wearing his ring." Her sharp tones made Sir William cringe and fall silent as she turned to her daughter. "Well, which of them is it to be?"

Susanna stared at her mother, and felt like screaming. Marry that fat fool Lord Digby! It was asking too much of her. She was prepared to marry to oblige her family, but this was unfair. Given time, she was certain she could have made a much better match. And one that she would have found acceptable. No, it wasn't possible. She could not do it!

The defiant words of refusal were on her lips as she looked at her father, but they died unspoken as she saw his abject misery. He had brought them to the edge of ruin with his unwise investments and his gambling, but he wasn't a fool and didn't deserve the scathing insults heaped on him by his wife. Suddenly, Susanna saw beneath the cheerful mask he habitually wore to the sad, tired man beneath. He believed himself a failure; he had lost the fortune he'd inherited and the respect of the wife he'd once adored, and now he was being forced to surrender his pride. His eyes were begging her to forgive him.

Blinking back the tears, Susanna felt a surge of love for her father, remembering the days of her childhood when she had climbed on his knees and felt the warmth of his love surround her. He couldn't help his nature; it was as much a part of him as his generosity. No beggar was ever sent hungry from the Hall, nor elderly servant turned out to starve in lonely old age. If he had been happier in his own home, perhaps he might not have felt the need to gamble so often.

"It's all right, Papa," she said softly, and saw him sag with relief. "Mama speaks truly. Lord Digby will ask me to marry him if I smile prettily and show him I'm willing."

"Then it's Digby." Lady Patricia nodded. "A sensible choice, Susanna. He is sure to be at Lady Carlton's soirée this evening. I shall find an opportunity to leave you together. If I were you, I should ask him to take you out on to the balcony for a little air. Say you feel faint. Once alone you should have no difficulty in bringing him to the point, but if he doesn't speak, I'll drop a few hints."

"I'm sure he will," Susanna said. "I've been holding him off for days."

"Then that's settled," Sir William sighed. "I'll be off then, m'dear."

His wife fixed him with a baleful stare. "I haven't finished with you yet, Warwick. Susanna, you may go to your room or take a stroll in the park with your maid. I want to talk to your father."

Susanna sat looking at herself in the mirror, her eyes dry and hot. She wanted to cry, but couldn't. Her mind kept trying to shy away from the horror she felt inside. She had agreed to marry Lord Digby! Even thinking about it sent a quiver through her and she was close to despair. It was so unfair of her family to demand such a sacrifice of her, and yet she knew she could not refuse to go through with it now. She had given her word to her father, and she did love him dearly despite his faults.

77

It wasn't as if anyone else had offered for her, Susanna thought regretfully. Nor had she met anyone that she would really like to marry. Perhaps it was her own fault for disobeying her mother and refusing to simper and smile sweetly as Miss Maddison and most of the other girls did. It annoyed her that young ladies were supposed to be interested in nothing but fashion and marriage. Not for the first time, she wished passionately that she had been a male child. Then she could do as she pleased, just as Stephen did.

Utterly miserable, Susanna wondered why her brother could not have been the one to marry a fortune. Yet knowing him as she did, it was clear he would be unlikely to rescue his father from gambling debts even if he married an heiress. He would want her fortune for himself.

Sighing, Susanna began to brush her long hair. There was nothing she could do about it now. She had no choice. Perhaps marriage to Digby wouldn't be so bad. She would be able to indulge herself with lots of pretty clothes and jewels . . .

Stephen was waiting for Maggie when she came through the meadows towards the woods. He had at last persuaded her to meet him and now knew that he was sure of getting his way with her. He had thought that she might not come, but the promise of a present had brought her after all. He bided his time until she was at the edge of the wood, then sprang out at her, catching her round the waist and pulling her roughly into his arms. As his mouth crushed hers, she wrenched away from him. Breathing hard, she looked at him angrily.

"I didn't say I was going to let you kiss me," Maggie said furiously. "Where's the present you promised me? The present you said I could have just for meeting you here."

Stephen took the string of glass beads from his coat pocket and dangled it before her eyes. She reached out but he drew it back, then dangled it again, tantalizing her.

"Give me one kiss," he said. "One little kiss and the beads are yours."

"They're not worth it." Maggie tossed her head, her eyes bright and challenging. "I wouldn't have come for a bead necklace. I can buy one at the fair for a few pence."

"Ungrateful little cat," Stephen said, watching her intently. "What would you give me for a red dress . . . a red velvet dress?"

"A red velvet dress?" Maggie was suddenly eager. She looked at him, trying to make up her mind whether he was teasing her or not. "You're just mocking me. You wouldn't buy me a dress."

"I might. Here." Stephen tossed her the beads. "I was going to give them to you anyway. I'll give you lots of presents if you'll give me what I want, Maggie Blackwell."

"Would you give me a dress for a kiss?" Maggie asked.

"You value your kisses highly," Stephen said, his eyes narrowed. "No, I wouldn't give you the dress just for a kiss. I'll buy you a pair of shoes for a kiss. A red satin pair to go with the dress . . ."

Maggie hesitated. She knew that if she agreed to the kiss he would become more and more demanding, but she did want that dress, and a pair of satin shoes to go with it. She knew that her fiancé would never be able to buy her the sort of dress she wanted.

"How do I know you'll keep your bargain?" she asked warily. "I've heard about you, Stephen Warwick. I've heard about your bad ways. There's many a lass regretted the day she set eyes on you."

"Come tomorrow and you shall have the shoes," he said. "If you keep your bargain, we'll decide what you have to do for the dress."

Maggie was in no doubt of the price. She stared at him, tempted to give in, then shook her head, backing away.

"Keep your shoes," she said. "And the dress. I don't trust you."

Stephen watched her go, his eyes gleaming. He had

sensed how near she was to capitulating and knew that he had almost won.

"Be here tomorrow, Maggie," he called after her. "I'll have the shoes and maybe a silk petticoat, too."

Stephen laughed as she began to run helter skelter across the field. Anyone would think the devil was after her. She wasn't afraid of him, though; it was herself Maggie Blackwell feared. He'd got the measure of her now, and he knew it wouldn't be long before she was willing to do whatever he wanted. And then, when he'd had enough of her, he'd be off to London in search of a compliant little heiress.

The ballroom sparkled beneath a thousand glass spindles which moved and tinkled as warm air fanned the intricate swags of the delicate chandeliers. In the light from the candles, magnificent jewels glittered about the throats of the ladies, adding to the brilliance of the occasion. With their silks and satins, exquisite lace and embroidered waistcoats, the men were almost as peacock-fine as their partners, and over all hung the heavy musk of body odours and perfume.

Susanna had no need to lie when she held a lavender-scented kerchief to her head and looked up into her companion's concerned face.

"Do you think we could go out on to the balcony for a few minutes, sir? My head aches and I feel most dreadfully warm."

"But of course, Miss Warwick." Lord Percival Digby looked at the girl with genuine sympathy, having felt the heat himself all evening. "It is a terrible crush tonight, is it not?" He offered her his arm. "Allow me to help you."

Susanna laid her hand on the sleeve of his puce satin coat, feeling the soft, fleshy arm beneath. He was at least three stones heavier than was good for him and she had noticed that his hairline was beaded with sweat. He was wearing a curled and pomaded wig, which must be very uncomfortable in this heat, and there were damp stains beneath his armpits.

They walked unhurriedly across the room, threading their way through the press of chattering guests. Many of the ladies were fanning themselves, and Susanna saw more than one man run a finger beneath the intricate folds of his cravat. People smiled and nodded, but they didn't stop to talk to anyone, and the girl knew that their progress had been remarked upon. The dowagers would be simpering and smirking behind their fans, for Susanna had given Lord Digby her undivided attention all evening.

It was much cooler on the balcony. Susanna sighed with relief, glancing up at the dark sky with its scattering of tiny stars. Her head really did ache, and she found herself wishing for the solitude of her own home. If only she could turn back the clock, if only Sir William had not lost so much money to the Marquis at cards . . .

"Miss Warwick." Lord Digby cleared his throat awkwardly and a little shiver ran through Susanna. She suppressed it at once and turned to him with a smile, knowing that the moment had come. He was going to propose to her. Encouraged, he seized her hand, holding it in a tight, moist grip. "Susanna, may I speak?"

She hesitated for the merest instant, then inclined her head regally. "You may speak, my lord."

He dropped heavily on one knee, looking so awkward and ridiculous that she had to hide her smile. Still gripping her hand, he gazed up at her imploringly.

"Susanna, you must be aware of the high regard I have for you?" She nodded very slightly and he seemed relieved. "Then dare I hope that you will consent to be my wife?"

"I should be honoured, sir." Now she allowed herself that smile. "Pray do get up. I fear you must be very uncomfortable."

Digby looked surprised, then pleased. She was exactly the sort of sensible girl he had thought her. He rose to his feet, dragging on her arm to steady himself as he gave a self-conscious laugh.

"So much for my attempt to be romantic! To be honest, my dear, I'm a plain-spoken man and no doubt I've made a fool of myself."

"Indeed you have not." Susanna saw for the first time that he wasn't quite the fool she had thought him. "It was romantic and sweet of you to go down on one knee, but I shall not ask it of you again. I – I hope that we can be easy together, sir."

He looked at her from beneath sparse, pale lashes, his eyes speculative. Percival Digby was aware of the impression he created. People generally took him for a fat buffoon, unless they had occasion to do business with him, after which they invariably changed their opinion. He was a bad man to cross, but treated with respect he could be both generous and kind, especially to those he cared for. And he had formed a real affection for Susanna Warwick. She was intelligent and she made him laugh, besides being a beauty. Never a man to bother much with the pleasures of the flesh in his younger days, she had stirred forgotten longings in his loins. No doubt he would pay a high price for wedding and bedding her, but it was a price he was well able to afford. He smiled at her and patted her arm.

"So it's settled between us, Susanna. I'll speak to your father in the morning."

It was a foregone conclusion. Digby knew exactly why the proud beauty, who had scarcely deigned to smile at him these past weeks, had suddenly become so amenable, but it bothered him not one whit. He was hardly likely to be her first choice of a husband, but the dice had fallen in his favour. He knew she detested the Marquis, and was pleased she had chosen him instead. She didn't love him; she probably didn't particularly like him, but she would stick to her bargain now it was made. And that was all he asked of her. With luck she would present him with a son to inherit his wealth and title, and that done he wouldn't stand in her way. By then he knew his own interest would in all likelihood have waned.

Maggie set out across the meadows. She had vowed she would not meet Stephen Warwick. All night she had fought with her own wicked desires. He was a devil and she would be a fool to get involved with him. Tom Sutton was a good man, even though he was coarse and dull-witted. He had asked her to wed him and she knew that he cared for her, but once they were married she would be tied to a tiny stone-dashed cottage with a parlour and kitchen, a few sticks of furniture and the brood of children they were sure to have. Her life would be even harder than her mother's and that was hard enough. At least her father was a craftsman. Tom was a farmer's son and the money he had was hardly enough to keep body and soul together. As his wife she would have no chance of getting a red velvet dress, nor a pair of satin shoes.

A kiss wasn't so very much to pay for a pair of shoes. At least, that was what Maggie told herself as she walked slowly across the meadows, with the sun warming her back. She loved the woods and she wasn't afraid of them. She wasn't even afraid of the gipsies, who came and went as they pleased. In spring the woods were a mass of wonderful mauve rhododendrons, which grew wild. It was summer now, but the woods were still beautiful, and there were secret places where you could go and no one would see you.

No one need ever know she had been with Stephen Warwick. She would make him promise never to tell anyone. Maggie wasn't a virgin. Tom had already had her more than once, so she wouldn't really be losing anything . . . and she might gain a great deal. Perhaps she could persuade Stephen Warwick to give her more than he planned.

Laughing, Maggie began to walk faster. She was anxious

to see those shoes and try them on. If they didn't fit her, she wouldn't give him anything, not even a kiss.

Sir William stared at Digby across the room, his conscience pricking him more than he cared for. The man was as old as he was himself, old enough to be Susanna's father. He felt the guilt weigh heavily on him as he realized his own foolishness had forced the daughter he loved into a marriage she could only hate. No doubt she would hate him, too, now that she was caught fast in the trap.

"It's like this, Digby." Sir William cleared his throat. "It's not that I wouldn't welcome your suit in other circumstances, but Brandon spoke to me about the girl last week . . . The thing is I owe him ten thousand guineas . . ."

"Miss Warwick has done me the honour of accepting my offer," Lord Digby said. "Naturally, as a member of the family I couldn't allow you to be beholden to the Marquis, nor to be reduced to selling your estate. If you will permit me, I shall make arrangements for my bank to transfer fifteen thousand pounds into your account. And I shall of course make a similar settlement on Susanna herself . . . say, twenty thousand pounds and a house in London."

"More than generous." Sir William's knees were shaky. "My dear fellow, I don't know what to say to you."

"Fortunately, I've never been one for spending money and I've increased the fortune my father left me sixfold, so it will not beggar me. I should make it clear, though, that I do not intend to go on settling your gambling debts. The fifteen thousand is all you will get from me."

Sir William felt the colour rise in his cheeks. Digby need not have put his offer so crudely. It left one no pride. He eyed the other man askance, thinking that he might almost have preferred the Marquis. At least he'd talked like a gentleman. Digby had the manner of a merchant. Tempted to refuse the offer, Sir William remembered the expression in Susanna's eyes when he had told her she must marry the Marquis. The girl had looked almost frightened. It was a damned coil! He wished he'd never sat down to cards with Brandon, yet at the time it had seemed a good idea. He'd had a winning streak, but it had suddenly deserted him, and instead of giving up when he ought, he had gambled recklessly, knowing he could not pay without selling everything. It had come as a relief when Brandon offered to forget the debt if Susanna would wed him.

Sighing, Sir William accepted the inevitable. He offered his hand, smiling fixedly as they sealed the bargain.

"I can only say thank you and wish you happy, my dear fellow."

"I shall be the happiest of men on the day Susanna becomes my bride," Digby said. "Now, I shall have my lawyer draw up the contracts for your signature and then the money will be forwarded to your account."

"Contracts?" Sir William frowned. "Oh yes, of course, the contracts . . ."

As Digby took his leave, Sir William felt a moment of unease. If Susanna were to change her mind, he would be ruined. He had hoped the matter could be settled between them like gentlemen, but Digby was leaving nothing to chance. He was obviously going to make sure that he got his pound of flesh.

"You came," Stephen said, a cunning gleam in his eyes. "I knew you would."

Maggie watched him warily, fearing his next move. That look in his eyes reminded her of pictures she had seen of beings who were half men, half wolves. She saw the hunger there and wondered just how far she could push him.

"Show me the shoes then," she said. "I bet you haven't got them. You just pretended you . . ." Her breath expelled sharply as he took something from inside his coat and she saw a flash of red. "Oh . . . oh . . ." She looked at him in wonder. "I've never seen anything so pretty."

The shoes were red satin, with waisted heels of about two and a half inches, which were studded with brilliants, and paste buckles on the toes. Maggie grabbed for them instinctively, but Stephen held them out of her reach.

"So what do I get then?"

"I want to try them on first. They might not fit."

"You can try one," Stephen said, his eyes glinting with mockery. "Then I want my kiss."

He watched as Maggie sat down on the dry bracken, tugging feverishly at the laces of her scuffed black boots. Her skirt had risen almost to her knees and he could see a tempting glimpse of pink flesh. She wasn't wearing stockings and it made him hot just to look at the shapely calves of her legs. How he longed to touch her skin, to feel its softness and see the whiteness of her breasts with their rosy nipples. Just thinking of it made him groan with anticipation. He could feel the throbbing in his loins and he knew that he just had to have her.

Maggie gave a cry of triumph as she slipped the shoe on her right foot and found it a perfect fit. It looked so elegant and pretty; she knew that she couldn't give it back now. She stood up, balancing on one foot as she looked at him.

"I reckon you deserve your kiss then," she said. "Only a kiss, mind."

Stephen reached for her. He was breathing hard, his senses spinning. Damn it! She was a tempting armful. No wonder she had driven him half out of his mind. She stood still as he caught her against him, his mouth seeking hers with a hunger he could not control. He kissed her feverishly, on the lips, the throat, at the corner of her eyes, her ears, and then her lips once more, ignoring her protests that she'd promised only one kiss. Then his hands moved feverishly at her breasts, squeezing and caressing her through the thin material of her gown.

"Maggie, Maggie," he murmured throatily. "You know how much I want you. I've never wanted a woman the way I want you."

86

Maggie pulled away from him. She saw the lust on his face and heard his ragged breathing. He was ready to do anything for her now.

"I want a red velvet dress next time and a silk petticoat," she said. "Then maybe I'll let you do what you want."

Stephen made a grab at her. He wanted her now, not tomorrow. There was nothing to stop him taking what he wanted, nothing to stop him having all he wanted from her now. Why should he pay for what he could take by force?

Maggie was too quick for him. Snatching up her boots, she darted back out of reach, her eyes bright with mischief.

"You don't want it like that," she said, taunting him now, "like a dog and a bitch. If that was all you wanted, you could have had me ages ago. You want me willing and eager, don't you, Stephen Warwick? You want me to do all the things to you that I do in your dreams."

Seeing her standing there laughing at him nearly drove Stephen wild, yet he knew that she was right. He did want her willing and eager. Rape would give him ease but no real pleasure. She wouldn't be the first one he'd taken that way, but it wasn't as good as when the girl was willing.

"I'll get you a dress tomorrow," he promised. "Let me have you now, Maggie. I promise I'll bring the dress tomorrow."

"I'll come tomorrow," Maggie said, her eyes dancing with excitement now. "Have the dress waiting and you'll get all you want and more, Stephen Warwick." She hopped out of range, taking off her precious shoe. "Now throw me the other one. You've had your kiss."

Stephen hesitated, then tossed her the shoe. He was calmer now. He could wait until the next day, but after that he would be the master. Maggie Blackwell would not get away so lightly again.

CHAPTER SIX

It was overpoweringly hot in the airless workshop. Adam had stripped to the waist, but the sweat still trickled over his muscled back and arms, and the curling black hairs on his chest glistened with moisture. Intent on carving an acanthus leaf on the leg of what was to be an important chair, he was aware of voices in the showroom – one of which was female and strident – but he took no notice as the door opened behind him.

Lady Helen Munford's first thought was that he was a magnificent specimen. With a body like that he could have been a prize-fighter. She already had in her employ two grooms and a footman who could have taken their place in any wrestling match or bare-knuckle fight in the country, but none of them had the wit to amuse her apart from the short time they spent in her bed. As Adam glanced up, she was struck by the intelligence in his eyes. So she had not been misinformed after all!

Her disappointment at being met by Robert Carter in the showroom had been intense though, having cast an experienced eye over the various tables, chairs and cabinets, she had seen that the work was very fine. In her estimation – and she had a reputation for being a woman of taste in such matters – very nearly as good as anything produced in Mr Chippendale's own workshop.

"Interesting," she had said, her manner haughty and slightly bored. "But not quite what I require. If I were to place an order with you, I should want something designed just for me. Have you someone who could do that?" She concealed her eagerness beneath heavy lids that gave her the look of a bird of prey.

Robert Carter inclined his head. "If your ladyship will wait one moment, I shall ask Mr Blackwell to step into the showroom."

"Stay!" she commanded as he turned away. "I have a fancy to see your craftsman at work."

"But the dust – your gown . . ." Robert Carter saw the imperious flick of her hand and bowed his head. She was an important customer and well connected. Her brother was Lord Digby and her husband was extremely wealthy. "As you wish, my lady. Please come this way." He led the way through to the back, holding the door for Lady Munford to pass before him.

Now she saw that her visit had been worthwhile. She approached the bench, smiling at Adam. He was hastily donning his shirt out of respect for her, but she had seen enough to know that she had found a new source of amusement. "And what are you working on now, Mr Blackwell?"

Adam caught the scent of her strong perfume as she leant towards him, the low sweep of her bodice affording him an intimate view of the soft, white mounds beneath. Although past forty, in her elegant gown and tall, pomaded headdress with its false ringlets, ribbons and laces, she gave an impression of youth and beauty. Once she must have been lovely indeed, though the colour in her cheeks was mostly rouge these days.

"It will be the leg of an important armchair," Adam said, his hands smoothing the wood, caressing it with the love he felt for his best work. "We always use the finest timber, my lady. See the grain and those swirls in the wood; they will show to advantage when it has been polished."

Lady Munford watched his hands, admiring the long, strong fingers. He stroked the chair leg as tenderly as if it were a woman, she thought, her bosom rising and falling as her breath quickened with excitement. Already she was imagining him in her bed. It was all she could do to keep her hands off him!

"I have been told you have some skill at design," she said, allowing him a glimpse of her neat ankle as she sat down on a chair provided by Robert. "Would you be prepared to do something for me?"

"I should be honoured, my lady. Would you care to look through a few sketch books?"

"Oh, la!" she cried, flicking his cheek with her lace kerchief. "It is far too hot to think of business now, Mr Blackwell. I fear I must go home and lie on my bed in the cool." She allowed him to picture the scene before continuing. "I should be grateful if you would attend on me at my home – shall we say at six this evening?"

Adam swallowed hard. The invitation in her eyes was plain enough, but she was not the first to look at him so rapaciously. From the age of fifteen, he had discovered that many women were willing, even eager, to lie with him.

"If your ladyship wishes." He inclined his head. "It will be my pleasure."

"Then we are agreed," she said, rising to her feet. "I shall expect you promptly. Do not disappoint me, sir."

She swept from the room with a curt nod at Robert. As they heard the showroom door shut with a snap, the two men looked at each other. Robert frowned.

"Be careful of her, Adam. She has an unsavoury reputation. They say she delights in breaking men's spirits."

"She is an aristocratic whore," Adam said dismissively. "But she could make us fashionable overnight if she chose."

"Or ruin us," Robert replied anxiously. "Be careful not to show your contempt, Adam."

"I shall be polite, naturally." Adam felt uneasy. There was something he had not liked about their visitor; he sensed something predatory about her, something unclean. Besides, he preferred to be the hunter. "You need not worry . . ." He broke off as the door to the living quarters opened and Jane Carter entered.

She brought a breath of fresh air with her, a clean wholesomeness that was particularly noticeable after the overpowering perfume of their previous visitor. Her soft brown hair was tied back off her face with a simple ribbon, and she was wearing a plain grey gown with a modest neckline and a white kerchief over her shoulders. She smiled at her father, and then, shyly, at Adam.

"Has your visitor gone, Father?"

"Yes, Jane." Robert looked at her fondly. "Did you want something?"

"Mother has prepared a cooling drink for you — would you like me to bring it in?"

"That was thoughtful of her," Robert said, mopping his brow and shrugging off the tight-fitting coat he had worn to greet Lady Munford. "What say you, Adam?"

"I should be grateful for a cool drink. Thank you, Miss Jane."

She smiled at both men and went out again. Robert looked at his employee.

"Have you thought any more about what we were talking about last week?"

Adam avoided his eyes, knowing that he was a fool even as he did so. "I've been so busy, sir. I . . ."

He was saved from continuing by Jane's return. As she poured the cool cider into two pewter mugs, handing one to her father and then turning to him, Adam wondered at his slowness at taking up her father's offer. She was comely enough and would make a comfortable wife.

Jane turned to her father once again. "Don't forget Mr Bennet is coming to dinner this evening."

She picked up her tray, nodded to Adam and went out.

Adam drew water from the well in the back yard, dousing his head and shoulders. It had been the hottest day he could remember in years, or perhaps it was only that it felt that way in the stuffy workroom. Drying himself on a coarse towel, he replaced his shirt and turned towards the scullery door. If he didn't hurry he would be late for his appointment with Lady Munford, and despite Robert's warnings he was excited at the prospect of designing furniture for her. Furniture that would be seen and remarked upon by her friends.

Seeing Jane emerge from the scullery with a bucket, he paused, waiting until she reached him. She smiled as he took the bucket and filled it for her.

"I could have done that, Adam. Father says you have an appointment this evening. I shouldn't delay you." She bit her lip, looking at him hesitantly.

Adam sensed her uncertainty. He knew that she must deliberately have sought him out, for there was a lusty serving-girl to do the menial tasks. He smiled at Jane.

"Is there something I can do for you?"

"I ought not to bother you with my foolish problems."

"Why not? We're friends, are we not?"

She gazed up at him then, her soft grey eyes anxious. "I can't talk to Father and Mother has enough to do ..." A faint colour tinged her cheeks. "I – I think Mr Bennet means to ask me to marry him." Now she raised her eyes deliberately to his. "I don't know what to say to him."

Adam frowned, uneasy as he met her frank gaze. Did Jane know about the offer her father had made him? He cleared his throat and averted his eyes.

"It depends on what you want, Miss Jane," he said at last. "John Bennet is a good man, though perhaps a bit old for you – and there's the children to be thought of."

John Bennet had been a widower for six months and he had two children under five years old. The most likely reason for his imminent proposal to a girl several years his junior, Adam thought.

"Yes, that's what's bothering me," Jane replied seriously. "Those poor mites need a mother. Do you think it's my duty to marry him for their sakes?"

Adam hesitated, knowing that this was his opportunity to speak. What was he waiting for? By the morning he could have his name on the sign outside Robert Carter's showroom. Surely he wasn't still thinking of Susanna

92

Warwick? Her image had haunted him, driving him to some restless nights in his own bed and causing Mary-Ellen Watts to eye him askance in the mornings. Yet Adam had realized long ago that such dreams were merely moon-madness; Susanna could be nothing to him. Their paths were set in opposite directions and he could not seriously hope for anything between them. No, his hesitancy was more likely just the temporary reluctance of a single man to settle down. He glanced at the young woman by his side.

"That's surely for you to decide," he said, as he carried the bucket of water towards the scullery. "It would certainly be the act of a charitable woman to take a mother's place. No doubt John Bennet would be grateful."

"So you think it's a good idea, then?" Jane looked at him earnestly.

"Now I didn't say exactly that." Adam smiled ruefully. "I think you should do as you please, Miss Jane – but if you'll heed my advice . . ."

"Yes?" There was a sudden betraying eagerness in her voice.

"I think you should take your time. Think about it for a while, just to be sure."

"Oh . . ." Jane found it hard to hide her disappointment. She had hoped for a more positive reaction. "Well, thank you for your advice, Adam. I shall think about what you've said." She smiled brightly. "And now I mustn't delay you any longer.'

Taking the bucket from him, she went into the scullery. Staring after her, Adam ruffled his thick, dark hair. Women were strange creatures to be sure!

Lord and Lady Munford's house in Henrietta Place was an impressive building, designed by the architect James Gibbs in the second quarter of the century. Descending from his hired carriage, Adam stared at the imposing front door before making up his mind. Then, quite deliberately, he rang the bell. Adam Blackwell was no longer to be summoned to the tradesman's entrance like a lackey.

He stared boldly at the liveried footman who opened the door. "Mr Blackwell to see Lady Munford," he said firmly.

For a moment their eyes met and clashed, then the footman's fell. "Will you please come in, sir? I shall inquire if her ladyship is at home."

Adam nodded, saying nothing as he followed the servant inside. Left to wait in a small chamber off the entrance hall, he amused himself by admiring the architect's fine arches and proportions. He was not kept waiting long before the footman returned.

"Her ladyship will see you, sir. If you would care to follow me."

Adam smiled inwardly. He had learned much since he was summoned to the Hall by Sir William Warwick, not least that respect for oneself demanded it from others. This was just the beginning. Adam Blackwell was going to be someone. One day he would own a house as fine as this, and he would be rich. The ambition that Lady Patricia's scorn had sparked in him had long since replaced his desire for revenge. Being sent to London as an apprentice was the best thing that could have happened. He was going to take his chances when they came, in whatever shape or form.

The footman led him up the main staircase with its intricate ironwork banisters and along a carpeted hall, one wall of which was panelled with dark oak and hung with family portraits. They stopped at the door right at the end, where the man turned to Adam, smirking slightly.

"You are to go in, sir."

Adam hesitated as the servant retreated soft-footed the way he had come. Something in the footman's eyes had made him faintly uneasy. Taking a deep breath, he knocked.

"Come in."

Turning the handle, Adam opened the door and went in. And then he understood the look in the footman's eyes. Decorated in cream and gold, with tall ceilings and intricate friezes, it was a woman's boudoir and Lady Munford was lying on a velvet-covered daybed, wearing only a thin silk robe that clearly showed the tones of her flesh beneath it. She smiled at Adam and held out her hand invitingly.

"Mr Blackwell," she said. "I've been waiting for you. Come, sit and talk to me. We have much to discuss . . ."

In the workshop, wearing her elegant gown and elaborate wig, she had given the impression of youth. Now Adam could see that her own hair was sparse and owed its bright colour to artifice. Her breasts sagged without the support of her corsets, and, bending to take her hand, he caught the unmistakeable stink of stale sweat. It was all he could do to stop himself recoiling in disgust.

Lady Munford patted the stool beside her, smiling at him. "Sit here and keep me company. The day has been long and I am weary of being alone."

Adam obeyed stiffly. "You wanted me to design some furniture for you, I believe?"

"I am bored with this room," she said, waving her hand to indicate the boudoir and bedroom beyond. "You may refurbish it for me entirely, and if your designs please me, my husband may ask you to furnish his new library. If you please me." The emphasis on the last few words was very deliberate. She reached for the fan lying beside her and held it out to him. "It's too hot for anything but talk today. Cool me, Adam – and talk to me. I could do so much for you if I chose." Her eyes glinted suddenly. "And I know you are an ambitious man, Adam Blackwell. So why don't you oblige me?"

Adam opened the fan, moving it to and fro with an awkwardness that made her laugh. He felt the swift colour rushing up from his neck to his cheeks. It was a long time since a woman had made him feel foolish. He closed the fan with a snap.

"I fear I have no talent for such things, my lady."

"No." She smiled from beneath hooded lids. "Your talents lie in other directions, do they not? So I shall excuse you this once. Instead you may talk to me. Entertain me, Adam."

"What would you like to know, ma'am?"

She lay back against the silk cushions, fanning herself languidly. "Tell me about yourself, Adam. Tell me about your ambitions – and your lovers." She laughed again as she saw his startled expression. "For shame, sir! You have the body of a prize-fighter but the stomach of a weak boy."

Adam saw annoyance in her eyes and knew he must retrieve the situation. "There was a time when I could beat any man in the county at wrestling," he said. "Would your ladyship care to hear about that?"

"It will do well enough for a beginning," Lady Munford said, her eyes glinting. "Entertain me for a while, and then we shall discuss business . . ."

Adam walked home, needing the solitude and a chance to breathe away from the stale odours of her ladyship's boudoir. The moon was almost full as he passed the plain brick building of the Oxford Chapel and turned towards the fine houses of Cavendish Square. As he reached the end of Portland Street, he saw a hire carriage pulled up beneath the flickering light of a street lamp, the horse pawing the ground impatiently with its front hooves. For a moment he hesitated, but decided against taking the carriage. He was in no particular hurry to reach his lodgings, and he carried a swordstick with which to protect himself from any attack by the Mohocks – robbers, who though often young bloods of quality, were so fierce that they had been named after savages – who sometimes roamed the streets at night to prey on the unwary. Unlike many a gentleman of fashion, Adam was well able to fend for himself and the dimly lit streets had no fears for him. He had been attacked more than once by footpads, but his spirited defence had soon sent them fleeing into the night for their lives.

In the distance he could hear church bells tolling the hour. It was nine o'clock. He had spent nearly three hours with Lady Munford, and found it difficult to escape even then. Had it not been such a warm night she might not have let him leave that early, he thought ruefully. Only her genuine fatigue had saved him from receiving her full attention.

After this evening, Adam was in little doubt of the price he would be expected to pay for her favours. Her ladyship was, to put it plainly, a lewd, corrupt woman hungry for the pleasures of the flesh. She had touched him at every opportunity, finding his embarrassment by turns amusing and annoying. Only his stories of wrestling victories had saved him from her anger.

Was he willing to pay the price she demanded? If he offended her by refusing to oblige her, she could use her influence to blight his hopes. Despite her loose morals, she had a reputation as a woman of good taste in all matters of fashion. Her opinions were listened to and respected by her contemporaries. If Lady Helen Munford said that Adam Blackwell's designs were desirable, he would be made overnight. She could ruin him just as easily.

It was unfair that a word from her ladyship could make or break him, but it was the way of things. Bribery and corruption were rife in public life; rich men often bought seats in Parliament for their friends, securing the votes of rotten boroughs with vast sums. Money and influence secured titles and favours for those who could afford it.

The morals of those in high places were often questionable. The royal dukes set a bad example. Cumberland had caused a great scandal by seducing the beautiful young Lady Grosvenor, whose husband started a court action against the duke. Cumberland promptly abandoned the beauty and began courting a Covent Garden actress, thus showing his disregard for public opinion. With such behaviour almost commonplace amongst the fashionable rakes, it was scarcely surprising that a woman like Lady Helen took lovers how and when she chose. The dowagers might whisper about her behind their fans, but Lady Helen never flaunted her vices in public and she was received everywhere. She was a powerful woman, Adam realized, and accustomed to getting her own way.

A personal sacrifice might have to be made in the interests of his career. She would no doubt tire of him soon enough. Sighing, Adam let his thoughts turn to his next most pressing problem. What was he to do about Robert Carter's offer?

Stephen was waiting in the usual place. Maggie was late in coming, but just as he was about to give her up, he saw her walking towards him across the fields. Her head was down, and there was something subdued about her manner. He felt his blood pound at his temples. She had made up her mind to take the dress. Three days she had come, and three times she had run away without accepting the bribe, but today she would give in. He knew it as surely as he knew the sun would rise.

She looked at him shame-faced, then said simply, "You've won, Stephen Warwick, but not because of the dress."

Surprised, Stephen could only stand and stare as she moved towards him, then she pressed her body against his, lifting her mouth for his kiss.

"You've won me," she said. "I've fought it with all my strength, but I can fight you no more. You be the victor, Stephen. Do what you want with me. I'll not resist you."

Moaning low in his throat, Stephen reached for her hungrily, covering her face and throat with feverish kisses. For a moment she was unmoving in his embrace, then she groaned and threw her arms about his neck, her fingers moving into his silky hair, stroking and caressing.

"Love me, Stephen," she murmured throatily. "Love me, for it's you I want . . . only you . . ."

His hands moved over her breasts, squeezing and caressing her. Then they were on the ground, and he was pulling up her skirts, opening his breeches in his hurry to have her. He found her wet and willing as he thrust into her without preamble, spilling himself far too soon in his haste.

"Damn it," he muttered. "See what you've done to me, you witch?"

Maggie lay laughing up at him, her eyes bright with mockery. "That's your dress gone," she said. "It's as well I've got the hots for you, Stephen Warwick, or you'd need a fortune at this rate."

"It was your fault." He glared at her. "Coming on so willing all of a sudden. I suppose you want something else from me now?"

"Yes, I do," Maggie said with a secret smile. "But it ain't a new gown . . . and I'm going to make it worth your while." Her eyes teased and tantalized. "Now, if you can wait jest a minute, I'll take me clothes off and we'll start from the beginning . . ."

It was another hot day. Adam went into the kitchen in search of a drink. Unusually, the large room was empty, though the fragrant aroma of meat simmering in the stewpot over the fire told him that Jane or her mother must be nearby. He was pouring himself a cup of cold water when the yard door opened and Jane came in, her cheeks glowing from the fresh air. She smiled at him and set down her basket of freshly picked herbs.

"Would you not prefer a glass of cider?" she asked.

"Water is fine, Miss Jane," he said. "It cools the throat on a warm day."

She smoothed back a lock of her fine, light brown hair, then took a bunch of rosemary from her basket and began to wash the stalks in a bowl at the table. "Did your business go well last night, Adam?"

"It's hard to say just yet. I've promised a new design for her ladyship's boudoir for next week. If she's pleased with my drawings, it could mean a big order for us – perhaps the first of many."

"I'm sure she will be pleased," Jane said, looking at him uncertainly. "Mr Bennet dined with us last evening ... Before he left, he asked me if I would consider marrying him."

"And what answer did you give?" Adam put down his cup to look at her.

"I said I would think about it."

Adam nodded. "A wise decision, Miss Jane."

She added the rosemary to the stewpot and came to stand in front of him. Her eyes were wide and innocent as she looked up. "It would be a good match for me, Adam. Mr Bennet is the owner of a fine house and carriage, and his business as an engraver is growing. Just last week he finished a set of Mr Hogarth's drawings and over one thousand prints have already been subscribed. He says Mr Hogarth's work has become more valued since his death than ever it was before."

"It is often the way," Adam agreed. "Your Mr Bennet will be a rich man one day."

"I do not care so much for riches," Jane said. "But he is a good man and the children need a mother . . ." She waited but when he said nothing, went on, "I have almost decided to marry him."

Adam nodded but his attention had wandered. Her remark about the Hogarth prints had put him in mind of something. An idea for her ladyship's boudoir.

"Well, you must do as you like," he said absent-mindedly.

"So you want me to marry him?" Jane's bottom lip trembled. "Then I might as well . . ." Tears started to her eyes and she suddenly turned and rushed from the room, leaving Adam staring after her in dismay.

Now what had he said to upset her?

"No, I tell you," Stephen said angrily. "You're asking too much, Maggie. I won't do it. I won't take you to London with me. I can't afford to set you up as my mistress. Besides, it's too risky. If anyone got to hear of it . . . You know I need to marry an heiress."

"I wouldn't get in your way," Maggie said with a wheedling smile. "I promise no one would know anything about us . . . and I'd be there whenever you wanted a little bit of this . . ." She bent her head, her tongue licking at his skin as she worked her way downwards from his navel to the object of her desire. Maggie laughed as he groaned and his manhood jerked into throbbing life once more. "See, you like it, don't you? You like what I do to you, so why won't you take me?"

Stephen gasped as her small white teeth nibbled at him, and then she took him into her mouth, sucking gently until he was willing to promise her anything.

"I'll see," he said hoarsely. "Damn you, Maggie, I'll think about it."

He was breathing raggedly as he thrust her back on the bracken and drove into her frantically. She was like no other woman he'd known and knew exactly how to drive him wild. He ought to give her what she wanted, but some devil inside him made him deny her. Yet for a few wild moments as he exorcised his lust, he was willing to consider her proposal. If he set her up as his mistress, she would be there waiting for him after he had married his boring little heiress. His own, hot-blooded temptress.

The temptation lasted only as long as the pleasure she gave him. Afterwards, as he was dressing, Stephen decided that it was time to call it a day. Maggie was worth all he'd given her, but it wasn't a challenge any more.

"I shan't be able to come for a while," he said carelessly. "I have to go to Norwich on business for my father. I'll see you when I get back."

Maggie stared at him, a little prickling sensation at the nape of her neck. "You will come back, won't you?"

"Yes." Stephen looked at her luscious body and sighed. He wasn't quite ready to give her up yet. He smiled at her and kissed her lightly on the mouth. "Of course I'll come back. And when I do, we'll talk about the future."

Maggie nodded, only partially convinced. She had meant to tell him today, but she wasn't quite sure. She was only ten days late. It wasn't definite that she was having a child, but one thing was certain: if she was pregnant the baby was his. Tom Sutton hadn't touched her for weeks. She hadn't let him, not since she'd started to meet Stephen.

CHAPTER SEVEN

"Is it not pretty?" Susanna held out her hand so that her mother might see the large sapphire and diamond ring on the third finger of her left hand, then she opened a flat leather box to show the matching necklace, eardrops and bracelet.

"Heirlooms, I presume," her mother said with a smile.

"No." Susanna looked at the jewels again. "Digby had them made specially for me. He said the family jewels were too old-fashioned and clumsy for me, though I shall have my pick of them when we are married. He says the sapphires cannot match the colour of my eyes, but he has hopes of the aquamarines he is having made up for my wedding gift."

"You will be utterly spoilt, no doubt," Lady Patricia snorted. "The marriage settlement on you was ridiculously large – and Lord Digby has been extremely generous to your father and myself."

"I know. Papa told me." Susanna met her mother's gaze. "So you are satisfied with me then, Mama?"

"I should be happier if you would agree to a wedding at Christmas. Digby is impatient to claim his bride."

"He has agreed to wait until the spring," Susanna said with a frown. "I've told him that I've always dreamt of a spring wedding and he has promised I may have it."

"Why the delay?" asked Lady Patricia suspiciously. "You're not being silly about this, Susanna? I've explained all you need to know. There's no need to be frightened of your wedding night. It won't be so very bad – and who knows, you might come to enjoy your husband's attentions."

"As you do, Mama?"

Lady Patricia had the grace to blush. "There was a time when I was not averse to your father's attentions. These days we choose to go our separate ways – and I see no reason why you should not find pleasure elsewhere. Once you have provided your husband with an heir, of course."

"Supposing I do not enjoy my husband's attentions?"

"Then you must endure them." Her mother looked at her unsympathetically. "So much fuss over nothing, Susanna. Think of all the pretty gowns you will be able to buy."

Susanna blinked hard, turning away. "Yes, Digby has been generous."

"After your engagement has been formally announced this evening, I see no reason to stay in town, do you?"

"No. I shall be glad to go home," Susanna said. "And Digby can visit if he chooses."

"Of course he will do so." Lady Patricia sounded pleased. "Then I shall leave you to rest for an hour or so. I shall tell the servants to start packing and we shall leave the day after tomorrow."

As her mother went out, Susanna's shoulders sagged. She genuinely appreciated the gifts Lord Digby had given her, but she was being asked to pay a terrible price. It was so hard to keep up the pretence when her heart felt as if it were breaking. The previous evening, when Lord Digby accompanied them to the gardens at Vauxhall, she had given a performance that would not be put to shame by one of Mr Garrick's actresses at Drury Lane, but at nights when she lay alone in her bed the tears were never very far away. Sometimes she thought she could not bear it, and she just wanted to curl up and die. Yet she knew there was no way to escape. She had given her word and must keep it – but she intended to delay the wedding for as long as she possibly could.

Now she was certain. This was the third morning she'd been sick. There was no doubt about it now. Maggie stared at her white face in the little dressing mirror her father had made for her last birthday and saw the fear in her own eyes. What would Stephen say when she told him she was having his child? Would he even believe that it was his? He must! He must know that she hadn't been with Tom Sutton since they became lovers. She hadn't wanted anyone but him.

"You're a fool, Maggie Blackwell," she said to herself. "You should have got all you wanted before you let him have his way with you."

All her life, Maggie had wanted something better than the existence that others of her class called living. She had envied her brother Adam his chance to go to London, wishing it was her. She wanted to be an actress and travel to big cities and perhaps even foreign lands. If only Stephen would take her to London and set her up for a while, just until she could have the baby and find herself a job on the stage. She wouldn't expect him to keep her forever; she knew he would tire of her sooner or later. It was her one chance to escape from the drudgery she feared, her one chance of finding something different.

Stephen had to believe her. He had to help her. She would make him. He was still wild for her, especially when she did things to him that none of the other girls had been willing to do. She would make him so mad for her that he would promise her anything. It was going to work. It had to work. The only alternative was to tell Tom Sutton it was his baby, and he would have to be a fool to believe her.

Going downstairs, Maggie saw her mother come out of the kitchen. Jeanie looked at her suspiciously and Maggie knew a moment of fear. Had her mother guessed already? Hot shame made her skin crawl as she looked at the older woman. It would kill her parents if she had a baby without being wed. She couldn't stay in Chorley Hale. She just couldn't. If Stephen wouldn't help her, she would run away and find work as a barmaid.

"Where be you going?" Jeanie asked. "I could do with a hand with the baking." She turned aside as a fit of coughing overtook her.

"I'll help you when I come back," Maggie said, unable to meet her mother's eyes. "I promise I will, but I've got to go somewhere now. I can't stay . . ."

"Maggie . . . You bain't in trouble, be you, lass?" Jeanie asked anxiously.

"No, of course not," Maggie said, forcing a smile as she ran past her mother and out of the house. "I shan't be long . . ."

She was breathing hard as she ran across the meadows, her heart thumping so madly that she could hardly breathe. Her mother knew! She knew the truth. It was only a matter of time before she made Maggie confess it. Brushing the hot tears from her eyes, Maggie drew a sobbing breath of relief as she saw Stephen was waiting for her as he'd promised. Today she would tell him. She would tell him she was having his child.

It was so good to be home! Susanna felt as though she had been let out of prison as she walked across the meadows with the wind blowing in her hair. Digby had gone to his estate earlier that day.

"To see that everything is in readiness for you, my dear," he had said, pressing her hand to his lips. "I shall be with you again within the month."

"I shall be impatient for your return," she had lied, keeping her smile in place until he had gone.

And now she was free! Free for a whole month. It was almost too wonderful to be true. She was happy again, so happy that she wanted to sing.

It seemed a lifetime ago that she had come this way to meet Edouard Dubarry. She had been an innocent child then, still untouched by the harsh realities of life, her head filled with dreams of romance. For a moment she wondered what might have happened if she hadn't run away when Edouard kissed her, but then she knew that it could only have made things worse. If she had consented to an elopement, she would have been fetched back in disgrace and married off to the first man who would accept spoiled goods. A little shiver went through her. At least she hadn't been forced to marry the Marquis. She had seen him watching her through his quizzing glass at the opera a few nights before they left town, and the look in his eyes had frightened her. She was certain he was angry because she had spurned his offer and accepted Lord Digby instead.

Recalling a scandalous affair where a young woman had almost been carried off from her own home by force after spurning the advances of a licentious rogue, Susanna glanced over her shoulder nervously. The Marquis would not pursue her here – would he?

Suddenly hearing a girl's shrill scream, Susanna spun round in a circle, looking for the source of the sound. And then she saw a village girl fleeing from a man who pursued her on horseback. A man she recognized as her own brother! Even as she watched, Stephen caught up with the girl, leapt from his horse and flung her to the ground, laughing wildly.

Furious at the sight of her brother behaving so wantonly, Susanna cried his name and began to run towards them. Stephen looked up, his face startled, and in that instant the girl escaped from beneath him, struggling to her feet and running off across the meadow. Stephen gazed after her, frowning, but making no attempt to continue the pursuit. He gathered his horse's reins and stood waiting for his sister to come up to him.

"What were you doing to that poor girl?" Susanna demanded furiously. "She sounded terrified."

Stephen glared at her. "What business is it of yours, miss? I was doing nothing that need concern you. Besides, she wanted me to catch her."

"It didn't sound much like that to me," Susanna said, still angry. "Surely you can find enough willing wenches without forcing yourself on a virtuous girl!"

"Virtuous!" Stephen grinned. "It's as well you came when

you did and not a few minutes later. I wouldn't want to sully your innocence."

Susanna looked at her brother with dislike. She had always felt this antipathy towards him, and she knew it was mutual. Stephen was selfish in the extreme, caring little who he hurt in pursuit of pleasure.

"One day you're going to get a sound thrashing," she said. "Father ought to have done it years ago!"

Stephen sneered. "My, my, we have come back from London the fine lady, haven't we?" He made her an extravagant, mocking bow. "Pardon me for breathing, milady."

"If it weren't for me you'd be out on the street and forced to earn your own living," Susanna cried, suddenly angry. Why should he be allowed to waste his time in drinking, gambling and seducing the village girls while she was forced to marry for the sake of the family! "And if it weren't for Mama and Papa, I'm damned if I would marry to oblige you!"

"Is that a profanity on those sweet red lips?" he mocked. "What have your fine friends been teaching you? Don't worry, Susanna, I'll find my own heiress when I'm ready. You won't have me hanging on your purse strings, begging for favours."

"That's just as well," she responded furiously. "For I'd not give you a shilling."

"You keep your money," he taunted. "You'll earn it the hard way — on your back like all the whores."

"You devil!" Susanna struck out at him in fury. "I hate you, Stephen."

He caught her wrist, holding her off, his mouth twisted in derision. "It's a high price to pay for fancy gowns, sweet sister, but never mind. You can amuse yourself with handsome lovers just as Mama does."

Susanna aimed a well-placed kick at his shins. He gave a howl of rage and let her go. She backed off, staring at him in disgust.

"You're a black-hearted devil, Stephen. One of these days someone will teach you a lesson — and I hope it's soon."

"You can dance on my grave, Susanna," he said, smiling insolently. "Just as I'll dance at your wedding."

She turned and walked away from him, her head high. As his loud, taunting laughter followed her, she felt the sting of tears in her eyes. Stephen was a cruel, tormenting devil — but the worst of it was that there was no escaping the truth of what he'd said. She had been sold to the highest bidder, exactly as if she were an exclusive whore.

"Maggie, I want to talk to you. Don't you be running off again, for I'll not be bamboozled. I mean to have the truth, my girl!" Jeanie pounced on her daughter as soon as she came into the house.

Maggie looked at her mother's face and her heart sank. There was no escape this time. She could hardly look at her mother as she said, "I know what you're thinking, and it's true. I bain't going to deny it."

"Oh, Maggie," Jeanie cried, her face crumpling as tears sprang to her eyes. "What your Pa's going to say, I daresn't think. He'll be fit to fly at Tom Sutton, so he will."

"It bain't Tom Sutton's," Maggie mumbled. "He bain't the father."

"Not the father . . . oh, Maggie!" Her mother stared at her in horror. This was far worse than she'd imagined. "What be you up to, my girl? What have you done?"

Suddenly, the tears were pouring down Maggie's cheeks and her story came tumbling out in a rush. "I bain't a bad girl, Ma. You know I bain't," she sobbed. "It were jest that I wanted a red velvet dress so bad, and then I went and lost me heart to 'im."

Jeanie looked at her sadly. "You be a silly girl, Maggie Blackwell," she said, but her tone was only mildly scolding now. "You couldn't have thought Squire's son would wed you, not Squire's son? Tain't to be thought of."

Maggie hung her head. "I thought he might take me to

London with him, set me up for a while, then I could go on the stage, be an actress . . ."

"Where be your head, Maggie Blackwell?" her mother asked, looking at her wonderingly. "Don't you know where girls like that end up? Start off as a rich man's whore and you'll die in the gutter, riddled with disease. I did think you had more pride in you."

"What am I going to do, Ma?" Maggie looked at her shame-faced. "Stephen Warwick won't take me to London. He says I should claim it's Tom Sutton's brat."

"Now that you bain't going to do," Jeanie said firmly. "You'll tell Tom the truth and then we'll see. Your Pa and me 'ull stand by you."

"Oh, Ma," Maggie wailed. "I can't tell Tom. I be too ashamed to face him."

"You'll tell him if I have to stand over you," Jeanie said, her expression stern. "That I be set on, Maggie. Tom Sutton be a good man and he be entitled to the truth."

"Yes, I know. I jest be feared to tell him, Ma. He be such a strong-tempered man."

"Then I'll stay with you while you tell him," Jeanie said. "He won't lay a finger on you while I be there, but tell him you will, my girl, or I'll take a strap to you meself."

"What are you reading?" Lady Patricia asked her eldest daughter as she saw her curled up to catch the warmth of the autumn sun on the window seat of the morning-room. "Something improving, I hope?"

"It's Mr Samuel Richardson's novel *Pamela*," Susanna replied with a little frown. "It was given to me by Lady Clarendon's daughter."

"Novels!" Lady Patricia pulled a face. "At least Mr Richardson sets a moral tone in his work, unlike Mr Fielding's parody."

"But, Mama!" Susanna protested. "You were amused by the *History of the Adventures of Joseph Andrews and His Friend Mr Abraham Adams*. I remember you saying to Papa that you

110

much preferred his irony to Mr Richardson's morality!"

Lady Patricia smiled wryly. "I keep forgetting that you are no longer a child. If you wish to read Mr Fielding's *Tom Jones*, I will make you a present of my own copy."

"Thank you." Susanna smiled back at her mother and stood up. "I should like to have it. And now I think I shall go for a walk."

Lady Patricia nodded and glanced out of the window. "Put your cloak on, Susanna; there's a cool breeze today."

Susanna left her mother and went upstairs to her own room. Lord Digby was expected any day now, and then her freedom would be at an end. Her mother had planned various entertainments with the neighbours and Susanna would have to accompany Lord Digby everywhere. She sighed deeply. He had written regularly, his letters telling of his impatience to claim her as his bride, and she was very much afraid he meant to retract his promise and press her to agree to a wedding at Christmas.

Opening her bedroom door, Susanna saw her sister standing by the dressing-chest. She had been holding the sapphire and diamond necklace against her throat, and admiring herself in the mirror. She blushed guiltily as she saw Susanna.

"I wasn't doing any harm," she said defensively. "I only wanted to see what it would look like on me."

"Why don't you try it on?" Susanna suggested with a smile. "And there are some gowns I took to London with me that I shan't be needing again. We could get Nanny Giles to take them up for you." She stood beside Beatrice in front of the mirror. "There isn't so very much difference between us now."

Beatrice fastened the necklace round her throat and clipped the eardrops to her lobes, her eyes bright.

"You're so lucky to have things like this." Her sparkle faded suddenly. "I'm going to miss you when you go away, Susanna. Mama is always out visiting her friends, and there's no one to talk to."

"You can come to stay with me, Bea." Susanna slipped an arm about her sister's waist. "We'll have lots of visitors and I'll buy you something pretty for yourself – a pearl necklace. Would you like that?"

"Susanna! Will you really?" Beatrice was all smiles again. "I'm sorry I was nasty to you before." She bit her lip. "I shouldn't have told Mama about Monsieur Dubarry kissing you – but I was jealous."

"Jealous of me?" Susanna was amazed. "Why?"

"Because – because you're so pretty and I'm plain . . ." Beatrice looked at her suspiciously as she laughed. "Why are you mocking me?"

"Oh, my dearest Bea," Susanna cried. "You're not plain. It's just that we're so different." She picked up her silver-backed brush and began to smooth her sister's thick hair. "When you're a little older you can wear your hair up like this. Now see how different you look."

Beatrice stared at herself. With a few deft strokes, Susanna had transformed her. She smiled as she saw the glitter of diamonds and sapphires around her throat.

"When I stay with you I shall find myself a rich husband," she said. "Someone like Lord Digby, who will let me do whatever I want. You're very lucky, Susanna! Your husband is so generous. I can't wait for you to marry him so that I can stay with you."

"Well, I don't suppose it will be long now." Susanna sighed as she laid down the brush. "If Digby and Mama get their way, I shall be married before the New Year."

Maggie looked into the eyes of the man she was promised to, the shame washing over her as she saw the disbelief turn to anger, disgust and then a blind misery that was worse than all the rest. She hadn't realized how much her betrayal would hurt him, and she discovered it made her own heart ache.

"The Squire's son . . . that rotten bastard," Tom Sutton said, sounding incredulous. "He's had every girl for miles around. How could you, Maggie? How could you let him?"

"He talked me into it," Maggie said defensively. "He bought me presents and . . . I didn't mean to do it. I fought him as long as I could . . ."

Tom's eyes glittered with fury. "You mean he forced you? If he raped you, I'll kill him, so help me, I will!"

"No . . ." Maggie couldn't look at him now. "It weren't rape, Tom, not that way. It were jest that he kept after me. He never give me any peace. He tempted me like the serpent tempted Eve in the Garden of Eden. He tempted me and . . ."

"You lifted your skirts for him like any common whore," Tom said bitterly. "All for the sake of a red velvet dress. You filthy little . . ." He moved towards her threateningly, but Jeanie rushed to stand in front of her daughter.

"You bain't a-going to hit her, Tom." Jeanie glared at him, then started to cough. It was several minutes before she recovered. "Maggie told you the truth. She's been honest with you. Some would have tried to pass the babe off as yours."

Tom's hands dropped to his side. There was sympathy in his face as he looked at Jeanie. She wasn't well, anyone could see it. Jeanie Blackwell had been a handsome, plump woman a few years back; now there wasn't a handful of flesh on her bones. For a moment his own pain was subdued as he thought of hers.

"That be true enough," he said. "And I dare swear I've you to thank for that, Jeanie Blackwell." He turned away to look out at the street, his shoulders stiff with anger.

"Maggie bain't expecting you to keep your promise to her," Jeanie said. "She can't hold you to it now, Tom. You be a free man."

For a moment Tom was silent, then he swung round, his face contorted with agony. "I ain't going to let her go," he said fiercely. "She be promised to wed me, and wed me she will, Squire's brat in her belly or no."

Jeanie looked at him in silence. Then: "You bain't going to take it out on her, Tom? Better you find another girl than start with bitterness in your heart."

113

"It's him I want to kill," Tom said. "The bastard that seduced her." He looked at Maggie. "I'll stick by you, lass. I bain't saying I can forget, but I'll do me best to forgive you."

Maggie looked at her mother and then at Tom. She began to shake her head and back away from them. "No," she whispered. "No, Tom, I'm too shamed to wed you. I'm too shamed . . ." She turned and fled from the room. They heard her running upstairs.

Tom moved to follow, but Jeanie stopped him. "Nay, Tom Sutton, leave her be for now, lad. She be sorry for what she's done and she needs to cry it out of her. You leave her to me. I'll talk her round." Jeanie had to turn away as the cough racked her once more.

"I'll call on Sunday as usual," Tom Sutton said. "That be a bad cough, Jeanie. You should ask the doctor to come."

"Bain't much he can do for me," Jeanie said with a sad smile. "Don't fret yourself, lad. I'll live long enough to dance at our Maggie's wedding."

"Aye." Tom nodded to her. "Reckon you will, Jeanie. Reckon you will. I'll be setting the banns on Sunday. You tell Maggie that."

"What are you doing?" Jane put down her tray and glanced over Adam's shoulder. On the bench in front of him were a series of sketches for the furnishings of a lady's boudoir. "These are wonderful! But it looks like . . ." She broke off and blushed as he glanced up at her.

"What does it look like, Jane?" Adam's eyes glinted with mischief as he saw her embarrassment. "A Sultan's harem perhaps?"

"Well . . ." Jane nodded, her cheeks pink. "It's almost as I would imagine a harem might look, except that I don't suppose they have cabinets or tables like those."

"Then I've achieved my objective." Adam smiled. "It is an English version of an Eastern potentate's harem. This is the daybed – see the tented effect with the pink silk draped overhead. And this painted commode, this bookcase, display

114

cabinet and the table top all portray scenes from Arabia. Each one follows the other – do you see?"

Jane stared at him. "They look a little – a little rude to me."

Adam laughed and nodded. "Exactly. You put the idea into my head when you mentioned Mr Hogarth's paintings. These cabinets are an Eastern version of the 'Rake's Progress'."

"But will Lady Munford like them?" Jane looked doubtful.

"They should amuse her," Adam replied. "She is easily bored. The paintings will titillate and intrigue her friends. See how I've carried the Eastern influence into the carved footstools and chairbacks. No one else will have seen anything like them."

Jane was still doubtful. She much preferred the plainer, more elegant style of furniture that Adam usually worked on, but she supposed he knew what he was about.

"When are you going to take your sketches to Lady Munford?" she asked.

"Perhaps tomorrow," Adam said. "I think they are finished at last. Yes, I shall send a note to Henrietta Place and ask if I may call tomorrow afternoon."

Susanna was reading when her sister came into the small sunny drawing-room that overlooked the park. She put down her book and smiled as Beatrice held out a letter.

"This just arrived for you."

"Thank you." Susanna glanced at the writing and laid it aside. It was another of Digby's long letters telling her every detail of the work he was doing at his house in Surrey.

"Aren't you going to read it?" Beatrice asked. "Aren't you in the least bit curious?"

"Not really." Susanna sighed. "I'll read it later."

"I wish someone would write long letters to me."

Looking at her sister's sulky face, Susanna realized that she was bored and restless. There was evidently to be no more peace for her that day.

"What do you want to do, Bea?" she asked. "Would you

like to ride or go for a walk, or try on some of my dresses? We didn't get around to it the other day, did we?"

Beatrice's eyes lit up. "Can I have the blue silk afternoon gown you showed me?"

"Yes, I don't see why not." Susanna stood up, linking her arm through her sister's. "When I'm married, Bea, you shall come to London with me and I'll buy you pretty new gowns of your own."

Beatrice gave a squeal of delight and hugged her. "You're the best sister in the . . ." She stopped speaking as Stephen came into the room. "Let's go now."

"Running away," Stephen sneered. "What a timid little thing you are, Bea darling. Afraid I might want to teach you a lesson for spying on me?"

"I'll tell Mama," Bea said, her eyes filling with tears. "I wasn't spying on you. I was in the tree and I couldn't help hearing you having an argument with . . ."

Stephen moved towards her threateningly. "You keep your mouth shut, you little cat. Tell anyone what you heard and I'll make you sorry!"

"Oh, I hate you. I wish you would go to London and stay there," Beatrice cried. Pulling away from her sister, she ran from the room.

Susanna looked at her brother scornfully. "Did you have to be so unkind to her? She doesn't have much to make her happy these days."

"She's a little sneak," Stephen said. "Always listening at keyholes or hiding in trees, spying on me."

"If you had nothing to hide it wouldn't matter," Susanna retorted. "Something on your conscience, Stephen?"

"Mind your own damned business," he muttered, and strode off.

Susanna frowned, then followed her sister upstairs. Stephen was definitely hiding something.

Adam dressed carefully for his appointment with Lady Munford. The plain cut of his dark cloth coat was in keeping with his situation, but it fitted him well, showing off the breadth of his shoulders to advantage, and the intricate folds of his starched white cravat would have been a credit to any affected Macaroni or fashionable gentleman.

Mary-Ellen Watts looked up from her baking as he came downstairs. She smiled as he paused for effect, his eyes quizzing her.

"Will I do then, Mrs Watts?" he asked, his mouth quirking at the corners.

She felt a spasm of desire in her stomach, but her smile was natural as she answered, "You look a proper gent. Too good for the likes of that harlot!"

"Now then, Mary-Ellen," he chided her softly. "You've no need to be jealous. Lady Munford is business."

"Business is it?" she snorted. "Business that's kept you from my bed these past two months or more!"

"Nay, she's not the cause," he said, slipping an arm about her comfortable waist. "Forgive me if I've hurt you, Mary love. I've had something on my mind."

She smiled and reached up to kiss his mouth. "Don't fret yourself, Adam. We've had a good run by my reckoning. If 'tis over, 'tis over. I'll not fall out with you because of it, sweeting."

He squeezed her waist and kissed her hard on the mouth. "You're a generous woman, Mary-Ellen, and I'm a fool to have slept alone these many nights."

"My door's not locked," she said. "But you come only if it pleases you. Now watch out for that highborn harlot. If she's not diseased, it can only be by the grace of God."

Adam nodded, his eyes serious. "I'll remember what you've said, Mary-Ellen. And now I must go or I shall be late, and that won't improve her ladyship's temper . . ."

This time Adam was not kept waiting. The footman again led him upstairs to Lady Munford's boudoir, where he was invited to enter as before. Her ladyship was wearing a loose sack gown of pale green silk with a laced bodice that opened down the front, scarcely covering her breasts, her thin hair caught up beneath a lace cap. A copy of the *Ladies' Diary* lay on the table at her side. She smiled at him, patting the stool beside her.

"So, Adam Blackwell, you have brought the sketches at last."

Adam inclined his head, presenting his leather folio with a little flourish. "These are preliminary, my lady. If they please you, I can make any adjustments you may require."

"Open the folder and show me," she said imperiously.

He did as she asked, declining to sit but watching anxiously as she studied the drawings. Had he misjudged her? Would she dismiss his ideas as a mere flight of fancy, or would she find them intriguing? She was silent for a long time, her expression giving nothing away as she went back over each plate several times, and then she glanced up and he breathed a sigh of relief as he saw his answer in her eyes.

"So, you have imagination and a sense of humour, Adam Blackwell. Your ideas intrigue me. I shall require a few changes. Pink is not a colour that becomes me. I find it too insipid, but a bright jewel colour — say shades of peacock blue and aquamarine — then yes, I think I would find your designs very pleasing."

Adam drew breath. "And the scenes from Arabia?"

Lady Munford looked at him. "Did you draw them yourself?"

"Yes, my lady. I should of course engage the services of a professional painter for the actual work."

"I suggest you produce a panel to let me see exactly how it would look — can you do that?"

"One small panel? I could have it ready within two weeks."

"Bring it to me then and if it pleases me, we shall agree the contract."

"Certainly, my lady." Adam bowed and turned to leave, but she laid her hand on his arm. He saw the flash of the emerald and diamond rings on her fingers and looked up into her glittering eyes.

"You do not mean to leave me so soon?"

"I thought you had dismissed me."

"For shame!" She flicked his cheek with her pointed fingernail. "I shall not allow you to run away, Adam. Come, sit beside me and we will share a glass of wine."

She waved him to a stool near her, pouring wine from a crystal jug into two large goblets and handing him one. Then she held up her own glass in salute, and drank.

"To success, Adam," she said throatily. "And pleasure. For one complements the other, does it not?"

Her words seemed to have a hidden meaning. He drank sparingly of the wine and set his glass down. She refilled both glasses, then patted the velvet seat beside her invitingly.

"Come, sit here at my side." As he obeyed, she leaned towards him and beneath the overpowering scent of her perfume, he caught the stale odour of an unwashed body. Instinctively, he recoiled. Her eyes flashed with anger. "So, you will not oblige me? You are too virtuous perhaps?" Her gaze narrowed as she read his mind too easily. "No, I think not. Then I do not please you."

"Nay, my lady." Adam felt the constriction of his cravat as a spasm of nerves caught his throat. "You – you are an attractive woman but . . ." He sought desperately for a way of escape that would not offend her. "Your husband . . . Lord Munford . . ."

"Is out with his friends and never ventures here." Her eyes glinted with malice now. "Patronage was never free, Adam. If you wish for mine, you must oblige me."

He hesitated, then moved slightly towards her. She responded by pressing herself eagerly against him, and as he still hesitated, entwined her arms about his neck. Her mouth was suddenly forced on his, her lips greedy and demanding, sucking at him as she kissed him, drawing his body down with hers on to the silken cushions of the daybed. He felt suffocated, his breathing restricted as

119

he tried to shut out the stale odour of her unclean flesh. She laughed up at him, her breath stinking and fetid as she revealed rotted teeth. And then she began to mock him, using language that he had hitherto heard only on the lips of harlots and guttersnipes.

Adam stiffened, revolted, hardly believing that a woman of quality could be so coarse. His stomach churned as she spewed out her filth, making lewd, obscene suggestions of what he should do to her that made him want to vomit. The picture of a young girl's beautiful face flashed into his mind and he knew that he could not do what this trollop demanded of him, no matter what the cost. With a cry of disgust, he broke free of her clinging arms, springing to his feet as the vomit rose in his throat. She lay laughing wildly, her breasts lolling out of her bodice where she had torn it open, and her legs spread wide, showing that she wore nothing beneath the robe. The stink of her private parts set him retching.

Suddenly her mirth was stilled. She sprang to her feet, knocking the wine glasses on to the floor. Watching the crimson liquid spread through the silk rugs, Adam turned to stone as before his eyes she changed into a spitting, venomous virago, beginning to scream and berate him in the language of the gutters.

"You will regret this," she said at last as the stream of filth abated. "You will rue the day you spurned me, Adam Blackwell."

Adam backed away from her, his face white as she suddenly ripped the bodice and then the sleeves of her gown, her eyes dark with hatred.

"Rape!" she cried. "You tried to rape me. My husband will see you hanged for this!"

"No! No, it was you who . . ."

Adam ducked as she threw a beautiful porcelain vase at him and then reached for its twin. He watched in horror as she stormed about the room, overturning tables and smashing everything that came to hand.

"You will come crawling on your belly before I've finished with you – and I'll see you hanged!" she screamed. "Now get out! Get out, you miserable excuse for a man. Spurn me would . . ."

Adam waited no longer. He was breathing heavily, his brain reeling from the shock of her attack. Unable to think clearly, he backed away from her, fumbling for the door handle as she threw a bronze figure at his head. That jerked him into action and he heard her wild laughter as he bolted from the room. Closing the door, he could hear her screaming and rampaging about.

Walking hastily along the hall and down the stairs, he was aware of a growing fear. Rape was a serious charge. Imprisonment or even hanging was not unknown if the man were convicted. Perhaps transportation – ruin at the very least. He cursed his own stupidity. He should have raped the whore as she'd wanted!

Stephen wasn't drunk when he left the inn, though he'd been drinking steadily throughout the evening. His mood was one of anger mixed with indecision. He'd told Maggie that he didn't believe the child was his, but in his heart he knew that she had told him the truth. He would have to do something for her, he supposed. Give her money, maybe. He knew what she wanted, and a part of him was tempted to give way. He could just about manage to set her up in lodgings in London, and pay her keep until after the brat was born. Yet he was afraid that she wouldn't keep to her side of the bargain. He needed to find that heiress. The estate was so heavily encumbered that even with the money Digby had paid his father, Stephen knew he had no alternative. The best thing would be to finish with Maggie for once and all . . .

Stephen blinked as the men moved towards him from the shadows. He hadn't seen them at first, but something menacing about them made a prickle of fear run down his spine.

121

"What do you want?" he muttered, then, looking into the angry face of the nearest of them, he understood. "Tom Sutton. So she told you then? The stupid bitch!"

"She told me." Tom Sutton grunted. "She told me what you done to her, you bastard. And now you're going to pay for it."

"Get out of my way, you fool," Stephen blustered. "Lay a finger on me and I'll see you before a magistrate in the morning."

"They can hang me if they like," Tom Sutton said. "But I'll teach you a lesson first, Squire Warwick's son or no."

"Put your fists up then," Stephen said. "We'll see who teaches whom."

"Nay, I'm not giving you the chance," Tom Sutton grunted. "A whipping's good enough for a dog like you."

Suddenly the other men crowded round him. Stephen saw that their faces were covered by mufflers. Only Sutton had been brave enough to show his true colours. Yet they were probably all known to him, village lads whose girls had been led astray by him.

Realizing he was trapped, Stephen tried to run, but they were all around him. As the first blows began to rain down on his body, he bit his tongue. They would like to see him humiliated, begging for mercy on his knees, but he would die first.

"Cowards," he taunted. "Not one of you is man enough to stand up to me alone."

"Don't listen to him," Tom Sutton warned. "Go for his body. We want to punish him, not kill him. We want him to remember this night for as long as the bastard lives . . ."

CHAPTER EIGHT

Susanna stood at the window of her bedchamber, staring out at the moon. Almost full, it cast a silver patch across the gardens, giving the night a magical mystery that set the girl's heart yearning. For a moment the picture of a man's face flashed into her mind. Adam Blackwell . . . She recalled the moment when they'd met outside the silk mercer's shop in London, and again later at Lady Maddison's, when he had seemed to snub her. Until then she had always carried a vague hope that he would keep his promise to come back for her. Of course he had only been teasing her, the way young men do. It had meant nothing. It was always she who had sought him out, she who had gone to the village just to see him. She who had dreamed foolish dreams. And yet he had risked his life for her once.

The memories stirred inside her as she thought about Adam rescuing her from the gipsies. He had been so brave, standing up to them the way he had. There had been so many of them. Now that she was older, she understood just what might have happened to her if Adam had not chanced to come that way.

Susanna smiled, remembering how innocent she had been then. For weeks she had visited the Blackwell family as often as she could manage to evade the watchful eye of Nanny Giles. How she had adored the serious-faced young man who had so boldly rescued her! She had looked up to him as the hero of her dreams, seeing him as Hercules or Apollo. But he had gone away without saying goodbye. She had wept into her pillow every night for a week. After that, she had stopped visiting the Blackwells, though she always stopped to talk to Maggie when she saw her.

Susanna's thoughts changed direction abruptly as she saw something in the gardens. A man was stumbling towards the house, almost falling and then recovering to walk unsteadily onwards. It was her brother!

Although still angry with him over their quarrel, Susanna didn't hesitate. Stephen was clearly in trouble and needed help. Slipping a warm robe over her nightgown, she picked up a lighted chamber-stick, left her room and began to walk quickly along the hall and down the back stairs, shielding the flame with her hand. Candles were still flickering in their sconces as she reached the lower regions, so some of the servants must still be about, though she knew that both her parents had long since retired.

Stephen entered by a little-used door at the side of the house seconds before she reached the hall. She saw him stagger and collapse against a wall, as if the effort of reaching the house had taken the last vestige of his strength, and hurried towards him. He glanced up as she anxiously bent over him.

"What's wrong, Stephen?"

"Come to gloat?" he asked, cursing as he tried to rise and fell back again, clutching his head.

Susanna saw that his mouth was cut and bleeding, his clothes mud-stained and torn.

"Have you had an accident? Were you thrown from your horse?" she asked, giving him her hand to help him stand up. He clutched at her arm, pulling on her heavily as he got to his feet. "You're bleeding, Stephen."

He wiped the back of his hand across his mouth and looked at the blood. "Damn those louts! They'll pay for this night's work."

Susanna stared at him. "Did someone attack you?"

His lips curled in a sneer. "You don't imagine one village lout could do this on his own? There were at least five of them, all armed with cudgels."

"But why?" Her eyes darkened with suspicion. "It was because of a girl, wasn't it? That girl I saw you

124

chasing the other day! Oh, Stephen, what did you do to her?"

"She was willing enough," he muttered defensively. "Maggie Blackwell is a lusty wench with an itch between her legs."

"Do you have to be so coarse?" Susanna asked. "Why did you press your attentions on the Blackwells' daughter, Stephen? You know Papa has always liked the Blackwells."

"I tell you, she was willing," Stephen insisted. "At least until the lout she was promised to became suspicious."

"So it was her fiancé who attacked you!"

"With some of his friends." Stephen grimaced. "He had the effrontery to threaten my life if I ever approached Maggie again. I should horsewhip the brute!"

"No, Stephen!" Susanna met his challenge. "Don't you think you've done enough damage?"

"I'll have my revenge yet." Stephen groaned as his head spun. "He'll make a mistake and then I'll see that he's left to rot in prison. But it will have to wait – I'm off to London in the morning."

His sister stared at him suspiciously. "You haven't told me everything, have you? What is it, Stephen? Why are you running away?" Her eyes widened in horror. "Maggie is having a child, isn't she? You're afraid of what Papa will say when he finds out."

"You said I should marry an heiress." Stephen avoided her accusing eyes. "It's best if I'm not around for a while."

"Coward!" How despicable her brother was. He had forced himself on the girl and now he was running off to London rather than face the consequences. "What about Maggie? What happens to her now?"

Stephen shrugged, pushing his sister's hand away as his head cleared. "Why should I care what happens to the whore?"

"But she's carrying your child. You must care what happens to the child?"

"I dare say she's not the first or the last. If she'd had any

125

sense she would have passed it off as Tom Sutton's brat."
Stephen laughed at his sister's shocked expression. "You're
mighty interested in the Blackwells — but then you always
were. That's why Father had to pack the son off to London
out of the way."

"What do you mean?"

"Didn't you know? Mama thought you were becoming
too friendly with the family, so she forced Father to do
something about it. He paid for Adam Blackwell to be
apprenticed in London from his winnings at the card table."

"So that was it." Susanna felt oddly betrayed. How could
her father have done that? She might have expected it of
her mother, but she hadn't expected her father to be so
unkind. She frowned at her brother. "You should at least
give Maggie money for . . ."

"You give her money if you're so concerned." Stephen
started to walk away.

"Don't you want me to help you? Your face . . ."

"Save your concern for those that need it." He shrugged
off her hand. "I can take care of myself."

Susanna stood back, watching her brother make his
way to the end of the hall and out of sight. She sighed,
shuddering to think of the commotion it would cause when
Sir William discovered what had happened. Perhaps it was
best that Stephen was leaving.

As for the money, she would go herself in the morning
and see what could be done to help Maggie.

"Where are you going, Susanna?" demanded Lady Patricia.
"I've been looking for your brother this past hour, but all
the servants will say is that he ordered the carriage and
went off this morning."

Susanna bit her lip. It was not for her to tell tales. Her
mother would discover the truth soon enough. "I thought I
would take a walk into the village," she said. "I want to visit
the church and place some flowers on Grandpa Warwick's
grave. It's his birthday today."

"Yes, I know." Lady Patricia frowned at her. She sensed that Susanna was making an excuse, though she would no doubt visit her grandfather's grave. "I thought we should have heard from Lord Digby before this."

"He spoke of a problem with the stone masons when he last wrote," Susanna said. "He has set some repairs in hand and I believe he wants to oversee the work himself."

"I see." Her mother nodded. "Well, I shall not keep you – but do not be late for dinner."

"No, Mama. I shall not be late."

Susanna left her mother and went out into the gardens. She made her way to the hot-house to beg some lilies from the gardener before setting off towards the village. Her errand in the churchyard took only a few minutes. Then she turned towards the house in the centre of the village, the one she had visited so often during that short period of her life. Outside, she looked up at the blackened timbers of the Elizabethan cottage with its overhanging windows and plastered walls. The Blackwells had lived in Chorley Hale almost as long as the Warwicks had been up at the Hall, and for as long as she could remember there had been a mutual respect between the families, though one was rich and the other was not.

Gathering her courage, she knocked at the door. It was several seconds before it was opened by a woman Susanna barely recognized as Jeanie Blackwell. Mrs Blackwell had been a stout, handsome woman, but now her cheeks were sunken and her eyes had a queer, dead look to them. It was obvious to Susanna that she was not well.

"Mrs Blackwell," she said. "I'm Susanna Warwick."

"I know who you are." Jeanie's eyes were resentful. "And I know who we've got to thank for our troubles."

"I am aware of what my brother has done," Susanna said quickly. "I saw him last night after Tom Sutton and his friends had thrashed him. No, don't look so worried," she added as Jeanie started to tremble. "He won't go to the

127

magistrate. He's gone running off to London with his tail between his legs like the coward he is."

Jeanie stared at her in silence for a moment, then nodded. "You'd best come in, Miss Susanna. Will you take a glass of my elderberry wine?"

"Thank you, I will," Susanna said, following her inside.

They passed through the workshop, which looked empty and deserted. Remembering it of old, Susanna thought it strange that it was so tidy and neat, as if no work had been done there for some time.

The kitchen was redolent with the aroma of cooking and herbs, which hung in bunches from a hook in the low ceiling. A kettle was boiling on the hob, but one glance was sufficient to show Susanna that no one else was there.

Jeanie saw her glance and frowned. "We're alone, miss. So you might as well say what you came to say."

Susanna looked at her, then inclined her head. "I don't blame you for being angry. You must hate all the Warwicks."

"Nay, I don't hate you — or your father. Sir William's not a bad man. It's just a pity he didn't take his belt to that brother of yours a long time ago."

"I couldn't agree more," Susanna said. "Before anything else, I must tell you that I am ashamed of Stephen. I told him last night that he is a coward and should face up to his responsibilities, but he has taken himself off to London in search of an heiress."

"I wouldn't expect him to marry our Maggie. Nor would she take him if he offered. Maggie bain't a bad girl, Miss Susanna. She were led astray by fancy words and a handsome face, so she were."

"Did — did he force her ..." Susanna broke off and blushed. "He swore she was willing but I didn't believe him."

"He bought her a pretty dress and a necklace of beads from the fair," Jeanie said. "She never meant it to go so far, but that be the way of things. I told her so and she knows it. Fair ashamed of herself she be."

"Will Tom Sutton still wed her?"

Jeanie frowned. "He says so but Maggie says she won't take him. Got some bee in her bonnet about being spoiled goods. Says she'll live with her shame . . ." Jeanie raised her apron to wipe the tears from the corner of her eyes. "She were always a bright, happy girl, Miss Susanna. Now all she does is lie in bed and stare at the wall. Says she'd rather die than bring more disgrace on us all. It's near broke her father's heart."

"And yours," Susanna said gently. "I wish I could do something to help you."

"There's nothing you can do for Maggie . . ." Jeanie regarded her hesitantly. "Mebbe you could have a word with your father . . . if he needs a new chair or something up at the Hall. Things haven't been so good recently and . . ." She broke off, too upset to continue. "My husband would die of shame if he heard me begging for work for him."

"Do you think your husband could make me a travelling cabinet?" Susanna asked. "I'm to be married soon and . . ."

"Why bless you, miss." Jeanie looked at her. "My old Tom, he's never forgot your visiting here all them years ago. He'd be mighty pleased to make you a cabinet."

Susanna smiled. At least this was something she could do to help the family, without it seeming like charity. Besides, she had been wondering what she could find as a gift for Lord Digby.

"Tell your husband I want something very elaborate with lots of drawers and fancy handles, and perhaps he could make a matching one that I can give to my husband as a wedding gift?"

"A pair of marriage chests, that be a commission to set my Tom on fire. He'll be right proud to make something like that for you, miss. A pair of marriage chests, now that be something special. Something you and your husband will always take a pride in."

Jeanie smiled, but then it faded and she pressed a handkerchief to her lips as a fit of coughing shook her.

"Are you ill?" Susanna asked in concern.

"Nothing but a cough," Jeanie said. "Don't you fret over me, Miss Susanna. I'll ask my Tom to start on them wedding chests for you as soon as he comes home."

"Thank you." Susanna hesitated, then took twenty gold guineas from her purse and laid them on the table. "A little present for Maggie, for the baby."

Jeanie stared at the money, her eyes anxious. "I'm not sure I should take that, Miss Susanna."

"It's not charity, Jeanie," Susanna said quickly. "Nothing can make up for the harm your family has suffered at my brother's hands, but perhaps this will help with the expenses. I know my father will want to . . ."

"Nay, my Tom won't hear of him being told," Jeanie said hastily. "He's a proud man, Miss Susanna. He says we've brought the trouble on ourselves by letting Maggie have too much freedom. It's Maggie he blames – and me for being so proud of her. And perhaps he's right. If I'd kept her at home instead of letting her fill her head with fancy ideas . . ."

"It's not your fault," Susanna said, her face grim. "We both know who's to blame, Mrs Blackwell. I'll make no excuses for Stephen. I'm only glad that Tom Sutton thrashed him."

Digby was not coming for another two weeks. She had two more weeks of freedom! The wind was cold and stung her cheeks, but she felt happy as she walked through the meadows. Digby had hinted strongly that he wished for a Christmas wedding and she knew she could not hold him off for much longer. Did it really matter? Acceptance had come to her slowly, but now she knew that a few months was neither here nor there. There was no escape from her destiny.

Becoming aware of someone walking towards her, Susanna

halted, shading her eyes to see more clearly who it was. She did not recognize him though he was plainly a young man of the village. A chill ran down her spine as she suddenly knew instinctively that it was Maggie's fiancé. What could Tom Sutton want with her? She kept quite still, waiting for him to reach her. For a moment they stood face to face, and she saw the terrible grief and anger in him.

"You've saved me calling at the Hall," he said gruffly. "I want to return this to you, Miss Warwick."

He held out his hand and she saw the glint of gold coins.

"That money was for Maggie and her child."

"I can take care of my wife. We shall have no need of charity from the likes of you."

Susanna felt the flush creep into her cheeks. "Do not tar me with the same brush as my brother, Mr Sutton. The money wasn't charity, but a gift from a friend."

"Take it back," he said, glaring at her. "We want nothing from you or your brother."

"My brother would not bother to offer it," Susanna said. "It was from me to Maggie. You have no right to take it from her."

"And you have no right to interfere in our lives," he growled. "We've suffered enough from the Warwicks. Stay away from Maggie – and keep your money."

He threw the coins at her feet. Susanna stared at him, saying nothing. Then she turned and began to walk away, leaving the money lying on the ground.

"And tell that brother of yours that if he ever shows his face here again, I'll kill him. I swear I'll kill him the next time!"

Susanna walked proudly, her head high. She did not bother to look round.

CHAPTER NINE

Adam's head had cleared by the morning. It was, he knew, unlikely that Lord Charles Munford would really believe his wife's story of rape, but even if by some good fortune he escaped arrest for the charge of assaulting Lady Munford, she would make it her business to ruin him. She had only to turn up her nose when his name was mentioned and imply that he was an inferior craftsman and the business that he had begun to build amongst the aristocracy would disappear overnight. Cursing himself for a fool, Adam set off for the house of his employer. Robert would not be best pleased at the news.

The wind was cold, and Adam shivered as he turned up his coat collar. Autumn had set in with a vengeance. Gloom hung over him as he walked along the street. He had had so many plans for the future and now they could all be ruined by the spite of a vindictive woman. Fool that he was! Why had he not given her what she wanted? And yet even as he cursed himself, he knew it had always been destined to end that way. His revulsion would have made it physically impossible to oblige her ladyship. He had no liking for whores, highborn or otherwise!

Letting himself into the workshop, Adam shivered again. He felt as if he were coming down with an ague, though he knew it was probably lack of sleep. What he needed was a tot of brandy. Robert kept a small barrel in the kitchen for medicinal purposes. He would not grudge his employee a measure of it.

Going into the kitchen, Adam halted as he saw Jane chopping vegetables. She looked up, frowned and went on with her work.

"I feel a little shivery this morning," he said. "Do you think I could have a tot of brandy to keep out the cold?"

At that, she raised anxious eyes. "Are you ill, Adam?"

"I didn't sleep well," he said. "I think I'm just tired, that's all."

"You look very pale." She left her work to fetch the brandy, pouring him a generous measure. "Drink this and sit by the fire for a few minutes. You shouldn't have come today."

"You're very kind to me." Adam smiled. "John Bennet is a lucky man."

"I haven't given him my answer yet."

Adam stared at her. As she looked into his eyes, he saw the mute longing in her and knew why she had delayed answering the widower. It was Adam Blackwell she wanted! In that moment he knew that he must speak now or lose her. His dreams of Susanna Warwick were simply moon-madness. If he threw away his chance of becoming a partner in Robert Carter's business for something that was so far out of his reach, he would be three times a fool. Jane was no beauty, but she was fresh and decent. And she was his only chance of realizing his ambitions.

For a moment Adam wrestled with his conscience. Was it fair to offer marriage to a girl he did not truly love? Yet it was more often that way than not, especially with plain-faced girls. Jane could hardly expect to find a love-match. It was either marriage to him, or a middle-aged widower with a ready-made family to raise. Undeniably, he would be gaining from the marriage, but equally so would Jane. Without Adam, her father's business would suffer and when Robert died she would be at the mercy of any fortune hunter that chanced her way.

Adam caught her hand as she would have turned away. She stiffened, and he felt her tremble. "Jane," he said. "If I offend you, say so plainly – but am I right in thinking that you would not be averse to becoming my wife?"

133

She looked at him then, her eyes bright. "Are you asking me to marry you, Adam?"

"Yes, Jane. I'm asking," he said. "I know I have nothing to give you, but I should be honoured if you will take me."

Her lips curved in a smile. "You are all I want, Adam. All I've ever wanted."

He stood up, reaching for her. She came to his arms shyly but willingly, lifting her face for his kiss. He took her lips with gentleness, brushing them lightly with his own. Then he stood back to look at her, his expression earnest.

"I'll be good to you, Jane," he vowed. "I swear you'll not regret making this decision."

She laughed and shook her head at him. "Oh, Adam. I never thought I would . . ."

Susanna looked at the pile of gifts in the library. Every day something new arrived from Digby. She felt overwhelmed by his generosity, and ashamed of her own emotions. She ought to be grateful to him, and of course she was, in her own way. It was very exciting to receive so many wonderful presents.

"Aren't you going to open them?" Bea asked, her eyes bright with excitement. "Oh, Susanna, do please open them. I can't wait to see what he's sent you this time."

Amused by her sister's enthusiasm, Susanna reached for a small parcel and handed it to her. "You open it," she said. "You can open all of them for me."

Beatrice threw herself on the parcels with unconcealed glee. "It's like Christmas only better," she said as she tore off the wrapping paper. "Oh, look, Susanna. What a pretty box!"

She was holding a delicate enamel patch box, the top coloured with pinks and blue with a picture of a young girl and a spaniel dog by her side.

"You may have it if you like," Susanna said generously.

"That's the third box Digby has sent me. I dare say he won't miss it."

"Thank you." Beatrice hugged her sister. "You're so good to me, Susanna."

She continued to pull the wrappings off one by one, exclaiming over the various gifts Digby had sent his bride to be. There were powder boxes and scent flasks, delicate fans made of ivory or painted chicken skin, one with an intricately worked gold handle. Silver-backed combs and brushes, diamond pins for her hair, a solid silver inkstand and quills to go with it. A beautiful gold box with a little singing bird inside, and a watch studded with pearls, sapphires and rubies to pin on her gown — so many precious trinkets that even Beatrice at last began to lose interest.

Susanna wandered away to the windows, looking out at the park. The trees had been glorious for weeks, their leaves a riot of autumn golds, browns and copper. Now they were beginning to fall. It would soon be winter, she thought. With every day, her wedding came nearer and she began to feel more and more trapped.

Beatrice came quietly up behind her, slipping her arm around her sister's waist. Susanna put her own arm around the other girl.

"You're so sad these days," Beatrice said. "Even those pretty things did not make you smile. Why are you so unhappy? Is it anything I've done?"

"No, of course not." Susanna kissed her sister's forehead gently. "You help me to bear it, Bea. Sometimes I think that if it were not for you . . ." She caught back the words, knowing that they would only upset the younger girl. "It's nothing, my dearest. Nothing that I can explain."

Watching the tender scene from the doorway, Sir William understood what his daughter would not say and his conscience smote him to the heart. Turning away, he sought the solace of his study and the brandy decanter that awaited him there.

*   *   *

135

Adam watched, shivering in the cool breeze as the new sign was hung in place: *Carter & Blackwell. Makers of Fine Furniture.* He felt pride stir inside him. This was something he had dreamed of, to see his name above the shop of a London cabinet-maker's establishment, something that on his own would have taken him years to achieve. He was tremendously excited to think of what the future might bring. Already he was beginning to be known, his work sought by some of the highest in the land. In time he could be as rich and famous as Mr Hepplewhite or Mr Chippendale. He had been given a chance to rise in the world, and he intended to take it with both hands, despite some lingering fears that Lady Munford might carry out her threat to have him arrested for rape. A week had passed since his visit to the house in Henrietta Place, and so far nothing had happened, but that might be a part of her ladyship's plan to torment him. Knowing that Adam would be ill at ease and forever looking over his shoulder, she might decide to play a game of cat and mouse with him.

He turned as Robert came out of the showroom, glancing up at the sign and smiling.

"A fine sight, Adam," he said. "This is one of the best days of my life. We must have a celebration this evening."

"I should enjoy that," Adam said. "We'll all go out to supper to the King's Head to mark the occasion."

"An occasion only a little less important than your marriage. Your wedding day will make me the happiest of men. I can die easy, knowing that you will be taking care of Lily and Jane." Robert adjusted his spectacles, rubbing the bridge of his nose.

"I wish you wouldn't talk of dying, Robert," Adam said seriously. "You know I'll look after the womenfolk. But I hope you'll at least be here to see your first grandchild born."

"My wish exactly," Robert replied. "But I'll not complain if I can see my daughter . . ." He broke off as Jane came out to them. "Have you come to see the sign, my dear?"

Then as he became aware of her concerned expression, "Is something wrong?"

"I'm not sure." Jane turned to Adam. "There's a letter for you, Adam, from your home. Mrs Watts sent it round by special messenger in case it was urgent."

"A letter from Maggie?" Adam frowned. "She only writes at Christmas. Something must be amiss."

"I don't think this is from your sister," Jane said. "I've never seen this writing before."

Adam took the letter from her, quickly examining the fine, spidery scrawl. "No, this isn't from Maggie. I wonder . . ." He broke open the seal, reading the brief message twice over before he could believe it. "The Lord have mercy!" He crossed himself, staring blindly at Jane and her father, overcome with emotion.

"What is it, Adam?" Jane laid her hand on his arm. "I was afraid it might be bad news."

"It's from the curate," Adam said, blinking stupidly as his mind struggled to take it in. "Maggie – Maggie is dead. He says . . ." His voice almost broke and his eyes were wild as he looked at her. "He says they think she drowned herself in the village pond."

"May I?" Jane took the letter as he nodded, scanning it swiftly. "Adam, this is terrible. Your mother is ill and your father is out of his mind with grief." She looked up at him. "You must go to them at once."

"But . . ." Adam was too stunned to think clearly. "The wedding . . ."

"Can wait," Jane said firmly. "Your parents must be in distress or the curate wouldn't have written. Your duty is to them now, Adam."

"Of course you must go," Robert agreed. "Take a few weeks – a month if need be. There will be things to settle and if your father cannot cope . . ."

Adam took Jane's hand in his, then raised it to his lips. "You are so understanding," he said. "I must go home, but I shall return as soon as I can."

Jane's smile was warm and gentle. "We have the rest of our lives, Adam. The wedding can wait for a few weeks."

"Yes." The shock had begun to wear off and now he was thinking positively. He turned to Robert. "There is nothing very urgent that you cannot manage. Mrs Saxon's table wants a final polish and that bureau for Mr Fox is finished. Everything else can wait until I get back. I shall pack at once and travel by fast coach to Norwich, then try to hire a horse."

"Don't think of the cost, Adam," Robert said at once. "If you need money . . ."

Adam shook his head. "I've a bit put by, sir. I can manage."

"Well, you have only to ask."

"I know." Adam's smile was stiff. "I must go now."

As he went inside to fetch his coat, father and daughter glanced at each other. Robert shook his head, tutting with distress.

"What can have possessed the girl to do such a thing?"

"The letter didn't say." Jane pressed his arm warningly as Adam came to the door once more. She went up to him, reaching up to kiss his cheek. "God be with you, Adam. I wish you a safe journey – and I'm so sorry. So very sorry about your sister. You were fond of her, I know."

"Yes." A little nerve flicked in his cheek. "I still can't believe it, Jane. She was such a bright, happy girl. I can't believe that she would . . ." He choked on the words and turned away.

Jane watched as he strode off down the street.

It had taken Adam the best part of two days to reach his home, though the fast coach had made the journey to Norwich in under twelve hours. He had dozed for a while as the coach rumbled over roads that were sometimes bumpy and rutted, though much better than they had been even a few years earlier, past stone-dashed cottages, ancient churches with quaint weather vanes and the lush green countryside of the Norfolk broadlands, wedged in between a morose-looking cleric smelling of peppermint and a thin-faced, poorly dressed woman who looked as if she might have been a governess. Pausing only to breakfast at the posting inn on some cold bacon and ale, he arranged for the hire of a horse to complete his journey. Unfortunately, the horse had cast a shoe a few miles down the road and some hours were lost in leading it to a blacksmith. So it was dinner-time when Adam lodged the animal with the village ostler and walked the last few yards to his father's house.

The Blackwells' house was in the centre of the village, some distance away from the pond, which was deep and usually had ducks swimming in it. Sometimes there was even a swan feeding at the reed beds at the edges. Because of its depth there was a small bridge across it. It must have been from the bridge that Maggie had . . . Adam closed his eyes for a moment as the picture that had haunted him ever since he read the curate's letter flashed into his mind. Maggie with her face a dead white and her hair floating in the water . . . a shudder went through him and he had to fight to steady himself. His little sister, dead long before her time. He could see her as she had been when he left for London, a bright, cheerful, pretty girl . . . What he wanted to know was why she had been so miserable that she had taken her own life!

He opened the door of his father's house and went in, struck as Susanna had been by the neatness of the workshop. It looked as if Tom Blackwell had begun to measure a length of timber, but there were no signs of any actual work having been done. The stove was cold and the glue had hardened in the pot. There was a forlorn, deserted air about the place he'd remembered as always being cluttered and busy.

"Ma — are you there?" Adam called, feeling uneasy.

The kitchen door opened as he approached it, and a woman he scarcely recognized as his mother stumbled forward into his arms for an emotional embrace. The shock left him stunned and bewildered, his throat tight. He caught her to him, feeling her painfully thin body tremble as she sobbed out his name.

"Adam," Jeanie wept. "Oh, Adam. Thank God you've come! Your father's near out of his mind with grief and . . ." She broke off as a fit of coughing overtook her.

Adam helped her back into the kitchen, where everything looked as normal, settling her into a rocking-chair by the fire. The quarry-tiled floor had been recently swept and the pine table top was damp from scrubbing. There was a new rush mat on the floor and the copper pans gleamed as brightly as ever, all evidence of his mother's industry, despite her ill health. Dumplings and meat were simmering on the stove, their aroma stirring nostalgic memories of childhood, but as Adam looked into his mother's eyes he felt her grief, and he knew that work was her only relief. She clutched at his hand and he knelt beside her, looking up into her face as she shed the tears she had held back until this moment. He was shocked by the ravages time and illness had wrought, and a sharp, stinging sense of guilt assailed him.

"Why didn't you let me know, Ma?" he asked gently. "Why didn't you send word before this that you were ill?"

"There be nothing you can do, Adam," his mother said, dismissing her own troubles with a shake of her head. "Don't bother about me; I can manage. It's your father I be worried about. This business with — with Maggie has broken him. Things haven't gone well in the workshop for a while now, and I do think this may finish him."

"You should have told me," Adam repeated, torn by remorse. "I could have sent money if nothing else."

Jeanie shook her head. "Your father wouldn't think of it. He wanted you to have your chance. He be that proud of you. You be doing so well in London."

"Robert Carter has taken me in as a partner. It's all signed and sealed," Adam said as he got to his feet. "Jane has promised to marry me."

140

"You're to marry Jane Carter?" Jeanie's worn face lit up with pride and pleasure. "That be the best news I've had in a long, long time."

"It means I can't come home for good, Ma." Uneasily, he remembered that for the past four years he'd hardly given his family a thought, except to send presents now and then.

"We bain't expecting it of you," Jeanie said. "You be here now and that be all we want."

Adam nodded, knowing that it was little enough. He ought to be here with his father. His hands clenched into tight fists.

"I should never have gone to London in the first place," he muttered. "If I'd been here, I might have prevented . . ." He glanced back at his mother. "Why did Maggie do it? Was it a man? Did someone let her down? What on earth possessed her to take her own life? I can't believe she would do it – not Maggie!"

Jeanie's eyes slid away from his. She was silent for a while, then, "She was so ashamed. That's why she couldn't bide with herself . . ."

"Ashamed?" His gaze narrowed as he realized what she must mean. "You mean she was . . ."

"She were three months gone," his mother said quietly. "Tom Sutton, he be still willing to wed her, but she be stubborn and wouldn't listen. She said it bain't right to saddle him with another man's child."

"Another . . . was she raped?" Adam saw his mother's uneasy look and the anger mounted inside him. "I want to know the truth. If some man raped Maggie, I'll kill him!"

"Tom Sutton thrashed him," Jeanie said. "Don't ask, Adam. Your father says there's to be no more trouble over it."

"Then Father is a fool!" Adam's eyes glinted with ice. At that moment he wanted to strike out in any direction, to wound as he himself had been wounded. "If you won't tell

141

me, I'll ask Tom Sutton. For God's sake, Ma, Maggie's dead! I have the right to know why she died."

Jeanie looked up then. "Maggie be dead and gone, son. You can't help her now. It be too late. Don't do anything foolish, Adam. We don't want to lose you, too."

"Maggie is dead. My sister is dead before she's had time to live." Adam's rage exploded and his fist crashed against the wall, making his mother jump. "Damn it, Ma! Someone is responsible and . . ." He stared at her. "There's only one family Pa looks up to . . ." Suddenly he knew, even before his mother began to speak.

"He pestered her, Adam," Jeanie cried. "There's not a girl in the village who hasn't been menaced by Stephen Warwick, but Maggie resisted him for a long time. She bain't a bad girl, no matter what anyone says."

"He forced her!" Adam cursed aloud. "I'll see him in Hell for it! I'll break his neck."

"No!" his mother cried, rising to her feet in alarm. "He seduced her with pretty trifles and sweet words, but she wasn't forced – that be why your father won't go to Sir William."

"If he won't, I will!" Adam moved towards the door as if he meant to act on his words immediately.

"No, Adam." Jeanie caught his arm, but he shrugged her off. "You can't bring Maggie back. Besides, Stephen Warwick bain't here no more. He be gone to London in search of an heiress. You can't do anything up at the Hall."

"Nothing can change what's happened," Adam agreed, his face grim. "But you and Father need help – I can speak to Sir William, tell him what's happened. The Warwicks can pay compensation for what they've done."

"Have you forgotten what Sir William did for you?" Jeanie looked at him sadly.

"I'm not likely to forget." Adam's laughter was harsh and unforgiving. "Don't fool yourself, Ma. It wasn't done as a kindness. I was packed off to London because it suited the Warwicks."

Jeanie gazed at him, her eyes dark with pain. "You sound so bitter, Adam. Things have turned out well for you, and it were always for the best. Gentry and common folk like us don't mix. If you'd stayed . . ."

"And you're not bitter?" He looked at her incredulously. "Well, you and Father can forgive and forget if you want to — but I intend to see that Stephen Warwick pays for his fun!"

CHAPTER TEN

"But you must be mistaken." Susanna looked at her sister in disbelief. "Maggie Blackwell couldn't have taken her own life. She just couldn't have . . ." She felt as if the world were collapsing around her. It was terrible news, especially as she believed she knew what had made Maggie do it. "To cause her parents so much grief . . ."

"That's what they're saying in the village." Beatrice sat on the edge of her sister's bed. "I heard the servants talking about it. They stopped when they saw me and looked at each other." She raised her puzzled eyes to Susanna. "It was almost as if – as if they were blaming me . . ."

"Not you, Bea. Don't think that."

Susanna felt physically ill. She knew who was to blame for the tragedy, and the servants must also be aware of the truth. It would be common knowledge in the village. Gossip would be rife and many would condemn the Squire's son, even if few were prepared to voice their opinions within the family's hearing. This time Stephen's selfish behaviour had gone too far to be condoned. It could only be a matter of time before her parents discovered what had happened, although Sir William seemed to live in a world of his own these days. Since his return from London, he spent almost every day shut up in his library, emerging only to eat a silent meal before disappearing again. Even Lady Patricia was worried about him, remarking to her daughter that it was unlike him to stay at home so long.

Susanna frowned at her sister. "You haven't said anything to Mama about this, have you?"

"I wouldn't dare. You know we're not supposed to listen to servants' gossip." Beatrice stared at her curiously.

"Do you know what this is all about?"

"Yes. Yes, I do." Susanna shook her head at the question. "I can't tell you, Bea. It isn't my secret – and it isn't very pleasant."

"Why won't anyone ever tell me anything? I should never know anything if I didn't listen to gossip." Beatrice pulled a sulky face. "I'm not a child – and it's not fair to treat me like one."

"No, it isn't." Susanna smiled at her sister. "I'm truly sorry, but I still can't tell you."

"Then I wish I hadn't told you!" Beatrice had been sprawling in a most unladylike manner on her sister's bed. Now she jumped up in high dudgeon and ran from the room.

Susanna gazed after her, sorry that once again they were quarrelling when she had thought their relationship was improving. But she had more important things to worry about. Maggie was dead. She had taken her own life because she was carrying Stephen Warwick's child. Jeanie Blackwell had told her how ashamed the girl was, but Susanna hadn't dreamt she would be so desperate. She felt responsible in some way, as though she ought to have done something to help Maggie. Instead of just leaving that money lying on the ground when Tom Sutton threw it at her, she should have gone back and talked to the girl . . .

Tears stung Susanna's eyes. It was terrible. She could scarcely believe it, and yet it must be true. Jeanie Blackwell had told her that all Maggie would do was to lie staring at the wall, wishing that she could die. Well, now she had her way. It was a sin to take your own life. Susanna wondered if Maggie had gone to Hell. Wherever she was, she had left a living hell for those who loved her – and it was all Stephen's fault. Susanna felt grief and shame as she began to realize just how dreadful it really was.

"Oh, Stephen," she whispered as the tears began to fall. "What have you done? What have you done to us all?"

The letter was lying on the silver salver in the hall. She

145

noticed it when she came down the following morning. Picking it up, Susanna saw that it was from Lord Digby. She broke the seal, reading the bold, clear writing with a little frown. Most people wrote in fine lettering, squeezing as much as they could on to the page to save the considerable expense of postage, but Digby took no account of such things, filling several sheets with his scrawl.

"A letter from Digby?" Lady Patricia asked as she came into the hall. "What does he say?"

"He should be here by the beginning of next week."

"At last." Lady Patricia smiled at her. "I was beginning to think he had changed his mind, though I should have known better. He has been a faithful correspondent . . ." Her smile faded as she saw her daughter was dressed for walking in a bronze velvet gown and heavy cloak. "Are you going out? It's very cold for a walk. We don't want you to take a chill, do we?"

Susanna refolded her letter and slipped it into the pocket of her gown. She met her mother's inquiring gaze with determination.

"I'm going to put flowers on Maggie Blackwell's grave, Mama."

Lady Patricia stared at her for a moment, then nodded. "She was fortunate to be buried in the churchyard. The vicar was undecided about that, you know. He asked me what he should do, and I told him I should be grateful if he would allow her to have a Christian burial. And he was disposed to oblige me. After all, it is not completely certain that she did in fact take her own life. It could just conceivably have been an accident. I thought we should show compassion."

Susanna stared at her in suspicion. Her mother had never bothered with the Blackwell family before. "You — you know, don't you? About the baby . . ."

"I am not quite a fool," Lady Patricia said grimly. "Stephen has behaved badly. I shall have something particular to say to him when he comes home."

"You haven't told Papa?"

"It would be unnecessarily cruel to burden him with something he can do nothing about," Lady Patricia said with a sigh. "I fear your father is not the man he was, Susanna."

"And never will be again." Susanna blinked back her tears. "We should give the Blackwells money, Mama. They are in need of it."

"I doubt they would take it. Tom Blackwell was always a proud man. If you want to help, Susanna, I should give money to the doctor to pay for medicines. He is a sensible man and would keep your confidence. You may leave it to me to see that they do not starve when you are no longer here."

Susanna looked into her mother's eyes. "You will be kind to them? Don't make them feel that it's charity."

"Jeanie Blackwell's cousin works in the kitchens. She can take food from time to time."

"Thank you. I know you think we should have nothing to do with the family but . . ."

"I may not have wanted you to become too friendly with the family, Susanna, but I am not without compassion."

"No, of course not." Susanna reached up to kiss her mother's cheek. "I must go now. I shall beg the best of the lilies from the head gardener."

"He will not be pleased with you," her mother said with a wry smile. "But if he resists, tell him that I have given my permission."

Susanna inclined her head and went on, through the hall and out of the front door. She crossed the lawns, pausing to look back at the many-windowed house with its graceful lines and rusty brick walls. Ivy was massed over the front façade, softening the rather austere aura of the building, a perfect foil for the urns of bright flowers that spilled over on to the terraces. The summer flowers were almost done now but the gardeners always managed to preserve them until the frosts came. A wave of nostalgia passed over

147

her. It was her home and she had loved it, but soon she must leave it for ever. But at least she was alive. Maggie Blackwell was dead.

"Is that from Adam?" Robert Carter asked his daughter as she came into the workshop, carrying a letter. He took off his glasses to rub the bridge of his nose. "What does he say?"

"It is even worse than he thought," Jane replied. "He says he may be longer than he'd hoped. Perhaps you would like to read it? It isn't a love letter. I think he intended you should."

Robert took the letter and read it carefully. It was a brief note and dealt mainly with business. Handing it back to his daughter, he said, "So you were right, it was a man. A terrible business, Jane. To take her own life . . ."

"We cannot be sure of that," Jane said. "You mustn't hold this against Adam, Father."

"No . . ." He looked at her uncertainly. "You are still satisfied with your bargain? You do not regret what I've done?"

"It was I who asked you to approach Adam," Jane said seriously. "I know he would never have asked me to marry him if you had not offered him a partnership. He was thinking of leaving us."

"And that does not upset you?"

"Why should it?" Jane asked serenely. "I have what I want, Father. I would have done anything to be Adam's wife."

Robert nodded, regarding his daughter with concern. Outwardly so meek and docile, underneath she was made of steel. He wondered if Adam really knew the woman he was marrying.

"And supposing he decides that he wants to stay with his family?"

"And give up his partnership with you?" Jane smiled confidently. "Oh, I don't think there is any danger of that, do you? Besides, he has signed a contract. It would ruin him if you were to hold him to it."

"You would not do that, Jane?" Robert was a little shocked. "I know it is legally binding, but for compassion's sake . . ."

"I'm sure it will not be necessary. I know Adam, Father. He is an ambitious man. No, at the moment he naturally wants to help his family, but he will come back to us. I am sure of it."

Robert watched as she walked from the room and sighed. He had done his best for Jane, but sometimes he wondered if she would be really happy once she had what she wanted.

Having decided to take her mother's advice and call on the doctor, Susanna was kept waiting until he returned from a visit to an outlying farm. It was almost an hour before he arrived and she was able to complete her business.

"You understand that I want no one to know about this," Susanna said, offering her hand as she rose to leave. "Use the money for the Blackwells' welfare in whatever way you think best."

He pressed her hand warmly between his own. "Trust me to see to it that they want for nothing, Miss Warwick. I am honoured that you have come to me – and I want to say how much I admire you for your generosity . . ."

Susanna shook her head, feeling embarrassed. "No, please don't make me a saint, sir. I have done little enough in the circumstances."

"Circumstances not of your making, Miss Warwick." The doctor shook his head sadly.

"I feel the burden of my brother's guilt in this." Susanna's hand trembled in his. "I only wish I could do more for Jeanie and her husband."

"I'm sure the whole village feels the same," he assured her. "Don't worry about the Blackwells, my dear Miss Warwick. They will be taken care of by us all."

Susanna smiled and took her leave. She walked to the

end of the village and commenced the climb up the steep incline to the churchyard. The trees had almost lost their leaves now, looking bare without their autumn glory. Mist had begun to curl across the damp ground, making the day bleak and cheerless. Her own mood was sombre as she thought about the woman who had so recently been buried. Maggie was only two years older than Susanna. She remembered her as a young girl, with her bright eyes and cheeky grin – the way she had been when they first met after Adam had rescued Susanna from the gipsies. It did not seem possible that she was dead. Sadness swept over Susanna as she thought of the waste of a young woman's life. If only she had been able to do more . . .

She began to make her way between the rows of mouldering tombstones, looking at the names of long-dead Warwicks. Then she saw the man standing beside the freshly dug grave and her heart jerked. His back was turned towards her, but she knew immediately who it must be. No one else in the village had such broad shoulders or hair that colour. Adam Blackwell had come back to Chorley Hale.

She ought to have expected it, but it was still a shock to see him standing there, his tall, powerful figure dominating the scene. She stood as if turned to stone, her flowers hanging limply at her side. She had wanted to bring her own tribute to Maggie, but now she felt it was an intrusion on his grief. She would come back another time. She was about to withdraw when he turned and saw her. For a moment he stared at her, anger blazing in those slate grey eyes, and then he took a step towards her.

"Susanna Warwick," he said bitterly. "You're the last person I expected to see here."

The shock ran through Susanna as she looked into his face. This was the man whose picture she had carried in her heart for so long, but she had never seen him like this, never seen such anger or hatred in his eyes. He looked as if he would like to kill her. She felt close to tears. Adam blamed her for what had happened to his sister, because she was a Warwick, and he must revile the very name. She looked away from those angry eyes, her heart aching for him in his pain.

"Forgive me, I brought flowers," she said, seeing that he too carried a floral tribute to his sister. She stepped forward and laid her lilies on the earth.

"We want nothing from the Warwicks!" With a sudden angry movement, Adam reached down and swept the flowers from Maggie's grave. "Stay away from here! Leave us alone."

Susanna stared up at him, stunned by the force of the fury in his face. "I know that you are grieving," she said. "But I came only from a desire to show my respect."

"Respect?" His lip curled. "The same respect as your brother showed her, perhaps? Do you think you can pay for his crimes with a few flowers?"

"I'm sorry for what Stephen did. I know how you feel but I . . ."

"How can you?" His voice had all the sharp, stinging cut of a whiplash, making her recoil. "You've been privileged all your life. You know nothing, Miss Warwick. You've never had to bow to your betters or say thank you when the master deigns to bestow a favour. You don't know what it's like to starve or sleep in the gutters . . ."

"Nor do you!" Susanna was riled by his accusation. "Your family has never starved, Adam Blackwell. Papa would never have countenanced it for a moment. He never turns a poor beggar from the door – and he has great respect and affection for your parents."

"Charity!" Adam snarled. "No man should have to take charity from another. It's men like your father who grow fat by grinding the faces of the poor . . ."

"Nonsense!" Susanna cried furiously. She was angry too now. No matter what Stephen had done, Adam had no right to speak to her this way. "You've been reading too many scurrilous rags and letting them poison your mind. My father is incapable of taking advantage of anyone. He

151

has been too soft-hearted all his life. That's why he . . ." She bit her lip, choking off the betraying words that would reveal her father's shame. "Stephen was wicked to seduce Maggie and then desert her the way he did, but even your mother doesn't blame my father. If Father knew he would be as angry as you are . . ."

"Sir William doesn't know?" Adam stared at her disbelievingly. "Then how do you . . ."

"I saw Stephen come in after Tom Sutton had thrashed him. I made him tell me what had happened. It would kill Papa if he . . . You don't know . . . You remember him as he was, but he has changed. He's not well. Sometimes he doesn't know what day it is. Can you not find it in your heart to have some pity for him?"

"What do you imagine this has done to my father?"

"I know, I know it must have hurt him badly. I wish I could bring Maggie back," she whispered. "Believe me, Adam. I'm sorry but you are so unforgiving . . ." She turned aside, the tears close as she began to walk away.

Adam gazed after her, the anger building inside him until he thought his head would burst. How dare she come here with her magnificent lilies when he had only a few straggling blooms from his mother's tiny back garden? Damn her and her condescension! Damn Stephen Warwick and his heedless lust for pleasure! He had seduced Maggie and thereby caused her death. Stephen Warwick had murdered his sister — and Adam would have his revenge. Now. This very minute. He turned and walked swiftly after Susanna, catching her arm and swinging her round to face him.

"Yes, I am unforgiving," he growled. "Your brother ruined my sister, and now I'll pay him back in his own coin. How will the mighty Warwicks feel when one of them is disgraced and ruined?"

Susanna felt a tingle of fear as she looked up into his glittering eyes. She caught her breath, pulling away from him as she realized what he intended.

"No — you can't," she whispered. "You wouldn't . . ."

"That's it," he snarled bitterly. "Beg, Miss Warwick. Beg as my sister begged for her virtue. You shall feel as she felt, suffer as she suffered at that devil's hands."

Giving a little cry, Susanna tried to break away from him. His grip on her arm tightened and she rounded on him, struggling, trying to fend him off. Adam laughed, wrestling with her and finally throwing her to the ground. The shock of finding him lying across her left her winded and slightly stunned, unable to fight any more. He had always been too strong for her; the struggle was unequal. She gazed up into his face, her eyes wide and questing, silently begging him not to hurt her. She saw his expression change. Suddenly, his face twisted in agony and he groaned as his mouth came down to possess hers in a hard, passionate kiss.

Stiffening, she tried at first to throw him off, but then she found that her betraying body was responding to his kiss despite herself. Her mind told her that she should fight to the last for her honour, but her senses were inflamed by the touch of his lips. She went limp beneath him, no longer fighting what must be. If he was determined on this revenge, she could not prevent it. He raised his head and looked down into her face, and she was shocked by his expression. He looked as if he were staring into the pit of Hell! Cursing loudly, he suddenly rolled away, lying prone beside her for a moment before getting to his feet. Then he was helping her to rise, his face grim and unsmiling. She looked at him uncertainly.

"Adam . . ." she whispered, trembling. "What changed your mind?"

"I find I have no taste for rape," he muttered. "So, Miss Warwick — will you inform your father and have me arrested for assaulting you?"

"Don't be foolish," she said, blinking hard. She should be furious. Why did she feel more like weeping than venting her anger on him? "You've done me no real harm. Why should I have you punished?"

"It is what I deserve," he said, his eyes narrowing as he looked at her flushed face. "I had no right to take my revenge on you – you are not responsible for your brother's actions."

"No," she said softly. "Nor are you, Adam. Don't blame yourself."

She had looked into his heart and seen the guilt he felt. He smiled wryly. "Am I so easy for you to read?"

"In this instance, yes." She looked up at him. "I understand because I too feel guilty. Stephen is my brother. I must in some way have contributed to what he is. Perhaps if I had loved him when he was younger . . ."

"I loved Maggie, but I doubt if I could have prevented her from doing what she did. We are masters of our own destiny, are we not?"

She smiled faintly. "That's not what you said just now, Adam Blackwell."

He nodded, his mouth twisting ruefully. "You are right to mock me, Miss Warwick. I was angry – and I said a lot of foolish things."

She offered him her hand. "Shall we part as friends, Adam Blackwell?"

"Friends?" He raised his brow. "You and I, Miss Warwick? Your mother would not care for that, I think."

"Then you would be revenged on her for her meddling, would you not, Adam Blackwell?"

"A sweet irony," he murmured and with a harsh laugh took her hand, bowing over it. "I believe we cannot be friends, Miss Warwick, but I thank you for the offer." His manner and way of speaking were that of the educated gentleman he had learned to be in London.

Susanna watched as he strode away. She felt a surge of annoyance. How dared he spurn her offer of friendship when she had forgiven him so magnificently for his outrageous behaviour? He had deserved her scorn but she had given him forgiveness and friendship. His manner was almost haughty. Who did he think he was?

154

It would serve him right if she went to her father after all!

Walking back to the village, Adam felt the sweetness of triumph as he recalled the look in Susanna Warwick's eyes just before he left her. She had seen him with new insight. His instinct when she first arrived had been to react like a wounded animal, striking out in pain. For a moment he had lost his head, but thankfully had stopped himself in time. Rape was a vile thing and he could not have forgiven himself if he had behaved so ill.

It was foolish to have lost control like that. As soon as he'd held her in his arms he'd known that he could never hurt her. His memories of her as a young girl were too deeply enshrined in his heart. It was much better to have left her in the way he had, retaining some semblance of dignity. She had offered friendship, but how could he take friendship from the daughter of a family he despised?

His mother was right. There was nothing he could do for Maggie now. In his first rage he would have killed Stephen Warwick or at least demanded compensation from Sir William, but now that he was calmer, he knew that there were better ways of taking his revenge.

Alone in her room some half an hour later, Susanna brushed the mud and débris from her gown. Her mouth still tingled from Adam's bruising kiss and she kept going over and over the incident, trying to make sense of it. She glanced at herself in the mirror. Her annoyance had faded now; it had been mere irritation of the nerves. Why couldn't Adam Blackwell have accepted her offer of friendship? And why wasn't she as angry with him as she ought to have been?

She remembered the moment when her heart had thumped with fright, a brief second later the fear becoming anticipation. She could not have wanted him to carry out his threat? Rape was a terrible crime, the action of a coward.

But when Adam groaned and kissed her everything had changed. He had kissed her in passion, not in anger. He had kissed her because he wanted her as a man wants a woman, not because he was determined on revenge. He had kissed her as though his very soul was in torment. That was why she had responded to him. He had wanted to make love to her. The look she had seen in his eyes had betrayed him.

Susanna smiled and touched her mouth wonderingly. She had run away in fright when Edouard Dubarry kissed her, but if Adam had not let her go she knew that she would willingly have surrendered her virtue. In those few seconds when his mouth had possessed hers, she had known desire. She had wanted him to take her innocence and make her his own. She had wanted him to love her. She could still feel that weakness, that longing to press herself against him and her hands shook as she ran a finger over her lips. This feeling inside her was almost like a sickness, a hunger that nothing but Adam Blackwell's mouth could assuage.

Staring at herself in the mirror, Susanna understood passion for the first time. Now she knew why her mother had taken lovers. Was she like her mother? Or was she truly in love with Adam Blackwell?

"What are you thinking about, Susanna?"

She jumped guiltily as her mother's voice spoke from the doorway. "Nothing, Mama."

"You have been gone longer than I thought," Lady Patricia said, her suspicions aroused as she looked at the girl's face. Something was different about her. Her gaze narrowed as she saw the damp stain on Susanna's dress. "You have mud on your gown. What have you been doing?"

Susanna flushed and looked down at her skirt. She hadn't noticed that damp patch at the back. "It was muddy in the churchyard," she said. "When I bent to lay the flowers on Maggie's grave, I slipped and fell."

"Are you sure that is all?"

"Yes, of course." Susanna could feel her cheeks growing warm. "Why should I lie?"

"I have heard that Adam Blackwell has come home." Lady Patricia saw the slight start Susanna could not conceal. "I hope you have not been foolish?"

"I have not seen Adam for years," Susanna lied. "Why should I want to? You wrong me, Mama. I simply went to put flowers on Maggie's grave. I had to wait for the doctor to come home, that's why I was so long."

"Very well, I shall take your word." Lady Patricia nodded grimly. "If I should discover that you have been foolish enough to meet this young man, I should be very angry, Susanna."

White-faced and trembling, Susanna watched as her mother walked from the room. She could only hope that no one had witnessed that little incident in the churchyard.

Leaving the church with Beatrice on her arm that Sunday morning, Susanna stopped to speak to the doctor and his wife. Lady Patricia had not attended the service, which was a memorial for Maggie Blackwell, but had insisted that Beatrice should go with her sister. Susanna realized that she was being guarded. Obviously, her mother was trying to make sure that she had no chance to speak to Adam alone.

"That was a touching service, was it not?" the doctor's wife said to Susanna. "I thought the vicar's sermon was excellent."

"Yes. Yes, it was."

Susanna saw Adam leaving the church with his parents, heading towards the graveyard at the back. Wishing she could follow and share their vigil at Maggie's grave, Susanna saw Adam stop and look back at her. For a moment his face was stony, then he smiled, a smile full of such sweetness that her heart turned over. It was the smile of the young man who had met her in the meadows. Instinctively, she knew that he had begun to forgive her. Tears stung her eyes, but she brushed them away.

"Can we go home now?" Beatrice asked, slipping her arm through her sister's. "I'm cold. I didn't want to come, but Mama insisted I must."

Looking down at her sister, Susanna knew that she must not blame her for tagging along everywhere she went. It was Lady Patricia who had set the younger girl to spy on her.

Escaping from the house two days later, Susanna managed to slip away before anyone else was aware of it. She hurried through the formal gardens and made her way towards the woods. Digby had arrived the previous evening and already she was fit to scream. He was always at her side, never giving her a moment to herself. It was unbearable. She could not stand another moment of Digby's company. His pawing hands made her shudder inwardly and she felt like fainting. How could she marry him? Remembering the thrill of Adam's kisses, she knew who she wanted. Adam Blackwell, the hero of her childhood. As a young girl she had adored him blindly, but now she was a woman and she had felt passion in his arms. How could she marry another man when her whole being cried out for Adam?

But it could never be. Even if Adam did not hate her, the idea of a marriage between them was impossible. She was promised to Digby. The wedding would take place very soon. If she refused now, her father would be ruined. He could never repay the money Digby had advanced him without selling the estate. It was useless. She was trapped, and there was no escape.

Sinking down on the trunk of a fallen tree, Susanna wept silently and bitterly. Her life was over. She would be better off lying in the churchyard like Maggie. She would rather be dead than married to Digby.

It was almost dusk when Susanna walked slowly back

towards the house. She had wept until she could weep no more and now she felt empty. There was nothing she could do. She was trapped and there was no way out of her misery. It was very cold but she was not yet ready to return to the house. She turned her steps towards the summerhouse, her favourite refuge in childhood days.

"Miss Warwick . . . Susanna, please wait."

Susanna's heart jerked and she glanced back in disbelief. Adam was striding towards her through the gloom. She waited for him to catch up.

"Yes?" she said, a little breathlessly. "Did you want something, Adam?"

He stood looking down at her, his eyes very intense. "I came . . . I wanted to apologize. You offered me friendship and I gave you scorn . . ."

"There was no need," she said. "You were upset. I understood why . . ."

"No," he interrupted harshly. "Let me speak. I have been in torment since that day at the church, though at first I was pleased with myself. I wanted to hurt you, but then I realized that it was unfair. I used Maggie's death as an excuse. I knew you weren't responsible – any more than you were responsible for my being sent to London four years ago."

"I didn't know you had gone until Maggie told me." Susanna smiled slightly. "It broke my heart. I cried myself to sleep for almost a week."

"Did you?" Adam stared at her, his breath quickening. The look in her eyes was unmistakeable. "I must admit I hardly thought of you after the first few weeks – until I saw you in London this summer."

"I wasn't sure it was you when you picked up my parasol," Susanna admitted. "I wanted to ask, but you looked so different . . . and the way you talk . . . I was afraid to speak. You've changed so much."

"For the better, I hope. I've used my time profitably," Adam replied, smiling wryly. "When I left here I could scarcely write my own name. I was given a chance to make something of my life and I was determined to do so."

"I always knew you would."

Adam took a deep breath. There was no doubt about the message in her eyes now. He had seen it often enough in the eyes of women who came to the workshop. It made him wary ... but this was Susanna Warwick. The blood pounded at his temples. He wanted to take her into his arms and kiss her. He wanted desperately to make love to her. It was impossible. He was promised to Jane and Susanna ... she was from another world.

"Well," he said awkwardly. "Perhaps I should be going ... It is growing late ..." His voice had become hoarse and his heart was beating so wildly that he could scarcely breathe.

"No," she cried. "Please don't go. Stay and talk to me for a while – we could go to the summerhouse. I was on my way there. Please, Adam. Please stay ..."

His gaze narrowed as he looked at her more closely. "Have you been crying?"

"Yes, a little," Susanna admitted. "Adam, I ..." She took a deep breath. Suddenly, she knew what she wanted. It was her one chance of a little happiness. She knew she must be the one to speak first. He would not dare. It was bold and wanton but she was desperate. If she could have only this one night to remember, it would ease the ache inside her. "I love you," she whispered, moving closer to him, her eyes liquid with desire as she gazed up at him. "I fell in love with you when I was fourteen and – and again when I saw you outside the silk mercer's ... The other day when you kissed me, I wanted you to make love to me. I want you to make love to me now, this evening ..."

"Susanna ..." Adam felt the desire move within him, yet could not believe this was happening. It was like something out of one of his dreams. "Do you know what you're saying?"

"Yes," she breathed. "Yes, I know, Adam."

"Susanna . . ."

As his arms closed about her, he shut out the memory of Jane's trusting eyes. Tomorrow . . . he would think about Jane and his promise to her tomorrow . . .

Suddenly sweeping Susanna up in his arms, Adam carried her into the summerhouse. It was dusty and unused, but to them it became more beautiful than a palace as they lay down together on an old velvet sofa. Kissing and whispering of their love, they touched and savoured, enchanted by the magic of what was happening to them.

"Susanna . . . Susanna, my darling," he murmured against her white throat. "I've dreamt of this ever since I saw you in London. I've wanted you so much . . ."

"Adam, I've always loved you. There will never be anyone else but you in my heart . . ."

"So beautiful . . . My sweetest love . . . so soft to touch . . . so warm and giving . . ."

The moonlight turned her skin to the palest gold. His eyes feasted on her loveliness, his hands caressing her with such tenderness that she melted into sweet surrender.

"Oh, Adam . . . Adam . . . Adam . . ." she gasped. "I love you . . . I love you . . ."

Susanna lay in bed staring at the moon through her window. She had not pulled the curtains because she did not want to sleep, not this night. Her body still tingled from Adam's caresses, and though she could feel the soreness between her legs, she could remember the pleasure his loving had given her. Now for the first time she understood why her mother had taken lovers. She knew what it was to be a woman.

There had been pain the first time, but Adam had been gentle with her. He had eased himself into her, trying not to hurt her but she had thrust herself against him, wanting to feel him inside her. In his own excitement, he had climaxed swiftly, but then he had begun to kiss and caress her all over again. He had taken her three times in all, and the

161

third time she had felt such sensation, such pleasure! She moaned, biting the sheet as the very thought of him set her longing for him again. She could hardly wait for the day to pass so that she could spend the hours of darkness in his arms.

"You must not come until midnight," she had said as she left him. "If we were seen . . ."

Adam had kissed her once more before they parted. "I'll be waiting for you," he promised.

Leaving the summerhouse first, Susanna had fled across the lawn, letting herself in by a side door. The house was in darkness. She had crept upstairs, expecting to be pounced on by her mother or Digby at any moment, but nothing had happened and she had reached her own room without incident.

Sighing, Susanna closed her eyes, reliving her encounter with Adam again. It seemed like a dream. A dream that had her head spinning with delight. If it had not been for the soreness between her thighs, she would have thought it was her imagination. Could it really have been so wonderful?

How could she endure the next day? How could she smile at Digby and pretend that everything was as it had been before? Suddenly, she realized that it did not matter any more. Adam loved her. He had said so over and over again. She could never marry Digby now. She would tell Adam that she wanted to go away with him.

Adam stood staring out of the window of his father's house, his expression grim. After what had happened in the summerhouse, he knew that he could not keep his promise to Jane. It would be unfair to her, and to Susanna. He wasn't sure what had been in his mind when Susanna gave herself to him. If truth were told, he had been too carried away with his own desires to think at all. He knew that she had been a virgin, and he believed that she loved him. But they were still worlds apart. Had she the courage to step down from her world to his? He would not have believed it possible until the moment she had given herself to him so freely.

Remembering the contract he had signed with Robert Carter, Adam groaned. Why, oh, why had he not waited a little longer? If only he had not asked Jane to be his wife. To jilt her would be unkind; she did not deserve such treatment. She knew nothing of her father's offer. It would be cruel to disillusion her . . . yet what else could he do? How could he marry her now when his heart belonged to Susanna?

Jane would be able to sue him for breach of promise if she so chose, but he believed she would release him. After that it would be best to go away. He would take Susanna and find a job somewhere, perhaps in France. He had always admired French furniture. He could find work there and no one would know that he and Susanna were fugitives. For fugitives they would be. The Warwicks would never allow their daughter to marry him. They would have to elope.

It would probably be the end of his hopes of having his own business, at least for years to come. Yet if Susanna was willing to give up so much for him, could he do less for her?

Beatrice had been crying. Her face still bore the marks where her mother had slapped her hard several times.

"You know where she is," Lady Patricia said, her eyes glittering like diamonds with anger. "Don't lie to me, Beatrice. I know you're hiding something from me."

"I'm not . . . truly, I'm not," Beatrice said, cowering away as her mother's hand was raised once more. "I didn't see her in the park . . . really I . . ." She gasped as she realized what she had said.

"You will tell me where she is." Lady Patricia shook her daughter until she was dizzy. "If you defy me, I shall have you whipped. Now, tell me, where is she and who is she with?"

Beatrice hung her head. Her mother would be furious with Susanna if she knew what she was doing. Watching for her sister to come home, Beatrice had witnessed the meeting between her and Adam Blackwell. She had seen them kissing, and had watched as he picked Susanna up and carried her to the summerhouse.

Frightened and a little shocked, Beatrice had returned home. She had no intention of telling her mother what had happened, and was silent all through dinner, but somehow she had betrayed herself. It was probably when she heard her mother tell Lord Digby that Susanna could not come down to dinner as she was unwell. She had seen her mother glance at her suspiciously as she flushed and looked down at her plate. All evening Beatrice had stayed out of Lady Patricia's way, but when she went to bed, her mother had followed her up.

Now, as she looked into her mother's furious face, she lied desperately. "She was just walking on her own. I didn't see anyone else."

"Where was she?"

"Near . . . Near the lake," Beatrice lied, and her mother nodded.

"Very well, I shall look for her myself," she said. "I'll deal with you in the morning, miss."

After she had gone, Beatrice cried and cried. She hadn't meant to get her sister into trouble, she really hadn't, but if Lady Patricia caught Susanna with Adam Blackwell . . .

Waiting by the window, Beatrice drew a sigh of relief as at last she saw Susanna slip into the house. It was all right. Their mother hadn't found her after all.

CHAPTER ELEVEN

Adam looked at his father, shocked not so much at how old he looked, though the years had taken more than their fair share from him, but at the emptiness in his eyes. Tom Blackwell looked like a man who was waiting to die; a man who had no purpose to his life. Adam was moved to pity. Somehow he had to reach through the wall of apathy, to touch the soul of the man he had respected and loved. His eyes moved anxiously round the room and then he bent down to pick up the length of timber lying on the floor, inspecting it with a critical eye.

"This is fine mahogany," he said. "What are you going to make with it, Father?"

Tom had been staring blankly into space, but he glanced up as his son spoke. "It was to be a travelling chest for Miss Warwick. She ordered one for herself — and one as a gift for her future husband."

Adam stiffened, feeling the pain twist in his breast. Susanna was to be married! It could not be true. There must be some mistake. He recalled the sweetness of her lips as she responded eagerly to his kisses. She had sworn that she loved him — and like a fool he had believed her. Now his father was telling him that she was to be married.

"Are you sure it was for a wedding gift, Father? Could it not have been simply a present for Sir William?"

"Your mother was quite definite about it, Adam." Tom frowned as he tried to remember. "Yes, the order was for a pair of marriage chests. She's to wed some lord or other I think. I did hear someone say who it was but I wasn't listening much."

If his father was so certain, it must be true. Susanna to

be married! Adam turned away, afraid that his father would see his anguish. He pretended to examine various pieces of timber as he struggled to come to terms with what he'd heard. What a fool he was. A ridiculous, love-sick fool. Of course! It was the reason for her visit to London. Naturally she would marry, and marry well. She was the daughter of gentry. Last night had meant nothing to her. She had been amusing herself – just as Stephen had amused himself with Maggie. What a blind, stupid fool he had been! He had been ready to give up Jane and his partnership with Robert to run off with Susanna. Knowing that the Warwicks would never agree to the marriage, he had spent a restless night planning their elopement. And all the time she had been laughing at him!

Cursing inwardly, he tried to convince himself that it meant nothing to him. So Miss Warwick had been playing a game. She was like her mother after all. He was just a man she had used for pleasure – so what did it matter? He would be married himself soon. This pain, this spreading numbness inside him, was ridiculous. Fool! Fool that he was. Susanna Warwick was not for him. He should forget her. He must forget her. He must forget the sweetness of her lips and the enticing, fresh scent of her body as she lay beneath him, looking up at him, inviting his love-making.

She had made a fool of him! Angrily he thrust the memory of her sweetness from his mind. He had other problems. His father was more important than a lying whore. No matter what he thought of her, he must get his father interested in work again.

"Shall we work on the chests together, Father? It would be a pity to disappoint Miss Warwick, would it not? Remember how fascinated she used to be watching you at work? It's an honour that she chose you for her wedding chests."

A flicker of interest showed in the older man's eyes. "Work on them together, Adam?" He smiled and nodded. "Yes, I should enjoy that."

166

"Good." Adam smiled at his father. "Now. What did she say she wanted?"

Susanna was dressing when her mother walked into the room. As soon as she saw her face, she realized something was terribly wrong. She watched while her mother turned the key in the lock, slipping it into the bodice of her gown. Susanna felt a prickling sensation of fear as Lady Patricia came to stand in front of her. For a moment they stared at each other in silence, the atmosphere thick with tension.

"Whore! You stupid, wicked girl! You have ruined us!"

Lady Patricia's hand snaked out, hitting her daughter across the face again and again in quick succession. Susanna staggered back, her eyes wide. She had believed she'd managed to keep her secret, but her mother knew. She knew what had happened in the summerhouse! Her face was very pale as she stared at the older woman, but she lifted her head proudly.

"You had no right to spy on me . . ."

"No right!" Lady Patricia was beside herself with rage. "What do you think would have happened if Digby had seen you? Tell me that!"

Susanna shrugged her shoulders, looking defiant. "It doesn't matter since I am not going to marry him. I've made up my mind. Why should I ruin my life just to pay Papa's gambling debts? It wasn't fair of you or Papa to ask it of me. I'm in love with Adam Blackwell."

"In love with that oaf!" Scorn was in every line of the mother's face. "He has no education, no intelligence . . ."

"That's not true," Susanna cried. "Adam has always been intelligent. He had no education but since he went to London, he has studied and . . ." She jerked back as her mother flew at her in a fury, trying to fend off the savage blows that rained on her face, neck and arms. Dodging out of the way, she said, "And I'm going to marry him whatever anyone . . ."

"You will marry Digby." Lady Patricia was suddenly icy

calm. "You will do exactly as I tell you. I shall not let you ruin us, Susanna."

"You cannot force me to marry him." Susanna looked at her defiantly. "I shall tell him that I've changed my mind and ask him to release me – I don't care what you do to me."

"You will care. Believe me, you will care."

Susanna sank on to the edge of her bed as her mother went to the door. Her face was stinging from the sharp blows, but she was still defiant. As soon as her mother left she was determined to run away. She would not stay here to be bullied and spied on. It was her life, why shouldn't she do what she wanted for once? She watched as Lady Patricia unlocked the door, surprised as she heard her speak to someone outside.

"She must be taught a lesson," the harsh voice said. "Bind and gag her."

Susanna's eyes opened wide as two of the grooms came in. They were big, burly men and they advanced on her purposefully. Giving a cry of alarm, she sprang to her feet and attempted to run past them but one of them caught her, holding her as she struggled wildly.

"Let me go at once!" she demanded imperiously. "My father will have you flogged for this."

"It's orders, miss," he muttered apologetically.

"My orders, Susanna." Lady Patricia came towards her as she was subdued, her wrists bound behind her back with a thin cord that cut painfully into her flesh. "You are to be bound and gagged and kept in your room until you come to your senses. I'm sorry about the gag but I can't have you screaming while Digby is in the house. I've told him that you were taken ill yesterday and that's why you didn't come down for dinner."

Susanna gazed at her mother's hard face in disbelief. "You can't do this. Even you wouldn't dare. Papa will . . ."

"Your father will do nothing," Lady Patricia said scornfully. "He hardly knows where he is most of the time. I have

168

told him you are too sick to see anyone, and naturally he believes me."

"I shan't marry Digby." Susanna's head went up proudly. "You can't make me."

"Can I not?" Her mother smiled slightly. "We shall see what a few days on bread and water will do. There are other ways of changing your mind, of course. Please don't force me to use them, Susanna." She turned to the groom who had spoken. "Put the gag on now."

Susanna struggled furiously, but she was swiftly over-powered. The groom lifted her on to the bed and then fastened the cord binding her wrists to one of the posts. She could change position but she could not leave the bed. Her eyes gazed angrily at her mother, rage and hatred making her pull uselessly at the ropes that bound her.

"You will soon tire of that," Lady Patricia remarked. "I shall return to bring water and bread – and allow you to answer nature's call at regular intervals. After all, I am your nurse and you must be attended to." She smiled slightly. "If I were you, Susanna, I should think very carefully. You might as well give in now as later."

Susanna stared defiantly at the door as her mother went out. She would never give in. Never! She would starve before she agreed to her mother's demands.

Perhaps he was a fool, but Adam knew he had to keep that appointment in the summerhouse. Striding across the meadows, his face was hard and as cold as the bitter wind that swept down from the north. He had to see Susanna just once more, if only to tell her what he thought of her. He would challenge her with his knowledge of her marriage, and if she laughed at him, he would smile and pretend that it meant nothing to him. He would tell her that he too was to be married, and make no mention of the foolish dream he'd had of running away with her. He would let her think that it had been a game with him too, that he had intended no more than a few nights in her arms.

It was a dark night, the moon shadowed by clouds, and freezing. Adam was too angry to feel the cold. All he could think of was Susanna's beautiful face. And her lying eyes. He had believed they reflected her love, but she had wanted only the gratification of her senses. She was no better than Lady Munford!

He could see the summerhouse now. The clouds had rolled back suddenly and in the moonlight it looked like an ancient temple – a temple of love! Adam knew that Susanna had been a virgin. Something moved in him as he recalled the sweetness of her surrender. She had given him the most precious of all gifts, he could not forget that. All at once, his heart began to beat faster. Susanna was waiting for him. Perhaps his father had been mistaken after all. Perhaps she had changed her mind about her marriage. Perhaps he was moon-mad – but now he wanted her. He wanted her so much that he was sick with longing. He sprinted the last few paces, wanting, needing to see her, to hold her.

"Susanna," he called, pushing open the door and going inside. "Susanna . . . are you there?"

He caught a whiff of strong perfume and then something hit him on the back of the head. He fell to the ground, his head spinning. Groaning, he tried to rise, but he was too slow and he felt another blow between his shoulders, then a heavy boot in his side. Rolling over, he opened his eyes. Everything was hazy but he could see three men and a woman. They were all masked, and the woman was wearing a blue dress . . . Susanna's dress.

"Susanna . . ." he whispered croakily. "Susanna . . . why?"

"Because you dared to rape her," a man said savagely. "And now you will pay for it, scum."

"No . . . that's a lie. I didn't . . ." Adam tried to rise as he protested, but another crashing blow on the back of the neck sent him sprawling. Then as the blows rained down on him, he lost consciousness and knew no more.

How many days had she been imprisoned in her room?

170

Susanna tried to count them ... was it five, six or only hours? She could not be sure. It seemed like a lifetime. At first she had not believed that her mother would really carry out her threat, thinking that she would come back at any minute and set her free. But the hours had passed and when Lady Patricia finally came, it was only to bring a cup of water and a slice of bread. Susanna scorned to eat the bread. If her mother intended her to starve she might as well die sooner than later. She would rather die than marry a man she didn't love. Yet a little voice in her head told her that her mother would not dare to let her die.

Lady Patricia returned and saw the bread uneaten. "Not hungry, Susanna?" she snapped. "You will be in a day or two." She took the uneaten bread and the cup of water away with her.

The second day Susanna again left the bread untouched, but she could not resist the water. Hunger was easier to fight than thirst. She drank it greedily, looking hopefully for more. Her mother smiled and nodded.

"You were thirsty," she said. "Why not stop all this nonsense? You can drink and eat as much as you like if you agree to be sensible."

"I would rather die," Susanna cried defiantly.

Lady Patricia shook her head sadly. "Then I'm afraid you will," she said. "As your grieving mother, I shall naturally turn to Digby for comfort. I'm sure he will be kindness itself – as long as he never knows that you were whoring in the summerhouse with that carpenter's boy."

"What good will that do?" Susanna asked. "He will still ask for his money back."

"Now that, my dearest daughter, is where you are wrong. If you break the contract your father signed, Digby will no doubt ruin us, but if you should die ... We cannot be held responsible for that. So you see, you leave me no choice."

"You must hate me."

"Hate you? No, I don't hate you, but you've let me down. I'm disappointed in you, Susanna. I thought you had more sense than to throw yourself away on a carpenter's boy."

"He isn't a carpenter's boy," Susanna cried angrily. "He's a very talented man and one day he'll be rich."

"How foolish you are." Her mother looked at her pityingly. "It must be the fever talking. You are out of your mind. It is obviously my duty to save you from yourself."

"Why can't I see her?" Beatrice asked tearfully. "She's my sister and I love her. I want to see her."

"She has a fever," Lady Patricia said, her face cold. "I'm afraid it might be catching. I don't want you to go down with it. I have enough to do nursing Susanna."

Beatrice turned away. She recognized that look in her mother's eyes and knew better than to press her further. She was certain Lady Patricia wasn't telling the truth. If Susanna was so ill, why had the doctor not been called, and why did her mother keep the door locked all the time? Once or twice she had been to her sister's door, pressing her ear against it, and was sure that she had heard Susanna call for help. She believed that her mother was punishing her for what had happened that night in the park . . . But what could she do about it? Even if she went to her father, it was unlikely that he would listen to her.

Jeanie gave a cry of alarm as she opened the door and saw the men outside. The three of them had carried Adam from the waggon drawn up in the road. His face was white and his lip was bleeding, his eyes tightly shut.

"What has happened?" she cried. "What have you done to him?"

"We found him," one of the men said. "He was lying at the edge of the woods. If we hadn't brought him to you, he might have caught his death of cold out there all night."

"But what happened?" Jeanie asked again. "He be hurt bad. Someone must have done this to him."

"Gipsies, I shouldn't wonder. Didn't he have a fight with them some years back? Rescued the Squire's daughter as

I heard tell. Bad blood in them gipsies. They harbour a grudge for years. Depend upon it, Mrs Blackwell, it was the gipsies what done it."

"Yes, it must have been," Jeanie said, looking at her son sadly. "Will you carry him up to his room for me?"

"We'll do that," the man said. "And when he wakes up, you be sure to tell him it was the gipsies, Mrs Blackwell. Don't forget now."

"No," Jeanie said. "I shan't forget. Thank you for bringing him back. I can look after him now."

"Sir! Please, sir, can I speak to you?" Beatrice cried as she saw Lord Digby walking in the gardens. It was the first time she had managed to find him alone, and she was determined to go through with her plan, even though her heart was thumping with fright.

Digby smiled at her as she approached and some of her fear abated. "Yes, Miss Beatrice, what can I do for you?"

"It's about Susanna . . ." Beatrice summoned her courage. "I'm so worried about her. I think she's going to die."

His smile faded. "Why do you think that?"

"Because I can hear her crying when I go to her door and listen. She says strange things, things that don't make sense, and she keeps asking for help. I think she is very ill."

"Yes, I fear so." Digby looked concerned. "What does the doctor say? I have been unable to catch him when he visits, or I should have asked for his diagnosis myself."

"The doctor hasn't been." Beatrice drew a deep breath as she saw him frown. "Mama says she can nurse her better herself, but I'm worried that she will die. Please, can you help her? Mama takes no notice of me, and she would be very angry if she knew I'd spoken to you but I love Susanna and . . ." Tears sprang to her eyes. "Please don't let her die!"

"She certainly shall not die if I can help it," Digby said, his face stern. "I shall send for my own doctor at once. He can be here within two days . . . and I shall insist on seeing Susanna myself."

Beatrice smiled, her tears vanishing as if by magic. "And you won't tell Mama that I asked you to help?"

"Indeed, I shall not." Digby smiled again. She was a pleasant little thing. Very biddable. "But you must excuse me for I shall talk to Lady Patricia at once."

Adam woke in bed to see his mother bending over him. She looked at him anxiously, her face grey with tiredness.

"How did I get here?" he asked, wrinkling his brow as he tried to remember.

"You were attacked by gipsies," Jeanie said. "The Squire's people found you and brought you home."

Adam sat up and looked at her. His body felt as if it had been beaten all over. He groaned as his head swam and he felt sick. Attacked by gipsies, that wasn't right . . . Suddenly, he remembered what had really happened. He had been attacked but not by the gipsies. He'd been beaten by the Squire's men, while Susanna watched! The vixen. What twisted pleasure had she taken from that? The anger moved inside him and he cursed his own stupidity.

"Adam!" Jeanie cried, alarmed as he threw back the patchwork quilt and swung his legs over the side of the bed. "What are you doing? The doctor said you were to stay in bed for at least three days."

Adam gritted his teeth. The pain was almost unbearable, but he wasn't going to give in to it. That would be to let her win – the bitch who had mocked him as he lay dazed on the floor, laughing as he was beaten and kicked. He wasn't going to give the Warwicks the satisfaction of thinking that they had humbled him. He pushed away his mother's restraining hand and scowled.

"I've work to do," he said. "Father has those chests to make and if I don't help him, he won't lift a finger."

"But, Adam," his mother protested. "You're in pain."

"Nothing that a glass or two of your wine won't cure," he said. "Leave me alone, Ma. I can manage."

Reluctantly, Jeanie left the room. He was suffering agony

174

but there was no arguing with Adam when his mind was made up. She knew that he was angry about something; it might have something to do with the Warwicks. She hadn't quite believed the Squire's men when they brought her son back home, though she'd faithfully repeated their story.

Left to himself, Adam dressed slowly, each movement causing him so much pain that it was all he could do not to crash back on the bed. His flesh was black and blue all over and his weakness made him sweat. His hands felt swollen and he could barely button his coat. Only his anger kept him going. Anger against all the Warwicks, but especially Susanna.

One day he would pay her back for this. One day.

Stubbornly, Susanna refused to eat. She drank the water but pushed away the bread. The gnawing pain inside her grew hourly, but she fought it. It had become a battle of wills between her and her mother, and she was determined to die or win. But now her mind was becoming hazy. She could not remember how long she had been here. Sometimes when she lay with her eyes closed, fighting the pain, she imagined she heard voices begging her to give in.

"It's not worth dying for, Susanna," someone said. "You hardly know him. Live for yourself. You're too young to die."

"Go away!" she cried, but when she opened her eyes there was no one there.

Then the voices became faces. Strange, winged monsters that floated out of the ground and attacked her, biting at her flesh and sucking her blood. They tried to drag her with them into that hellish pit in the ground. She cried out in fear, begging them to go away. Someone was bending over her, laying a cool hand on her brow.

"My poor child," the voice said. "You are dying. Say that you will do as I ask you, Susanna. You've fought well, but you're too young to die." A hand steadied her, holding a cup of water to her parched lips. "Just say yes," the gentle voice went on. "That's all you have to do and then it will all be over."

What was it she had to say yes to? Susanna couldn't remember. All she wanted was to be left alone to die. Perhaps if she said yes, they would leave her alone. Her lips formed the word, a whisper that could hardly be heard but was understood.

Looking down at her daughter, Lady Patricia was amazed that she had won. Another day and she would have had to give way. Digby was being difficult. He had insisted on sending for his own doctor . . .

Adam looked at the design he had drawn with satisfaction. It was exactly the kind of thing that would appeal to someone like Susanna. He showed it to his father, who nodded agreement.

"That's very fine, Adam. It should please Miss Warwick."

"We're agreed then, Father. I'll work on one chest and you on the other. I'll help you all I can before I go back to London. I want to see these finished before I leave."

"I could do them myself," Tom Blackwell said. "But it will be good to have you working with me, son. Almost like old times."

There was a flicker of pain in his father's eyes, and Adam knew that nothing would ever be the same for him again. With him in London and Maggie gone, there would be little for either of his parents to look forward to but a lonely old age.

"Why don't you come to London, Father?" Adam asked. "You and Mother could live with Jane and me. You could help me out with the polishing."

For a moment Tom's eyes lit up, then he shook his head. "It's good of you to offer, Adam, but I reckon me and your ma will bide here. It's what we're used to. We be plain folk, your ma and me. I reckon we're best here with folk who understand us."

176

Adam nodded, knowing in his heart that his father was right. Jeanie Blackwell would find London harsh and bewildering. She would be happier living out her days in Chorley Hale. He felt a surge of anger as he thought that she ought to have had her daughter and grandchildren to keep her company.

"Well, we'd best get on with these marriage chests," he said, turning back to his designs. "I'll start work on the chests and leave the stands to you. I might be able to finish at least one of them before I go."

Adam's expression was grim as he thought of the message he meant to send Susanna Warwick. His whole body was sore from the beating he had been given, and it was taking him all his time to stand on his feet, but pride kept him going. He would design and execute the most splendid marriage chest he was capable of, to make sure that Miss Warwick never forgot him. In one corner of a certain drawer, he intended to leave a clue that she could not fail to notice: a tiny broken heart that would lead her to the hiding place he had planned for his note. A few bitter lines that would tell her of his hatred and his anger.

Jeanie embraced her son, tears glistening in her eyes. She knew in her heart that this might be the last time she would ever see him. This wasting sickness, whatever it was, and the doctor knew very little about it, was gaining on her. The only blessing was that she had no pain, or none that she took account of.

"It was powerful kind of you to come," she said, lifting her face for Adam's kiss. "It's done your father a world of good to have you here. It be clever of you to get him working again, Adam. He be almost back to his old self."

"He needs to work, Ma." Adam looked down into her face. She looked so exhausted that his heart was wrenched with pity for her. "But I think he'll be fine now. When the chests for Miss Warwick are done, there's a set of chairs for the doctor, and the vicar has asked for a breakfront bookcase for his parlour. Father has enough work to keep him going well into the New Year."

Jeanie nodded and smiled. "Folk be kinder in times of trouble," she said. "My cousin brought a basket of baked meats and a quince tart yesterday. She's never bothered to visit before, not since she got took on at the Hall, but it were a kindness, though with your father working again we'll not need charity."

Adam nodded and looked down at her. "Father will manage now. But what of you, Ma?"

"Doctor Mason brought me a new medicine," she said. "It be powerful strong and he wouldn't take a penny piece for it. I feel better already. Don't you worry about me, Adam. My old gran lived to be near on ninety, she did. I doubt me I'll do as well, but there be a few years left in me yet."

She was lying to comfort him, just as she had when as a child he'd been afraid of having a tooth pulled by the tooth-drawer at the fair. She had sworn it wouldn't hurt but a mite. It had hurt like hell, Adam remembered, but he hadn't cried because she'd stood with him, smiling and saying it would soon be over. He'd forgotten how much he had once loved her, and now his love returned to smite him with guilt and regret.

"I should stay here," he said. "You need me – you and Father."

"You be mazed in the head!" Jeanie said, frowning at him. "Neither me nor your pa would rest easy in our beds if you threw away all your chances for our sakes." She shook her head as he would have protested. "No, Adam Blackwell. You listen to me awhiles. I be a simple woman with no learning, and if you hadn't gone away to London you would have been jest like me. Oh, I know you be good with your hands, lad, but it bain't enough. You've learned to talk proper and you know so many wonderful things since you went to London. You've got a chance to make something of your life now. You do it, Adam. You do it for me, for your pa – and for Maggie."

178

Adam could never remember his mother having made such a long speech before in her life. He stared at her in silence for several minutes, and then nodded. She was right. He could do very little for either her or his father if he stayed. Besides, there was a deep need in him, a need to succeed. His bruises had almost healed, but the pain inside him went deeper. He had been beaten and ridiculed by Susanna Warwick and the bitterness was like an ulcer festering inside him. One day he was going to rise in the world. He would be rich and famous, like Thomas Chippendale. Then he would look back on his experiences at the hands of the Warwicks and laugh. The need to succeed, to show Susanna and her family that he was not a man to be sneered at and treated like a dog, was so strong in him at that moment that it became an ache in his guts.

"I'll make you proud of me, Ma," he said. "I promise you. One day you'll be proud of your son."

"I be proud of you now," she said. "Now be off to London and your Miss Jane. That's where you belong."

Adam bent his head to kiss her. "I'll say goodbye to Father and then I'll go."

Jeanie smiled and nodded. She stared at the door long after it had closed behind him, her smile gradually fading. It had cost her a lot to let him go. Tom had his work now. He would get through, but it was going to be lonely without Maggie's cheerful face popping round the kitchen door.

Jeanie threw off her mood of self-pity as she went to the pantry and fetched eggs, milk and flour. A good nourishing meat pudding was what her Tom needed to set him up. She would never cease to grieve for her pretty daughter, but Adam had got Tom working again, and he was to make a fine marriage in London. Perhaps one day her son would bring his wife and children to see her. At least the future looked bright for him.

CHAPTER TWELVE

"You look better," Beatrice said as she perched on her sister's bed. "You were very ill. We've all been so worried. I wanted to visit you before, but Mama wouldn't let me."

"No," Susanna said weakly. "I don't suppose she would. I might have been infectious. It was some sort of a fever, wasn't it?"

"Yes, I expect so," Beatrice said, smothering her doubts. "Lord Digby insisted on bringing in his own doctor. We all thought you were going to die."

"I almost did." Susanna reached for her sister's hand. "It was nice of you to worry about me, Bea."

"I don't want you to die," Beatrice said, blinking back the foolish tears. "I do care about you, Susanna. Besides, you promised me I could come and stay with you. You said we would have lots of parties, don't you remember?"

"Did I?" Susanna pressed her hand to her forehead. "I can't remember very much at the moment. Sometimes I think the strangest things, but the doctor said I was hallucinating during my illness. I thought Mama was trying to starve me to death."

"Oh, Susanna," Beatrice cried. She must try to keep her sister's spirits up, that was what the doctor had told her. Otherwise, Susanna might slip into a decline. "What a silly thing you are. Mama was devoted to you all the time you were ill. She wouldn't let anyone else nurse you, not until she was sure you were getting better."

Susanna frowned. "I suppose it was just bad dreams, though they seemed so real. How long was I ill, Bea?"

"Almost three weeks," Beatrice said. "But you're much stronger now, the doctor said so."

180

"Of course she's stronger," Lady Patricia said, rallying her daughters as she came in. "It was just a very nasty chill, but it is all over now. Susanna will soon be up and about again – and ready for her big day, won't you, darling?"

"My big day?" Susanna stared at her mother.

"Your wedding day," Lady Patricia said serenely. "It has been arranged for the week after Christmas. The doctor says you will be quite well then. Besides, Digby is so considerate. He's going to take you down to the country and cosset you until you are strong again."

"He has been so kind." Susanna's eyes strayed to the baskets of fruit and flowers in her room. She tried to remember . . . She hadn't wanted to marry Digby but she couldn't remember why.

"Of course he is kind," her mother said in a bracing tone. "He adores you. You are a very lucky girl, Susanna."

"Yes, I suppose I am." Susanna closed her eyes. "I'm very tired. I should like to sleep now."

"May I walk with you, Susanna?" Lord Digby looked at her as she came downstairs wearing a heavy cloak over her gown. "Don't you think it's a little cold for you to go out, my dear?"

Susanna stifled her annoyance. She was finding his constant fussing tedious, but he had been very kind, so she tried to hide her impatience. She was feeling so much better that she was desperate to escape for a while.

"I want to see someone, Percival," she said, pouting at him prettily. "It concerns a surprise for you."

"For me?" He raised his brows.

"Yes." She smiled up at him. "A wedding gift. I want to see if it's ready yet."

He looked surprised but pleased. "Then I suppose I must let you go alone – but do not stay too long in this chill wind."

"I shall be an hour at most," she promised, reaching up to kiss his cheek. "There, that is for being a dear, kind Percival." She stepped back out of his reach.

Digby's smile faded as she walked away. Susanna never refused his company, but he was aware of a change in her. A change that had begun before she was ill. In London she had seemed happy enough with their bargain, but now he was not so sure. He had tried to embrace her more than once, but she kept him at a distance. Of course she was very young, and her mother was strict, but a chaste kiss was not so very much to ask from the woman he was soon to marry. Things would alter then. He was prepared to abide by her rules for the moment, but once they were married . . .

It was very cold. Susanna pulled the hood of her thick cloak up over her head. She had been determined to escape this morning. Her memory was still hazy, but things were beginning to come back to her. She had strange dreams, dreams in which she was in Adam Blackwell's arms. In her dreams they had gone to the summerhouse and . . . but was it all imagination? She remembered the kiss in the churchyard; she remembered Adam's anger and the way she had responded to his passion. Perhaps the dreams were just that. Hallucinations, just like those she had had about her mother trying to starve her. She must have been very ill. Sometimes it seemed to her that it had all been real.

Tucking her head down against the wind, Susanna walked faster. If she could just see Adam, perhaps she would remember everything. It was important to remember.

She knocked at the Blackwells' door, her heart racing wildly. If she could just see him, speak to him. The door was opened by Jeanie, who smiled and drew her inside.

"Come you in, Miss Warwick," she cried. "Why, you be fair frozen! What made you walk all this way on such a day?"

"I wanted to see if my travelling chests were ready." Susanna's cheeks flamed as she made her excuse.

"Come you in to the fire," Jeanie said, taking her through to the kitchen. "My Tom be up at the vicar's measuring for a bookcase, but he'll be back soon. I believe he be nearly finished them cabinets you ordered. Adam did give a hand with them afore he left."

"Your son has gone?" Susanna's heart sank at the words. She was too late.

"He went last week," Jeanie said, as she poured a glass of elderflower wine. "Get that inside you, Miss Susanna. That be powerful good, though I says it myself."

Susanna sipped the wine. She felt it warming her through and sighed gratefully. "It is good, Mrs Blackwell. The best I've tasted. I – I thought Adam might stay with you for a bit longer?" She felt like weeping with frustration. It hadn't occurred to her that Adam would return to London so soon.

"He wanted to bide by us another week or so," Jeanie agreed. "But Tom be better now and Adam belongs in London, alongside of that girl he be promised to wed."

"Adam is to be married?" Susanna swallowed hard, trying to keep the shock from her face.

"Aye, that he be, to Miss Jane Carter." Jeanie beamed with maternal pride. "Rare pleased the Carters be too, I can tell you. They sent me a fine tea chest filled with the best leaves, and a letter telling me how clever our Adam be. Curate read it to me, Adam being too bashful. Mr Carter can't manage without him so he's made him a partner in the business. His name's on the sign outside the shop, and they're going to buy another house with a showroom and a workshop for Adam to train up his own apprentices. *Carter & Blackwell* that sign says – now what do you think of that?"

"It's very exciting." Susanna managed a smile despite the ache inside her. She must have imagined that night in the summerhouse after all. "I'm very pleased for all of you. I wonder . . ." She broke off as the door opened and Tom Blackwell came in, puffing and blowing on his hands to warm them.

"There you be, Tom." Jeanie gazed fondly at her husband. "Look you who's come to see us."

Tom Blackwell nodded and smiled. "Miss Susanna. You've grown right pretty, not that you bain't always been a sight for sore eyes."

"Thank you." Susanna remembered his kindness to her years before. He was just the same despite the sorrow her brother had caused. "I came to see if my cabinets were ready. You see . . ." She drew a deep breath. "I am to be married soon after Christmas."

Once it was said, she felt relieved, as if a weight had been lifted, or some kind of a threat. At least Mama and Digby would be pleased. And what did it matter? She had imagined that Adam had held her in his arms and vowed he loved her, but it was all part of her strange illness. It couldn't have been true. Adam was already promised to Jane Carter.

Susanna had the travelling chests carried up to her room. Digby had gone up to London to make some last-minute arrangements for their wedding. Or so he had said as he kissed her goodbye. She guessed that he had planned some surprise for her. He became more indulgent as the days passed and their wedding drew nearer.

She looked at the cabinets as they stood side by side. In size they were exactly equal, being eighteen inches deep, three feet in length and standing some three feet high on shaped bracket supports, from which they could be removed for travelling. The front was split into two and the doors opened outwards to reveal the drawers inside.

Outwardly plain and serviceable except for the gleaming brass locks, the insides made her gasp in surprise and pleasure. The surround was cross-banded with rosewood and satinwood stringing, and there was a different motif inlaid into the centre of each drawer front. Several different types of wood had been used for the marquetry, and the colours ranged through yellow, green, black and pink, blending into a pleasing whole. Some of the motifs were of musical instruments, others of singing birds and flowers.

Adam and Tom must have put in hours of work to get them done so quickly for her. She thought that she had never seen anything quite so exquisite. As she looked closer, however, she saw that the workmanship on one cabinet was much finer than on the other, though it was not discernible at first glance.

Susanna knew that this must be the chest Adam had worked on while he was staying with his father. This was the chest he had made for her — her wedding chest. It had been made for her by the man she loved for her marriage to a man she could never love! The irony of it was a cruel blow that made her heart ache. Yet despite her pain, she could take delight in the beautiful workmanship.

She examined both chests again, finding tiny details she had missed the first time. She noticed that in the corner of one of Adam's drawers there was a broken heart. The design of the motifs on the drawer fronts of the second chest was not quite as intricate and there was no sign of the broken heart. For a moment she wondered if Adam had had some purpose in adding it to his own chest, but then she decided that Tom had simply missed it. He had made a brave attempt to copy Adam's designs, but they were not as cleverly done.

She ran her fingers over the smooth wood of the chest Adam had made himself, closing her eyes as she remembered the way he had made love to her in her dreams and felt again the sensual pleasure she had experienced. If only it had been true. But he had gone, back to London and the woman he was promised to wed. Tears rolled down her cheeks, but she brushed them away. If Adam had loved her, he would never have left.

Susanna's heart ached as she looked at the cabinets again. She would keep the best chest for herself, she decided. Digby would never notice the difference, if he even bothered to give it a second glance. She would keep it to remind herself of what might have been.

*　　　*　　　*

Jane's face lit up with pleasure as she saw Adam enter the kitchen. Wiping her hands, she left the delicate china she had been rinsing in cold water and went to meet him.

"So you're back then," she said. "How is your mother? And your father?"

"Father has started working again," Adam said with a slight frown. "But my mother is far from well. She has a wasting sickness and cannot live long."

"I'm truly sorry." Jane looked at him, her face serious. "Then we are united in sorrow, for I fear my dearest father is ill. He hides it from my mother and me, but I've seen him when the pain strikes and I know he suffers."

"I'm afraid it is so, Jane – though he would not want you to know it."

She smiled up at him. "I shall not add to his distress by letting him see I am aware of his illness. He will be happier now that you are back. He was afraid that you might decide to stay with your family."

"I could not do that, Jane." Adam took her hand. "My promise was given to you and your father." He put the memory of that night in the summerhouse from his mind, relieving his conscience. It had been a moment of madness, nothing more. A night of pleasure for which he had paid dearly. What a fool he would have been to desert Jane for that lying whore!

Jane saw the shadows in his eyes, but she understood them. He was grieving for his sister, and for his mother. She gave him a sympathetic look.

"It would have grieved me," she said. "But I should not have held you to it had you felt your duty lay elsewhere." She could say it now that he was back, knowing she would not be called upon to stand aside. It was better always to be meek with a man, at least until they were safely wed. Jane knew she was no beauty. She also knew that Adam thought her pleasant but weak-willed. He would learn the truth in time, but by then they would be husband and wife and accustomed to each other's ways.

"There was nothing I could do for my mother if I stayed – and there's not enough work in the village for both father and me these days. It was best I came back."

"And I'm glad of it," she assured him; then as he turned to go through into the workshop, she called him back. "Oh, Adam, I was forgetting. Lord Charles Munford asked for you while you were away. Father sent word that you were out of town, and promised you would call as soon as you returned."

Adam felt a spasm of fear in his stomach. It had come at last, the summons he had dreaded. For a moment he wanted to run away, to evade the trouble he knew must await him at Henrietta Place; but he knew that whatever it was, he must face it. He was innocent of the charge and would swear it even as they put the noose around his neck. He forced himself to smile at Jane, regretting the shame and misery his arrest and imprisonment must give her.

"I shall send word that I am back and ask Lord Munford if I may call tomorrow afternoon," he said. "But for now I want to catch up on what has been happening while I was away. There must be a deal of work to do."

"So, madam, your brother is to marry that pretty little chit from Norfolk." The Marquis of Brandon looked at Lady Munford through his quizzing glass. "I had thought him a confirmed bachelor."

"Did you want the little bird for yourself?" Helen Munford taunted him, unable to resist the opportunity to pay him back for old scores. They had once been lovers, but he had tired of her. He was one of the few who had left her, and she had never quite forgiven him for it.

"As a wife, heaven forbid!" the Marquis said, his light tone belying the anger he felt inside at the way he had been cheated. All the trouble he'd taken to court Warwick's company, to make a friend of a man he despised and lead him on to his destruction. His plans so carefully laid, and the chit had refused him! "As a temporary amusement, perhaps."

Lady Helen knew him too well to be deceived. "We shall have to see what can be done when Digby brings her up to town, my lord. Someone must take the chit under their wing; why should it not be me?"

Brandon's eyes narrowed as he looked at her. It might be useful to have her co-operation. The Warwick girl was too proud for her own good. She had to be humbled, and if Helen Munford were willing to help him, so much the better. However, he was not ready to share his confidence just yet. Helen was greedy. She would demand far more than her services were worth. Besides, the hunt was half the fun. Only if he could find no other way would he enlist her help.

"That is a matter for you," he said and yawned behind his hand. "I am not sure that the chit is worth the trouble."

He was lying. His pride had been wounded when Susanna Warwick refused his offer. It was the first offer of marriage he had made to any woman, and it would be the last.

"Well, perhaps you are right," Helen said, seeing that he would not be pressed further. "And now, my dear Brandon, I must speak to Lady Clarendon. You will excuse me?"

He bowed and she walked away, smiling to herself. She had known when Brandon sought her out at this boring little soiree that something was on his mind. He was furious that Digby had won the girl, and would not be satisfied until he got his revenge. Brandon was not to be parted from his money without some persuasion, but she could wait. He would pay handsomely when the time came.

The wedding presents were arriving every day now. Susanna and Beatrice opened them together, after which the servants arranged them on tables in the library.

Silver epergnes, delicate Sèvres china, little coffee cups studded with pearls and garnets, wafer-thin glass goblets with fragile stems twisted through with a twirl of glass that looked like lace. A huge silver gilt tea and coffee service from Lord and Lady Munford. Tea caddies, writing boxes inlaid with mother of pearl and silver. A black lacquer commode with delicate paintings of birds and flowers, and gilt mountings, a pretty miniature of a hunting scene set in a gold frame, fine linen edged with lace, silk carpets and scent bottles made of Bristol blue glass with gold mounts; so many beautiful gifts that Susanna was kept busy writing thank-you notes and had no time to brood.

It was Beatrice who opened the case of stuffed birds. As the wrappings fell away, she gave a cry and tears welled up in her eyes. Susanna looked at her in surprise.

"What's wrong, dearest?"

"They're beautiful," Beatrice said. "But who would be that cruel? They look perfect – almost as if they had been killed just so that they could be put in this glass dome . . ."

Susanna felt a coldness inside as she examined the case. Why had anyone sent her such a gift? It was almost as though it were some kind of warning, yet that was nonsense, a mere irritation of the nerves.

"I'm sure you're wrong," she said, to reassure herself as much as Beatrice. "Who would want to kill such beautiful birds? Why, there's a robin and a goldcrest, and a wren and a tom-tit, all such delicate little things." A frown creased her brow. "I do not much care for it. Who sent it to us, Beatrice?"

Her sister looked at the card. "It was from the Marquis of Brandon," she said, then as Susanna went pale, "What's the matter?"

"Nothing." Susanna took a deep breath to steady herself. "I – I do not like the Marquis. I must acknowledge his gift, of course, but I shall not take it with me. I could not bear to have it in the house. Nanny Giles can put it up in the attic."

"It's horrible," Beatrice said with a shudder. "Such a strange thing to send as a wedding gift, don't you think?"

"Yes. Yes . . ." Susanna tried to ignore her feeling of foreboding, but found it difficult. "Yes, not as useful as most of the others, I must admit. Cover it up, Beatrice, and look at this. Lady Maddison has sent me a set of beautiful silver coasters, was that not kind of her?"

Beatrice had covered the offending dome and was once more intent on discovering what was inside all the exciting parcels. No more was said about the birds, but Susanna could not quite rid herself of the feeling that there had been some deeper meaning behind the Marquis's gift.

CHAPTER THIRTEEN

Adam drew a deep breath as he stood across the road from the Munfords' house and stared at it. His request for an interview with Lord Munford had been met with a polite invitation to call at three-thirty. It wanted five minutes to the half hour. Adam replaced his watch in his waistcoat pocket, squared his shoulders and crossed the road. He would put up no physical resistance to his arrest, he decided, but would defend himself in a dignified manner that must command respect.

A footman he had not seen before opened the door to his knock. He was invited to enter, and left to cool his heels while the servant went to inquire if his master was in. It was more than ten minutes before he returned. Adam spent the time pacing up and down the small room, his nerves fraying.

"His lordship will see you now, Mr Blackwell." He was led through the hall to a ground-floor apartment at the rear, the footman throwing open the double doors to announce him. Going in, Adam paused, startled to discover that he was in an empty room. The floor was boarded and highly polished, but there was no carpet and not a stick of furniture. As Adam stared in bewilderment, a door at the far end opened and a man entered. He was small, no more than five foot six in height, thin, with sticklike legs that bowed outwards, making him look almost deformed. His knee-breeches and coat were fashioned of a pale grey cloth, and as plain as Adam's own, though his stock was of the finest Brussels lace. Apart from a diamond pin at his throat, he wore no jewellery or ribbons and his hair was cut straight above his collar with no powder or false pieces.

He stood staring at Adam with frank curiosity, his hazel eyes bright and inquisitive. He could not have been called an attractive man, for his nose was long, his cheeks pinched and pale, and there were heavy bags beneath his eyes that made him look rather like a sorrowful bulldog. As Adam waited in silence, a malicious smile touched his mouth.

"So, Adam Blackwell," he cackled suddenly. "What's this I hear about your disrespect towards my wife?"

Adam looked him in the eyes. "I must defend myself, sir. I did nothing wrong. Lady Munford . . ." Words failed him as he realized how impossible it was to tell this man that his wife was a disgusting whore who had begged him to rape her.

Lord Charles Munford nodded, his eyes fixing Adam's with a piercing stare. "Nothing wrong, you say? Lady Munford complained of you to me for nearly an hour, sir. Can you not be more explicit? Tell me, Mr Blackwell, why was my wife so angry with you?"

Adam cleared his throat. It had seemed easy enough to defend his own honour when he was on his way here, but face to face with this hawk-eyed little man, he found it more difficult than he had expected.

"I can say only that I neither did or said anything dishonourable, sir."

"Damn me if he isn't trying to protect her!" Lord Charles chuckled with malicious delight. "Correct me if I'm wrong, Mr Blackwell, but I have it on good authority that my wife offered you her patronage if you would — oblige her in her bed."

Adam drew breath, nodding stiffly. "Yes, my lord. That was exactly it. When I refused she flew into a temper and threatened to tell you that I had raped her."

"Oh, indeed she did tell me," Lord Charles said. "At some considerable length. It was most diverting . . ." His eyes leapt with humour as he saw Adam's start of surprise. "I know Lady Helen too well, Mr Blackwell. If you had indeed raped her, she would have been only too delighted.

192

She is often bored and seeks new experiences in sexual encounters as other women might seek for a new gown or a precious bauble. Her other lapdogs have grown too tame for her; they grovel for her favours and she hoped for much from you. I fear you sadly disappointed her. She believed that you would come back and beg for her forgiveness. She wanted to break you to her will – and if she had, she would have thrown you out like a discarded shoe."

"I had hoped for Lady Munford's patronage, but the price was too high, sir."

A high-pitched laugh broke from his lordship and he slapped his thigh. "Bless my soul! I never thought to see the day that Helen was crossed. You've courage, sir. She could ruin you with the flick of an eyelid if she chose."

"I am aware of that, sir."

"And yet you refused her." Lord Charles nodded, looking pleased. "Well, you may rest easy on the charge of rape, Mr Blackwell. I made it clear to my wife that I would not support her in it. Indeed, I should have been forced to support you, and that would have caused much scandal and a great deal of laughter amongst her cronies."

Adam felt the relief surge through him. "I am greatly indebted to you, my lord."

The other man nodded, his eyes bright. "I cannot guarantee that she will not try to ruin you. It is easily done with a frown or a word, but in place of Lady Helen's patronage, I offer you mine."

"Yours, sir?" Adam stared at him, not quite able to take it in.

"You gave me the best laugh I've had in a long time," Lord Munford said, his lips twisting in a malicious grin. "If I were a vindictive man, I could divorce my wife, Mr Blackwell. God knows, I have cause enough! But she is the mother of my sons, for I know well she did not betray me until the succession was safe. I kept her in seclusion to make sure of it, and her taste for grooms did not develop until later. For the sake of my sons and their families, I put up with Helen and her little fancies. But she knows better than to push me too far. So she will not bother you again, and you may work here in safety." His eyes danced with mockery. "If you would care to design and build me a library . . ." He indicated the empty room. "As you see, you have a clear field."

Adam stared and then his expression lightened. Suddenly he was laughing, and the laughter was echoed by Lord Munford.

"I should be glad to design and build your library, sir."

"Then here's my hand on it. Bring your preliminary sketches to me as soon as you can, Mr Blackwell, and then we shall discuss terms."

Lord Munford offered his hand and Adam took it.

"I cannot tell you how grateful I am, sir."

"Just build me a library that compares with the best, and I shall be satisfied."

"You won't be disappointed, my lord. I give you my word."

Adam was walking on air as he left the house. He felt as if a great burden had been lifted from his shoulders. Lady Munford no longer had the power to hurt him. He felt so good that he decided to take a drink with a few of his friends. It was seldom that he visited a tavern, but this was cause for a celebration.

Helen Munford alighted from her sedan chair just as Adam was departing. She frowned, tempted to call him back. Had he decided to accept her offer after all? The thought excited her. She had been angry with him, but she was prepared to forgive him on her own terms. She was bored with her present lovers and craved a new amusement.

As she entered the house, a footman bowed and approached her, saying, "Milady. Lord Munford begs the pleasure of your company in the green drawing-room."

It was on the tip of her tongue to reply that she had a headache and could not see her husband at that moment, but curiosity overcame her. Munford seldom asked her to step into his apartments.

Nodding to the servant, she walked briskly through the hall and into the magnificent room at the rear of the house. The walls were hung with shaded silk in a dark green and there were many pictures and gilt-framed mirrors. The furniture was dark mahogany, designed and made by Thomas Chippendale. Helen had commissioned it for her husband when they were still on reasonable terms.

The look of malice on Munford's lips told his wife that he had been brewing some mischief. She was on her guard at once, watching him suspiciously.

"Helen my dear," he said. "How gracious of you to spare me a few minutes of your time."

"You sent for me. I was curious. We have so little to say to one another these days."

"I knew you would want to hear this. I have just been talking to your cabinet-maker, my dear. The one you claimed tried to rape you. He denied it, of course."

"Naturally." Her lip curled. "Would you expect him to admit it?"

"If it were true he might; he seems an honest fellow. I rather liked him." Munford's eyes were bright with triumph. "I've engaged him to build my library."

"You what?" Helen stared at him furiously. "How dare you? How dare you offer me such an insult? To invite that man into my house . . ."

"My house," Munford reminded her. "You surprise me, Helen. Only a few weeks ago you were extolling his virtues. As fine a craftsman as Chippendale, you said, and half the price."

Her eyes narrowed. "You've done this to insult me," she said. "I shan't forget, Munford."

Turning on her heel, she walked swiftly from the room.

*   *   *

Adam's steps were unsteady as he bid his friends goodnight and entered his lodgings. He had stayed too long at the King's Head Inn and drunk too much of the landlord's fine French wine.

"Is that you, Adam?" Mary-Ellen called. She came downstairs in her nightgown, carrying a lighted chamber-stick. Staring at him in silence for a moment, she smiled. "So that's the way of it, is it?" she said, her voice soft with amusement. "Well, now, here's a fine carry on."

Adam looked at her. In the pale glow of the candle she seemed comely and inviting. His senses stirred as he felt desire. He lurched towards her, slipping an arm about her waist.

"What's wrong, Mary love?" he asked, squeezing her and kissing her cheek. "What's the matter? Did I wake you?"

Mary-Ellen shook her head. "Nay, I wasn't asleep," she said in her good-natured way. "Have you been celebrating, Adam?"

He pressed a finger to his lips, swaying slightly on his feet, a look of mischief in his eyes. "S-shall I tell you a secret?" he asked, his words slurring. "I've been given a commission by his lordship – and I've been playing whist with my friends. I won five shillings, what do you think of that?"

"Did you indeed?" Mary-Ellen's brows rose. "That was clever of you, considering the state you're in. Beginner's luck, I shouldn't wonder."

She slid the bolts on the door and came back to look at Adam, who was staring owlishly in front of him. It was the first time she had ever seen him the worse for drink and it worried her. Drinking and gambling had never been his way. It wasn't like him, not the Adam Blackwell she knew. In the four years he'd lodged with her, she had never before seen him the worse for drink. The best place for him was bed! She put her arm about his waist, and he gave her a wicked grin.

"Fancy me do you, Mary love?"

Mary-Ellen hesitated. He was promised to Jane Carter, but they weren't wed yet. Why not once more for old times sake? She smiled at him, her eyes warm and inviting.

"My bed's always open to you," she said, laughing as he nuzzled her neck. "Why not then, Adam? For the last time."

"You're a tasty armful for any man," Adam said. "I envy the man who shares your bed when I've gone."

"Do you, Adam?" Then why haven't you shared it for months? The question was in her mind, but she did not ask it.

At the top of the stairs they turned as one towards her room. Adam leaned heavily on her but he seemed in an amorous mood, nibbling at her neck and whispering the funny, endearing little things that had made her take to him from the first. This was the man she had cared for so dearly for these past four years; the silent, brooding stranger of the last few months was someone she did not recognize. She sat him down on the bed, bending to pull off his boots. He was struggling with his coat buttons, his fingers stiff and clumsy.

"Can't seem to manage it, Mary love." His face had a foolish, vapid look as she bent to unfasten them for him and pulled off the coat. Then, his expression changing to one of mischief, he laughed and leapt on her, pinning her to the bed. "Had you fooled, didn't I?"

She shrieked with laughter, realizing that he wasn't as drunk as he'd made out. "Oh, you're a wicked one," she cried, pretending to push him away. "Just for that I shan't . . ."

And then his mouth was on hers and she was silenced. A fierce, hot desire surged in her and she clutched at him, responding to his urgent need which she sensed. Adam had always been the most considerate of lovers, taking pains to see that she enjoyed their love-making as much as he, but for the first time ever he took her

197

as she lay, fully dressed and unready, hurting her with his savage thrusting. Surprised, she lay unresisting, letting him have his way, understanding that this was something that had been building in him for a long time. That he could not control his actions and was not himself was plain enough to Mary-Ellen. Afterwards, he rolled away from her, lying face downward. His voice was muffled as he said,

"Forgive me, Mary. I never meant it to be that way."

"It doesn't matter," she said.

For a while she lay in silence, thinking. Something had been eating at him for some time now. She sighed, then she turned on her side, stroking his hair. He stirred but did not move and she realized that he had fallen asleep.

"Poor Adam," she whispered. "Who is she? What woman has done this to you, my lovey?"

There was no answer. Her eyes were sad as she lay staring into the darkness. For her it was just a momentary pain, a disappointment that would soon be forgotten. She had other, sweeter memories of Adam to comfort her. But she wondered about the girl who was to be his wife. She didn't know who had hurt him so, but it was not for Jane Carter's sake that he had needed to be half drunk to climb into bed with Mary-Ellen Watts.

Waking to find himself lying alone on Mary-Ellen's bed still fully clothed, Adam recalled his selfish act the previous evening and groaned. He didn't know what had come over him. It was true that he had drunk more than he was used to, but that didn't excuse his behaviour. He had needed the physical relief, but then a picture of *her* had come into his mind and he'd lost control. The memory of Susanna's smiling face followed by the humiliation of his beating had driven all else from his mind. It was Susanna he had wanted to hurt.

Ashamed, he got up and went into his own room, stripping to wash quickly in the ice-cold water from a

198

brass jug. The muzziness cleared from his head and he was clear-sighted as he went downstairs to find Mary-Ellen slicing cold cooked bacon and fresh bread. She smiled at him, just as if nothing untoward had happened.

"Would you like some eggs with your breakfast, Adam?"

"Thank you, no," he said, the feeling of shame growing as he recalled how good she had always been to him. "This will do fine . . . Mary-Ellen, I want . . ."

"Nay, Adam," she said. "There's no need. I've known for a while that something's been eating at you. Last night it all spilled over. And maybe it was best that way."

"Well, I'm sorry for it," he said, making a mental note to bring her a present that evening. "As you said, I've had something on my mind – but I shouldn't have taken my frustrations out on you. You've been good to me, Mary-Ellen, and I'm more grateful than I can say."

She smiled and nodded. "Would it help to talk about it, Adam?"

He hesitated, then shook his head. "No one can help me with it," he said. "It's just something I have to conquer myself." He gave her a self-conscious glance. "To tell the truth, Mary, I'm a damned fool and there's an end to it. I ought to have learned my lesson, but . . ."

"There's a woman, isn't there?" Mary-Ellen looked sympathetic as he remained silent. "She's hurt you and you've discovered that love is sometimes painful."

"Love?" Adam considered the idea. Was he still in love with Susanna Warwick? He dismissed the notion as foolish and laughed at himself. "If this is love, give me lust every time," he said. "We had some good times, didn't we, Mary love?"

"Oh yes," she said. "Now eat your food, Adam, and be off with you or you'll be late for work."

"That would never do." Adam frowned. "Robert is taking Jane and me to see the new house today. We'll have a showroom and a workshop there so that Jane and me can be on our own. Robert will keep on the old showroom, but he's not fit to work much any more so the old workshop can be used for storage space. We were always a mite short of that."

Mary-Ellen looked at him. "You are happy about what you're doing, Adam? If not, well, I've often thought that you could have had a little workshop here until things came right for you. I've plenty of room and I shouldn't have charged you until you were on your feet."

Adam stared at her. He had never dreamt of such a thing, though he realized now that it might have worked. For a moment he knew a pang of regret. Mary-Ellen had never put strings on him. He might have had his own business and been completely independent. Before the idea could even begin to take shape, he acknowledged that it was much too late. The partnership papers were signed and sealed, and he'd given his promise to Jane.

"You're a generous woman, Mary-Ellen," he said. "But I'm happy enough with my bargain."

Yet as he walked to work some twenty minutes later, Adam wondered about what might have been. With his own business, in a year or two he might . . . Then he saw where his wayward thoughts were leading and he laughed out loud. Fool that he was! It would take years before he had anything to offer a girl like Susanna Warwick, and even then there was a world between them. Besides, she was a lying whore, just like her mother. He had been used and humiliated. Susanna had wanted nothing more than a fling before her marriage to a man old enough to be her father — and the sooner he accepted that the better!

Adam glanced through the designs for Lord Munford's library once more then laid them aside. Tomorrow he would deliver them in person, but today was his wedding day. Since they would have their own home, Adam and Jane had decided to dispense with a wedding trip. The weather was cold and neither of them were keen to spend several days in inns with inadequate heating when they could be warm and cosy in their own house.

"Perhaps in the spring we might spend a day or two in the country," Jane said. "But I confess I would rather begin our marriage in our own home. Mother has given me some of her preserves, but I like a well-stocked pantry and I shall be busy filling the shelves for weeks. And you have so much work to do, Adam."

Jane's sensible attitude had found favour with Adam. Their new home was still thin of furniture, for they had chosen to make do with only what was necessary and build up the interior as they went along.

"Father has given us quite enough," Jane said. "Besides, I would rather you made what we want as and when you have the time."

"It will be best that way," Adam agreed. "We can decide on the designs together."

Jane had been adding to her dower chest since she was fourteen. Each year on her birthday she had asked her father for a sensible gift, perhaps some linen for her to make into sheets, or lace to edge a tablecover. She was clever with her needle and had worked industriously over the years, dreaming of her wedding, so they had plenty of linen and china, and presents of plate, glass and even a few silver trinkets had been arriving from relatives and friends. Mary-Ellen had given them a splendid candelabra, and Jane's mother had presented them with a fine Sheffield kettle on a stand, to be used in the parlour when they took tea with their friends on a Sunday. Adam's father had sent a trinket box for Jane, filled with silver-topped bottles, brushes and combs. He had made the box himself, lining it with blue velvet. She was delighted and showed it to Adam with pleasure.

"It was kind of him to make this just for me," she said. "I shall always treasure it."

For a moment Adam thought of the marriage chests he had designed for Susanna Warwick. He had done all the intricate work on the drawer fronts of one of them himself. Would she keep that one for herself, he wondered? He dismissed the thought with a laugh. Susanna probably hadn't noticed the difference, nor would she guess how much effort he had put into making it special for her. It had been done out of pride, to prove that he wasn't the talentless oaf Lady Patricia had thought him. But his efforts would in all likelihood be wasted, and Susanna might never find the secret drawer, or its contents. Perhaps that was for the best now.

For Jane's wedding gift, Adam had made a small ladies' writing desk. Knowing her taste for plain things, he had concentrated on clean lines and quality. He had backed it with polished mahogany so that it could stand out in the room if she wished, rather than against the wall, and the top was lined with green leather with gold tooling round the edges. It had one long drawer at the top and three small ones at each side. On bracket feet, it was just three feet wide and twenty-three inches deep. Adam knew it was one of the best things he had ever made, though not as pretty as Susanna's marriage chest, nor as lovingly done. Even so, it was the best quality he could produce. Perhaps because guilt had made him strive for excellence. Jane was entitled to the best.

Recalling his wandering thoughts, Adam studied his appearance in the mirror. He'd had a new coat and breeches made for the wedding. They were pale grey, and he had gone to Lord Munford's own tailor, paying far more than he could rightly afford. The fit was superb, and he knew that he made a fine figure, fine as any gentleman of fashion. Jane would not be ashamed to stand by him at the altar. Glancing at his pocket watch, Adam saw that it was time to leave. The reception was to be at the Carters' house, just a few friends of his and several of Jane's relatives. It was too far for his parents to come. But now he must be on his way to the church. As he went downstairs, Mary-Ellen and the friend he had asked to be his witness were waiting to greet him. He drew a deep breath; there was no turning back now.

"Shall we go then?" he asked. "It's the bride's privilege to be late, but I think the groom should be on time, don't you?"

Laughing, they went out of the house together.

"I think it all went well, don't you?" Jane gave her husband a shy look. They were alone now in the kitchen of their new house, and the guests had all long departed for their homes. "Mother's cake was delicious, wasn't it? Everyone said so."

Adam nodded in agreement. "I fancy a slice of it for my supper," he said. "Lily sent some for us, didn't she?"

"Yes, indeed she did. A goodly piece," Jane said and went into the pantry, bringing out the cake and unwrapping the filmy layers of muslin. "There, Adam, that should fill you, though I don't know how you can eat any more."

"Won't you have some?" Adam asked as she set a plate before him.

"I couldn't swallow another morsel," Jane said, her gaze downcast as she rewrapped the cake. "I'm a little tired after all the excitement. I think I shall go up now, Adam."

Adam didn't look at her as he nodded. "That's right, Jane," he said. "You go up. Take your time. I shall be a while yet."

"Thank you."

Jane's cheeks were pink as she left the kitchen. How considerate he was, she thought. Yet he had no need to be anxious for her sake. She had looked forward to her wedding night with pleasure and was not afraid of what was, after all, only right and natural. Her mother had warned her that it might be uncomfortable the first time, but had told her not to be squeamish.

"Adam's a good man, Jane," she had said. "He's sure to be gentle with you, and it's a comfort to have a husband beside you on a cold night. Never say no, no matter how tired you are, and you'll have a good marriage."

Unaware of his wife's thoughts, Adam's smile faded as she left the room. Throughout the reception he had been haunted by his memories of Susanna Warwick. Try as he might to put her out of his mind and think only of Jane, Susanna's lovely face had seemed to float before his eyes, mocking him every time he looked at his wife. Jane was looking almost pretty in her simple gown of cream silk, with the knot of ribbons at her waist, but as the hours wore on she had begun to appear plainer and plainer to Adam. He was desperately ashamed of his thoughts, knowing that they were a betrayal of the girl who had given him so much, yet he was unable to control them.

After Jane's footsteps had died away, he went to the pantry and took out the small barrel of brandy Robert had given him, pouring a measure into a glass. It would warm him and put some fire in his belly, he thought. He wouldn't drink too much, just enough to enable him to perform his marital duties with credit.

It was more than an hour later when Adam finally found the courage to go up to the bedroom. He had fortified himself with three small glasses of brandy, not enough to make him drunk by any means; but enough on top of the wine he had taken at the wedding to dull his senses sufficently to shut out the tantalizing image of Susanna Warwick lying beneath him, her mouth soft and inviting. God, how he wanted her! It moved in him like a sickness, nagging at him as he glanced towards the bed and saw Jane sitting up against a pile of pillows. In her high-necked bedgown and lace cap, with her hair tucked beneath it, she looked ugly. Or perhaps any face but Susanna Warwick's would have looked ugly to him then.

He didn't speak as he went into the privy closet and relieved himself, undressing and pulling on the clean nightshirt that Jane had placed there for him. He could not put off the moment of consummation any longer. Jane was waiting for him. He had hoped she might have fallen asleep, but one glance had been enough to confirm

204

that she was wide awake and expecting him to do his duty.

He went back into the bedroom, drew back the sheets and got into bed. Then he blew out the candle. Turning towards his wife, he moved on top of her, pulling her nightgown to waist height.

"Well, Jane," he muttered. "We'd best get on with it."

Adam was snoring beside her. Jane lay wakeful, tears on her cheeks. It was not so much the pain, though she could still feel the tearing soreness between her legs, but the cold, emotionless way he had penetrated her, thrusting a few times before emptying himself inside her and then slid off her body, falling asleep almost at once. Somehow she had not expected him to be so unthinking, so selfish. She had thought they would talk for a while of their hopes for the future, and then come together with tenderness. Surely he knew how much she loved him?

Jane had never deceived herself into believing that Adam loved her. She knew why he had married her. It had been entirely her idea that her father should offer him the partnership, and she was not upset that he had in fact bought her a husband. She was aware that she wasn't beautiful, but neither was she ugly. She might not inspire men to romantic dreams, but a warm and loving heart beat within her. She believed she was capable of passion. She had welcomed Adam's touch and wished that he had given her time to show her response. His kisses had been brief, but even so she had felt the beginning of desire. If only he hadn't been in quite such a hurry to get it over with, she thought with regret. She had hoped that Adam might learn in time to love her as she loved him; his lack of concern for her was deeply hurtful.

Yet the warmth of his body close to hers was comforting. Being a sensible girl, she decided that she would not hold Adam's clumsiness against him. He had been nervous, trying not to hurt her too much as he penetrated her

205

virgin body. Wiping away her tears, she sighed and turned to press herself up against Adam's back. She inhaled the scent of his skin, liking the freshness mixed with a slight muskiness of sweat. At least he was here beside her. In time it would all come right, she thought as her eyes closed. It had to, because she loved Adam with all her heart and she wanted to be a good wife to him. She wanted to bear his children and share his hopes, triumphs and sorrows.

Adam was polishing a pair of elbow chairs he had just finished making to go with a set of ten shield-backed dining-chairs that had been commissioned by one of his most valued customers. They had thin tapered legs and satinwood and ebony stringing, with a design of feathers in the centre of the back. The seats were padded and would be covered in a rich crimson and silver stripe, to match the sofa and wing chairs that would accompany them in Mr Sawston's drawing-room. The work was satisfying and rewarding, and Adam enjoyed seeing the grain of the wood come to life beneath his hand.

He looked up as his wife entered the workshop, carrying a tray with bread, cheese, onion and a jug of ale. She set it down on a side table, out of the way of his work and stood watching him in silence for a moment. Adam carried on with his polishing.

"I'm just about to go to the market," she said. "I thought you wouldn't want to stop for your lunch, so I brought it in here."

"Thank you, Jane, that was thoughtful of you. I want to get these finished today if I can."

"Yes, I know," she said, waiting for a moment. Still he did not look at her. "Well, I'll be off then."

"Yes. I might be late this evening. I'll pop in for my supper at about six, but then I'll get on with the upholstery."

"If that's what you want," she said and went out.

Adam frowned as he heard the front door shut. He ought to have said something to her, to have apologized or asked

206

her forgiveness, but somehow the words had stuck in his throat. He was embarrassed. Ashamed of the way he'd behaved on his wedding night. Jane had deserved better. He would have to think of some way to make it up to her . . . when he had time.

Jane sat at the writing desk Adam had made her as a wedding gift. She had had it carried upstairs to their bedroom and set in the window so that she could look out from time to time as she did her accounts. The window overlooked the busy street below and she liked to watch folk coming and going, and to listen to the cries of the costers crying their wares. If she heard the cry of fresh fish or ripe apples, she could lean from her window and ask the young lad or old woman to wait. It took but a minute to run down and see if the fish carried in baskets were indeed fresh.

Although married only a week, Jane had settled into the routine of her new life. She delighted in keeping the house spotless, and it was washed from top to bottom twice a week. Her mother had taught her the art of preserving, and of making simple cures for various aches and pains. Already the shelves in her still room were beginning to look crowded. Jane cleaned, cooked and scrubbed, seldom feeling in the least fatigued. And she was never too tired to welcome Adam to bed, though he came only when it was very late and went straight to sleep after kissing her on the cheek.

Jane was disappointed that he had made no further attempt to consolidate their marriage, but she knew that he was working hard. Adam had taken his first set of designs to Lord Munford, and though they had been approved in principle, certain adjustments had needed to be made. Always busy in the showroom and workshop during the day, Adam had begun work at night on a chest of drawers for their bedroom, seeming as though he could not relax for a moment. He never went out to the coffee houses

207

that she knew he used to frequent before his marriage, nor did he go to cockfights or the taverns that abounded in the city as so many men did. So perhaps she would be unreasonable to complain of neglect. Perhaps men did not need physical release very much, she thought. It might be unladylike of her to suggest to Adam that she would be more than willing to oblige him.

Sighing, Jane returned to her accounts, wondering if she dared ask her mother how often it was usual for a husband and wife to accommodate each other.

Adam washed his hands in the copper, which was still full of the soapy water Jane had been using earlier to boil the sheets. It was well past ten in the evening, and he had just finished dove-tailing the drawer fronts of the chest he was making for their bedroom, working by the light of several candles. He had a feeling of deep satisfaction as he reviewed his progress; he had used good mahogany for the fronts and a slightly cheaper wood for the linings. Tomorrow, when the glue was dried, he would be able to begin polishing and . . . As Jane came in, Adam looked up, surprised. She had gone up an hour since and was in her nightgown.

"Is something wrong?" he asked, with that odd twinge of guilt he experienced every time he looked at his wife. It was three weeks now since their wedding night and he had not attempted to touch her intimately once. "Are you not well, Jane?"

Jane hesitated, feeling a spasm of nerves in her stomach. She had been driven by her disappointment in his continuing abstinence to come in search of her husband, but now she was finding it difficult to begin.

"I – I might ask the same of you, Adam," she said at last. "Is it your health or something else that keeps you from our bed? We have been wed three weeks now and . . ." She stopped and blushed, mortified that it had come to this.

Adam glanced at her and felt her distress. "I know I've neglected you," he said. "To tell the truth, I've been ashamed to approach you, Jane."

"Ashamed?" She stared at him in astonishment. She had thought of everything that might keep him from her: ill health, tiredness, a dislike of physical contact, but not this. "Why should you be ashamed, Adam?"

He came towards her then, looking down into her eyes. She had not put on her nightcap and her hair was hanging round her face. It was soft and straight but thick and luxuriant. He had not realized quite how attractive her hair was until this moment, and it smelt faintly of a flowery perfume. In the gentle glow of the firelight, she looked young, fresh and almost pretty. He reached out to touch a strand of her hair, feeling genuine regret for the way he had treated her.

"My shame is for the way I behaved on our wedding night," he said. "I was selfish and hasty, and I fear I must have hurt you."

"You hurt me a little, it is true," Jane agreed. "But that is natural for a virgin, is it not? You hurt me more, Adam, by your refusal to be a proper husband to me. I thought when you wed me that we could be comfortable together – that you wanted all the natural things of marriage. I had hoped to bear your children."

"And so you shall, Jane," Adam said. "Forgive me, dear wife. I shall try to do better by you in future." Suddenly he laughed and swooped down to catch her up in his arms. "And why not begin as I mean to go on?"

Jane laughed too, her arms going willingly around his neck. As his lips touched hers, she kissed him back, tangling her fingers in his hair to hold him when he would have withdrawn. Sensing the passion in her, Adam chuckled. So Jane wasn't quite the milk-and-water miss she had appeared.

As he carried her up the stairs, he felt a stirring of desire and knew that he wouldn't find it so difficult to perform his marital duties that night. Laying her down on the bed, he stripped off his clothes, not bothering with a nightshirt. It pleased him that Jane did not blush and turn her head aside. Instead she looked at him with evident pleasure in what she saw. And then with one economical movement, she removed her own nightgown, revealing a body that was sweetly plump and pleasing. Bending over her, Adam began to kiss her breasts.

"Soft, pretty Jane," he whispered. "This time it will be better, my love. I do promise you that . . ."

CHAPTER FOURTEEN

Susanna's head moved restlessly on the pillow. She was dreaming of her wedding. Dressed in the beautiful gown of ecru silk and lace with tiny diamonds sewn into the skirt, which had been delivered the previous day from London, she was walking towards the altar. A man was standing there, waiting for her, his back turned towards her. She was trembling, reluctant to take the final steps, then he turned towards her and she saw his face. All at once her doubts fled and she ran towards him, holding out her arms.

"Adam," she murmured. "Oh, Adam . . ."

And then she woke in the darkness. Getting out of bed, Susanna shivered in the chill of her room. The fire had been allowed to go out and the cold bit into her flesh. She went to the window and looked out at the moonlit night. There was a frost and everything was white. Hugging herself to keep out the chill, Susanna remembered her dream and felt a choking sensation in her throat. How could she marry Lord Digby when it was Adam Blackwell she loved? It was clear in her mind now. Her dreams were all true. Adam had made love to her in the summerhouse. They had arranged to meet the next evening, but her mother had bound and gagged her. No wonder she had been so ill. She had almost starved to death! How could her mother have been so cruel?

For a moment she thought wildly of running away, of refusing to go through with the wedding, but then she remembered that Adam, too, was to be married – no doubt to a young woman of his own choosing. It must already have been arranged when he came back to Chorley Hale for Maggie's funeral. Adam had known he was promised even as he held her in his arms and swore he loved her. Yet he could not have expected anything more than a night of passion. He had been wiser than Susanna, realizing that their feelings for one another were hopeless.

Even if she had not been forced to marry for her father's sake, there could never have been anything between them. Even if Adam had loved her as she loved him, their families would never have countenanced a marriage. The divide was too wide, too deeply entrenched in the minds of their contemporaries to be bridged. Susanna truly believed that her mother would have let her die first.

Despair overwhelmed her as she wished with all her heart that she had died. Then she would not feel this pain inside. Tears ran down her cheeks as she opened the large closet, looking at the gown she was to wear for her wedding in two weeks' time. Such a beautiful gown, but she would be wearing it for Lord Digby, not for Adam Blackwell.

Casting herself down on the bed, she began to weep as though her heart would break.

Susanna took the large leather box that Lord Digby offered her, hesitating for just one moment before she opened it. Nestling against the bed of black velvet was a magnificent collar of filigree gold set with the blue-green beryl *aigue-marine*, meaning sea water. The stones were very large and an elaborate cross set with slightly smaller stones hung as a pendant from a little gold loop that could be removed. There were also eardrops and a bracelet in the case.

"I thought the colour might match your eyes," Digby said, "but now I see that the stones fade into insignificance. But perhaps the design may please you?"

"They are beautiful," Susanna said. "Thank you very much, Digby. I – I shall wear them for – for our wedding."

He shook his head. "I have something else for your wedding gift," he said. "These are just to express my gratitude at your having agreed to give up your dream."

212

"My dream?" Susanna blushed. "Oh, you mean of a spring wedding. It was just a girlish fancy."

He took her hand, holding it in a playful manner and kissing each fingertip. "Well, now you see how much you have pleased me, my dear. If you continue to please me, you will find me generous."

Susanna looked at him, her heart fluttering. Was there a concealed warning behind the teasing words? "I hope I shall always please you, my lord," she said, avoiding his penetrating gaze. "Surely that is my duty as a wife, to please my husband?"

Digby bit the end of her forefinger. The sudden pain made her gasp but instinct prevented her from crying out. Now she was certain. He was warning her that though he could be generous, she would be unwise to cross him. As though to soothe her, he kissed the finger he had bitten.

"And so, my dear," he murmured. "In two days' time you will be my bride."

Susanna said nothing as he bowed and walked away. A prickle of apprehension went through her as she understood that Digby would not be quite the manageable fool she had imagined . . . He would demand much more from her than she had expected to give.

As she came downstairs the next morning, Susanna saw her brother standing in the hallway. Still booted and cloaked, he had clearly just arrived and the servants were hurrying to take his hat and gloves. He turned as she spoke his name, giving her a mocking grin.

"Surprised to see me?" he asked. "Didn't I tell you I would dance at your wedding, sweet sister?" His tone was sharp with sarcasm.

Susanna frowned, holding back the angry words until he followed her into a small parlour to the side of the hall where they were alone.

"Have you no thought for anyone else, Stephen?" she demanded. "Can you not imagine what the Blackwells will

213

feel at seeing you in church? She has hardly been laid to rest in her grave, and your child with her . . ."

Stephen's smile faded and he glared at his sister. "You should not blame me for Maggie's death," he said. "I know I was at fault – but I am not responsible for that. I wasn't even here."

"She killed herself because she was ashamed," Susanna cried, furious now. "She was too ashamed to go on living after what you did to her. And you say you are not to blame!"

"Nonsense!" he said, dismissing her assertion with scorn. "When I last saw Maggie, she begged me to take her with me to London. She said that she would rather be a kept mistress than the wife of Tom Sutton – that's why she told him the child was mine. Maggie was no shy virgin when I had her. She had already lain with Tom. She could have told him the brat was his and no one would have been the wiser. She told him, because she was trying to blackmail me into taking her to London. She was bored with village life and she talked of running off herself if I would not take her. She said she would be a barmaid or starve in the streets rather than wed him."

Susanna stared at her brother. She wanted to reject his words as careless lies, but somehow she believed him. There had always been something hidden and secretive about Maggie. It would be just like her to want to escape from the village. Susanna frowned as something struck her.

"If what you say is true – why would she kill herself?"

Stephen shrugged, his face sullen. "How should I know? I told her I would give her a hundred guineas when the brat was born. I'm not quite as heartless as you thought me. She was going to put it out with a foster mother and leave the village." His expression was dark with annoyance. "Maggie Blackwell had a fancy to be an actress. Don't imagine her as a meek, ignorant girl. There was nothing innocent about Maggie! She talked of playing Shakespeare at a theatre in London – and she would have made a good actress. She could be as meek and prudish as she liked one minute, and a firebrand the next. I don't believe she killed herself. She had too much to live for. In London she could have found herself a protector and . . ."

"What are you saying, Stephen?" Susanna asked him with a new intentness. "If Maggie didn't take her own life, what happened?"

Stephen's frown deepened. "Who knows? She might have done it in a fit of temper. Or, more likely, Tom Sutton did it for her. She told me he had a violent streak in him — as I know well enough. I've not forgotten the beating he and his friends gave me. He'll pay for that before I'm through."

"You think Maggie was murdered?" Susanna stared at her brother in horror. This changed everything. No one had even considered murder. "What are you going to do about it?"

"Do? Why should I do anything?" Stephen shrugged and turned away. "I've come a long way, I want to change . . ."

She caught his arm. "Surely you will do something? For Maggie's sake. You must have liked her once."

For a moment something like regret flickered in his eyes. "She was a comely lass, and I liked her well enough. If she had kept quiet and married Tom, I'd have given her money, but she was a fool. She thought she could blackmail me into taking her to London and keeping her as my mistress — and that would have proved expensive and awkward." All at once his features brightened. "You should wish me happy, Susanna. I've found myself an heiress. Her father's a merchant, of course, but I could hardly look for blue blood in my circumstances, could I? Rosemary is a pretty little thing, and so grateful to me for asking her. Her father can't quite aspire to Digby's fortune, but he's promised to settle a sizeable sum on me on our wedding day, and when he dies, there'll be a nice little fortune coming my way."

Susanna felt a surge of disgust. "You really are selfish, aren't you?" she cried. "Don't you ever think of anyone besides yourself?"

"The pot calling the kettle black?" Stephen's brows lifted and his voice was sharp with sarcasm. "It's all right for you to marry a fortune but . . ."

"That has nothing to do with it." Susanna glared at him. "And I had no choice, as you well know. I'm talking about Maggie. If you believe she was murdered, it's your duty to do something about it. She was carrying your child. Whoever killed her, killed your baby, Stephen. Besides, the Blackwells would be able to hold up their heads again if . . ."

"The Blackwells." Stephen snapped his fingers. "Why should I bother? Maggie's dead, we can't bring her back. I can't afford to get involved in a scandal now."

"But you are involved!" Susanna was very angry now. "If you don't do anything, Stephen, I shall tell your fiancée that Maggie killed herself because you deserted her when she was carrying your child. I doubt if she or her father would be happy about the marriage then."

"Damn you!" Stephen moved towards her threateningly. He was breathing hard and his eyes had a brittle shine. "I should break your neck."

Susanna gasped and stepped back from the malice in his face. This time she had pushed him too far. He might really seek to harm her.

"Please moderate your language." Lady Patricia spoke from the doorway. "I shall not allow you to threaten your sister, Stephen."

"Mama, I did not see you." His cheeks coloured. She was the only person he had ever had the least respect for in this house. "Of course I did not mean it."

"I heard enough to know whether or not you meant it," his mother said, icy cool. "You will do as Susanna asked, Stephen. At the moment everyone blames you for the girl's death, and it brings disgrace on this family. If Tom Sutton murdered her, it would clear you and our name."

"But it's too risky," Stephen said, sullen now. "Sutton and his cronies damned near killed me the last time."

"Have you no friends, Stephen?" Her eyes flashed with contempt. "If you are afraid of a village lout, take a few of the grooms with you. Or wait until you can find him alone. Take a pistol with you if you're nervous."

"I'm not afraid." Stephen directed a look of angry pride at his mother and sister. "Oh, very well. I'll do my best. I'll ask a few questions. Someone must know where he was that night. But I can't promise anything."

"Of course not." Lady Patricia was calm as she kissed his cheek. "It is as much for your sake as ours, Stephen. Now, tell me about this heiress of yours — is she presentable?"

Susanna turned and walked from the room. She had hardly spoken to her mother for days. Remembering the days and nights of torture she had endured, it was all she could do to be civil when they met. It would be a relief when the wedding was over and she could leave this house forever.

Her wedding day! Susanna woke to a sense of dread. She had known it must come but in her secret thoughts she had nurtured a desperate hope of a reprieve. It was not to be. As Beatrice came running excitedly into the room to bounce on her bed, Susanna resigned herself to the inevitable. In another few hours she would be Lord Digby's wife.

Hot water was carried up to her room by a succession of servants. One of the maids poured a generous measure of attar of roses into the porcelain hip-bath and Susanna climbed in.

Left alone, she soaked in the water until it was almost cold, then dried herself and summoned the maids. She had just slipped on her bodice and under-petticoat of fine linen when Lady Patricia walked in, dismissing the servants.

"You may return in a few minutes," she said. "I wish to speak to my daughter alone."

When the maids had gone, Susanna turned bleak eyes on her mother. "Have you come to make certain that I shall not refuse at the altar?"

"So you have remembered." Lady Patricia nodded. "I thought as much. I hope you intend to be sensible?"

"What choice have I?"

"Exactly." The older woman's eyes were wary, watchful, as if expecting a tantrum. "Why not make the best of it? You will be the wife of a wealthy man. Please him, and Digby will refuse you nothing."

Susanna did not reply. She was so angry that she did not trust herself to speak. Lady Patricia sighed, then laid a blue silk garter on the dressing-chest.

"For good luck," she said.

Susanna ignored the garter. She looked rigidly at her mother. "After today, I never want to see or speak to you again," she said. "Papa and Bea will be welcome in my house. You will not."

There was a strange expression in the older woman's eyes. Susanna could not tell if it was anger, regret or a deeper, more complicated emotion.

"Very well." Lady Patricia inclined her head. "I do not expect you to believe this, Susanna, but I acted for your own good. One day you may understand."

"Never!" Susanna's cry was sharp and bitter. "You have ruined my life. I shall never forgive you. Not for as long as I live."

"Then I am sorry for you." With that, Lady Patricia left her daughter's room.

Susanna was pale but beautiful as she walked up the aisle on her father's arm. Sir William had made a great effort with his appearance for his daughter's wedding and he looked almost his old self, except for a certain slowness in his movements and a vagueness that had not formerly been there. During the carriage drive to the village, he had talked cheerfully to his daughter, telling her how lovely she was, but Susanna was aware of the change in him. He was suddenly an old man, who seemed to have lost the will to live. How ironic it would be if he were to die soon. Her

218

sacrifice would then have been made in vain. Silent, bitter laughter shook her.

Sir William glanced at her in concern. "Are you cold, m'dear?"

"No, Papa." She smiled at him. "Just a little nervous."

Sir William's eyes darkened with grief as he looked at his beautiful daughter. His hand moved to cover hers, and there was pleading in his face as he looked at her.

"Forgive me, Susanna?"

"There is nothing to forgive," she lied. "Don't worry, Papa. I have accepted my destiny. This is what I want now." She gave him her hand and he helped her down from the carriage.

It was a cold, crisp day but the sun was breaking through at last. Inside the church, Susanna made herself concentrate on the altar with its shining brass candlesticks and the hot-house lilies that made the air heavy with their overpowering scent. She did not want to look at her bridegroom, an obscene figure in his purple satin breeches and coat, which was already beginning to show damp patches of sweat. She did not want to think of the consummation of her marriage or the long, empty years ahead. What must be, must be. Susanna would bear it somehow. Instead, she thought about all the new gowns she would buy and all the dinners, balls and musical evenings she would give. Susanna would make herself the most popular hostess in London. Her life would be one round of social pleasure so that she never had time to think, never had time to remember.

Susanna managed to smile as the vicar pronounced them man and wife. Digby kissed her on the mouth. It was the first time she had allowed him such an intimacy since her acceptance of his proposal. She could barely repress the shudder of revulsion she felt at the touch of his moist lips, but she managed to keep her remote smile in place. Then she was leaving the church on her husband's arm as the bells rang out joyfully.

Outside, the wind had risen and it was colder than before. They were showered with dried rose petals and presented with little gifts from the villagers: a straw doll for fertility, a horseshoe tied with ribbons and gloves for both bride and groom.

"God bless you, Lady Digby."

Hearing herself addressed by her title for the first time, Susanna blinked. It was done. She was tied to Percival Digby now for good or evil. She smiled as Tom Blackwell offered a small wooden box. It was prettily inlaid and crossbanded on the lid, opening to reveal an interior padded with quilted satin.

"For keeping buttons and bits of lace," Tom said. "I made it and Jeanie did the padding. It be with our love, Miss Susanna." He coloured and retreated quickly as Susanna thanked him.

He and his wife had been invited to the Hall with the rest of the villagers. There was to be cider, cakes, cold meats and ale for them in the servants' hall, while the guests dined upstairs on roast goose and venison. Susanna had wanted the Blackwells invited to the main reception but her mother refused her request, saying, "It would only embarrass them, Susanna. They will be more comfortable with their friends."

Seeing that Tom and Jeanie were happy enough when she paid the bride's customary visit to the servants' hall, Susanna admitted to herself that her mother had been right. She joined in a lively country dance with Tom and some of the other local lads, then returned with her husband to the drawing-room upstairs, where most of her mother's friends were fast becoming intoxicated on the fine wines Digby had provided.

"I think you should change your gown now." Digby took out his gold pocket watch and glanced at the engraved dial. "I want to leave in an hour."

There was a hint of imperiousness in his tone. Susanna tensed, feeling annoyed, but something in his eyes made her hold her tongue.

"Very well, Digby," she said in a meek tone. "I shall not keep you waiting."

He smiled and patted her hand. "What a considerate wife you will make," he said. "I was proud of you today, Susanna. You look very lovely."

She glanced up at him, feeling a little guilty. After all, she had encouraged him to propose to her, and it wasn't his fault that she had fallen in love with another man. She was certain that he knew nothing of the way her mother had bound and gagged her. Indeed, it was most likely his insistence on sending for his own doctor that had saved her life. She gave him a diffident smile. Perhaps it would not be so very terrible to be his wife.

"If I look pretty it has much to do with these." She touched the magnificent diamonds at her throat. "You spoil me, Digby."

"I live only to serve you, my angel," he responded, pleased with the first genuine smile he had had from her that day. He checked his watch as a longcase clock in the hall began to strike the hour. "Don't forget, Susanna. I want to leave by three."

"I shall miss you so much." Beatrice was crying as she clung to her sister. "I wish you didn't have to go away."

Susanna kissed her forehead, lifting her chin to look into her face. "We shall see each other often," she promised. "As soon as we are settled, I shall ask Digby if you may come to us. In a few months you will be seventeen, and then I shall take you to London with me. We'll find you a nice husband. Someone young and handsome who will adore you."

"That will be nice," Beatrice said, her tears drying miraculously. "But he must be rich, too."

Susanna laughed and shook her head. "You want it all, dearest, don't you? Well, we shall see what we can do when the time comes. Now, I must not keep Digby waiting any longer."

Hand in hand they walked downstairs together.

Susanna dismissed her maid. She was wearing a silk night-chemise and her hair had been brushed until it shone, hanging loose on her shoulders in a golden cloud. For a moment she stared at herself in the small mahogany dressing mirror that had been her brother's wedding gift.

"So that you can see what you look like when you prepare for bed," he'd murmured in her ear as he pretended to kiss her. "Sweet dreams, sister mine."

How Stephen had gloated as he watched her walk down the aisle. She knew that he had never cared for her. Now he was angry because their mother had prevailed upon him to find out what he could about Maggie's murder.

The mirror had been carried up to the inn chamber together with the travelling chest Adam Blackwell had made. Turning away from her brother's gift, Susanna let her fingers stroke the smooth, polished wood of the cabinet. How different it would have been if she'd been spending her wedding night with the man she loved. How eagerly she would have awaited her bridegroom then.

They had reached the inn, the finest on the Norwich road, in time for dinner. Digby had previously arranged for the best rooms to be reserved, and there was a cheerful fire waiting for her when she went up. He had said that he would join her in a little while.

Rising, Susanna went to the fire and held her hands to the flames. She was trembling, her knees shaking. This was foolish. Breathing deeply, she took control of her nerves, steadying the tremors. At least she was not ignorant of what was to happen as were many young girls in her situation. She knew what was expected of her. Walking over to the four-poster bed, which was piled high with feather mattresses and a quilted, patchwork cover, she climbed in, sitting up against the pillows with the sheet folded back. When Digby came he would not find a frighted child. She was ready to do her duty.

It was over an hour before the expected knock came at her door.

"Please come in," she said, sitting up once more. She had been drifting towards sleep. Schooling her lips to a smile as Digby entered, she said, "I was beginning to think that you had forgotten me."

"So impatient, my love?"

Digby was wearing a long silken robe over his linen nightshirt and a cap with a tassel. He carried a chamberstick with a lighted candle, which he set down on a table near the fire. For a moment he stared at his bride, then he took off his robe and blew out the candles, leaving just one small flame burning.

Susanna's nerves jumped as he climbed into bed beside her, grunting a little at the exertion. Would he know that she was no longer a virgin? He would be angry if he thought he had been cheated. She remembered the sharp pain she had felt as Adam penetrated her for the first time. If she cried out, Digby might not guess the truth.

His body felt soft and spongy and he was very hot, sweating profusely. She closed her eyes as he reached for her, and then she felt his hands pulling at her nightgown, lifting it and tearing it off her. Susanna fought to control a shudder as she felt his fingers probing between her legs. She stiffened, lying tense and unresponsive as his podgy hands pawed at her breasts, and then he was on top of her. His weight almost crushed her and she found it difficult to breathe, but she was relieved that he had not removed his own nightshirt. She did not think she could have borne to feel his moist flesh against hers. Now his mouth was covering hers, wet and slobbering and his finger pushed up into her softness, invading and hurting. He rubbed frenziedly, moaning in frustration and grunting. She became aware that something was wrong.

Digby took her hand, forcing it down between their bodies. Now she understood. Adam's maleness had throbbed and pulsated as he thrust into her, its smooth hardness

223

penetrating her easily. Digby's hung soft and lifeless in her hand. He held her fingers, making her close them tightly on him.

"You've got to help me," he muttered. "Rub it, damn you."

Susanna obeyed, performing the required action with a mechanical detachment. She made herself think about other things. When they reached Digby's country home, she would lose no time in calling on her neighbours. She would give a large dinner party to . . . There was a slight firming beneath her hand. Digby pushed it away impatiently and thrust himself between her legs. He jabbed at her twice and then moaned in frustration as he went limp again.

He pushed her hand down the bed. This time she understood what was required of her. Her hand moved back and forth, but nothing happened. He made her rub harder and faster, but there was no response. He still hung limp and lifeless in her hand.

At last he rolled away from her. For a moment he lay beside her, then he got up, put on his robe and picked up the chamber-stick.

"Goodnight, madam," he said and went out.

Susanna lay staring at the fire, watching as the logs were gradually consumed and began to crumble into ashes. Tears slid from the corner of her eye, trickling down her cheek. She brushed them away. There was no point in thinking about another man's touch, or the way her body had come tinglingly alive in response to his loving. At least it was over for a while. It had been unpleasant and humiliating, but she could bear it. She thought that it could not have given Digby much pleasure. Perhaps it would not happen very often . . .

She got out of bed and went over to the travelling chest, running her hand over the silken surface of the polished wood. The memory of that wonderful night in the summerhouse with Adam swept over her, raising longings that made a mockery of what had just taken place. She

224

knew herself to be a passionate woman; yet here she was locked into a sterile marriage with a man who could not even be a true husband to her.

"Oh, Adam, Adam," she whispered, as the sharp pain twisted inside her at the waste of it all. Suddenly her unhappiness was too much to bear. She threw herself across the cabinet and began to weep as though her heart would break.

Stephen left the inn when he saw Tom Sutton come in. Stephen had drunk far more than was good for him and he was angry. The whole village was treating him as if he were a leper, as if he were responsible for Maggie's death. No one had spoken to him all evening, yet as soon as Tom Sutton arrived, they clustered round him, offering to buy him a tankard of ale. Even the young bloods who had been Stephen's friends had turned their backs on him.

Resentment at the unfairness of it all was deep in him. He couldn't deny that he had seduced Maggie, but she'd been willing enough in the end. More than willing. It was she who had prolonged their loveplay, she who had begged and pleaded with him to take her to London. He wished now that he had given in to her. Although he would never have admitted it, it hurt Stephen to think of the girl buried in the cold earth. Maggie had been so alive, so hot-blooded and vital. He remembered her husky laughter and the way she had mocked him, the way her touch could heat his blood and bring him such pleasure. It was such a waste of all that passion. His thoughts were gloomy as he walked towards his waiting horse.

"Warwick, I want a word with you!"

The cry halted Stephen in his tracks. For a moment he stood immobile, furious, his fists clenched at his sides. How dare that village lout speak to him like that? He whirled round, his face haughty, eyes flashing.

"What do you want, Sutton?" he asked. "Have you come to murder me the way you did Maggie?" The

225

accusation crackled in the frosty air, shocking them both.

For a moment Tom Sutton stared at him, his face white. Then he began to move very slowly forward, his eyes reflecting the hatred that was consuming him.

"Yes, I killed her," he said. "I killed the bitch . . . I killed her because she refused to wed me. She laughed in my face and said she would rather be your whore any day of the week than my wife. You bewitched her, Warwick. You bought her with your pretty . . ."

Seeing the anguish in Tom Sutton's face, Stephen threw back his head and screamed his scorn aloud. His eyes were filled with the devil's laughter, bitter, angry and taunting. "It wasn't just for the dress or the shoes," he said, his voice sharp with spite. "I satisfied her, that's what she told me. She said you had as much idea of love-making as a bull, but that you lacked the bull's stamina. You bored her, Sutton. She found you dull-witted and . . ."

With a roar of agonized rage, Sutton sprang at him, going for his throat. They wrestled desperately, knowing that it was a fight to the death. At first Sutton's rage fuelled him and he seemed to overpower Warwick simply by the force of his onslaught, but Stephen began to fight back. His fist exploded in the villager's face, sending him reeling on his heels. Seizing his advantage, the Squire's son followed with another blow and yet another, causing Tom to stagger and fall. Then Stephen kicked him in the ribs, again and again, jeering and laughing with a wild, insane light in his eyes. He was beyond control now as he vented his anger, pain and frustration on his victim. This was sweet revenge for the beating he had taken.

"Not such a big man when you're on your own, are you?" Stephen cried. "Not so clever when you haven't got some of your bully-boy friends to help you out. Oh, you can murder women all right, that's about your mark, isn't it?"

Tom lay retching and groaning on the ground. A little group of villagers had gathered outside the inn to watch. Stephen looked at them in triumph.

"This is the man you were all so sorry for," he said. "This bastard killed Maggie. He killed her because she didn't want him. She wanted me . . ." Something snapped inside him and he screamed out, "God damn you, Sutton! I wanted her . . . I loved the silly bitch, as much as I could love anyone . . ."

As he said the words, Stephen realized they were true. He turned away as the wave of despair overtook him and let out a demented howl. It was the howl of a demon, some said afterwards, or an animal in pain.

No one knew what Tom Sutton meant to do. All at once he was on his feet. Something flashed silver in the moonlight as he sprang and the knife buried itself deep into Stephen Warwick's back. Stephen half turned, surprise in his eyes as the blood trickled from the corner of his mouth. Then he fell like a stone to the ground.

Lord Digby's country estate was some five or six miles from the village of Bletchingley in Surrey. Susanna stared out of the carriage window as they drove through the village on their journey, catching a glimpse of the wooden ramparts of a Norman castle set amongst young trees at the top of the hill. The houses were fine, timber-framed buildings and the big, sandstone church presided imposingly over the open country of the North Downs.

Lord Digby's estate was not huge, consisting of two or three tenanted farms, the parkland and a small manor house. The house was old with blackened timbers and a deeply sloping roof over the dormer windows of the upper floors. Ivy grew up the walls and there were attractive gardens with little sheltered walks, besides a large park that bordered the wide expanse of the downs. Susanna was surprised and pleased. She found it charming, much prettier than her own home. She exclaimed in delight.

"It's beautiful, Digby. I had not expected it to be so charming."

"I'm glad that something pleases you, madam."

Susanna saw his scowling look and turned away. She understood the cause, but it was not her fault that he had been unable to penetrate her. They had spent several days and nights on the road, and each night he had gone through the same ritual without success. She had not complained once or refused his requests, and though some of them disgusted her, she had nevertheless done what he asked. None of it had been of the slightest use. He could not sustain an erection for more than a few swift thrusts.

Susanna knew that he blamed her for her lack of response. As his frustration grew, he had become increasingly vindictive towards her, seeking revenge for his failure. It was her fault for being an unnatural woman, he said.

"How can I behave like a normal man when you lie there like a dead thing," he complained when he failed for the fourth time. "You could at least pretend to welcome me to your bed, madam. Any whore would do as much for those diamonds I gave you."

By this time Susanna had begun to feel sorry for him. It was now he who suffered the most humiliation, not she. The next night she had genuinely tried to help, going so far as to put her arms about him when he climbed in beside her and kiss him. He had become very excited and she had felt him growing hard in her hand, but before he could even mount her, he ejaculated. He had almost screamed in his disappointment and frustration, venting his fury on her as he called her every filthy name he could think of.

Susanna had listened calmly, untouched by his spite. She had discovered that she was not afraid of him even when he was angry. She could even feel some sympathy for him. It was becoming much easier to detach herself from his fumblings, to remain aloof from his taunts.

Digby's servants were waiting outside the house to greet the couple when they arrived. The housekeeper took Susanna up to her rooms, fussing over her like a mother hen. Digby mumbled something about having business to attend to, and so she was left to explore at her leisure.

Her own apartments consisted of a sitting-room, which had been newly refurbished with crimson hangings, display cabinets containing delicate porcelain, and velvet-covered sofas in a rusty gold; a bedroom that was decorated with rich wall-hangings of deep blue with a design of exotic birds, and a small dressing-room that connected to Digby's own apartments. She noticed that there were no keys to the locks that connected her rooms to his.

A pretty ladies' desk stood in front of the window of her sitting-room. Spread out on its leather top was a variety of silver trinkets, all of them inscribed with the letters SD and attractively embossed with cherubs and flowers. A box containing writing paper, ink bottles and wax also had her new initials engraved on the top. There was an impressive seal for her letters. In the bedroom there was every imaginable comfort; she saw that the initials had been embroidered on sheets as well, and woven into the bed hangings. She could not help being touched by Digby's thoughtfulness and told him so at dinner that evening.

For the first time in a week he looked at her with approval. "I told you I had prepared for your coming," he said. "You are my wife, Susanna. You shall be denied nothing for your comfort. I believe you will discover your allowance adequate when we reside in town, but you will not find me unreasonable if you require more. I expect you to entertain and keep up a high standard."

"Thank you, Digby." She looked at him uncertainly. "If I have been at fault . . ."

"I was perhaps too impatient," he said. "Now we are at home, things may improve. I shall not however trouble you tonight."

Susanna warmed to him. "I'm sure it will be better soon," she said. "I hope to be a good wife to you in all ways, Digby."

Digby's mood softened as he looked at her. Even if he could not bed her, he could appreciate the sight of her and touch her whenever he wished. She was a beautiful

229

object he owned, something to be admired and envied. He would enjoy knowing that other men wanted her. She was another possession to add to his collection. And when she was happy she had a charming way of smiling and teasing him that he liked. He decided that he was satisfied with his bargain after all.

"You will make an excellent hostess," he said at last. "I think we should wait a week and then hold a dinner for our neighbours. You will want to get to know everyone as soon as possible. We shall stay here until the spring, then go up to London."

The scream penetrated Sir William's fog of apathy. For days he had been sitting at his desk in his library, staring at nothing in particular. He had consumed several glasses of brandy, but was not drunk. It would have been a relief to lose himself in the mists of intoxication, but so far relief had not come. All he could see was his daughter's white face as she was driven away in Digby's carriage. Now, hearing the screams coming from the hallway, Sir William roused himself enough to investigate. That sounded like Patricia, but surely it could not be his wife making that terrible noise . . .

As he came out into the wide entrance hall at the bottom of the main stairway, the scene that met his eyes sent a chill running down his spine. Instantly he was sobered. The blood-stained body of his son was lying on the ground and Patricia had thrown herself across it as she wept with demented abandon.

"Good Lord!" he muttered, moving towards her. "Patricia, my dear. What has happened? Has there been an accident?"

She made no reply, continuing to scream and weep as she clung to the limp body of her dead son, pulling at his coat and lifting him off the ground in a frenzy as she begged him to speak to her.

"Stephen! Stephen!" she screamed out in her agony. "You can't die. You can't leave me . . . I won't let you . . ."

"Patricia ... Patricia my dear ..." The mild, gentle Sir William was embarrassed by such an unseemly display of grief. At a loss to know how to comfort her, he stood looking down at her. "Please, my dear. I know you were fond of him, but you must try to control yourself. It is a loss to us both ... I feel it as much as ..."

She looked up at that, her eyes wild. "Don't you dare to say it, Warwick!" she cried. "You never cared for your son. You've never cared for anyone but yourself. It is your excesses, your stupidity that has killed my son."

"Patricia!" Sir William reeled before her fury. "I don't understand you. How can I have caused Stephen's accident?"

"It wasn't an accident." Her eyes were dark with pain. "He was murdered by Tom Sutton ... Maggie Blackwell's fiancé." Lady Patricia got to her feet, her first wild spasm of grief over as she stared at her husband. "It was your fault for encouraging that family to think too highly of themselves. They should have been put in their place long ago."

"I don't understand you ..." Sir William was bewildered. "What are you talking about?"

"I'm talking about your son and Maggie Blackwell," she cried. "That wanton seduced my son, then she tried to blackmail him into taking her to London as his mistress. When that didn't work, she told her fiancé she had been seduced and he killed her ... and then he murdered my son by plunging a knife in his back."

Sir William blanched with shock. For several seconds he could not speak. Then he sighed and looked at her with sadness. "I know Stephen too well, my dear. I fear that he inherited the worst of both of us. It was he who seduced the girl and then deserted her. Don't lie to me, Patricia. I am not quite the fool you have always thought me."

She looked into his face, and seeing a quiet dignity there, knew herself defeated. Without another word to him, she turned to the shocked and silent servants who had witnessed the terrible scene.

"You may carry my son up to his room," she said with an icy calm. "I wish to be alone with him."

Her face remote and proud, she walked away, not even bothering to glance at her husband. Sir William watched her go. About to return to his study, he checked himself. He had indulged in self-pity for too long. There was something he had to do in the village. Something he must say to Tom Blackwell.

Digby looked at his wife as she opened the letter brought to her in their drawing-room on a silver salver. It was from her mother and had been delivered by special messenger. Her face paled as she read it and he heard the sharply indrawn breath. The letter fell from her hand as she gave a cry of distress.

"No . . . No, it cannot be true . . ." Horrified, she looked at him. "This is terrible . . ."

"What has happened?" he asked. "Has your mother bad news of your father?"

"Not of Papa . . ." Susanna stared at him, too shocked to take in the full meaning of her mother's letter. "My brother . . . Stephen has been murdered. It was Tom Sutton. He was a farmer from Ludham way who was engaged to that girl who died, Maggie Blackwell. You may have heard my mother mention her . . ." Choking on her emotion, Susanna put a shaking hand to her mouth. It was a moment or two before she could continue. "Stephen and Maggie's fiancé quarrelled and fought, and then Tom stabbed my brother in the back. He died almost instantly. Tom has been arrested and charged with murder." Her voice broke and her eyes were dark with grief and guilt. "I think it may have been my fault for asking Stephen to challenge Tom over Maggie's death. I called him a coward and . . ." Tears sprang to her eyes as she remembered the quarrel. Stephen had never cared for her and she had often found herself disliking him, but he was her brother . . .

Digby saw her deep distress. "If I remember rightly you

232

told me that your mother had insisted he try to clear his own name."

"Yes, but it was my suggestion. I thought it might help the Blackwells." Susanna bit her lip. It was she who had called Stephen a coward and demanded that he do something.

"You have nothing to reproach yourself with. Your brother's behaviour was shameless. Having seduced the girl, he should have made sure she was provided for before running off to London."

"Yes," Susanna agreed. "That cannot be denied. But for Stephen to die like that . . ." Her voice faded to a whisper as the guilt struck home. She had known that Tom Sutton had threatened to kill her brother, but never believed he would carry out his threat. "I believe I am in part responsible. My mother must be distraught. Stephen was always her favourite child."

Digby frowned as she passed the letter to him. "It is a terrible thing, Susanna. Do you want to go home?"

Susanna thought for a moment, then shook her head. "No, I don't think so, Digby. The funeral has already taken place. There is nothing I can do – to tell the truth Stephen and I were never friends. I am upset by his death, of course, and sorry for Mama, but my sympathy lies mainly with Papa and Beatrice. Particularly poor Bea. It must be awful for her at home now."

"Do you want to ask her to stay for a while?"

Susanna smiled. "Would you mind? I know we have only been married a few days but . . ."

"If it makes you happy, my dear." Digby got to his feet. "Well, I have business to attend. What are your plans for this morning?"

"I shall write to Mama, of course, and then I think I shall go to church. A little quiet prayer may ease my mind."

"The carriage will be ready for you in an hour," he said. "Yes, ask your sister to stay, Susanna. It will be good for her to get away from a house in mourning, and company for you."

"How good you are to me, Digby." Susanna jumped up and kissed his cheek. "I shall write to Mama straight away."

"Oh, Susanna," Beatrice cried as she sprang from the carriage and ran to embrace her sister. "You cannot imagine how glad I am to be here."

"Poor Bea." Susanna smiled. "Has it been very bad at home?"

"Mama hardly speaks to anyone. You know Stephen was always her favourite," Beatrice said. "And poor Papa can do nothing to please her." She looked at her sister thoughtfully. "Yet in a way it has done him good. He has begun to ride round the estate again and take an interest in things. It's as if he feels he has to atone for Stephen's death."

"It must have been a terrible shock for him," Susanna agreed. "I suppose he knows about Maggie now?"

"Everyone knows," Beatrice said, rolling her eyes. "Tom Sutton has confessed to Maggie Blackwell's murder. She didn't kill herself at all. He hit her and she fell in the pond and drowned. He has been imprisoned and they say . . . they say he will hang for the murders."

"Yes, poor man. I can't help feeling sorry for him despite his crimes." Susanna turned to her sister, her eyes wet with unshed tears. "It has all been such a dreadful tragedy. I wish it hadn't ended this way but at least the Blackwells can hold up their heads again. Maggie didn't take her own life. In a way it exonerates Stephen, too. He didn't drive her to kill herself. Maggie wanted to be his lover; it was her choice. He was not to blame for her death."

"Don't let's talk about it any more," Beatrice begged. "I can't bear it. I just want to be with you and to forget all the nastiness."

Susanna tucked her arm through her sister's. "We can't hold any large parties for a while, my love, but I agree with Mama that you are too young to wear black. We shall both wear lilac gowns and I see no reason why we shouldn't drive out and visit my friends. I've made lots of new friends, Bea."

Beatrice looked happier. "Are there any nice men?" she asked. "Shall you find me a husband, Susanna?"

"Oh, Bea," Susanna laughed. "You are much too young to be married. Perhaps next year, after you've had a Season or two to make up your mind."

Beatrice pulled a face. "I wish I need never go back home. I would much rather be married."

"Well, you need not go home just yet. I intend to take you to London when we go," Susanna said, squeezing her arm. "And I shall find you a nice husband, Bea. You've grown so pretty now that I'm sure you will have all the gentlemen swooning at your feet."

Beatrice laughed up at her sister. "I do envy you, Susanna. You are so lucky to be married. You can do exactly as you please now."

"Well, not quite, but it is not as bad as I had feared." Susanna glanced at her sister. "And now I have a present for you, Bea. Do you remember I promised you a string of pearls?"

Susanna felt a warm glow inside at her sister's cry of pleasure. There were certainly compensations in being the wife of a wealthy man.

CHAPTER FIFTEEN

Adam finished fitting the shelves to the first bookcase he had made for Lord Munford's library and stepped back to admire his work. They were fashioned out of dark mahogany and polished to a warm richness that gave a feeling of elegance and comfort. The top rail reeded and lipped to form a pediment; four graduated shelves separated the rail from the spacious cupboards beneath, each of which had a shell pattern inlaid in the centre panel. One wall was now complete. The opposite wall would match exactly and the shorter walls would have painted panels above the cupboards. It was beginning to take shape. When the table, chairs and steps were all in place it would look as elegant as Lord Munford could wish.

Lost in thought, Adam at first took little notice of the voices. It was not until he heard a name mentioned followed by Lady Munford's shrill laughter that he began to listen.

"She was a Warwick before she married Digby," Lady Munford said. "She only married him because Sir William was ruined at the tables of course. He paid a high price for the privilege of bedding her, but he can afford it."

"You say he's bringing her up to town next month?" a second female voice asked.

"My poor besotted brother is a fool if he does," Helen Munford murmured with another laugh. "Munford kept me in the country until his sons were born. Digby isn't exactly a young girl's dream. She'll have a lover before the year's out."

"If she hasn't already . . ."

236

The voices drifted away. Adam realized he had been gripping his hammer so tightly that his knuckles had turned white. They had been talking about Susanna. Suddenly, he was remembering. He could almost smell her perfume and taste the fresh sweetness of her lips. He could feel the satin smoothness of her flesh beneath him. For a few moments he was weak with longing, the desire churning within him. How he wanted her! He fought against it, remembering the beating he had endured the following night.

She was a lying whore and he was better off without her!

Jane looked up as Adam entered the kitchen. She smiled, getting up from her chair to greet him. As she did so, the faintness swept over her and she gave a cry, pressing a hand to her forehead.

"Are you ill?" Adam asked, coming to support her. "What's wrong, Jane?"

She smiled again as the room steadied. "It was just a little dizziness, Adam. Nothing to worry about."

"Nothing to worry about?" he cried. "You sit down and I'll fetch the doctor to you."

Jane laughed teasingly. "I've already talked to the midwife, Adam. She's confirmed it – I'm to have a child. Our first child . . ."

"A child . . ." Adam was stunned and Jane's eyes sparkled with amusement.

"Oh, Adam, don't look like that! It was bound to happen sooner or later."

"Yes . . ." He began to relax as he saw her pleasure. "It's just a shock, that's all."

"A pleasant one I hope?"

"Yes, of course." He watched anxiously as she moved a heavy kettle on to the fire. "Should you be doing that?"

"It won't hurt me. I can work for a while yet, Adam."

"We should get a girl in to help you."

"Can we afford it?"

"I think so. The order books are beginning to fill up. There was that bureau for one of Lord Munford's friends and his library will bring us nearly a thousand guineas. If this keeps up, I shall need a second apprentice."

Jane's eyes were full of pride as she looked at him. "You're so clever, Adam. Everyone says your work is the equal of Mr Chippendale's."

"Is that what they say, Jane?" Adam grinned at her. "I dare say I put Mr Hepplewhite in the shade then?"

"You go on and laugh at me," Jane said, shaking her head at him. "One day you'll be as rich and famous as the best of them."

"Yes," Adam said, his face suddenly serious. "I certainly intend to be."

He regarded his wife thoughtfully. He knew that Jane was right, people were starting to take notice of his work, important people who could make his name. He had begun to believe that his dreams were coming true. Yet something inside him was still unfulfilled.

As Jane moved away to see to their supper, Adam sat in the rocking-chair by the fire. For once he was in no mood to work on the various pieces of furniture he was making for their home. He was remembering the snatch of conversation he had overheard and thinking about Susanna Warwick. He wondered what she thought of her bargain now. Did she enjoy being married to a man old enough to be her father?

Damn Susanna Warwick! Adam's thoughts returned to his wife. Now that a child was on the way, he would insist that Jane had help in the house.

Susanna sighed as the footman handed her down from the carriage. They had been some hours on the road and she was tired, though pleased to be in London at last. Digby had put the journey off twice, but now they were here she was eager to see the house. Beatrice was almost asleep on her feet, and Susanna handed her over to the housekeeper, with instructions to take her straight to bed. Having seen her sister safely upstairs, she began to look around her with interest. She would need to make some changes here!

"I thought you might enjoy refurbishing the London house," Digby had said a few days earlier. "Perhaps not at once, but when you are ready. I shall give you carte blanche."

She thought she understood what he meant as she looked around the house for the first time. It was Jacobean, with a predominance of heavy, dark oak, making the whole interior rather dull. The preference these days was for lighter, more elegant furniture.

"I see what you meant about refurbishing, Digby," she said to her husband as they went up the staircase to the main salon on the first floor. "The whole house needs to be brightened up. It isn't just the furniture. It needs a great deal of thought."

"Exactly so." Digby's face was indulgent as she walked about the room, opening cabinets and prying into drawers. "It's your house, Susanna, you may do as you please with it and send me the bills." She was already planning changes. He was pleased that she could see the potential; it would give her an interest, keep her from straying for a while.

Susanna was aware of him watching her but she was not uncomfortable. Their relationship had settled into something approaching companionship over the past months. From time to time, he came to her bed, but he was often content just to fondle her for a while. Only on rare occasions did he attempt anything more. It was on those occasions when his true nature showed through, and she felt his spite.

Away from the bedroom, however, they dealt very well with one another. Susanna had been quick to realize that her husband was not the fool many people thought him. She discovered that his business interests ranged far beyond the few farms he let to his tenants. Although he did not care to have it generally known, preferring people to think of him as a simple country squire, he owned several mills in the north of England and he had an interest in a tin mine in Cornwall. It was the woollen mills that provided him with the bulk of his fortune.

"My grandfather started them," he told her once he saw that she was interested. "My father bought this estate. He was ashamed of the mills. During his lifetime they became run down, but when he died I built them up and bought more. So now that you know where the money comes from, Susanna, what do you think about it?"

"I think you must be very able, Digby. You are clearly an astute business man."

"And it does not disgust you that I should dirty my hands in trade?"

Susanna touched the diamonds at her throat. "No, it does not disgust me, Digby."

He laughed, pleased with her answer. "I was not mistaken in you," he said. "You are a sensible woman. We shall do well together."

In the London house, Susanna was examining the carved panelling above the fireplace. "I think this must come off, Digby," she said. "I shall have silk wall hangings and . . ." She looked at him in surprise. "What is it?"

He was frowning over a letter he had just opened. "This is from Helen. She has invited us to take tea with her tomorrow."

"Your sister . . ." Susanna waited, knowing that there was little affection between them. He had used Lady Munford's hospitality during his courtship of her, but Susanna had not expected to visit so often now that they were married. She did not much like the older woman. "Shall we go?"

"I have some business of my own, but you must go, Susanna. Helen is not someone you can afford to offend. You must cultivate her even if you dislike her. She has so much influence with the Ton."

"She did not come to the wedding . . ."

"Helen refuses to leave London these days." Digby smiled maliciously. "She probably thinks that if Munford ever got her to the country, he would lock her up and throw away the key."

"That is unkind, Digby." Susanna looked at him. "Why should he do that?"

"Apart from the fact that she has had every groom, footman and prize-fighter in London in her bed at one time or another, I have no idea." Digby's amusement faded and his eyes became hard. "Do not let her corrupt you, Susanna. Munford is a weak fool. I am not."

Susanna lifted her head with pride. "I am not a fool either," she said. "And I have no interest in grooms or footmen." There was only one man she cared for.

"I'm glad to hear it, my dear." Digby's face softened. "Do not let us quarrel, Susanna. It was simply a warning. I am satisfied with my wife."

Seeing the look in his eyes, Susanna knew that she could expect a visit from him that night. It no longer bothered her now that she was able to detach her mind. She had so much to think about, so much to look forward to now that they were at last in London . . .

"Very well, I shall go," she said. "But I do not believe I shall take Beatrice. I think she would be better employed enjoying a stroll in the park with the maid you've engaged to look after her. It is her first visit to town and I know she is anxious to see the sights."

Beatrice admired her reflection in the mirror, her eyes sparkling. She was wearing a very smart walking gown and pelisse of dark bronze velvet trimmed with gold braid, and a matching bonnet with a high crown and feathers. She looked very different from the young girl who had climbed trees in the garden of her home, and she knew that it was all due to her sister's generosity. She turned to Susanna with a cry of delight and hugged her.

"Thank you for my new gown, Susanna. I'm so glad it was finished in time for our visit to London."

Susanna inspected her ensemble with a critical eye. The gown had been made by a provincial seamstress and was not as smart as some of her own gowns, though an improvement on anything Beatrice had previously owned. "It looks well enough for the moment," she said. "But we shall buy you lots of pretty clothes now we are in town, dearest."

Beatrice hugged her sister once more. "I'm so lucky," she said. "But I wish you were coming with us to the park, Susanna."

"So do I," Susanna said with a little sigh. "But Digby wants me to visit Lady Helen, so of course I must do so. He has been very generous, allowing you to live with us, Bea."

"Yes . . ." Beatrice wrinkled her brow, doubtful. It was true that Lord Digby gave Susanna lots of presents, and he had forced her mother to have the doctor when Susanna was ill – she would never forget that – but she had discovered that she didn't much like him. He wasn't really kind to Susanna. She had observed things . . . little things which made her think that in the privacy of their bedroom, he was sometimes rather cruel to her sister. Not that Susanna had ever said a word against him, but Beatrice had noticed a few bruises on her sister's arm and had seen Digby pinch her once or twice. "Yes, of course you must do as your husband says."

"We shall have lots of outings together," Susanna said. "Don't look so disappointed, my love."

"Oh, I'm not upset," Beatrice said. She didn't want Susanna to get into trouble on her account. "It's a lovely day for a walk, and Maria is very pleasant, even though she's older than I would have liked. Why couldn't I have a younger maid?"

"Because Digby thought Maria suitable," Susanna said firmly. "And so do I. She will do very well as a chaperone for a madcap like you!"

242

Beatrice pulled a face. "As if I needed one," she said, and then laughed. "Very well, Lady Digby. I shall be on my best behaviour. After all, I'm going to marry someone rich and important, aren't I?"

"Well, we shall see," Susanna said. "Now, I really must go . . . I must not keep Digby's sister waiting."

Susanna was invited to wait in the small front parlour while the footman went to advise Lady Munford of her arrival. She glanced out of the window, wishing that Digby had come with her for this first visit to his sister. She had met Lady Munford when she was in London the previous year, of course, but she had been Susanna Warwick then and not Lady Digby. She was bound to be scrutinized severely, her clothes commented on and her manners noted. Much of her success in society might depend on whether or not her husband's sister approved of her.

Hearing footsteps in the hall, she swung round, just as someone entered the room. She stared in disbelief, the colour draining from her face as she saw him. It could not be! She was dreaming . . .

"Adam . . ." she whispered. "Adam Blackwell – what are you doing here?"

For a moment he stared at her in silence, a stunned expression on his face. Susanna made an involuntary movement towards him, but then he suddenly came to life and she halted, hardly daring to breathe.

"I beg your pardon," he said with stiff politeness. "I came only to look at the design of a chair. Lord Munford wants me to copy it for his library."

He walked past her and began to examine a very elegant elbow chair. The design was unusual in that it had a coat of arms carved into the centre strut of the back.

Susanna stood as if turned to stone, feeling as if he had slapped her in the face. She wanted to ask him about his wife, and to explain why she had not kept their assignation in the summerhouse, but his turning his back on her was so clear that she could only stand and stare out of the window in mortified silence.

How could he be so cold and uncaring? Surely that night had meant something to him? He had sworn that he loved her and now . . .

"Lady Munford asks if you will come up, Lady Digby."

The footman's words cut into Susanna's confused thoughts. She inclined her head and followed him from the room. Her heartbeat was erratic, and she felt close to tears but she knew that she must control her emotions. She could not afford to let anyone guess what that chance meeting with Adam Blackwell had meant to her.

Adam could not think clearly until she had gone. Her beauty had set his senses whirling, making him react defensively. Memory assailed him and he remembered the softness of her skin, the sweetness of her kisses. He had been overcome with an urgent longing to bear her to the ground and possess her, the desire moving in him so fiercely that he had almost groaned aloud. Then he had recalled the beating and the way she had stood watching, mocking him.

He had been only just conscious and in agony, seeing her through a haze, but he knew that she had been there. He remembered the dress she'd worn. The one she'd had on the previous day when . . . He groaned as the memory of that glorious night came back to haunt him once more. Would he never be free of her?

"Damn her," he muttered angrily. Adam forced himself to concentrate on his work. She wasn't worth all this pain!

Susanna sat on the edge of her chair, sipping tea from a fine Worcester porcelain cup, aware of her hostess's intent scrutiny. She lifted her chin, her face unconsciously proud.

"Your first priority is for a new wardrobe," Lady Helen

244

said at last. "That gown does very well for the country, but it won't do for the wife of Lord Digby in town. Not if you want to be well thought of in the right circles."

Susanna's irritation was tempered by her realization that the older woman was right. Swallowing her annoyance, she said, "Perhaps you could direct me to a suitable dressmaker?"

"If I do, you must follow my advice. No half measures."

Helen Munford's eyes gleamed with sudden interest. It might be amusing to mould and shape this young beauty. Digby was a fool to bring her to town so soon. The girl would have her pick of lovers. It could be diverting to teach her how to conduct her affairs.

"Everyone says you have perfect taste, madam," Susanna replied. "I should be happy to be guided by you."

Lady Munford was wearing a very elegant Petenlair jacket with a sack back, short elbow sleeves and a stomacher front. Edged and frilled with the finest laces and silk ribbons, it reached over her hips, allowing her full skirts to billow out around her in a most attractive manner. Susanna's own bodice was much plainer and far less stylish.

"Then that's settled. Tomorrow morning I shall call for you. It's time Digby was parted from some of his money."

Some of it would find its way into her pocket in the form of commissions, Lady Munford thought with satisfaction. Munford had made a generous settlement on her when they married but she had expensive habits and was always short of money. Her vices included a passion for the gaming tables, where she was often reckless, losing far more than she could afford. Studying the girl's pretty face, she thought that there might be more than one way of making money from her innocence.

"And later," she continued with a smile, "I can promise you a most amusing diversion. I have arranged to visit Bethlem hospital with some of my friends."

"Isn't that where they house the lunatics?"

"Don't worry, Susanna." Helen Munford's eyes flashed with scornful laughter. "It's quite safe. They are all securely

245

chained. I promise you, it is the most entertaining sight to watch them trying to get free. Some of them actually foam at the mouth and scream. Almost as good as following the procession from Newgate to Tyburn to see a hanging."

Susanna felt sick at Lady Munford's glee. She had no desire to visit Bedlam, but she dare not refuse. She was certain that her sister-in-law was testing her. If she showed her disgust openly, she would find herself being ridiculed in front of Helen's friends. The story of a rift between them would spread like wildfire, and she would find it that much harder to establish herself. Much as she disliked her husband's sister, she would for the moment have to humour her whims, unpleasant though that might be.

"I shall look forward to tomorrow then." Susanna rose to take her leave.

Lady Munford's look was sly. She took up a long-handled ivory back scratcher and slipped it down the neck of her jacket, rubbing at an irritation. "That's better – I believe I shall enjoy our little outing," she said. "It promises to be the start of an interesting acquaintance . . ."

Something in her eyes made Susanna uncomfortable, but as the footman arrived to conduct her downstairs, she dismissed all thought of the next day. Her heart was racing wildly as she walked down the stairway. Would she see Adam again?

All through her tête-à-tête with Lady Munford, her thoughts had kept returning to that chance meeting in the parlour and what she would say if it happened again. Susanna decided that Adam must have kept his distance because he believed that she had never intended to meet him that evening following their night of passion. Perhaps he thought she had merely been amusing herself, as her mother did with various lovers. If he knew that she had been locked in her room because of her love for him . . . Yet it could make little difference now. They were both married.

There was no sign of Adam as Susanna left the house. She was disappointed, even though she knew it was for the best. With a heavy heart, she was driven back to the house in Bedford Row. Until she saw Adam, spoke to him, felt the sudden surge of longing his presence in the same room had aroused in her, she had believed she was adjusting to her new life. She had thought she might find a certain contentment in being a society hostess. Now the ache had begun inside her once more.

It was so exciting to be in London. Walking in the park with her maid, Beatrice was conscious of a feeling of adventure. So many people promenading in the sunshine, and all so splendidly dressed. Her eyes sparkled as she watched the elegant dandies and the fashionable young women. Although each young lady had a chaperone with her, she noticed that they managed to stop and talk to the gentlemen every now and then. Hearing the sound of laughter, Beatrice watched a group of young people talking and making jests, and wished that she had some acquaintance in London.

Susanna and Digby would of course include her in their own entertainments, but Beatrice would not be invited out much for a while, because her sister had only a few friends in town herself. Wistfully Beatrice watched some children playing with a ball. They were accompanied by two adults, whom she took to be their older sister and brother. They were all having a wonderful time. Including the rather attractive young man.

Suddenly the ball rolled towards her. Beatrice swooped on it and picked it up, then threw it to one of the young children, a boy of perhaps six or seven, who immediately entered into the spirit of things, throwing it back to her, and applauding as she jumped to catch it.

"Bravo, bravo," he cried. "You're a good catcher, miss."

"Thank you . . . My name is Miss Warwick," she said. "Miss Beatrice Warwick."

Ignoring Maria's frowns, she threw the ball again; it was tossed back to her and she caught it neatly once more. This time she was congratulated by the boy's older brother.

"Well done, Miss Warwick," he said, with a look of approval. "Would you care to join us? We were just about to play a game of cricket, but we need an extra hand. Sylvia is hopeless at catching . . ." Then he laughed and shook his head. "Forgive me, you don't know who Sylvia is . . . Come and meet my family, Miss Warwick."

Drawn by the sweetness of his countenance, Beatrice walked over to join the happy group. There were five of them in all: two young girls of between eight and ten years of age, the boy, his older sister and brother.

The man who had spoken now made a stylish bow. "May I present Miss Sylvia Browne, a young lady of taste and beauty, but no sporting ability. My sister Phillipa, a tomboy of the first class. My sister Anna, her devoted slave . . . and this young tearaway whose name I seem to have forgotten . . ." His eyes were teasing as the boy exclaimed indignantly.

"Oh, don't tease him," Sylvia Browne cried in agitation. "You know what he is and we don't want Miss Warwick to get a bad impression of him."

"That would never do. Not now that we've finally found someone who can actually catch a ball." He ruffled the boy's hair. "Ah yes, of course, his name is David . . . and mine is John."

Beatrice laughed. What a delightful family they were, and how happy she was to have made some acquaintances on her very first day.

Maria frowned at her and shook her head, but Beatrice turned her back deliberately. These people were well spoken and John Browne was a gentleman. There could be no possible objection to her forming a friendship with them.

"You can sit on the bench and watch, Maria," she said. "I think I shall play for a little while."

"Lady Digby will be expecting you home for tea," Maria pointed out.

248

"No, indeed she will not," Beatrice replied. "I need not be back until it is time to change for dinner. There's hours yet, so do not pull such a face."

Her expression a mask of disapproval, the maid retreated to the bench and sat down to watch. She had done her duty and no one could blame her if Miss Warwick got herself into unsuitable company. Even she could see that the family, though genteel, were not of the first quality. Poor as church mice she wouldn't wonder. You had only to look at the frayed cuffs on Mr Browne's sleeves to know there was no money. His sister was better dressed, but Maria had her own ideas about her. A companion or governess on her day off was about the size of it, wearing her mistress's castoffs. No, not at all what she'd been led to believe was expected, but it wasn't her responsibility. She'd done her best . . .

And that was what she duly reported to Susanna later that afternoon.

Susanna listened to her rather prim report of the encounter in silence. It all sounded very innocent, and she was a little annoyed that Maria should come to her behind Beatrice's back, but knew it would be unwise to show it. Next time it might be something serious.

"Thank you for telling me," she said in a pleasant tone when dismissing the maid. "No great harm was done this time, Maria, but I shall speak to my sister."

After Maria had gone, Susanna was thoughtful. She didn't want to make a big issue out of the affair, but she really would have to speak to Bea about it. She sighed, remembering her own disappointments. Whatever happened, her sister must not be allowed to fall into the same trap.

"Did you enjoy yourself today, my love?" Susanna asked her sister just before they went down to dinner that evening.

"Oh yes," Beatrice replied, her face glowing. "I met such a nice family, Susanna. Miss Sylvia Browne, her brothers

John and David and two younger sisters. We played cricket in the park."

"Did you indeed?" Susanna's brows rose. "I dare say no great harm was done, but you must remember that you are not at home now, my love. Young ladies of quality seldom play cricket in a public park. It isn't done."

"Isn't it?" Beatrice looked uncomfortable. "Maria did scold me on the way home, but I told her you wouldn't mind."

"For myself I don't mind at all," Susanna said. "I am merely concerned for you. Some of the Society hostesses are very strict. If one of them should get to hear of what she might consider undignified behaviour, you might not be invited to all the best houses."

"Oh . . ." Beatrice's face fell. "I'm sorry, Susanna. I didn't think. Miss Sylvia Browne didn't seem to mind being seen."

"Perhaps Miss Browne isn't expecting to be invited to the Ton balls this Season."

"No . . ." Beatrice was thoughtful. "I don't suppose she is. I did notice that her gown was a little old-fashioned, and John . . . I mean Mr Browne's cuffs were frayed. Maria said she thought Sylvia might be a companion or a governess, though she was obviously very well spoken."

"It could be that she comes from a good family who have fallen on hard times," Susanna said. "As we might have done had I not married Lord Digby. If Papa had been forced to sell the estate, we might all have been forced to work for a living." Susanna sighed, realizing that her dreams of running away with Adam Blackwell had been doomed from the beginning. Could she really have done it, knowing what it might mean for her family?

"Poor Sylvia," Beatrice said. "It must be awful to be poor. I wonder who she really is?"

"She didn't tell you where she was staying or speak about any dances she was hoping to attend this Season?"

"No. We had some fun together and then parted, saying how nice it was to have met."

"Then I would suppose Maria to be right," Susanna said. "She is obviously a well brought up young woman, and she didn't wish to press her acquaintance with you further. I am sure it was all just an innocent affair. You enjoyed yourselves, but I doubt you will meet again."

"Yes. Yes, I expect you are right," Beatrice said, secretly a little disappointed. She had liked all the family, and Mr John Browne in particular. She had hoped they might meet again at one of the many parties she would be attending, but of course Susanna was right. The Browne family did not move in the circles from which she expected to find a rich husband . . .

"Oh well," she said with a sigh. "I shall make lots more friends soon. Can we go shopping tomorrow, Susanna?"

"Tomorrow I must go out with Lady Helen," Susanna frowned. "She has promised to take me to her own dress-maker's. I would much rather go with you." Seeing the disappointment in her sister's eyes, she added, "Instead we shall go to Ranelagh in the afternoon and take tea. That will be much nicer, won't it? And then I'll take you shopping another day."

Susanna was examining one of her new gowns when Digby came into her bedchamber. She held it up for him to admire. It was a blue and silver evening robe, open in both bodice and petticoat with a wide stomacher, and was to be worn over a small hoop. It had silver lace ruffles down the bodice and serpentine ruchings which softened the elegant but slightly severe line of the overdress.

"This has just arrived, Digby," Susanna said. "Helen helped me to choose it. I thought I would wear it for her soiree tomorrow – what do you think?"

"The gown is very fine. It will suit you." Digby pulled at his cravat. "You are seeing a great deal of Helen recently, Susanna."

"I thought that was what you wanted?"

Susanna lifted innocent eyes to his. She had allowed

herself to be drawn into Lady Munford's circle more than she had intended, because each time she visited she had hopes of seeing Adam. Indeed, she had caught glimpses of him on several occasions. As yet, she had not managed to see him on his own again, but there was always the chance that she might do so one day. For that reason alone, she was prepared to put up with the rather lewd and bawdy behaviour of some of Helen's friends.

"I said that you must not offend Helen," Digby said. "I did not tell you to make her your bosom friend."

"Then I shall not do so," Susanna replied. "Already we have more invitations than we can possibly accept. But I cannot drop her altogether, Digby."

"No, of course not. That would be most unwise." His frown eased. "We hold our own ball next week; after that you will scarcely have time to visit Helen more than once a sennight."

"Hardly that," Susanna agreed. "Please do not be concerned, Digby. I intend to form my own circle of acquaintances. Your sister has merely helped me to become fashionable."

"As long as that is all." He nodded, his humour restored. "And now, my dear. I came to give you these." He presented her with a flat leather case.

Opening it, Susanna discovered a long string of creamy pearls. "They are beautiful, Digby."

"They belonged to my grandmother," he said. "I had them restrung for you. You can wear them tomorrow evening if you wish."

"They will be perfect with my dress." Susanna went to kiss his cheek. "Thank you."

"They are a going-away gift," he said. "I have some urgent business in the north. I may be away for some days, but I shall return for our ball. In the meantime I suppose you must rely on Helen if you wish to attend some of these affairs." He waved his hand to indicate the cards piled on her desk and propped up on the mantelpiece. "Just be cautious in her company, Susanna. I should not trust her too much if I were you."

"I shall be careful," Susanna promised.

"That's a nasty cough," Susanna said, looking at her sister in dismay. "I was going to suggest that you come to Lady Helen's party with me, but I think you should stay at home and go to bed early, don't you?"

"Yes." Beatrice bit her lip. She did not want to tell Susanna that she had been caught in a rainstorm in the park. Maria had warned her it looked like rain, but she had deliberately wasted time, hoping to catch sight of Sylvia Browne and her family. They had not been there and she'd taken a soaking for nothing. "Yes, perhaps it's a good idea."

Susanna thought it was unusual for Beatrice to be so meek. "Don't be disappointed, dearest," she said. "I don't think you would enjoy Lady Munford's card party very much. Besides, we want you to be well for our own ball next week, don't we?"

"Yes, of course." Beatrice cheered up. "Yes, I'm looking forward to it, Susanna. I shall be seventeen two days after that."

"So you will," Susanna said, laughter in her eyes. "I wonder what surprises that day will bring . . ."

"Oh, do tell me," Beatrice begged, but Susanna shook her head.

"Off to bed with you," she said. "I must get changed and then I must be on my way."

Susanna was a little anxious on her sister's behalf as she went to get ready. She hadn't been able to spend as much time as she'd planned with Bea and thought her sister must be rather bored. Perhaps that accounted for the look in her eyes. If she didn't know better, she would almost think that Beatrice had fallen in love, except that she'd scarcely had a chance to meet any young men yet.

Sighing, Susanna dismissed her sister's problems. At the moment, she had enough of her own.

*   *   *

253

Susanna entered the main salon alone. Digby had left early that morning and she did not need an escort to attend her sister-in-law's card party, though she wished that Beatrice could have come with her as they'd planned. She paused on the threshold for a moment to survey the glittering scene. There were twenty to thirty guests. Lady Helen had said it would be just a small, intimate party of some of her closest friends.

"Nothing special, Susanna. Just some music, cards for those who wish it and a little refreshment."

Everyone was richly dressed in silks and satins, the colours a vibrating kaleidoscope of pinks, oranges, lavender, purples and crimson. Jewels flashed from the throats of the ladies and the fingers of the gentlemen, sparkling in the light of the huge glass chandeliers. It was a scene Susanna had seen many times before and yet as she hesitated at the door, she felt that there was something different, something hidden beneath the surface.

"Ah, my dear Susanna," Helen said, coming forward to embrace her. "Pray do not stand there as if you were doubting your welcome. Come and meet my friends."

Susanna had already met some of them. As she progressed from one painted fop to another, her sense of disquiet increased. Most of the men were wearing as much paint on their faces as the ladies. A heavy scent of musk and perfume hung in the air and beneath it was an unclean odour. Looking into faces that were sly and depraved, their eyes knowing, calculating, she felt a sickness in her stomach. They looked at her as if they were stripping her bare of her clothes, assessing what lay beneath. She was suddenly very glad that she had not brought her young sister. It would have been better if she had not come herself.

The women were all of a similar age to Helen Munford. Susanna looked in vain for any young women or men. Now she was beginning to be uneasy. This was not quite what she had expected. These men and women were not the elite of the Ton, though they were all titled and accepted into society. There was something unsavoury about them and she wondered how long she must stay before she could leave without causing offence.

Having introduced her to everyone, Lady Munford went off to greet more guests. Susanna smiled and nodded, moving away to the window to stand alone staring out at the night. The moon was shining and it was quite light. She wished that Digby had been with her, sure that he would not have stayed more than half an hour or so. Behind her the laughter had become harsh and she heard a few lewd remarks that made her cringe inside. Although there were many in society who condoned this coarseness, Susanna intended to set a code of manners for her own circle. She would cultivate only people of good sense and taste. Her salon would become a meeting place for men and women of intellect, who would prefer witty conversation to this excuse for drunken debauchery.

"Lady Digby, I believe?" The smooth voice spoke behind her. "What a pleasure. I had not hoped to find you here this evening – and all alone, I think?"

Susanna's nerves prickled as she turned to find herself looking up into the face of the man she feared more than any other. The Marquis of Brandon! She stared at him in dismay, feeling trapped as she saw the predatory expression in his eyes. He looked as if he would like to devour her.

"Sir." She inclined her head stiffly. "Excuse me please."

She made as if to go by him, but he moved to block her path, his hand just touching her sleeve. A huge ruby and diamond ring flashed on his third finger. "Surely you do not mean to leave already? Everyone is talking of your beauty, Lady Digby. We should all be devastated, not to say offended, if you were to go."

Susanna heard the subtle note of warning in his voice. It was true, she could not leave so suddenly or Helen Munford would be angry. A few words from her and

Susanna could find herself the laughing stock of society. She felt a surge of anger as she thought how unfair it was. Lady Munford was lewd and depraved, but because of her connections, because of the position she had won for herself, no one dared to cut her openly. Forcing herself to smile, Susanna said, "I was merely intending to find something to eat, sir."

"Then you will allow me to escort you, madam. You can always be sure of a fine supper at the Munfords'. Perhaps some cold chicken or a slice or two of a fine York ham?" The Marquis's fingers clasped her arm, forcing her to go with him. "I shall be privileged to serve you myself."

Glancing across the room, Susanna saw the mockery in her sister-in-law's eyes and guessed that Lady Helen had deliberately arranged this meeting when she knew Digby would not be present. Anger made Susanna's head go up. She had been put in an impossible position, but there was little she could do about it. She could not leave for at least an hour, and until then she must just accept the Marquis's company. Hearing the raucous laughter of some of the other men present, she thought at least she would be protected from their attentions. He was not likely to yield his place at her side to anyone else . . .

"Very well, my lord," Susanna assented, her face proud as she laid the tips of her fingers on his arm. "Since you insist."

"I do, my dear Lady Digby," he said. "I do indeed insist . . ." There was something menacing about his manner. "You may deny me that which I most desire, but not the pleasure of your company."

"I beg your pardon, sir. I do not think I understand you." Susanna's voice was stifled by his overbearing presence.

"Indeed?" His brows rose. "I had thought you understood me very well, madam. But if you wish me to speak more plainly . . ."

"No, sir. I forbid it."

Susanna's cheeks were hot. The look in his eyes could

256

not have been clearer. His gaze seemed to strip her naked, leaving her exposed and vulnerable.

Seeing that he had disturbed her, a smile of satisfaction touched his thick lips. "A woman as beautiful as you should not be afraid of taking lovers," he murmured. "You were made for passion, surely you know that?"

"Please, sir. You are embarrassing me," Susanna said.

"Then perhaps we should go into supper?" The Marquis was amused but concealed it behind a mask of politeness. "You will discover that I am a patient man, Lady Digby. I am prepared to wait until you are ready to . . . shall we say, look for new amusements?"

"That will never be," she replied, her face haughty. "But you may take me into supper now."

Susanna wished that she could leave at once, but there was no immediate escape. Short of abducting her by force, there was little real harm the Marquis could do in the house of her husband's sister, but as soon as possible she would send for her carriage and go home.

Susanna was relieved to find that Beatrice was feeling very much better the next morning. When Susanna told her she was taking her to meet Lady Maddison's niece, who was now the Earl of Grafton's wife, she was very excited. Dressing quickly in her very best gown of yellow watered silk, she went downstairs to meet her sister, full of anticipation.

"Do I look all right?" she asked as Susanna's eyes went over her. "Is my bonnet straight?"

"You look very pretty, dearest. The carriage is waiting for us, shall we go?"

"Yes." Beatrice nodded happily. "Tell me about the Countess again. Is she nice? Will I like her or is she one of those haughty dames you told me about?"

"Angela Maddison was not in the least haughty when I met her at her aunt's," Susanna said. "Of course, she wasn't married to the Earl then. However, when we met the other afternoon, she remembered me and seemed pleased to see me. I mentioned you were staying with me and she said she has a distant cousin visiting her. She suggested that I bring you to meet her. She thought it would be nice for you to be friends since you are of a similar age."

Beatrice raised her eyes to meet her sister's. "You didn't tell me about the cousin before."

"I had forgotten," Susanna said. "I've had a lot on my mind. But if the Countess's cousin is your own age it will be nice for you to have a friend you can visit without me sometimes. I fear I've not had as much time to spend with you as I'd hoped."

"It doesn't matter," Beatrice said. "You take me with you as much as you can."

"I'm glad you didn't come last night," Susanna said. "I didn't stay long myself."

"Why?" Beatrice was curious.

"Oh . . . there was someone there I didn't like. He pressed his company on me and I found it uncomfortable."

"Why didn't you tell him to leave you alone?"

"The Marquis of Brandon isn't an easy person to snub. He seems impervious to hints."

"The Marquis of Brandon . . ." Beatrice tried to remember, then it came to her. "Didn't he send you those stuffed birds?"

"Yes." Susanna tucked her arm through the younger girl's. "Let us forget about him. You will like the Countess of Grafton. I hope her cousin is pleasant; it will be nice for you to have a friend, Bea."

"I'm so glad you could come." Angela, Countess of Grafton, kissed Susanna's cheek warmly. "And this is Beatrice. I'm so glad to meet you, my dear. I want to introduce you to my cousin, Miss Sylvia Browne . . ." She looked at Beatrice's incredulous face. "Is something wrong?"

Sylvia moved forward, her hand outstretched. "Miss Warwick, how wonderful to meet again like this. I've thought of you often since that day ..." She turned to her cousin with a smile of explanation. "This is the young lady I told you of, Angela – the good catcher we dragooned into playing cricket the day we arrived in London. You may well stare, Miss Warwick. We must have looked a rag and bobtail company that day. John had brought us all up to town in the hope of finding me a position as a companion. I had held such a position to an elderly lady in Bedford. When she died, I asked her relatives to give me a letter of recommendation, and they did so. When I came up to meet the Countess of Grafton, I had no idea she was a distant cousin, indeed, we only discovered it as we were talking. Our mothers were second cousins, so the connection is slight and we hardly knew of each other's existence."

"I had heard of Sylvia through my mother." The Countess took up the story. "But she had no idea of my identity. It was a surprise and pleasure to both of us."

"Angela very kindly took me in as a friend," Sylvia said. "As you can see, Miss Warwick, she has given me pretty gowns and a wonderful home."

"I've given her very little," the Countess said modestly. "It is pleasant for me to have a companion I can trust. Especially when the Earl is out of town on business. He is a very busy man, of course."

"But so devoted to you," Sylvia said. "I've never seen a more loving husband."

The Countess blushed delicately. "The Earl is very thoughtful," she said.

"And your brother," Beatrice asked Sylvia. "Is he not with you?"

"He had to go back to the country, but he will return in a few weeks." Sylvia glanced at the Countess, who inclined her head, giving permission for the girl to carry on. "The Earl has a living that he thinks will soon come vacant and he has promised it to John. So he will come up to visit us then ..." Sylvia paused, then continued, "I shall tell him

259

we've met again when I write next. I know he will want to meet you when he comes . . ."

Beatrice was silent, but Susanna was surprised to see the colour high in her cheeks. Beatrice turned away as she noticed her sister's gaze and Susanna was suddenly alert. Beatrice could not really be interested in this young man, could she? She had always said she intended to marry for money, but there was something in her eyes . . . As the Countess began to speak again, Susanna decided she must have been mistaken. Bea would never think of marrying a penniless clergyman!

CHAPTER SIXTEEN

"I've heard Lord Munford is building a new library," Digby said to his sister as he, Susanna and Beatrice took tea in her drawing-room. "I should be interested in seeing it, wouldn't you, Susanna? We are thinking of refurbishing the house I bought, Helen. Would you mind if we had a look?"

"If you wish." She shrugged her shoulders in an expression of unconcern. "I would not recommend using the firm, but you are welcome to see." She rose to her feet and the others followed suit. "I should warn you that the tradesman is a surly fellow."

Susanna's heart was jumping as she followed just behind her husband and his sister. Beatrice looked at her inquiringly and she put a finger to her lips, warning her to stay silent.

As they walked into the library, Adam was using a hammer to fix the runners in one of the bottom cabinets. Lying on his side, he had his head inside it so that he could not at first see who had entered.

"What are you doing?" Digby asked. "You look most uncomfortable."

Adam edged out and glanced up, frowning as he saw who had addressed him. His eyes went past Digby to Lady Munford and then Susanna. He looked away at once, afraid of betraying himself. Standing up, he brushed sawdust from his breeches.

"It needed a slight adjustment," he said. "His lordship changed his mind about the position of the shelves."

"Why don't you admit that you made a mistake?" Lady Munford's voice was sharp and biting. "Your work simply isn't up to the standard my husband had imagined."

Adam's cheeks flushed with anger, but he bit his tongue. To argue with her now would be foolish. "As you prefer," he muttered. "His lordship seems satisfied."

"His lordship has little taste in such matters," she sneered.

"Oh, I don't know about that, Helen," Digby said, examining the workmanship and running his fingers over the smooth wood. "I think it is rather fine . . . What do you say, Susanna? Shall we ask Mr Carter to give us a price for the house?"

Susanna's throat felt as if it were closing up. "If you wish, Digby," she murmured. "We could at least have a look at some designs."

Digby turned back to the other man. "My card, Mr Carter. Perhaps you would call on me?"

"Certainly, Lord Digby. My name is Blackwell, sir. I'm Mr Carter's partner."

"Blackwell . . ." Digby wrinkled his brow. "I've heard that name somewhere. Isn't that the name of that girl . . ." His eyes narrowed as he looked at Susanna and saw her pink cheeks.

"Mr Blackwell is Thomas Blackwell's son," Susanna said. "Yes, you are quite right, Digby."

Digby nodded, understanding her embarrassment perfectly. It was an awkward situation. "I see . . . Well, that's all over now. I shall expect you one day next week, Blackwell. Shall we say Thursday morning?"

"At twelve thirty, if that would be convenient, sir."

Digby nodded and turned to leave. "Come along then, Susanna. We mustn't keep Mr Blackwell from his work."

Susanna obeyed, saying nothing. She walked ahead of her husband back to the salon, trying to subdue her emotions. She must not let Digby see how distressed she was.

"That was a damned silly thing to let me do," he said irritably as they reached the drawing-room. "Why didn't you tell me it was Maggie Blackwell's brother?"

"I didn't know," Susanna lied. "I had no idea he was working here. Surely it doesn't matter, Digby. Maggie's death had nothing to do with us."

"Well, as long as it doesn't embarrass you," he said. "I thought the workmanship was damned fine, and cheaper than some of the other cabinet-makers in town, so Munford was telling me. Isn't that right, Helen?"

His sister didn't answer him at once. She had seen Adam's face as he looked up and noticed Susanna. A keen observer of others' emotions, Helen Munford had recognized that expression. Watching Susanna now, she suspected that there was more here than Digby realized.

"Carter and Blackwell are cheaper than some," she said, hiding her annoyance as best she could, "if you find the workmanship to your taste."

"Then that's settled," Digby said. "You need not speak to him much yourself, Susanna. Give me a list of what you want and I'll show him over the place. When the designs are ready, you can decide if you want him to do the work or not."

"Yes, Digby," Susanna said meekly. She was aware of Lady Munford's bright eyes watching her. "I think that is much the best idea."

Susanna went to her sister's bedchamber and knocked at the door. "May I come in, Bea? Are you dressed yet?"

"Yes, I'm ready," Beatrice called. She turned as her sister entered, twirling round to show off the full skirts of her pretty blue gown. "This is so elegant, Susanna. I really love it."

"It suits you," Susanna replied. "I'm glad we chose that style for you."

The dress was made of a pale blue satin. It had wide overskirts that were looped in small panniers each side of a petticoat of cream silk, and was heavily embroidered with silver and pearls. The heels of Beatrice's shoes were also encrusted with pearls, and she wore the necklace Susanna had given her. Her hair had been brushed until it shone and was piled up on top of her head beneath a tiara of pearls and diamonds, which Susanna had lent her for the evening.

Susanna's own dress was a pale gold satin and of a much narrower style. The overskirt was draped towards the back and fell to the floor in little tiers of frills. It was plainer, with no embroidery or embellishments, but was extremely elegant. Her hair fell in two shining ringlets onto her shoulder and she wore a band of diamonds round her forehead. She had on the magnificent diamond necklace Digby had given her as a wedding present and a pair of matching eardrops.

"You look beautiful," Beatrice said admiringly. "I think you are the most beautiful woman in London, Susanna."

Susanna shook her head. "You are prejudiced, my love," she said. "There are many other lovely women in London, as you will see this evening."

"Not as lovely as you," Bea said, taking her arm as they went out together. "I'm so looking forward to it, Susanna. My first dance in London. I'm glad Mama didn't come up for it."

"I thought it my duty to ask her," Susanna said. "But I too am glad she refused."

For a moment she remembered her own first dance, when she had met Digby, little thinking that within the year she would be married to him. So much had happened in that year that it seemed much longer. A sigh rose to her lips, but she held it back. Lifting her chin, she put her problems to the back of her mind. She was determined that this should be Beatrice's evening. Her sister was going to find someone nice, someone who would love her and whom she could love in return. No one would force Beatrice to marry a man she despised . . .

Perhaps it was because Beatrice was still such a child that she instantly attracted so much attention from the young men. From her first dance, she was never without a partner, and her happy laughter rang out again and again. Watching her carefree manner, Susanna could not subdue a pang of envy. How different her sister's introduction to society was from her own!

Of course, everything was different now. There was no pressure on Beatrice to marry a rich man, though she seemed determined to do so. It was much easier for her with only an indulgent sister as her chaperone. Lady Patricia had been so very strict with her elder daughter. Now she had abandoned Beatrice to Susanna, saying that she was not well enough to be bothered with finding her a husband.

"I'm sure you can manage very well without me," she had written in her letter. "I know that you would prefer I did not come. I have not forgotten that I am not welcome in your house."

Sometimes Susanna regretted that she had been so harsh to her mother on her wedding day. She could never forget what Lady Patricia had done, of course, but Stephen's death had more than punished her. Now, when she thought about it, Susanna believed she might one day be able to forgive, even if she could never forget. Yet she was glad that her mother had not come. It was better for Beatrice this way . . .

"Lady Digby." Helen Munford's voice startled her. "Your sister looks very well this evening. I should think you will have little difficulty in finding her a suitable match."

"Beatrice is in the fortunate position of being able to choose for herself," Susanna said. "She is very young. Her marriage can wait for a year or two yet."

"Yes, a child still," Helen agreed. "I do not see the Marquis of Brandon here this evening."

"No." Susanna hesitated. "I believe I did not invite him."

"That was cruel of you." Helen tapped her with her fan. "You know he is your most devoted admirer."

"I do not care for him," Susanna said. "Excuse me, I must go to my sister."

As she walked away, Lady Munford stared after her with eyes narrowed to slits in jealousy. Who did that little upstart think she was to snub her? Remembering the expression she had seen on Adam Blackwell's face, Helen felt the envious anger stir inside her. He had dared to refuse her, yet he looked at Digby's wife as if he would kiss the very ground she walked on.

Watching Susanna laughing with her sister, Helen decided that she would be revenged on the pair of them.

"I love your gown," Sylvia Browne said to Beatrice. "It was so kind of your sister to invite me to her dance. Angela includes me in all her entertainments, of course, but I am not always invited to accompany her when she goes out. I shall have no dowry and some of the dowagers ignore me. Angela gets very cross about it."

"I'm not sure that I shall have a dowry," Beatrice admitted. "Or only a very small one. Susanna didn't have one at all."

"But she is so beautiful," Sylvia said. "And your father is Sir William Warwick. My father was only a Reverend. It makes a difference."

"Yes, I suppose so." Beatrice squeezed her arm. "Don't give up, Sylvia. You might meet a rich lord who will fall madly in love with you."

"They all seem to be falling in love with you," Sylvia said, but without malice. "I've hardly been able to get near you all evening."

Beatrice laughed with delight. "I'm having such a good time." She blushed and looked down as she saw the man coming towards them. "I do believe he's going to ask me again. I've already danced with him twice. Susanna said I mustn't dance more than twice with anyone . . ."

"But that's Lord Farringdon," Sylvia said. "The Countess told me that he's one of the wealthiest men in London."

They both stopped talking as the tall, distinguished-looking man approached. Although in his middle years, Lord Vincent Farringdon was attractive and had a pleasant smile. He bowed politely as he asked Beatrice for the honour of the next dance. For a moment she hesitated, then gave him her hand, knowing that it would set the tongues wagging.

Seeing them dance by soon afterwards made Susanna uneasy. Beatrice must know that by accepting Lord Farringdon as her partner for a third time, she was practically inviting him to be a serious contender for her hand?

Susanna had nothing against Lord Farringdon. Indeed, she thought him a gentleman and his manners were perfect. Yet she could not help feeling that Beatrice would be making a mistake if she allowed him to propose to her. He was far too old. Susanna decided she must talk to her sister. Beatrice must take her time and wait for the right man to present himself. A man who could give her happiness . . .

Relaxing, Susanna concentrated on her task of being a good hostess. She meant to cultivate all the dowagers with young, pleasant sons or nephews on her sister's behalf. Beatrice was going to be given every chance to find a husband she could really love and respect!

Moving amongst her guests with an almost regal assurance, Susanna was unaware of the angry eyes watching her from across the room. Unaware that her husband's sister was already planning her downfall and humiliation . . .

"Well, Munford, your library is almost finished," Lady Helen said as she walked into her husband's bedchamber. "And are you satisfied with it?"

Lord Munford was suspicious. She was up to something. It was years since she had visited him here. They had given up the physical side of marriage long ago.

"What do you want?" he asked. "If it's money, I refuse to extend your allowance yet again. It's costing me enough to build that library."

Money was his weakness. Lady Helen looked at him calculatingly. He'd always had a mean streak in him. She knew that he had engaged the services of Adam Blackwell because he believed it would annoy her. Would he listen to her now, or turn his back? Charles was unpredictable.

"I've been thinking," she said. "I believe I know of a way

in which you could save yourself at least some of the cost of your library."

"I've already paid for the materials," he grumbled. "The man refused to use anything but the best."

"Then it would serve him right if you tricked him," Lady Helen said, her eyes intent as she saw that she had caught his interest. "Why should you pay so much for workmanship that is not of the highest quality? I believe he has overcharged you. It would be only fair if you were to come off the winner in this, Charles. After all, he has benefited from all the orders that have come his way because of it."

"That's true," Munford muttered, still wary of trusting her. "What are you trying to say, Helen? Out with it. I've an appointment in half an hour."

"Adam Blackwell has ideas above his station," she said. "He wants to be a gentleman. I think that he would be flattered if you asked him to take a glass of wine with you . . . and then . . ."

"And then?" her husband demanded irritably. "I don't see how that will help me recover the cost of the library."

How stupid he was, she thought. Did she have to explain everything to him? With a few words, she outlined her plan, watching as comprehension and then amusement showed in his eyes.

"Damn it, Helen," he chortled. "I like it. I like it very much . . ."

Beatrice tore the wrappings off the parcel her sister had given her, exclaiming over the pair of pearl bracelets inside. She jumped out of bed and hugged Susanna.

"They're beautiful," she said. "They will go with my necklace. I'm so lucky."

"There is a pile of cards for you downstairs," Susanna said. "Someone seems to have told our acquaintances that it is your birthday."

"Not me," Beatrice said. "At least, I only told Sylvia."

"Then she has been busy," Susanna said. "Some floral tributes have arrived, and a parcel. I believe that might be from Lord Farringdon." She hesitated as her sister blushed. "Don't be in too much hurry, Bea. There's plenty of time."

"What do you mean?" Bea's cheeks were hot.

"I'm not criticizing you," Susanna said. "Just be sure you know what you want, dearest . . ." She relaxed as Beatrice played with her bracelets. "I shan't say any more. It's your birthday and I know that Digby has something for you, too. He is impatient to give it to you."

"I shall dress at once and come down to breakfast," Beatrice said, her moment of embarrassment gone. "Not that I'm hungry. It's too exciting."

Susanna smiled but said nothing as she went out. Digby had bought the girl a present that could not be carried upstairs. She had been surprised and touched by his thoughtfulness, especially as he knew that she had already bought the bracelets for Beatrice.

"I like the girl," he'd said when she raised her brows. "She was the only one of your family who seemed to care when you were ill. Besides, she's an innocent, biddable child."

His bleak tone told Susanna that he was angry with her again. Angry that he had failed once more in his most recent attempt to penetrate her. Her arms were covered with bruises where he had pinched her afterwards, taking out his disappointment on her as usual. He wasn't exactly violent towards her, not in a way that made her fear for her life, but he was increasingly spiteful, both in actions and manner. Sometimes, when he left her, she felt that she could not bear it any longer. No matter how many pretty gowns she bought, it could never make up for the misery she was forced to suffer at his hands.

Beatrice was soon down. Digby gave her an indulgent look; evidently his bad temper did not extend to his wife's sister.

"Now, miss," he said. "Come outside and see what I have for you."

"You are very good to me," Beatrice said, excited despite her private unease concerning his treatment of her sister. "I cannot imagine what it can be."

"Just you wait and see." Digby enjoyed teasing her. He was always at his best when he felt he was being looked up to by someone as innocent and sweet as this girl. He sometimes thought that it would have been better if he had married her instead of Susanna. Perhaps then he would have been able to act like a man, instead of being frozen by his wife's coldness.

Beatrice followed him outside, and saw the beautiful chestnut filly being held by a groom. She looked at Digby in astonishment.

"Is she really for me?" Her pleasure showed on her face as he nodded. "What is her name?"

"That's up to you, miss. I heard you tell your sister that the one thing you missed in town was being able to ride — so there you are. Now you will be able to canter in Rotten Row and have all the gallants after you!"

"Isn't that where the courtesans go?" Beatrice dimpled. "My mother would have a fainting fit if she thought I was riding there."

"You would not ride alone, of course," Digby said. "We can't have you losing your reputation, but I dare say I can spare a groom to take you now and then, or Susanna might go with you. I might even stir myself."

Beatrice thanked him, but was uneasy. Sometimes she disliked the way he looked at her . . . almost as if . . . but she must have imagined it. He was in love with Susanna. Why else would he have married her?

"I shall ride her today. I'm sure Susanna will spare the time to come with me; if not I can take a groom." She looked at Digby, her cheeks a pale rose. "It was very kind of you to buy the filly for me, sir."

"And what do I get?" Digby asked. "Will you not thank me properly?"

Beatrice hesitated, then kissed his cheek, which pleased

him. He seemed about to speak again, but then Susanna came out and he turned away, telling the groom to stable the horse.

"Have her ready for Miss Warwick in an hour," he said. He gave his wife a stony look. "I have business to attend, madam. I shall not be here for dinner this evening, so you need not wait for me."

Beatrice linked arms with her sister as they went back into the house. Feeling Susanna tremble, she glanced at her sideways.

"Is something wrong?"

"No . . ." Susanna attempted to look cheerful. She couldn't tell her sister how unhappy she really was. It would spoil her pleasure in the trip to London. "No, nothing is the matter, Bea. I'm just a little tired. I didn't sleep very well . . ."

For a moment the pain struck into her heart as she remembered her husband's unkindness in their bedroom the previous night. She wished yet again that she had not been forced to marry him. If only . . . tears filled her eyes as she thought of Adam Blackwell, but she blinked them away. She had loved him so much but it was obvious from his behaviour the last time they'd met that he had never truly cared for her. All Adam was really interested in was his work . . . his ambition to be a famous cabinet-maker, to rise in the world and earn a fortune. It was for this that he had left Norfolk, breaking her heart when she was still a child.

Susanna found it difficult to believe that Adam could be so uncaring, but he was no longer the young man who had rescued her from the gipsies. Something had changed him . . .

"So, it is finished at last." Lord Munford looked round the library with satisfaction. The last shelf was in place; a magnificent circular table, with a top that had been inlaid with different coloured woods to resemble a sunburst, graced the centre of the room and all the various steps and chairs were assembled. "You've done a good job, Blackwell."

"Thank you, my lord." Adam accepted the compliment with a smile. It was his best ever commission and he was genuinely pleased with the results. Such work could not fail to attract more commissions and already he had begun to receive new orders on the strength of it. He glanced at his silver pocket watch. "I think I should be getting home. My wife will be expecting me for supper."

"We must take a glass of wine together before you go," Lord Munford said. "Come into the back parlour, Blackwell. My friend Wexford was talking about commissioning a set of dining chairs from you. There are a few of my friends visiting with me. We were just about to play a hand of cards." He paused, then, "Perhaps you would care to join us? We play for small stakes. Just a guinea or two."

Adam hesitated, knowing that he ought to leave at once. Yet it was a rare honour to be asked to sit down with a member of the aristocracy. And he must not offend his host. As yet Lord Munford had paid only for the materials, which amounted to no more than a half of the cost. He was owed over five hundred guineas.

"Well, perhaps a glass of wine," he said. "I wonder if I could ask you to pay something on the account . . ."

"Of course." Lord Munford smiled at him. "All in good time, Blackwell. A glass of madeira first and then perhaps a hand or two of whist . . . then I shall settle in full. There, you can't refuse such an offer, can you?"

Adam gave in reluctantly. The aristocracy were not always the best of payers. One wrong word at this moment and he might have to wait months or even years for his money.

"No, my lord," he said. "Of course not. I shall be delighted to take a glass of wine with you."

Adam's face was expressionless as he laid down his cards three hours later, but inside he felt sick and angry at his own stupidity. How could he have been such a fool as to go on playing when he had gone down heavily time after time?

"I believe that is five hundred guineas I owe you, my lord," he said. "I'm afraid I cannot raise that much immediately."

"By my reckoning it just about covers the amount owing for the work you've done, Blackwell," Lord Munford replied with a little shrug. "Give or take a few guineas. I suggest we call it quits – what say you?"

"Perhaps that would be best if you are agreeable," Adam said as he rose from the table. "And now if you will excuse me, gentlemen." The room seemed to be spinning and he felt a little hazy. Lord Munford's madeira was too strong for his taste. He had drunk only one glass and it had gone straight to his head.

He walked from the room, his back stiff, shoulders squared as the laughter began behind him. They were laughing at him, of course. No doubt they had thought it a fine joke. He suspected that he had walked straight into a trap. He had been allowed to win over the first few games to keep him at the table. He could hardly rise a winner when they insisted on playing on and for ever higher stakes. But then he began to go down again and again. Still, he had tried to keep his head and it was not until the last hand that he had risked more than fifty guineas in a desperate attempt to regain what he had lost, and of course he had been trumped by Lord Munford. The amount of his losses had astounded him and he realized that it had been planned from the start. Probably the cards had been marked and he had been cheated, but he could not prove his suspicions.

Leaving the house, Adam walked slowly, anger building inside him. What a damned fool he had been, allowing himself to be flattered into joining Munford's friends at the gaming tables. He ought to have known that they were using him, amusing themselves at his expense. No doubt they had been laying bets on whether or not he would be stupid enough to lose all the money that was due to him. And he had walked straight into the little trap Munford had set for him.

Surely he had learned his lesson this time! Cursing, Adam swore that he would never again be taken in by offers of friendship from the aristocracy. In future he would keep his dealings with them on a strictly business level. His heart sank as he realized that he had to tell Robert what had happened. He had thrown away the whole of more than six months' work!

But he felt so strange. There was a hammering at his temple and he swayed as the pavement seemed to come up to meet him. Surely he could not be drunk! He had taken only one glass of wine . . . strong wine that had made him feel odd. Suddenly, Adam bent over and vomited in the gutter. As he tasted the bitterness in his mouth, he knew what was wrong. He had been drugged. Not enough to make him lose control, but sufficient to cause him to be hazy so that he could not think clearly, to keep him sitting at the table until he had lost the required sum.

Ruefully, Adam sat down on the pavement as his head swam. Lord Munford would never have thought of such a cunning plot on his own. He knew who he had to thank for this. How she must be laughing now . . .

"I'm sorry, Robert," Adam said. "I was a fool and there's no more I can say. I'll make it up somehow, but I don't know how."

Robert coughed, clutching his chest as the pain struck. His face was grey and the evidence of his illness was deeply ingrained in his face, making him look much older than his years. The pain was getting much worse now. Sometimes he brought up blood and it was becoming harder and harder to breathe.

"It's an unkind lesson to learn, Adam," he said when he had conquered his coughing. "But it could have been worse. I've known master craftsmen who've worked for years on the house of a nobleman and died without ever receiving a penny piece for their trouble. If this teaches you to be sharper in business, then it was money well spent. Remember in future to arrange for stage payments and stop work if you're not paid your dues. Most folk are honest, but it's always best to ask a few questions before you take on a large commission."

"I don't know what to say." Adam's face was angry. "I feel such a fool. I'm sure I was cheated. They drugged the wine. It made me ill in the street."

"You would be a fool to say that in public. No, Adam, you acted in the only way you could, with dignity. We must swallow this loss. Lord Munford has put several customers our way, and I'm sure there will be more. This is just something we have to accept."

"Thank you, sir." Adam looked at him gratefully. "I'll work harder until . . ."

"You already work all hours," Robert said with a faint smile. "I've not regretted our bargain, Adam. And this does not change my mind. When I'm gone, I shall rest easy in my grave knowing that Jane and Lily have you to look after them."

Adam frowned as he saw the dark shadows beneath Robert's eyes. "Is the pain worse again?"

"It's bad enough," Robert said. "I've accepted it can't be long now."

"Is there anything I can do for you, sir?"

Robert shook his head. "Just go home to your wife, Adam. She is approaching her time now and women get moody when their bodies become heavy and ungainly. She needs your support now."

"Yes, I know." Adam sighed inwardly. Jane had become irritable and sharper-tongued of late. He knew it was because of the child she was carrying, but the atmosphere in the house had become more and more strained.

"There's no need for Jane or Lily to know what happened

at Munford's," Robert said. "Women don't understand these things. It will remain our secret, Adam."

Adam felt relieved. He had not welcomed the prospect of telling Jane what a fool he had been, especially in her present mood.

"Thank you, Robert," he said. "I've learned my lesson now. I'll not be taken in again like that."

Adam heard the cry from upstairs as soon as he entered the house. It was Jane. He started for the stairs but was stopped before he reached the upper landing by the little servant girl he had hired to help his wife.

"It's the baby, isn't it?" he asked. "It's come early. What happened, Mabs? Did Jane fall and hurt herself?"

"She took a tumble in the yard," Mabs said. "But the doctor said there's nothing to worry about. It's only a few days too soon. He's sure everything will be all right."

Adam thanked her and hurried on to the bedroom. The doctor and midwife were working on Jane, encouraging her to push harder. Just as Adam moved towards the bed, Jane screamed in agony and he was in time to see the arrival of his son, who came into the world with a little whoosh and began to cry lustily. As the midwife whisked the bawling infant away to cleanse and dry it, Adam anxiously bent over Jane.

"Forgive me for not being here sooner," he said. "I was delayed at the Munfords' and then I went to see Robert."

"Is something wrong?" Jane asked. "Father isn't worse, is he?"

"Stop worrying, Jane," Adam reassured her. "Robert is as always. It was a business matter."

"Oh, business . . ." Jane sighed, closing her eyes as the midwife came back to cover her up. "It's always business with you, Adam."

"You shouldn't be here, sir," the midwife said, a scolding note in her voice. "Go away now and let me look after your wife. You can come back later."

Realizing he was in the way, Adam walked to the cot and looked down at the child wrapped in a linen cloth. The baby's face was red and ugly and his hair was bright ginger. Adam felt a surge of repulsion, which was swiftly replaced by shame. How could he dislike his own son on sight?

Leaving the room, he felt oddly shut out. Jane had been exhausted by the pain and effort of giving birth of course, but there had been a tone of rejection that had nothing to do with either. It had been creeping in for a while now. She seemed to resent the hours he spent at his work.

Shrugging, Adam took off his coat as he went downstairs. It was just that he had arrived at a bad moment, he thought. Everything would be as it had been when Jane was on her feet again. Meanwhile, he had work to do . . .

It did occur to him that he might have had different feelings about the birth of his first son if . . . but that was foolishness. He would do better to put that night with Susanna right out of his mind. She was married now to a wealthy man, and that of course was what she had always intended. It would not have altered anything if she'd found that foolish note he'd placed in a secret drawer of her marriage chest. It had been a whim, just as was the tiny broken heart he'd woven into the design of the drawer fronts. A message that might have changed their lives if she had cared . . . but of course she had not. She was no doubt quite happy in her new life.

And he had work to do!

"Do we really have to go this evening, Digby?" Susanna asked with a sigh. Her husband looked at her inquiringly and she pulled a face. "It's just that I don't much care for Helen's friends."

"Nor I," he agreed. "But we cannot avoid this dinner, I'm afraid." His eyes narrowed at her expression. "Is there any particular reason for your reluctance, Susanna?"

She hesitated, then, "I understand the Marquis of Brandon will be there. He – he frightens me, Digby. I told you about that evening when you were in the north. He forced his company on me and would have insisted on escorting me home if your sister had not intervened."

"You cannot imagine he meant to abduct you?"

"I – I don't know." Susanna felt chilled as she thought about the Marquis's behaviour since that night. "He has made suggestions, Digby. Sometimes he seems to imply that I should become his mistress . . . Oh, he says nothing that I could rebuke him for. It is all innuendo. An inflexion in his voice or a lift of his brow."

"Men of the Marquis's stamp are simply a nuisance," said Digby with a shrug. "You must learn to cope with them. Be cold and distant. He will soon tire of his game."

"Perhaps."

She smothered her sigh, glad that at least Beatrice would be saved the necessity of going with them. She had been invited to spend a few days in the country with the Earl and Countess of Grafton. Lord Farringdon would also be a guest, and Susanna believed that he might make an offer for her sister. His attentions had become more and more marked of late, and scarcely a day passed without him calling to at least leave his card. Susanna knew that Sylvia teased Beatrice unmercifully about his devotion, but as yet he had not come up to scratch. Susanna hadn't said any more on the subject to her sister but she hoped that Beatrice would give the matter careful consideration.

Susanna stood passively while Digby placed a heavy velvet cloak about her shoulders. Several weeks had passed since that evening at Lady Munford's when Brandon had forced his attentions on her, and she had tried many times to discourage them. It had not deterred him in his pursuit of her. Indeed, he seemed amused by her efforts and more than ever determined to overcome her resistance. She was convinced that he believed he would prevail in the end.

Susanna was silent throughout the drive to her sister-in-law's house. She hoped that she would not be forced to sit beside the Marquis at dinner, but her fears were realized when he claimed the privilege of taking her in.

"I persuaded Lady Helen to rearrange her table so that I could have the pleasure of your company," he said.

Glancing across at Lady Munford, Susanna saw the gleam of sly amusement in her eyes. She had done it deliberately, knowing how much Susanna disliked the Marquis, as punishment because Susanna had refused several invitations to visit her of late.

There was nothing Susanna could do but smile and accept the Marquis's arm. She was forced to sit beside him for the next two hours, listening to a stream of malicious gossip and moving her leg away every time he pressed his knee against hers. His predatory manner made her feel like a tethered sheep who senses the approach of a wolf.

"And so the Duke found himself saddled with another bastard," he said at the end of one of his anecdotes. "But what is one more when the world knows each of his three younger sons has a different father?"

"How can the world know?" asked Susanna, irritated by his slanderous tales. "Has the Duchess ever admitted her infidelity?"

"She would not be such a fool." The Marquis shrugged, his hooded eyes speculative. "Provided she is discreet no one really cares, except perhaps her husband – but he was a fool for marrying a young and beautiful girl when he's in his dotage. She was bound to cuckold him. And the succession was secured by his first wife, so it hardly matters who fathered these brats."

"Well, I think it's a shame," Susanna said. "I've seen him looking at her. He dotes on her."

"Ah, you are too virtuous, Lady Digby. You would have us believe that you intend to be faithful to your own husband."

Susanna's cheeks grew warm under his scrutiny. "I think that is my own affair, sir," she replied, her voice aloof and cold. "Please change the subject."

"Very well." A smile of disbelief played across his mouth. "Munford was telling me an amusing story about his library."

"Oh?" Susanna saw the malicious gleam in his eyes. "I believe it is very fine. It was all the work of one craftsman, was it not?"

"So I was told. Munford got it for a fraction of its worth."

"How was that?"

"The fellow was a gullible fool. Munford invited him to sit down with his cronies at the card table. Foolishly, the man was flattered and became embroiled in their little schemes. Of course they let him win small sums for a start. He ended by losing almost five hundred guineas to Munford."

"Five hundred guineas!" Susanna cried. The glee with which he told the story disgusted her. "How could he afford to lose so much?"

"He could not pay, of course." The Marquis smirked. "So Munford took the library in lieu. Rather neat, don't you think?"

"What a cruel trick," Susanna said. "All those months of work gone for nothing."

"Serves the fellow right for getting ideas above his station. If he had been less blown up in his own conceit, he must have known they were laughing behind his back. A tradesman should not try to ape his betters."

Susanna was silent. She could not deny that what the Marquis said made sense. She wondered at Adam's recklessness in sitting down with Munford and his friends. He ought to have known that they had not truly accepted him as one of them. Her father had liked and respected Tom Blackwell, but he would never have thought of asking Tom to dine at the Hall. Had Adam really imagined he could cross the divide so easily? Perhaps when he had established himself and become wealthy enough . . . But even then he would need to buy a country estate and cultivate his neighbours. Perhaps even buy himself a title . . .

Susanna was thoughtful as she followed her hostess from the room at the end of the meal. For a while at least she was free of the Marquis's attentions. No doubt he would seek her out when the gentlemen had finished their port, but for now she could relax. Her thoughts were with Adam Blackwell. To lose five hundred guineas must have been a serious setback for him. She had heard that he was gaining a reputation for the quality of his work, but five hundred guineas . . .

"Susanna, why so sad?" Lady Munford appeared suddenly at her side. "Are you feeling neglected?"

"I beg your pardon?" Susanna stared at her in surprise.

Helen winked knowingly. "Shall I send someone to bring the gentlemen from their port?"

"Not on my account, ma'am."

"So modest!" Helen seemed in a good humour. "You need not fear that I shall breathe a word to Digby. Your secret is safe with me."

"Secret?" Susanna was wary now. "I have no secrets from my husband."

"La! How serious she looks." Lady Munford rapped her playfully with a painted fan. "The Marquis is devoted to you. He talks of you constantly, Susanna. I should be the last one to criticize you if you were to . . . shall we say amuse yourself?"

Susanna's cheeks burned. "I have no interest in the Marquis, ma'am."

"Then you should have." Helen Munford's eyes narrowed. "Do not tell me that Digby's attentions are enough for you. You are young and beautiful. You should have lovers, Susanna. The Marquis would be an excellent tutor. He could teach you so much . . ."

"Lady Munford!" Susanna cried, shocked. "How can you suggest that I should cuckold Digby?"

"You are a fool if you don't," came the sharp reply. "Why be faithful to a man who cannot satisfy you? Life is there for the taking. Eat your fill of its fruits, Susanna. Gorge yourself on its pleasures while you may. One day it will be too late for anything but regrets."

As she moved away, Susanna stared after her. Her suggestion was shocking. To come from Digby's own sister . . . And yet something inside her was echoing the sentiments, outrageous though they were. Her marriage was no marriage. Digby seldom came to her bed these days. She would never have children, never know the sweetness of a lover's touch. Unless . . . Memories swept over her, twisting at her heart, making her weak with longing.

Seeing the gentlemen returning, Susanna recalled the main theme of Lady Munford's words and turned away in disgust. She wanted nothing more to do with the Marquis. The very idea made the vomit rise in her throat. Neither he nor any of the other men present appealed to her sufficiently to make her consider risking Digby's displeasure. There was only one man she had ever wanted, but he had made his feelings towards her plain.

Remembering the coldness of Adam's eyes, Susanna wondered just what she had done to make him look at her that way. What sin had she committed that would make him hate her? He must have loved her a little that night in the summerhouse . . . or had he? Sometimes she thought that she could bear anything if only she knew that he had loved her once.

"Do not keep the horses standing, Maxwell." Susanna pulled the hood of her thick cloak up over her head. "You may return for me in half an hour."

"Yes, my lady."

Susanna hesitated on the pavement outside the shop as her carriage was driven away. She had spent a restless night deciding whether or not to come. Adam's designs had lain on her dressing table for weeks while she delayed her decision. They were all that she could ask for and more, but it would mean him actually working in the house and she was not sure she could bear that. She glanced up at the sign above the workroom door – *Carter & Blackwell. Makers of Fine Furniture*. Why was she so nervous? After all, it was Digby's suggestion that she should use this particular firm. Yet that was not why she had come. The Marquis's spiteful tale had aroused her anger and concern. A large commission from her might help to make up for what Adam had lost, and despite everything she wanted to help him. Drawing a deep breath to steady her nerves, she lifted the latch and went in.

No one was in the shop. Seeing a little brass bell on a table just inside, she rang for attention. Her eyes moved round the room. It was not large but of a sufficient size to display a satinwood card table with a D-end, which could be folded and stood against the wall when not in use, a set of mahogany dining chairs with shield backs, a walnut bureau, a sideboard with painted panels and eight tapered legs, besides many small pieces. She was examining a brass-bound wine bucket when a door opened behind her.

"Forgive me," the voice said. "I hope you have not been waiting long? My wife has just risen from her confinement and I . . ."

Adam's words died on his lips as he looked into those wonderful blue eyes, the eyes that still haunted his dreams. The eyes he'd thought of when he'd looked at the reddened face of his firstborn son and felt nothing but disappointment.

"Lady Digby," he said at last. "This is an unexpected honour."

"Mr Blackwell," she replied, the words sticking to her tongue. She turned away, forcing herself to appear calm. "I have come about those designs you did for me. It has taken me some time to decide. I am thinking of having the walls hung with silk and the old panelling replaced, which would mean you working in the house. I'm now ready to commission the furniture. I want to make a start with my salon. Some elegant chairs, occasional tables, a few mirrors . . . Your designs were exactly what I require, but

283

I need much more than I had at first thought. I believe I shall furnish the whole house this year instead of doing it gradually. If you could show me some more of your designs . . ."

"Of course," he replied with a coldness he was far from feeling. "If you will tell me what style you had in mind. I have several folders of designs I have made for other people. Naturally, I could always work to your own specifications."

Susanna was hurt by his tone. Was he still angry because of Maggie? Had that turned him against her? She had thought he had forgiven her for Stephen's treatment of his sister. How could he be so unfeeling towards her after what had happened between them that night in the summerhouse? Even if it had meant nothing to him, there was no need for this anger. She hesitated, then took a step towards him, holding out her hand in unconscious supplication.

"You know that Stephen was murdered soon after my wedding," she said, a break in her voice. "Your sister's lover confessed to her murder at his hanging – you cannot still blame my brother for her death?"

"No – Maggie knew what she was doing. It seems it was as much her fault as Stephen's. And he paid a heavy price for seducing my sister. It was a tragedy for both families."

"Then – then why do you hate me?"

Adam stared at her in disbelief. "You can ask me that – after what you did?"

"What I did?" His anger made her determined to explain. "I promised to meet you in the summerhouse that night, but I could not. I did come to the cottage to apologize when I was well enough but . . ."

"When you were well . . ." Adam's eyes were hard. "But you were there that night. I saw you before they knocked me senseless."

"Before . . ." Susanna's heart jerked. "What are you saying? Who knocked you senseless? I don't understand."

"I came to the summerhouse even though I had learned you were to be married. They were waiting for me . . . Three of them armed with cudgels . . ." His look challenged her, daring her to deny her involvement. "But you were there. I saw your dress . . ."

"I was not at the summerhouse, Adam." Susanna's face was very pale. "You must believe me. My mother had me bound and gagged the morning after . . . the morning after she saw us together in the summerhouse. I was locked in my room and given only bread and water . . . I almost starved."

"Your own mother did that to you?" Adam drew a sharp breath as he realized it was the truth. "The devil take her! Then it must have been she who had me beaten."

Susanna recoiled as though he had slapped her. "You thought it was I who . . . You thought I would do that after . . ." Stricken, she turned away.

Adam stood in silence, looking at her rigid back. It was difficult to take in what she had said. He had been so sure that she had betrayed him.

Susanna forced herself to face him and saw the shocked disbelief in his eyes. He still doubted her. He still thought that she . . . The pain was like a sudden knife thrust, making her gasp.

"Excuse me, I must go."

Adam moved to prevent her flight. "Please," he said, his voice throbbing with urgency. "Please don't go, Susanna. Forgive me. I've been a fool. I thought you were like her. I thought you were using me, that you wanted a diversion before your marriage to an older man."

"You are insulting, sir." Susanna's face was suffused with hot colour. "Pray stand aside and let me pass."

"In a moment." Adam's grip tightened on her arm. "That night you said you loved me – did you mean it?"

Furious, hurt that he could compare her to Lady Patricia, that he could believe she had been using him, Susanna would not look at him as she said, "At the time I may

285

have done. I was very young and foolish. Pray let me go now."

"I meant it," he said, his voice deep with emotion. "I meant every word."

She looked up then, her eyes wide. "Adam . . ."

The door from the workshop opened and an anxious-looking young lad of perhaps fourteen came in. He was carrying the arm of an elbow chair.

"I can't seem to get the bend right . . ." Becoming aware of Susanna, he faltered and then stammered awkwardly, "B-Beg pardon, ma'am. I'm sorry, Mr Blackwell, I didn't know anyone was with you."

"It's all right, Jem," Adam said. "Lady Digby was just looking round. You go back to your bench. I'll be with you in a moment."

"Yes, sir. Beg your pardon, my lady."

Susanna shook her head, and moved towards the door. "I was about to leave. We shall discuss the designs another day, Mr Blackwell. When my coachman returns, you may tell him that I've gone to the mantua-maker's in the next street."

With that, she went out. It had been a mistake to come, she thought as she walked away. She ought to have known that it was useless. Even if Adam had not believed she could be so cruel . . . that he could believe it for a moment! But even if he had not, it was hopeless. She was married. Adam was married. His wife had borne him a child. They could never be anything to each other. She must forget him. She must never go back to his shop again . . .

After a restless night, Susanna was in her boudoir when the maid brought her a letter from her sister. Susanna grew anxious as she read the scribbled message. Beatrice begged her to forgive her, but the Countess had asked her to stay on for a few days longer and she had agreed. Susanna puzzled over the last two lines, which looked as if they had been scribbled at the last moment.

"Sylvia's brother John has arrived unexpectedly. We are all going for a picnic by the lake. Yours in haste, Bea." Then at the very bottom. "I wish I knew what to do! I think perhaps you were right. I'll tell you when I come back."

Remembering her sister's blush when the Reverend John Browne was mentioned at the Countess of Grafton's house, Susanna wondered. What ought she to do if her suspicions were right? Lady Patricia would expect her younger daughter to marry well, but if Bea were in love with a poor clergyman . . . As she put the letter away, Susanna vowed she would never allow her sister to be forced into an unhappy marriage. Beatrice should never suffer as she was suffering now.

Feeling the sting of tears, Susanna wiped them away impatiently. It was no use looking back. After what Adam had said to her . . . No, she could not face him again. There was no point.

Closing the lid of her spinet, Susanna walked to the salon window and looked out. The streets were almost deserted; even the hawkers were silent for once, and there was not an organ grinder or a ballad singer in sight, no one she could summon to entertain her for an hour or so. She had not had one visitor that day. Even Digby had gone to see some sporting friends, leaving her alone. She was bored and restless, unable to concentrate on her books or her embroidery.

Suddenly, she pulled on the bellrope, summoning a servant. "Have my carriage brought round," Susanna said, when he asked her pleasure. "I'm going out."

"Shall I inform your maid, my lady?"

"No." Susanna ignored his look of surprise. "I don't need Dulcia today."

Leaving him staring, she went upstairs to put on her cloak.

*   *   *

Susanna dismissed her coachman outside the mantua-maker's she had visited the previous week, telling him to return at a certain time. She spent only ten minutes in the shop. It was no use, she had to see Adam, just once more. After a week of restless nights, she had finally reached her decision. She would see him and talk to him, and then she would forget him.

It was early autumn now. In July of that year, Captain Cook had returned to England after a long sea voyage. London had talked of little else but his discoveries for weeks. He had spent several months in Tahiti, then sailed on to claim a new colony for Britain, which he named Botany Bay. It had been an exciting time as people wondered at the strange tales he told of this new land, the wild savages who inhabited it and the even stranger creatures Captain Cook had seen there. But now it was September, and London was becoming thin of company as people's thoughts turned to the country and hunting. Digby talked of returning to Surrey soon. The winter would be long and lonely, and Susanna might be snowed in for weeks at a time with only her husband for company. She had to see Adam before they left.

Lost in her thoughts, Susanna was not aware of the man who had just left a tavern across the street. She walked with care, avoiding the ruts where puddles remained after a storm the previous evening, lifting her gown so as not to muddy the hem.

"And where are you going, my pretty one?"

Susanna was startled. Giving a cry of alarm, she looked up into the hooded eyes of the Marquis of Brandon, experiencing the familiar surge of revulsion. Where had he come from? She had not seen him. As he leant towards her she could smell the brandy on his breath. He was drunk! Instinct made her recoil from him. Sober, the Marquis was difficult enough. Who knew what he might do in this condition? And Susanna was alone! She had dismissed her servants so that they could not carry tales to Digby.

She pulled away in fear as the Marquis took hold of her arm.

"Pray let me go, sir."

"Damn me, if it isn't Lady Virtue herself," the Marquis muttered, almost more surprised than she. He had seen a pretty face and followed his instincts without realizing who she was. "What are you doing here?"

"Visiting a mantua-maker," Susanna said. "Please release my arm, sir."

The Marquis's eyes gleamed. Though he'd drunk deeply at the tavern with some persons of doubtful character he liked to cultivate for their usefulness, he was still alert enough to sense a mystery. Ladies of quality did not roam the streets alone. He looked for a carriage or sedan chair, his excitement rising as he realized that she did not even have a maid with her. She must have an assignation!

"So you're not quite the innocent you would have us all believe," he murmured. "It's a lovers' tryst, I'll be bound."

"Sir, you are mistaken."

Susanna tried to wrench away from him, but his grip tightened on her arm. His fingers were digging into her, hurting her tender flesh. She saw the leering grin on his slack mouth and felt a frisson of fear.

"Well, my pretty one, your lover will have to wait his turn. You've given me the opportunity I've been hoping for."

Susanna gave a cry of alarm as he began to force her across the street towards his own coach, which she now saw was drawn up at the side of the road. This was desperate indeed. Once the Marquis had her inside she would have little chance of escape. It was a golden opportunity for him, and Susanna had handed it to him on a plate. She would never dare to complain to Digby, because she could not explain her own conduct.

"Let me go!"

Susanna struggled furiously, tugging and kicking at his shins. There were a few people in the street; a baker's boy carrying a basket of loaves on his head went hurrying by, hardly glancing their way. A man driving a dray cart looked at them and then grinned, obviously thinking it a quarrel between husband and wife. Two women cleaning their front steps frowned and then went indoors, closing their doors firmly as if to shut out the indecent sight.

Susanna screamed out, "Help me! Please help me! He's trying to abduct me!"

"Be quiet, you little vixen," the Marquis said, clasping a hand over her mouth. Susanna bit him and he cried out. "Damn you!"

Taking advantage of his surprise, she jerked free of his hold and began to run down the street. He gave chase almost at once. Now people had begun to take more notice. Some of them looked uncertain whether or not to interfere, then she ran straight into the arms of a man who had stepped out into the road. She glanced up, relief sweeping over her as she saw his face.

"The Marquis . . ." she gasped, trying to catch her breath. "He – he was trying to get me into his carriage . . ."

Adam saw the fear in her eyes. He nodded, pushing her behind him as the Marquis stopped and looked at them, hesitating.

"Go into the shop and wait for me there," Adam said. "I'll handle this."

Susanna did as he ordered without arguing. She watched through the window as the two men met in the road, holding her breath. The Marquis was carrying a swordstick – would he attempt to use it? Adam was unarmed and vulnerable. He could easily be killed. She waited anxiously as the seconds ticked past. They appeared to be talking, but from inside the shop she could hear nothing. Now the Marquis was walking away. It seemed that he had given up without much of an argument. She watched as he climbed into his carriage. Adam stood outside on the path until the coach drove away. As he came into the shop, she drew a deep breath.

"What did you say to him?"

"Nothing much." Adam looked grim. "He said he had mistaken you for a doxy. He sent his apologies. He had drunk a little too much, that's all."

"No . . ." Susanna shook her head. "He lied to you. I know him, Adam. He – he has always wanted me. He was trying to abduct me."

"Then you must be careful of him. I didn't like the look of him, Susanna."

"No one would help me," she said, moving towards him. "If you hadn't come . . ."

"They probably thought you were his mistress," Adam said seriously. "It is not usual for a woman of your quality to be walking the streets alone. Where are your servants?"

"I – I sent them away." Susanna glanced down. "I was coming here . . ." She hesitated, then looked at him directly. "This is the second time you've saved me from being abducted, Adam."

Something in her eyes made him catch his breath. He felt the desire swirling inside him, a fierce longing that made him ache with the need to hold her in his arms. His need of her made him forget caution.

"Susanna," he breathed, reaching out for her. "Susanna, my darling."

"Adam . . ." She gazed up at him. "If my mother had not locked me up I was ready to run away with you. I love you. I have loved you since I was a child – you must believe me."

"Yes," he said. "I do."

He was about to take her into his arms when he became aware of a customer at the window. He moved away and began to show Susanna the intricacies of a small revolving bookcase, pointing out the elegant reeded spindles.

As the customer moved away, Adam's manner became urgent. "I have to see you," he said. "In private."

"Yes," Susanna agreed eagerly. "Somewhere we can be alone."

"I will find a place," Adam promised. "Will you visit me again?"

"Will you furnish my salon for me?" she asked. "I loved those designs you did in satinwood and ebony. They were so original and elegant. It will give me an excuse for coming here – and you are one of the finest craftsmen in London. I really want you to work for me."

"Come next week at the same time." His voice was soft with love. "It will be my pleasure to do whatever you wish . . ."

CHAPTER SEVENTEEN

Adam could hear the baby crying when he walked into the kitchen. Feeling hungry, he looked for signs of supper but the stewpot was empty. Jane didn't seem to have started to prepare their meal as yet. Sighing, he pulled off his shirt, took a kettle of water from the fire and poured it into the sink. Adding some cold from a jug on the floor, he began to wash to the waist. He had just finished drying when Jane came in. Her face looked flushed and she was obviously tired.

"What are we having for supper?" Adam asked.

"For goodness' sake, can't you wait five minutes?" Jane snapped irritably. "I've only just got Robert to sleep. He's been crying all day. I think he has a colic."

"You should have sent for the doctor."

"That's right, blame me," she said. "I haven't had time to think of anything, what with all the washing and . . ."

"Where is Mabs? You shouldn't need to do so much now that you have a girl to help you."

"She's ill," Jane replied, scowling. "Besides, she's hopeless at cooking. I have to watch her all the time."

"Then perhaps we should employ a cook as well."

"We can't afford it," Jane said. "My father made you a partner in the business, he didn't hand it over to you lock stock and barrel. He says things have been bad recently, that you've lost money on a commission. I'm not sure what he means, but anyway, we can't afford to pay for more help in the house."

Adam felt the colour rise in his cheeks, annoyed that Robert had mentioned the Munford affair to Jane. It still rankled that he'd been made to seem a fool. Robert hadn't

293

disclosed the details, but Jane obviously blamed him.

"Several commissions have come in recently," he said defensively. "We're not as poor as you would have me believe. Good grief, I work all hours."

"You don't need to tell me that." Jane glared at him. "I hardly see you. If it wasn't for the child, I wouldn't know I was married. I thought marriage was a part of the bargain."

Adam stared at her. This wasn't the first time she'd thrown his bargain with her father in his face. When she talked like that, it made him feel as if he'd been bought. Turning away, he picked up his coat and put it on.

"Where are you going?" Jane cried. "I'm just about to get supper."

"Don't bother," Adam muttered. "I can buy a pie at the tavern." Without looking at her, he went out of the house and slammed the door.

Walking through the darkened streets, Adam bitterly regretted his hasty decision to accept Robert Carter's offer. Although Jane was a good wife in her way, if he'd waited and thought a bit more, he might have had a workshop at Mary-Ellen's and been free to marry where he pleased. Adam had been uneasy in his mind about his arrangement with Susanna, but after Jane's behaviour this evening, he no longer felt guilty. If their marriage was a failure, it was more Jane's fault than his . . .

This time Susanna told her coachman to wait while she went into the shop. She was nervous and on edge as she waited for the bell to be answered. Supposing someone else came?

Susanna need not have worried. Adam was swift to answer and she knew by the look in his eyes that he had been anticipating her arrival. Her heart did a little skip and she knew that whatever happened in the future she was going to take what little happiness she could.

"Is it all arranged?" she asked in a breathless whisper.

"I've written it down for you," Adam said, pressing a tiny scrap of paper into her hand. "I was afraid you would change your mind."

"I almost did," she admitted. "But then I knew that if I did not come, I would regret it all my life." She looked up at him pleadingly. "Surely we are entitled to a little happiness?"

Adam was filled with a desperate hunger as he looked into her eyes. His desire to take her into his arms then and there was almost overwhelming. Restraining himself, he nodded to some passers-by who had stopped to glance in at the window.

"I must go," Susanna said. "My coachman is waiting. My servants think I have come to approve your latest designs."

"They are ready." He handed her a sheaf of drawings of cabinets, tables, chairs and mirrors. "I think this is what you wanted."

She examined them, then agreed. "Exactly. You're so clever, Adam. I'm sure Digby will like them and place the order with you himself. It's best that he doesn't think I've been here too often."

Adam stood looking at the door as it closed behind Susanna. He had been afraid she would not return as promised, or only to say it was impossible to meet, despite his having made all the arrangements.

For a moment his conscience smote him as he realized what he was planning to do. When he'd met Susanna in the summerhouse they had both been free. Now she was married and he had a wife and child. He knew that he had no right to betray the woman he had married. She had given him his chance in life, yet he was tired of being reminded of it. Jane acted as though she had bought him as a husband, when it was really a business contract between him and her father.

Despite the fiasco with Lord Munford, the business was building steadily. He knew that Jane was often tired, but it was her own fault. She insisted on doing too much herself and refused to let him employ another servant to help with the baby. Besides, other women had children and coped. Adam could not understand why she found it so difficult. If she was tired and the baby was crying, she should let the house go.

It was Jane's fault that he had turned away from her. She hardly ever stopped complaining these days . . . Adam smothered his guilt. Jane didn't really love him or she wouldn't nag the way she did. It wasn't as if what he was doing would actually harm her or his son. Besides, he wanted Susanna so badly that he knew nothing on earth would stop him meeting her as they'd arranged.

It was dusk when Susanna slipped from the house, wearing a gown and cloak she had borrowed from her maid. A hood was pulled up over her head and the top half of her face was hidden behind a velvet mask. Dulcia had had to be bribed, but with several golden guineas put aside for her marriage dowry, Susanna was sure that the maid was to be trusted. Dulcia had also arranged for a sedan chair to carry her 'friend' to a spot near the river, where Adam would be waiting with a boatman.

It was Adam who had insisted on enlisting Dulcia as their agent.

"Taking her into your confidence is a risk," he said, "but you cannot walk through the streets alone at night. Nor should you come dressed as Lady Digby. If you are simply gowned it will arouse less suspicion."

As her chair was carried through the dimly lit streets, Susanna's heart was beating very fast, though whether from excitement or fear she could not tell. She was longing to see Adam, longing to be alone with him so that they could really talk, and yet she was fearful of discovery, as much for his sake as her own. Digby could be vengeful when he chose. If he even suspected . . . But he must never know.

It was dark by the river, the only light that of a few stars. As the chair halted at last, Susanna saw a black-cloaked figure standing at the top of some stone steps leading down to the river. She paid the men who had carried her chair and walked with quick steps towards the shadowy figure, her pulses jumping as Adam came to meet her. He took her hands and looked searchingly into her face.

"I was afraid you would change your mind, or that he would prevent you from coming."

"I would have managed it somehow," Susanna said in a low voice. "But he left urgently for the north this morning. He will not be back for several days."

"Come on then, guv," the boatman cried from below. "I ain't got all night."

Adam did not rebuke him for his rudeness. The boatmen were well known for the way in which they insulted the passengers they ferried across the Thames. Anyone who took umbrage or argued was likely to be marooned midstream until they paid an extra shilling or two.

Taking Susanna's hand, Adam helped her down the steps to the water's edge. The boatman gave her his hand to steady her as she climbed into the small boat, then, when she and Adam were seated, he took up his oars and began to row them downstream.

Susanna sat in silence, listening to the gentle plopping sound of the oars and watching the lights from the houses on either side of the river. Occasionally, she saw the bobbing of a lantern as they passed boats going in the opposite direction. Adam and the boatman were discussing a huge hue and cry in the streets earlier that day, when the Bow Street runners had chased and finally caught a highwayman.

"He'll be for the nubbing-cheat, mark my words," the boatman said with unashamed glee. "They said it were his doxy that turned the nose on him. Trust a mort to gag every time, say I."

"No doubt he's tucked up at the King's Head Inn tonight,"

Adam said, using the man's own slang for Newgate Prison. "So it was his sweetheart who turned informer then?"

"Aye, they say she was jealous of a heavy-swell mort he'd taken up with on the side. So he'll wear a Newgate garland afore many moons 'ave passed."

Susanna shivered as she heard the boatman chuckling at the prospect of a hanging. She wondered who the highwayman was, and whether he had ever been rowed downriver to a secret assignation with the fashionable lady who had become his lover and thereby sealed his fate. Suddenly, she was attacked by nerves. Supposing Digby discovered what she was doing? She would not put it past him to have Adam attacked and beaten one dark night. There were plenty of rogues who would cut a throat for a handful of guineas.

"You're trembling," Adam said as he took her hand. "Are you cold?"

"Just a little."

"We'll soon be there. A few minutes longer, that's all."

As they rounded the bend in the river, Susanna saw the dark shape of an inn and a jetty jutting out from the bank. Hardly any light was showing at the back of the inn, but as they approached a young lad ran out with a lantern to guide their steps.

"This way, sir," he said to Adam. "Everything be ready."

Adam paid the boatman and took Susanna's arm. She had stopped shaking at last. He raised his brows and she nodded.

"I'm fine now," she whispered as the boy led them through a back entrance. They were in a tiny hall at the bottom of a narrow stairway. From somewhere deep within the house, Susanna could hear the sounds of laughter and singing. Then she was following the boy upstairs.

They were shown into a cosy parlour where a supper of cold meats, bread and wine had been laid. Beyond the parlour was an open door leading into a small bedroom.

"There you are, sir," the boy said, pocketing a coin Adam

298

gave him. "These be private apartments. You'll not be disturbed."

As he departed, Adam removed his cloak and warmed his hands at the fire. Susanna stood uncertain and tense, watching him. Adam turned to her. "Are you regretting this?" he asked. "It seems sordid, I know, but I wanted somewhere private."

Susanna took a deep breath, threw back the hood of her cloak and removed her mask. She walked to the fire, rubbing her hands in front of the flames, then she looked up and smiled at him.

"No, I'm not regretting it," she said. "It was cold on the river and all that talk of the highwayman and his lover made me nervous. Do you think he suspected anything?"

"Our boatman?" Adam shook his head. "I told him your mistress refused to let you have a follower. He thinks we're planning to marry when we can afford for you to leave your employment."

"I wish we could," Susanna said. "I wish I were a maidservant. I wish we could run away together."

"Oh, Susanna. How I wish that I had known what was happening to you when you were locked in your room!" Adam moved towards her, his hands gripping her shoulders as he looked down into her face. "I would give anything if we could go back to that night in the summerhouse and begin again."

"Would you?" Her breath came in a little rush as she gazed up into his eyes. "Adam, I . . ."

He reached for her then. As his mouth moved urgently on hers, Susanna gave a little groan and pressed herself against him. She forgot that she had come only to talk as the desire surged through her and her body leapt with joy. How often she had dreamt of this, of being with him, in his arms . . . She slid her arms up around his neck as she arched into him, almost swooning with pleasure as she felt his lips on her eyelids, her cheek, her neck and then her mouth once more. She opened to the insistent probing of his tongue, her hands in his hair as she returned his kiss with equal fervour.

"I want you so much," he murmured. "I've thought of nothing else all week."

"Adam," she gasped. "Adam, I love you. I want you . . ."

Adam reached out, unfastening the ties of her cloak, then her velvet jacket and the thin wool bodice that laced over a silken petticoat. One by one the layers slid to the ground until she was clad only in a simple linen shift; he removed it with slow deliberation, making her tremble in anticipation. For a moment Adam just looked at her, his eyes feasting hungrily on the creamy perfection of her slender body and the rose-tipped peaks of her breasts. He kissed first one shoulder, then the other, his mouth moving down to her breasts, sucking gently at the nipples to send a ripple of sensation through her, then on down to her navel. Susanna groaned aloud as he knelt before her, burying his face in the damp hair that covered her mound of Venus, his hands squeezing her buttocks as his tongue probed and flicked, making her knees tremble. Then he lifted her in his arms, carrying her into the bedroom and laying her on the bed. She smiled up at him as he threw off his own clothing.

His body was so firm, the flesh satin smooth and taut over his stomach and legs. Susanna felt the hot liquid run between her thighs as she looked at him and gloried in his masculine beauty. The evidence of his own desire was plain enough, making her tingle with excitement and anticipation. She held out her arms to him, begging him to come to her.

"Adam," she whispered hoarsely. "Adam . . ."

He knelt beside her on the bed, his mouth moving with reverence over her quivering body inch by inch, kissing, licking, tasting her. He kissed her toes and the soles of her feet, making her jerk and laugh as his hot breath tickled her. She was on fire, longing for him to possess her and make her one with him, but he continued to touch and caress her, taking his time as he told her how lovely she was and how much he adored her.

". . . dreamt of you . . . tormented by memories . . . no one was ever like this . . ."

His words and his touch raised her to fever pitch. Tiny beads of sweat glistened on his skin in the candlelight as he lowered himself on to her, the burn of his flesh sending a shock of delight winging through her. Susanna moaned, writhing and arching as she lifted herself to meet his thrust. He was so hard and hot as he drove into her, stretching her, filling her so that she cried out, the shock of his entry almost as painful as that first time, but then the exquisite pleasure swept through her and she was gasping, her nails raking his back as she moaned beneath him.

His movements were slow and rhythmic, teasing her as he left her for a moment and she cried out in mourning for the loss of him, before plunging deep inside her again. Susanna clung to him, her head moving from side to side on the pillow as she lost all control. She was his completely and utterly, surrendering her very being as the world seemed to explode within her and she cried his name in ecstasy.

Afterwards, he lay slumped against her, their sweat mingling as they rested, limbs still entwined, reluctant to part even for a moment.

"Never felt like this . . ."

"So happy . . ."

"I love you. I love you . . ."

"I wish it could always . . ."

"Hush, my darling."

His mouth was on hers again. Susanna felt the desire stir within her. Once again she gave herself up to him without restraint. He took her with a swift urgency this time, his thrusting almost savage as he drove into her. Susanna's response was eager, her hands clutching at his back, climaxing over and over as something inside her seemed to reach out and hold him while he emptied the warm sperm deep inside her. It was quite unlike the first time, a special feeling that brought tears to her eyes.

"If you should have a child . . ."

"I want your child, Adam. I want your baby . . ."

"My darling . . ."

He held her as she wept into his shoulder, his hands moving gently at the nape of her neck, tangling in the damp gold of her hair. Gradually, she was comforted. She smiled through her tears. Pushing him back into the pillows, she looked down at his body, marvelling at the strong, muscled limbs. She ran her fingers through the dark curling hair on his chest, then bent her head, beginning to kiss and lick at his nipples. He groaned as she slid down the bed, kissing and sucking him, nibbling with her sharp white teeth.

"You're insatiable," he laughed. "Not again, Susanna. I'm exhausted."

He lied. His manhood sprang to throbbing life once more as she kissed and caressed him, taking him into her mouth to suck and tease him. Then with one graceful movement, she sat astride him. Susanna laughed as his hands spanned her waist, lifting her and then bringing her down hard as he slid into her, making her gasp. She arched her slender body, riding him triumphantly as they gloried in the strength of their young bodies. Bodies that were beautiful and perfectly matched. Lion and lioness. Stallion and mare. Made for one another, moving in harmony to the final climax of love.

For a long time afterwards they lay side by side, sleepy and contented, talking in whispers.

"If there was some way we could be together . . ."

"It is so difficult. I have Jane to think of and the child . . ."

"I know. If only we had run away together that first night."

"You don't know how often I have wished the same. I could leave her but . . ."

"You would feel guilty. Besides, Digby would pursue us. He would ruin you, Adam. You would never be able to work in London again, perhaps not in England."

"We might go to France. I have thought of it."

"It could not be yet, because of the scandal. Beatrice might be going to marry Lord Farringdon. I would do nothing to ruin her chances."

"Then we have no choice but to wait."

"We can go on meeting like this?" She bent over him, looking into his face, her eyes dark with anguish. "This isn't the last time, Adam?"

"How could you ask?" he said, kissing her mouth as once again desire stirred. "I shall never have enough of you, never . . . Susanna . . ."

Reassured, she gave herself up to passion once more. And then at last they both slept, exhausted, satiated, and finally at peace.

Susanna looked into her dressing mirror the next morning, noticing the new shine in her eyes. Would anyone else see the difference in her? Would they guess that she had a lover? What she had done frightened yet thrilled her. She felt so alive, so wonderfully alive.

If Digby ever discovered the truth . . . for a moment joy was replaced by fear and she tried to shut it out, not wanting anything to spoil her happiness. She was an adulteress . . . She had betrayed her husband, broken her marriage vows.

Yet she had never wanted to marry Digby. It had been forced upon her against her will and he had made her suffer for his own inadequacy too many times. He had given her material things, but made her pay for them with tears. Lifting her head in pride, Susanna dismissed any feeling of guilt. She was only doing what many other women who had been forced into unhappy alliances did, what Digby's own sister had advised her to do . . .

Susanna smiled as she wondered what Lady Munford would think if she knew that she had taken her advice, but with a lover of her own choosing.

* * *

"You have failed me," the Marquis said, his fingers tapping against the wooden arm of his chair. "You said you could persuade her to take me as a lover."

"And I shall," Lady Munford replied, her eyelids drooping. She hoped he wasn't going to be difficult. It would be impossible to repay the money he had given her. "You are too impatient, sir. Susanna is afraid of upsetting Digby. She will come to realize how dull her life is and then . . ."

"She has a lover," the Marquis interrupted. "She has met him every night this past week."

"Impossible!" Helen stared at him, her disbelief beginning to falter as she saw his certainty. "I can't believe it. How do you know?"

"I have my informants," he said. "I suspected it so I have had her watched. She goes dressed as a maid and they are rowed to an inn downriver. They have private rooms and the bed is used. There is no doubt, madam."

It had been the easiest thing in the world to have Susanna followed. There were a legion of fools ready to do the Marquis's bidding, both in the drawing-rooms of society and the streets. Many of London's poor were ruled by their desire for the oblivion they found in cheap gin, and willing to sell their soul for a shilling to buy drink. Steeped in every vice imaginable, Brandon had tired of the stupid wenches who squandered their youth and freshness for a few coins. His pursuit of Susanna had begun in a moment of pique, but now she had become an obsession. He was determined to have her at any cost.

"Digby would kill her if he knew." Lady Munford's eyes gleamed. She had never liked the little upstart. "It might be amusing to tell him."

"That would ruin everything." The Marquis glared at her. "You will say nothing to Digby, do you hear?"

"As you wish." Her look was sly. "You know I always try to please you."

"You have been well paid, but there's a thousand guineas for you if you keep your mouth shut and do as I say."

She smiled, leaning back against the silken cushions of her daybed. "But of course, my dear Marquis. I begin to see what you mean. I shall be delighted to help you . . ."

Adam glanced at the note that Susanna's maid had delivered and frowned. Digby had returned sooner than expected and their arrangement for that evening was cancelled. Susanna would be in touch when they could meet again.

"Who was that just now?" Jane asked as he returned to the workshop from the showroom. "Was it a customer?" You weren't with her long."

"No one important," Adam replied. "Just a tradesman's daughter."

Seeing the look on his wife's face, Adam thought it was just as well he would be spending a night at home for once. Jane had become increasingly suspicious about his business appointments in the evenings, and he'd found it more and more difficult to find excuses for her.

He yawned and stretched. "I shall be glad of an early night," he said, smiling at her. "And how is Robert today?"

Jane stared at him suspiciously. He seldom mentioned his son, except to tell her if he heard Robert crying.

"A little better, I think," she said. "Are you really going to stay in this evening?"

"Yes." Adam smiled again, wanting to please her. "We'll spend a quiet evening together, Jane."

Her suspicion eased a little. Her mother had told her that men often went out more when the children were small. "Let's hope that Robert sleeps tonight."

"He's been a trial to you, I know," Adam said, with a pang of guilt. "If he wakes tonight, I'll go to him."

"No you won't." Jane's smile finally banished her mood. "You work hard enough as it is. I'll tell Mabs to prepare something special for this evening . . ."

Watching her leave, Adam sighed. He didn't want to hurt Jane, but what was he to do? Perhaps he ought never to have started to meet Susanna, yet the thought of never seeing her again was a tearing pain in his breast. He must go on seeing her now and then, even if it was not as often as it had been this past week. Otherwise his life would seem pointless . . .

He wondered unhappily how Susanna was managing now that her husband had returned. She'd hardly mentioned Digby, except to say that he was a jealous man, but Adam had an idea that she suffered more than she would say. He hoped that their meetings at the inn would not mean trouble for her.

What a mess it all was. Adam shook his head as he took off his coat and rolled up his sleeves. It was time he started work. He had an order for a library table and two sets of steps that were promised for next week and still needed a final polish.

Susanna was in the drawing-room when the note was delivered. She glanced at it then read it a second time before screwing it into a ball and throwing it into the fire. Lord Digby looked at her with mistrust. Something was bothering her. He had sensed it as soon as he returned.

"Is something wrong, Susanna?"

"It was from Helen. She wants me to take tea with her this afternoon."

"Shall you go?"

Susanna tried to hide her anxiety. The note had been almost imperious, threatening. "I suppose I shall have to. She says I've neglected her and she will be offended if I do not go."

"Have you neglected to visit her, Susanna?"

"I have so many friends, Digby. It is impossible to please everyone. Besides, I told you, I've been unwell these past few days. I didn't go anywhere in the evenings. I spent most of the time in my room, in bed."

"What did the doctor say was the matter?"

"I didn't send for him. It was just a little chill."

"A chill can so easily become pneumonia," Digby said. "You ought to take more care of yourself. I remember how ill you were just before we married — that began as a chill, I think."

"Oh, it was nowhere near as bad as that," Susanna said stiffly. She was restless and on edge. It was all she could do to sit still in her chair. "I'm quite recovered now."

"Then there is no reason why you cannot have tea with Helen, is there?"

None that she could put into words. Yet even as she complied, a feeling of foreboding was stealing over her. That letter had been very odd. It was almost a command . . . Helen could not have discovered her secret, could she? No, that was impossible. It was just another of her little tricks. No doubt some of Helen's closest friends would be there, including the Marquis of Brandon. Susanna paused before asking, "Will you come with me, Digby?"

"I have business of my own," he replied. "I've told you before, Susanna. You cannot afford to offend Helen. Now I must go. I shall dine at home this evening. I trust you have no other engagements?"

"None that need concern you," she said. "There is a small, informal affair at Lady Wexford's, but I can go later if you are going out yourself?"

"I thought we might spend the evening together, Susanna."

Susanna turned her cheek for his kiss, suppressing the shudder that his touch aroused. She felt a rush of protest as he kissed her. How could she bear it if he came to her room that night? How could she bear his clumsy fumblings after she had gloried in Adam's loving night after night?

Dismissing the prospect with a little shrug, Susanna knew that she would cope when the time came. She was used to Digby's spiteful ways now. What worried her more at the moment was Lady Helen's note.

Susanna followed Lady Munford's footman upstairs with growing unease. She knew she was being conducted to her sister-in-law's boudoir, and that meant she would probably be the only guest. Just why had Helen summoned her here today? She felt a spasm of nerves in her stomach. Supposing Helen had discovered her secret?

The footman had stopped outside the boudoir door. He turned to her, inclining his head with deference.

"Her ladyship asks that you go in, Lady Digby."

"Thank you." Susanna hesitated as he walked away, then knocked at the door. "May I come in, Helen?"

There was no answer. Helen must have stepped into her bedroom, Susanna thought. She turned the handle and went in. The room was in semi-darkness, the windows heavily draped; she could just see the dark shapes of tables and chairs scattered around the room. Susanna blinked in surprise. What was happening?

"Helen," she said, her movements awkward and un-certain as she tried to adjust to the unnatural gloom. "What is the matter? Are you ill? Why have you closed the curtains?"

She heard someone move behind her and then an odd sound like the turn of a key in the lock. She spun round, her heart jerking with fright.

"What are you doing?" she cried. "Who is there?"

"There is no need to be afraid. I was merely taking a precaution."

The man's voice sent a thrill of horror through her. She gave a little cry, then as the drapes were suddenly pulled back she saw him standing by the window.

"What are you doing here?" she demanded. "Where is Lady Munford?"

"She has been forced to make an unexpected visit to an ailing friend," he said, smiling as he came towards her. "So we are alone, Susanna."

She backed away from him, her eyes widening as she saw his predatory expression. "Unlock that door at once, sir," she cried. "How dare you address me so familiarly? I refuse to be alone with you. Let me go at once."

"And if I do not choose to let you go?" He raised a brow. "What then?"

"I – I shall tell my husband that you have insulted me."

The Marquis smiled. "I hardly think so, my dear Lady Digby. For if you were to tell him that, I might have to tell him what I know . . ."

"What you know?" Her heart was racing as she gazed into his eyes. They were like the eyes of a stoat as it prepared to spring on a rabbit. "And – and what is that, sir?"

"Come, Susanna," he murmured, his voice soft and persuasive. "There is no need for this. Surely we can come to terms without threats? I want to be your friend . . . your intimate friend. Can we not be pleasant to each other?"

Susanna retreated once more, her face pale. "I think you know my sentiments towards you well enough, sir. I prefer you to speak plainly. What is the meaning of this charade? Why have you gone to such lengths to trap me?"

"Trap you, Susanna?" He lifted his quizzing glass to survey her. "I merely wish to put a little proposition to you."

"The answer is no," she cried. "Now please unlock this door and let me go at once."

His eyes were as hard as granite and she sensed the suppressed anger in him. "Very well, since you will have it so – I know that you have a lover. I know who he is and where you meet him."

"And . . . unless I do what you want you will tell Digby." Susanna proudly raised her eyes to his. "Do you imagine that I shall give in to your blackmail, sir?"

"I believe you will," he said in a measured tone, "when you have had time to think. Perhaps if it were only Digby's censure you might be brave enough to defy me, but think carefully, my dear. Your lover is a common tradesman. If he were a duke or an earl society might titter behind their hands and condone your little indiscretion – but a carpenter . . ."

Susanna flushed. "A carpenter is no worse than a groom or a prize-fighter."

"You do not imagine that you can flout the laws of society the way Helen Munford does?" His brows rose in incredulity. "You are a little nobody from the country. The case is quite different. You will be ruined, my dear. Digby will have no choice but to send you back to the country and forget you ever existed."

Susanna turned away, suppressing her desire to shout and scream at him. He was right. She could not hope to ride out such a scandal. Her hopes of becoming a fashionable hostess would be over. Digby would send her away in disgrace ... But it need not be like that. All at once, she realized that it did not matter. She would leave her husband. She would go away with Adam. It was what she truly wanted. With triumph in her eyes, she turned to face her tormentor.

"Tell him," she said. "Tell Digby. Tell everyone the truth. I care nothing for society or anyone in it!"

For a moment the Marquis stared at her in disbelief, then understanding dawned. "You little fool," he said. "You would give up everything, ruin yourself for him!"

Susanna lifted her chin, her face defiant. "I love him," she said. "I love him and I would rather die than become your mistress."

His eyelids drooped, hiding the rage inside him. Susanna trembled inwardly, fearing that he would attack her. He read the expression in her face and shook his head, a cruel smile playing over his thick lips.

"No, Susanna," he said, his voice rasping with menace. "That is not my way. Oh, I would have abducted you that day in the street if your lover had not interfered, but I had been drinking. An unusual occurrence, I assure you. I am quite sober now. I could rape you if I chose . . ." He laughed as he saw her start in fear. "Rape does not interest me. If I had wanted so little, I could have had you at any time this past week. A few guineas and your chair would have been carried to a different place. It amused me to let you have your little affair. Now it is over. No, my dear, I want you to come to me willingly."

"I shall never do that!"

"That depends on whether or not you value your carpenter's life," he said smoothly. "If your virtue means more to you . . ."

"No!" Susanna's hand crept to her throat. Fear smote her as she saw the evil in him. "Even you wouldn't dare . . ."

"You underestimate me, Susanna." There was malicious amusement in his face. "I have many friends, friends who move silently in the darkness. A sudden thrust of a knife, a blow to the head or . . ."

Instinct told her that it was no idle boast. He had had her watched. He could just as easily have had her killed . . . or Adam . . .

"*No!*" she cried. "You must not! He must not die . . . I beg you . . ." Her voice broke on a sob. "I beg you, sir. Do not harm him."

"How sweetly you beg for his life." The Marquis looked into her tear-drenched eyes. "Almost I am moved to grant your plea . . ."

"Please," Susanna wept. "Please, do not harm him."

She forced herself to be passive as he came towards her. He stood for a moment looking at her pale face, then bent to kiss her. She shuddered as his mouth possessed hers greedily.

"You will have to do better," he said. "If you want me to be merciful, you must show me kindness. I want you warm and eager in my bed, Susanna."

Anger moved in him as he saw her instant recoil. She had been too proud. Before he was finished with her, she would crawl at his feet. It would be amusing to break her little by little until she was no longer of any interest, then he would sell her as a whore.

"Do what you want with me," she said, feeling as if she were suffocating. "I shall not deny you."

"That is not good enough," he said. "But you are shocked and I am not an uncivilized man, Susanna. Indeed, you will find me generous if you please me. I shall forget all your unkindness to me. You will meet me tomorrow evening at the same place as you met your lover. We shall go to your little love-nest by the river and there you will show me just how willing you are to please me."

Susanna lifted her eyes to his. "And if I do, how can I be sure that you will keep your part of the bargain?"

His brow arched with a hint of indignation. "Because I am a man of my word, my dear. You can be quite sure that if you do not meet me, you will never see your carpenter alive again."

"He would not dare to carry out his threat," Adam said as he saw the fear in Susanna's eyes. "Even the Marquis must think twice about murder."

"But you do not know him," Susanna cried. "Please, Adam, you must take this seriously."

"And let you pay such a price for my safety?" Adam's expression reflected his outrage and pride. "You must not keep your appointment with him, Susanna. I forbid it."

She looked up at him then, feeling a tenderness inside as she saw his fury. "I know you want to protect me, but . . ."

"There are no buts about it," Adam insisted. "You were right to come to me, Susanna. I shall deal with this."

Susanna hesitated, uncertain now what to do. Her first instinctive reaction had been to visit Adam at his shop and tell him of the Marquis's threats, but now she wondered if she had been wise. Adam was strong, but the Marquis was a ruthless devil.

"He carries a swordstick, Adam," she warned. "And he is an evil man. He told me himself that he has friends who move silently in the darkness. I believe he would kill you himself if he felt threatened."

"You must not worry . . ." Adam's smile of tenderness was swiftly hidden as the door from the workshop opened

312

and Jane entered. He looked at her in surprise; she seldom came into the showroom. "Is there something wrong, my dear?"

Jane was staring fixedly at Susanna's beautiful face. As she turned to her husband, her jealousy and suspicion were all too evident.

"I came to tell you that there is a message from my mother. Father is worse. She has sent for the doctor."

Adam's concern was immediate and genuine. "I'm sorry, Jane," he said. "You must go to him at once. I shall come as soon as I can."

"He will want to see you, Adam." Jane looked pointedly at Susanna. "I am sorry to interrupt your business with my husband, ma'am."

Adam reluctantly made the introduction forced on him. "Lady Digby, this is my wife Jane. Her father is very ill and may be dying."

Susanna nodded, her face stiff as she turned to Jane. "I am sorry to hear of your father's illness, Mrs Blackwell. I shall delay your husband no longer. I believe our business was finished for now, was it not, Mr Blackwell?"

"As you say, Lady Digby." Adam's tone was polite and formal. "You may leave your commission in my hands."

Susanna murmured her thanks and left the shop. As her carriage was driven away, urgent questions tormented her. Dare she leave everything to Adam? Or must she keep her appointment with the Marquis that night?

After Susanna had gone, Jane turned to her husband. "She has been to the shop several times recently, hasn't she?"

Adam heard the sharp, querulous note in her voice. After their talk that morning, he had hoped they could be on better terms, but now he knew that they were on the verge of yet another quarrel.

Despite his passion for Susanna, Adam was fond of Jane in his own way. He was grateful to her father and he felt guilty because of his betrayal. Now, seeing the hurt in her

313

eyes and knowing how upset she was over her father, that guilt struck hard. He drew Jane into his arms, kissing her forehead.

"I'm working on a commission for Lady Digby," he said. "Run and put on your cloak, Jane, and we'll go to your father's house together."

Adam was thoughtful as he left the house that evening. Jane had been upset at being deserted when she was so worried over her father. Near to tears, she had accused him of going to meet a lover.

"You promised me you would stay home tonight," she'd cried bitterly. "You promised, Adam!"

"I would not leave you if it were not important, Jane," he had said, but she had looked at him coldly.

"If you cared for me at all, you would not go."

"If you had respect for me, you would not question my decisions."

Adam was angry as he left the house. He had not broken his promise lightly. Jane would have to learn that he meant to be master in his own house, but for the moment he had other problems.

What was he to do about the Marquis? If Susanna was right, it would be useless to reason with him. All he could do was to face him man to man, to answer his threats with scorn and show the Marquis that he would not be intimidated.

The moon had slipped behind some heavy clouds and it was almost dark when he reached the river. Seeing the heavily cloaked figure standing alone at the top of the steps, Adam hesitated. Until that moment he had not in his own mind believed the Marquis would be there, thinking the threat at worst a cruel jest, at best a misunderstanding. Now, for the first time, he realized the danger of his situation. Adam was unarmed and the Marquis carried a swordstick. He must be alert and ready to defend himself. There might be servants on hand to help their master. As he

314

walked across a patch of open ground, the Marquis turned and saw him. For a moment they looked at one another in silence. The Marquis was the first to speak.

"So she told you. That was unwise of her." In the dim light the Marquis's face showed incredulity and disbelief. He had been so sure he had Susanna this time. So sure that he had come to meet her alone, without his servants.

"Susanna would have given way to your threats. I forbade it. I would not allow her to degrade herself by meeting you."

The Marquis's thick brows rose. "Did you indeed? I had heard you were a brazen upstart with ideas above your station. I see that my information was correct. You will, I fear, regret the day you interfered with my plans, master carpenter."

"I am what I am," Adam replied, unruffled. "You and some of your kind may despise me for it if you will, but I am not afraid of you. I believe myself your equal, sir, mayhap your better."

"Insolent dog!" the Marquis snarled. "I'll deal with you myself."

With a twist of the silver knob, his elegant walking cane revealed its more sinister purpose. The clouds had moved away and the moon sailed across a suddenly light sky. As the thin blade flashed in the silver light, Adam stepped back quickly, his body tense. The Marquis's sword lashed out, its deadly tip slicing within inches of Adam's shoulder as he nimbly dodged aside. He was forced to retreat before it.

The Marquis laughed, his thick lips curling in scorn. "Now, master carpenter, now admit who is your superior!"

Adam's keen mind sought desperately for something to use as a weapon. He could see nothing suitable as a cudgel to beat off the Marquis's attack. He had nothing but his wits and his quick eye to help him.

He retreated step by step, avoiding the cut and thrust of the Marquis's attack only by his ability to move faster than the older man. Brandon had begun to pant and sweat, his anger at being thwarted making his swings ever more wild and erratic. His sword slashed and whistled through the air as he tried desperately to wound his quarry. Still Adam retreated, carrying the Marquis with him, slowly, purposefully, towards his goal. Behind them was a wood and iron bench which had been placed by the river for the benefit of the elderly by some generous philanthropist.

Judging his moment, Adam suddenly sprinted the last few feet, taking cover behind it. Mistaking his action for panic, the Marquis gave a grunt of satisfaction.

"Run you coward," he cried. "Run like the craven scum you are."

The seat was between them. The Marquis saw the river bank was at Adam's back, with a steep drop to the murky water. The fool had trapped himself, he could go no further. He had him now! Brandon paused to catch his breath before a last deadly onslaught. Then his eyes widened in disbelief as Adam lifted the heavy seat off the ground and with one huge effort thrust it forward. Unable to credit what he saw, the Marquis stood immobile, his mouth open. He was struck by the falling bench, dropping his weapon and crying out as he staggered back in an effort to avoid being caught beneath it.

Then Adam was on him. Brandon went down beneath the flying tackle, hitting out with a flurry of wild blows. The struggle was unequal. He was a big man but his bulk was fat, built through years of excesses. Adam was all muscle and bone, with the strength of a raging bull, his anger driving him to a mindless ferocity. The Marquis knew one terrifying moment of fear as he felt the powerful hands enclose his throat. His eyes opened wide with surprise as he understood he was going to die. He tried to speak, to plead for his life, but it was too late. Aroused to the point of madness and fighting for his own life, Adam forgot his own strength. Only when he heard the sharp cracking sound and felt the Marquis suddenly go limp did he realize what he had done. His hands fell away and he let go, staring in

316

horror as the Marquis's head lolled horribly to one side, his eyes wide and staring.

Stepping back, Adam looked down at the man whose neck he had just broken. He was dead. He had killed the Marquis! For a moment he felt a chill of horror sweep through his body. He had committed murder. He would hang for it! Sheer terror almost drove him to flee in panic. He fought the impulse, looking round for any sign of a witness. Had anyone seen the fight?

His nerves steadied as he saw he was alone. He had originally chosen the spot for his meetings with Susanna because of its isolation. There were one or two houses on the other side of the river, but their windows were dark, shuttered against the night. The nearest buildings on this side were warehouses, locked and deserted at this hour.

Taking a deep breath, Adam set the bench back in its place. Then he bent over the Marquis, taking a large ruby ring from his finger. The huge red stone lay in his hand like a drop of blood, sending a shudder through him. Fighting his revulsion at robbing the dead, Adam put the ring in his pocket and removed a small purse of gold from the Marquis's coat. As he straightened up, he heard a shout from the river steps. The boatman! He had forgotten the boatman. The Marquis would have had a boat waiting at the foot of the steps. Dropping the gold, Adam turned and ran. He heard another cry, but he did not look back as he sprinted across the open ground towards the shadows of the warehouses.

CHAPTER EIGHTEEN

"You will not leave this house without giving me an explanation, madam."

Susanna looked at Digby and felt a flicker of fear. He had caught her trying to leave the house wearing Dulcia's gown and dragged her back to her room.

"Where were you going dressed like that?"

Susanna was unable to think of an explanation. Knowing it was useless, she faced him in proud defiance.

"Answer me, Susanna!"

As she remained silent, he slapped her across the face. Susanna blinked, her eyes smarting with tears, but remained silent.

"So you will not tell me." Digby's gaze narrowed. "Then I must make what I will of it. Your maid will be questioned and if I find that you . . ."

"She knows nothing," Susanna cried. "I gave her money for the gown, that's all."

"Why were you sneaking out like that?"

"To — to meet the Marquis," Susanna whispered, her face very pale. "He — he threatened to — to kill you if I did not."

Digby stared at her suspiciously. He thought she was lying, but she was certainly very frightened. "Why should he kill me? You cannot expect me to believe that, Susanna?"

She lifted her eyes to his, pleading with him. "Have I not told you that he is ruthless, Digby? He hates you because I took you instead of him. He is determined to have his revenge."

"Are you lying to me, Susanna?" Digby was swayed by her tears. He had grown fond of her despite his frustration at his own failure in their bed. He took her hand and kissed it. "Forgive me. I have been a fool to doubt you. You have warned me of him so many times. I had heard of his unsavoury reputation, of course, but I did not believe he would dare to threaten you."

Susanna moved towards him in entreaty. "He frightens me, Digby. Can we not go home tomorrow? I fear he will ruin us somehow."

"I am not afraid of Brandon," her husband said. "You may leave this to me, Susanna. I have neglected my duty towards you, but no more. Tomorrow the Marquis shall hear from me."

"No," Susanna cried, her fear real enough now. "He is evil, Digby. He will kill you. Let us go to the country."

"Your concern pleases me," Digby said with an indulgent nod. "We shall go home soon. Now, take off those unbecoming clothes, my dear, and join me downstairs. We shall spend the evening together . . ."

As he left her to change, Susanna stared at her face in the mirror. She had no doubt that the Marquis would tell Digby everything. And then what would happen?

Adam locked the shop door behind him, standing with his back against it while he fought for control. As his breathing eased, he told himself there was no cause for undue alarm. The boatman had not seen his face, he had made sure of that. After that first shout, he had made no attempt to follow Adam. There was nothing to connect Adam Blackwell with the Marquis of Brandon. No one but Susanna had any idea that he had gone to meet Brandon that evening. She must know that she could be accused as an accomplice if Adam was charged with murder. It must and would remain their secret.

His mind went round and round as he thought it all through. He had taken a ring. It would look as if the Marquis had been attacked by footpads. The boatman would testify that he had seen someone robbing the body. For a moment

Adam felt the sickness swirl inside him. He had killed a man. He was a murderer.

In another moment his head had cleared. He had killed in self-defence. It had been his life or the Marquis's. His conscience was clear. Panic had made him take the ring. If he had told the truth . . . But that was impossible. It would have ruined them all. No, he had done the only thing he could. With luck no one would ever suspect him. He would carry his secret to the grave.

As he began to think more sensibly, he saw that this would be his cross. He must live with his secret. He had taken another man's life. It had been in self-defence, and yet in one part of his mind he might have seen it as a way of safe-guarding Susanna, of saving himself from ruin or assassination. He would never be quite certain, even in his own heart. Had there been a moment when he had made a conscious decision to kill? He could not be sure.

"Adam . . . Adam, is that you?"

Jane opened the door from the workshop. She stood on the threshold, a lighted chamber-stick in her hand. Her long hair hung loose on her shoulders and her face looked pale and anxious in the yellow light.

"Adam, are you all right? Is something the matter? Why are you standing here in the dark?"

Adam took a deep breath and went to her. "Nothing is wrong, Jane," he said. "I was just thinking . . ."

"Oh, Adam." She caught back a sob. "Are you angry with me for what I said earlier? I shouldn't have gone on to you like that. I know you have to see customers. You work so hard."

Jane's eyes were red and sore, and Adam could see that she was very unhappy. Her face looked plainer than usual.

"No, Jane, I'm not angry," he said. His expression was serious as he looked down at her. She was a good wife. He had almost ruined all their lives because of his lust for another woman, a woman who should never have been more than a dream to him. "It is you who has every right to be angry with me. I have been neglecting you of late."

"Adam." Jane's smile lit up her plain face. "It doesn't matter. Come to bed now, Adam. Come to bed . . . please."

Adam said goodbye to his dream then. He had thought for a while that he could defy the whole world. Holding Susanna in his arms, he had almost believed that there was a way, a chance for them to escape their destinies, to make another life somewhere else, but now he knew that chance had gone. Susanna was the only person who could connect him to the Marquis. It was safer for both of them if they stopped seeing each other.

The Marquis was dead, his neck broken. His naked body had been found in the river several days after he was known to have disappeared. Everyone said it was the work of footpads.

"The motive was obviously robbery," Digby said when he heard the news. "It must have happened the night you were to have met him, Susanna. It is a mercy you did not go. You might also have been killed."

"Yes," Susanna agreed. "Yes, I am thankful you prevented me from leaving, Digby."

She got up and went to look out of the window as he picked up his news-sheet again. Had it been the work of footpads? She had not seen Adam since that night. She had sent Dulcia with a note asking him to meet her, but the shop was closed. Robert Carter was dead and all business was postponed until after his funeral as a mark of respect. By that time she might be in the country.

Susanna realized that her brief love-affair was over. She could not go to Adam's house and ask to see him, especially at such a time. Besides, she believed that Adam was avoiding her. He would have found a way of contacting her if he had wanted to see her. In her heart she knew that it had been bound to end this way. Even when they had been together at the inn, he had never actually said that they would go away together. It was she who had talked of leaving Digby. Adam's answer had always been to kiss her until she could think only of him and the pleasure he gave her. They loved each other, but the chasm was too wide, the circumstances too difficult.

Blinking back her tears, Susanna admitted the truth she had tried so hard to deny. Their love was hopeless. It had been doomed from the beginning.

Adam could hardly believe it when he read the account of the Marquis's death. His naked body had been found in the river . . . of course! The boatman must have taken advantage of the situation to help himself to the Marquis's money, and his clothing, which would fetch several pounds at the second-hand stalls of London's markets, with no questions asked. He must have put the Marquis's body in the river, and by doing so, he had made it appear that the motive was robbery. No one would be likely to connect either Adam or Susanna to the incident.

Adam felt a little easier in his mind after that. If the boatman had enriched himself, he was not going to report having seen a man bending over the body. It seemed that Adam was in the clear after all. He hadn't been able to sleep since that night, but now his nerves were less tightly strung. He had been afraid that his wife might notice his restlessness and question it, but Jane had been too upset by her father's last painful hours to take much notice of him. Nor would she have guessed what was on his mind.

Adam had been lucky. No one need ever know the truth. All he had to do was to keep his head and the incident would be forgotten. Just as long as he didn't talk in his sleep or disturb Jane with the nightmares that haunted his dreams . . .

Adam was working on a new set of chairs for a Mr Henry Monkton. He had already glued them together and applied clamps; now they were ready for him to begin the polishing. With splat backs and plain cabriole legs that ended in attractive claw and ball feet, they were made of good quality mahogany that promised to have a hint of red when polished. He picked one up, turning it upside down to examine the joints. He was pleased with the way this particular commission had turned out. Mr Monkton had wanted quality rather than elegance and they were a good, honest set of sturdy chairs, suitable for a merchant's house.

More and more of his work was coming from wealthy businessmen these days, Adam reflected with satisfaction. Although there was not quite as much prestige attached to a commission from someone like Mr Monkton as there had been from the aristocracy, he had decided he preferred to deal with men of his stamp. Monkton would pay as soon as the chairs were ready.

Adam's eyes moved round the crowded workroom. A large partners' desk for a long-established firm of solicitors was finished and waiting for collection. It too was solid, good quality mahogany with plain loop brass handles and nicely shaped back plates on each drawer. The top was covered in a dark green leather and tooled round the edges with gold; altogether an impressive piece. There was a sideboard in mahogany, too, with six tapered legs, three neat drawers and two cellarets; the customer had asked for Dutch drop handles on the drawers, though Adam personally would have preferred a plainer ring style. It was for the customer to decide, of course, though increasingly many of them were relying on his advice. Besides the desk and the sideboard, there were many small tripod tables, one with an attractive piecrust top, mirrors, writing boxes, a ladies' work table and several torchères, on which would stand ornate candelabras. He had recently made six matching ones for Lady Carlton.

Hearing the bell ringing in the shop, Adam nodded to his apprentice and picked up his coat, slipping it on. "You can take the clamps off, Jem. We'll start on the polishing when I come back."

He went into the shop, pausing on the threshold as he

saw who was waiting for him there – the last person he had ever expected to call. A prickle of apprehension ran down his spine.

"Lady Munford," he said. "How may I serve you?"

"I do not know that you may serve me at all," she said in a haughty tone. "I was looking for a small item of furniture as a gift for a friend, but I'm not sure that anything here pleases me enough."

Adam stiffened at the insulting tone of her voice. "What exactly was it you were looking for, ma'am?"

"A giltwood pier glass or perhaps a pretty table . . ."

Adam thought of the piecrust table he had recently finished, but said nothing. He would prefer not to sell to this particular customer. He had an uncomfortable feeling that she had not really come to buy furniture.

"I'm afraid I have nothing suitable at the moment," he said. "If you would care to see some designs?"

"No, I think not," she said. "It was just a whim. I shall visit Mr Robert Adam's showrooms. I believe I shall find something more to my taste there."

Adam was polite as he inclined his head. "As your ladyship wishes," he murmured, refusing to rise to her bait. There was something in her eyes. A calculating look . . .

She walked to the door, then turned and looked back. "I have just come from the memorial service for the Marquis of Brandon," she said. "I wonder, Mr Blackwell, if you have heard of him . . . He was a friend of mine. A very dear friend."

Adam stiffened. There was a deeper meaning beneath her casual words, but she could not know. She could not know that he . . . He took control of his nerves and looked at her directly.

"I do not believe that I have ever had the honour of meeting the Marquis, Lady Munford."

"No?" Her brows rose. "He knew you, Mr Blackwell. Good-day, sir. I may return if I can find nothing to please me elsewhere."

After she had gone, Adam stood very still, staring at the door. Had he imagined it, or had there been a veiled threat in her voice?

Lady Munford angrily paced about the elegant drawing-room. The business with Munford's library had not ruined Blackwell as she'd intended it should. The fool had let him get away too lightly. Why could not Charles have played on until the cabinet-maker was deep in debt? She could then have forced him to do exactly as she wanted. How it would have amused her to see him grovel at her feet. Looking around his showroom, she had realized that he was indeed one of the best craftsmen in London. No matter what she did or said, he would continue to prosper as his work became known.

Then there was the matter of that little upstart, Digby's wife. Digby would soon be taking her to the country for a while, but Helen had not forgotten that first snub or the others that had followed. Susanna Digby would pay for that one way or the other. It was such a nuisance that Brandon was dead. She had been shocked to read of the manner of his dying. What on earth had he been thinking of to venture into that part of the city alone at night?

She knew that he carried a swordstick, and he had boasted often enough that he was a match for any footpad. It was, however, the way he had died that puzzled her most. His neck had been broken. It must have taken a great deal of strength to do that; Brandon was not a weak man by any means. What sort of footpad would kill in that way? It was usually a swift blow to the back of the head with a heavy cudgel and then a hurried search of the body. The intention was to rob not to kill ... Whoever had killed Brandon had been intent on murder. The robbery could have been an afterthought or even the work of someone else ... Helen Munford's eyes narrowed as she remembered Adam Blackwell's expression when he saw Susanna come into the library.

Of course, that was it! She had been a blind fool, half suspecting but unable to make the connection. Now she saw exactly what must have happened. It had been obvious that Susanna and Adam knew each other. Brandon had told her that Susanna had a lover, but not his name. Now she knew what had taken place that night beside the river. The Marquis had tried to blackmail Susanna into becoming his mistress and she had gone running to Blackwell. He had met Brandon and . . . killed him. She remembered how strong Adam was. He had told her of his victories in the wrestling ring. He was just the kind of man who would kill by brute strength . . . It was that hint of ruthlessness in him that she found so exciting. She knew the truth now, but what use could she make of it?

Suddenly, her eyes were alight with triumph. At last she had him where she wanted him. The means to ruin both Blackwell and that upstart from the country was within her grasp . . .

Susanna was sitting alone in her boudoir when the door opened and someone came in. The words of rebuke died as she saw it was Beatrice and she gave a little cry of pleasure instead, getting to her feet to embrace her sister.

"So you're back, my dearest," she said. "I quite thought you had abandoned us for the Countess of Grafton."

Beatrice looked at her uncertainly. "I'm sorry, Susanna. It's just that . . . just that . . ." Her words died away and she sighed, tears starting to her eyes. "I'm so unhappy!"

Susanna quickly took her into her arms as she began to weep. "What is it, my love? Please tell me."

Beatrice's story came tumbling out, her words falling over themselves as she explained the cause of her despair.

"Oh, Susanna, I don't know what to do," she sobbed. "Lord Farringdon is so kind and good and he swears he loves me but I . . ." She gulped and looked at her sister helplessly. "I'm in love with Sylvia's brother John."

"Come and sit down, my love." Susanna gave her her

own handkerchief to wipe her tears. "Now, tell me again, slowly. Lord Farringdon has made you an offer – what did you say?"

"I – I told him I needed time to think about it." Beatrice looked at her woefully. "I do like him, Susanna. I think he would be kind to me and he is rich. That's what I thought I wanted but now . . ." She drew a shaky breath. "John is so wonderful. So kind and considerate."

"Are you sure that you love him?"

Beatrice nodded, her cheeks pink. "He – he kissed me once, then apologized. You see, he couldn't afford to marry me for years and years so he feels he doesn't have the right to ask me to be his wife, though he loves me and . . ."

"Slow down," Susanna said, her manner warm and indulgent. "What I want to know is what will make you happy. If you could marry your John – say next summer – what would your answer be?"

"I – I should marry him," Beatrice said. "Lord Farringdon is very kind but . . ."

"You don't want your marriage to be like mine." Susanna nodded as she saw her sister's flush of embarrassment. "Lord Farringdon would not be like Digby, dearest, but I do not think you should marry him when your heart is given to another. You are a little young to marry anyway, but perhaps next summer."

"But John has no money . . ."

"I shall settle five thousand pounds on you," Susanna said. "It isn't a huge fortune, but it should be sufficient . . ." She broke off and laughed as Beatrice hugged her. "Well, don't strangle me, then."

"Oh, Susanna." Bea's eyes were shining. "I don't know how to thank you . . . It means that we can marry years sooner . . ." Her face fell as she thought of something. "But what will Mama say?"

"You may leave her to me," Susanna said. "We shall all go down for Christmas. Say nothing of this in your letters until then."

"No," Beatrice said with a shudder. "She would come up to town and demand that I go home at once – or say I must marry Lord Farringdon."

Susanna's expression was grave. "You were a little foolish to encourage him, Bea. You will have to give him a proper answer, you know."

"Yes." Beatrice bit her lip. "It was very wrong of me to encourage him, wasn't it?"

"It wasn't kind," Susanna said. "But you are very young so perhaps he will understand. I shall ask him to call and explain that you were carried away by your first visit to town, but you must see him yourself and apologize."

"Yes." Beatrice nodded soberly. Then her eyes lit up with excitement. "But please, I may write to John and tell him our news . . ."

"Yes." Susanna kissed her cheek. "Tell him to call on me before we go to the country. I want to meet this young man of yours."

Later, after Beatrice had left her, Susanna sat down to compose her letter to Lord Farringdon. It would not be an easy task to tell him that her sister had given him false hopes, but she would far rather be embarrassed than allow Bea to make a terrible mistake.

Lady Patricia was not going to be pleased either, but Susanna was stronger now. She would speak to her father if need be, tell him how she had been forced into marrying Digby. If he gave his permission for Bea's marriage to John Browne, Lady Patricia could do nothing to prevent it.

When her letter to Lord Farringdon was finished, Susanna hesitated, then penned a few lines to Adam, asking him to meet her. She read them through, then screwed the paper into a ball. It was too difficult to write. She would find an excuse to visit Adam at the shop.

Adam was uneasy as he saw the woman who had come into his showroom just as another customer was leaving. Helen Munford seemed very pleased with herself and that look in her eyes boded no good. She was planning some mischief. He would stake his life on it.

"I am glad to find you alone, Mr Blackwell," she said. "I have decided that I shall commission a table from you."

"Very well," Adam said, inclining his head. "What had you in mind?"

"That we shall discuss when you call on me at my home," she said. "I believe we have much to discuss, Mr Blackwell. You will need to visit me frequently."

Seeing the malicious glee in her eyes, Adam had no doubt of her meaning. "I fear I am unable to oblige you," he said. "I may not be able to work on a commission for you for some time."

She moved towards him then and he caught the scent of stale sweat beneath her perfume. Her eyes snapped with temper and her hand snaked out, her long nails digging into his hand as she caught it and held it to her bosom. She laughed at his shocked face.

"Just so that you understand what is required of you," she said as he jerked back. "I have you now, Adam Blackwell. You spurned me once, but now you will do as I command. I am your mistress and you shall be my slave."

"Have you lost your senses?" Adam said. "I am a respectable married man with a business to run . . ."

"Then you should have remembered that before you bedded my brother's wife and murdered Brandon," she cried, laughing as she saw the colour leave his face. "Do not try to deny it, my foolish friend. It was an easy thing to discover the whereabouts of your little love-nest, and the rest was not so difficult for anyone with half a wit. The boatman saw you robbing the body. His description would convict you with any jury. He was frightened to tell me at first, but one of my servants loosened his tongue. Gold will make him wag it at your trial . . . Unless of course you decide to be sensible . . ."

Adam's head felt as if it would burst. He looked into her serpent's eyes and knew that she would carry out her threat unless he did exactly as she asked. He was caught fast in her trap and there was no way out.

"Perhaps I may find time for your commission," he said, the words forced out of him. "At what time may I call on you, Lady Munford?"

Helen beamed in triumph. "I shall expect you at six," she said. "Do not be late."

Susanna wiped the vomit from her mouth and looked into a mirror at her white face in fright. For days the fear had haunted her and now she could no longer deny the truth even to herself. She was having a child. Adam Blackwell's child!

What was she to do? Did it show yet? No, it was much too soon. She pulled the folds of her loose-wrapping gown over her stomach with a protective gesture. Was she imagining the slight rounding of her body? There was no possibility of the baby being Digby's. He would be furious with her when he discovered her condition and there would be a return to the spiteful pinching that he had indulged in less of late. He had such a vindictive temper when roused. It was certain that he would find some way of punishing her.

Wild thoughts of running away went through her mind. She would go to Adam and beg him to leave his wife . . . but he had a son and was building a successful business. When Digby had recently asked him to begin the commission they had planned, he had said that he could not begin for at least six months.

Adam had made no attempt to contact Susanna. She hadn't seen him since she told him about the Marquis's threats, which she felt could only mean that he did not want to see her again.

Susanna had never been sure that the Marquis had died at the hands of footpads. Adam had promised to take care of the problem and the Marquis's neck had been broken. Very few men would be strong enough to do that, she thought. Of course it could have been an accident. If the Marquis

330

had fallen ... Adam Blackwell could snap a man's neck with his bare hands. Was that what had happened? If so, it might explain why Adam had deliberately stayed away from her. She was the only link ... If someone realized that there was a connection ... Susanna felt a prickle of fear. Adam could be hanged. She might even be accused of plotting with him to murder Brandon.

Helen Munford knew that she'd had a lover, and had hinted as much at their last meeting before Susanna left for the country. She had also insinuated that there was more to the Marquis's death than anyone knew. He must have taken her into his confidence when she allowed him to use her boudoir to lure Susanna into a trap. Lady Helen was already suspicious, but she didn't know the name of Susanna's lover. If she ever put the last piece of the puzzle in place ... Susanna believed that her husband's sister would not hesitate to accuse her of complicity in the murder. Helen would take pleasure in exacting revenge for what she thought of as Susanna's insolence in refusing her favours.

Susanna knew that she must speak to Adam alone, but what she had to say must be said in private. She would wait until she was sure Digby was out for the day and then ask him to come to the house.

What was he to do? Adam rubbed hard at the chair leg he was polishing, putting all his frustration and anger into his work. He could not think straight, because his head was whirling so fast. That highborn bitch had him caught in a trap. It seemed as if he would have to give in to her this time, and yet he stubbornly refused to accept that it was the only way.

"Adam, are you coming in for your supper? It's on the table."

Adam looked up as Jane came into the workshop. There was an anxious air about her, and he knew that she had not yet forgotten their last quarrel. If he started to visit

Lady Munford regularly, she would think he was betraying her again, and she would be right. It would be a far worse betrayal. He had never forgotten Mary-Ellen's warning and he knew it was possible that Helen Munford carried the whores' disease. If he did what she wanted, he would risk bringing that foul sickness back to his wife. Jane certainly did not deserve that, however much she nagged.

"I'll be in in a few minutes," he said, nodding to his wife. "I've just about finished these now."

As Jane turned and went back into the house, Adam put down his polishing cloths. His expression hardened into one of determination. He would not do what Lady Munford wanted. Hanging would be preferable ... And yet, there was one way he might escape. He would send a message that he could not come to the house at six and ask her to meet him by the river. Then he would kill her and dispose of the body.

A shiver went through Adam as he realized that this time he was actually planning cold-blooded murder. Yet she had left him little choice. It was either her death or his.

Lady Munford glared wrathfully at the footman who had brought the note on a silver salver. How dare that common tradesman defy her so openly? To demand that she should meet him instead of coming to the house as she had ordered!

"When did this arrive?" she asked, her temper mounting. "Who brought it?"

"It was a young lad, milady. He didn't give his name."

So Blackwell had sent his apprentice, had he? Well, he would soon learn the error of that! "You may take my answer to him when I have written it ..." Her gaze narrowed furiously as she saw his expression. "The boy is waiting for my answer?"

"No, milady. He said no answer was wanted."

"No answer wanted ..." Her rage flaring, she flew at the unfortunate servant and struck him across the face.

"Imbecile! Fool! You should have made him wait. Am I served by idiots?"

"I beg your pardon, milady." The footman looked at her resentfully. She was the cause of all his problems. For a few weeks he had shared her bed, then she had discarded him as she would an old shoe. Now he was suffering the most excruciating pain in his genitals and it was all her fault. She had given him the whores' disease. "I did not think that you would want to send an answer."

Seeing his bitterness, Lady Munford's rage exploded in a ball of fire in her brain. How dare he look at her that way? She owned him body and soul. He was a mere creature she kept to amuse herself, a thing she had bought and could do with as she pleased. Now he was looking at her as if he hated her, as if he had a right to his own opinion. Suddenly something snapped in her head. It was all part of a plot against her.

"Wretch! Imbecile!" she screamed at him, snatching up a candlestick and beginning to beat him about the head with it. "You are not paid to think, only to serve. You are my dog, my slave. You will do as I say, not as you think . . ."

The footman retreated before her, putting up his hands to protect himself. She was a devil. A witch. He had never wanted to bed her in the first place but she had threatened him with prison, vowing that he'd stolen a brooch. He had given in to her threats, but now he thought that prison would have been a sweeter alternative. Her eyes were wild, frightening. He thought this time she had really lost her mind.

Backing away from her, he found himself against the wall. His hand reached out and encountered a table. On the table was the pair to the candlestick she had in her hand . . .

"Adam, you're not going out tonight?" Jane cried as he got up from the table and put on his coat. "You promised me you wouldn't meet customers at night again. You promised faithfully."

"This is the last time," Adam said grimly. "I have to go, Jane, but I swear that it will be the very last time. You know how busy I've been these past weeks. I have to go tonight. I really do."

She pulled a face as he kissed her, but said no more. Adam smiled, promised not to be late and left the house. He walked with a measured tread, knowing that there was time enough to meet Lady Munford. He had told her not to be at the appointed place before eight o'clock that evening. His letter had been unsigned, but she would know who it was from, and she would be angry. Oh yes, she would be angry, but she would come, because she thought she had him at her mercy and she could treat him like one of her wretched lapdogs. She believed that he would submit to her threats and grovel like one of those poor devils she employed, but tonight she would discover how wrong she was. It would be an easy matter to snap her scrawny neck, and he would do it without compunction.

Lady Munford was herself merciless, so why should she expect any better than she gave? It was a wonder that someone had not been driven too far long before this. Murder was a terrible crime, but if he did what she asked he could be condemning his wife to death from the disease the she-devil carried.

His face grim in the dim light of smoky street lamps, Adam walked towards the river and his appointment with destiny. After this evening he would have two deaths on his conscience or he would be in prison . . . One way or the other it was up to Fate.

Susanna gave the note to Dulcia. It was to Adam, asking him to call the following afternoon, when Digby would be out on business.

"You understand," she said, "you must give this to Mr Blackwell himself, no one else."

"Yes, of course, your ladyship." Dulcia accepted the handful of gold coins and slipped them into her pocket. "What shall I do if he isn't there . . ."

Susanna was about to reply as the door opened and her sister came in. She waved Dulcia away with a meaningful look. "Bring it back to me," she said, then to the younger girl, "What is it, my love?"

"John is here." Beatrice couldn't hide her pleasure. "He is waiting downstairs to meet you."

Susanna stood up. "Then I suppose I must come," she teased. "I've heard so much about Mr John Browne that I scarcely believe such a paragon exists."

"Oh, Susanna," Beatrice cried. "I'm so happy."

"Are you, my love?" Susanna kissed her cheek, suppressing a pang of envy. How much she wished that she was in Beatrice's position. Determinedly, she crushed her feelings of sadness and bitterness. This was Bea's day. "Then so am I. Now, let's go down before Mr Browne wears out my carpet . . ." Her face was serious for a moment. "He is going to have to ask Papa formally for your hand, Bea. You realize that I cannot guarantee anything, though I shall do everything in my power to help you both."

Bea nodded, confident of success. "I know that Papa will listen to you," she said. "Besides, when he meets John he will like him."

Susanna was supervising the packing of her gowns for the imminent visit to her parents' home when Digby walked into the room. She saw the look on his face and gave a little cry of alarm.

"Something is wrong," she said. "Is it my father?"

He shook his head. "I've just received a letter from Munford," he said. "Helen was murdered yesterday evening . . ."

Susanna went white. "Murdered? How? What happened?" Her heart was beating very fast as she waited for his answer. Could it be that Helen had discovered the truth and tried to blackmail Adam?

335

"Apparently she lost her temper with one of the footmen," Digby said. "She flew at him with a candlestick, beating him about the face and head. In the end he retaliated. Killed her with the pair to it. Ironic, what?"

"One of her servants killed her ..." The relief made Susanna weak and she sat down. Adam wasn't involved! Looking at her husband she said, "That's terrible, Digby. I'm so sorry."

"I can't say I'm shocked, Susanna. She always had a terrible temper on her, and she treated those servants of hers like animals. I'm only surprised one of them hasn't turned on her before."

Susanna had stopped trembling now. Anxiously she asked, "Does this mean that we must cancel our visit to my parents?"

"No, I don't think so," Digby said. "I shall of course have to stay in London for a while and support Munford, but I see no reason why you should not go down to Chorley Hale without me. I shall join you for Christmas."

Susanna stood up and kissed his cheek. "How thoughtful of you, Digby. You are very good to me."

"Am I, my dear?" He studied her carefully. There was a new bloom about her of late, rendering her more beautiful than ever. For a while he had thought he might have made a mistake, but now he was satisfied with his bargain after all. Beatrice was a pretty child, but Susanna was perhaps the most beautiful woman of his acquaintance. It gave him pleasure to know that there were at least a score of men in London who would give anything to be in his shoes. "Well, I have an appointment now and shall not be back until late this evening. Give my best wishes to your sister and ask her what she would like as an engagement gift from me."

Reading the letter handed to him by Susanna's maid, Adam nodded, his face revealing nothing of his inner turmoil. The note simply said that Lady Digby wished to discuss the furniture for her new salon, but he knew that it must be important for Susanna to ask him to go to her house.

"Please inform Lady Digby that I shall be there this afternoon," he said.

After she had gone, Adam frowned. He hadn't been able to believe it when he'd read the news-sheet. Lady Munford dead! Murdered by her servant, who swore that he had killed her in self-defence. Now the man had been taken off to Newgate Prison to await his trial.

"There but for the grace of God go I," Adam thought, feeling sorry for the poor wretch who was now facing hanging or a transportation order at the very least. Self-defence or not, the courts would never condone an attack on a member of the aristocracy by a servant. It might set a dangerous precedent. Lady Munford wasn't the only highborn personage to mistreat her unfortunate employees.

Remembering how close he'd come to committing cold-blooded murder, Adam drew a deep sigh of relief. He'd waited that night by the river for three hours until he was sure that Helen Munford would not come, before returning home with a heavy heart. He'd been on edge all night, thinking that retribution would fall on him at any moment. Now he knew he was safe. She was dead. At long last he was free of the threat of the spiteful Lady Munford, leaving him free to pursue his growing business interests . . . But not his affair with Susanna.

Jane had a hand on the purse strings. The reading of Robert's will had shocked Adam. Robert had left his share of the business between his wife and daughter. Jane was to have full control of both their shares until her mother died, when she would inherit her mother's portion.

Adam had stared grimly at the lawyer. "You're sure that there is no mistake?" he asked. "It was my understanding that Robert had made a will in my favour. I was to have full control of the business when he died."

"I'm sorry, Mr Blackwell." The lawyer shook his head. "Mr Carter spoke to me about it only a few days before he died. He added a clause to make sure that Mrs Blackwell had as much say in the business as you. He said that his wife would have been content to leave her affairs in your hands, but that Jane had a mind of her own and would stand up for her rights."

"So I must ask my wife's permission before I make any decisions?" Adam felt a surge of outrage as the lawyer looked awkward. "This is most unusual, sir."

"It was Mr Carter's express wish, Mr Blackwell."

Adam nodded, holding back the angry words that rose to his lips. This wasn't what Robert had promised him. He must have altered his will at the last moment. He was humiliated and furious at the restrictions imposed on him by Robert's change of heart. Jane had the power to refuse any ideas he might have for expanding the business. He knew she would be unlikely to interfere in the everyday running of the workshop, but her temper was uncertain and the knowledge that he must consult her at every step rankled in his heart.

Putting Susanna's note into his breast pocket, Adam groaned to himself. In future Jane would have the right to question every commission he undertook, which meant that it would be impossible to meet Susanna at the inn again . . .

Susanna had dressed in her favourite gown, a pretty pale blue silk with delicate lace ruffles crossing the bodice and wrapping round the skirt at the back. A dozen times she went to her dressing mirror, tucking a stray hair behind her cap of lace and silver thread. Had she begun to look matronly? Would Adam know that she was carrying his child?

This was too ridiculous! She was as nervous as a young girl, but she loved him so. Her pulses fluttered as the expected knock came and Dulcia showed him into her sitting-room.

"Mr Blackwell to see you, milady."

"Ah, Mr Blackwell." Susanna rose to her feet with a cool smile of welcome. "How good of you to come."

As soon as the maid had left, Susanna's expression changed. She ran towards Adam, her face alight with eagerness.

"Oh, Adam, I've been in agony. I dare not come to the shop and . . ."

Adam placed a finger to his lips, then went to the door and glanced outside. "We can't be too careful," he said in a hushed voice. "You heard what happened to the Marquis?"

"Yes . . . Was it . . ." Her voice died away as she saw his face. "Oh, Adam, I should never . . ."

He hushed her with a shake of his head. "We both did what we had to do," he said. "Don't ask for details. It is best that we forget what happened, Susanna. Best for both of us."

"Yes, I know." She looked at him, awkward with tension. "Did you hear about Lady Helen . . ."

"She knew," Adam interrupted. "She was blackmailing me. If her servant hadn't . . ." A nerve twitched in his cheek. "I thank God that it isn't me in Newgate."

Susanna crossed herself, feeling a little faint. This was what their affair had cost Adam. Because of her he had killed a man; he had almost been forced to kill a second time. The sheer horror of it swept over her and she knew that she could not tell him about their child, nor could she beg him to run away with her. She had already asked too much of him. For her sake he had committed a terrible sin. To ask for more would be unforgivable.

"I'm sorry," she said, her throat catching with emotion. "It was my fault . . ."

"Ah, no," he said gravely. "Promise me that you will not blame yourself, Susanna. The man was evil. He had no doubt destroyed many lives. You need not reproach yourself."

"It was of you I was thinking."

His smile was so tender then that it almost tore the heart

339

from her body. "I can bear it," he said. "It was the price I paid for knowing what was the greatest happiness of my life. Those few nights we had . . . they will live in my memory for always."

Looking up into his eyes, Susanna knew that it was over. He was saying goodbye.

"We shall never be lovers again, shall we?"

"I cannot desert my wife and child, even though I have never loved her," he said, a tiny nerve beating in his throat. "I thought perhaps I could, but . . ."

"I know." Susanna's voice was regretful but steadfast. "I could not leave Digby either. Beatrice hopes to be married next summer. If I caused a terrible scandal it would ruin her chances of happiness. So we have no choice . . ." Tears stung her eyes but she fought them back. "We never really had a choice, did we, Adam?"

For a moment he thought of the note in the secret drawer of the marriage chest. If she had found that before he was wed to Jane . . . The thought died unspoken. There was no point in telling her now. If she hadn't found the drawer before this, she probably never would. He had hidden it too well.

"I should go," he said. "I have much to do."

"Adam . . ." She took an involuntary step towards him, her eyes pleading.

A groan broke from him and he reached for her, drawing her into his arms to kiss her with hungry, bruising lips. Then, almost thrusting her from him, he turned and strode from the room without another word. For a moment Susanna stared at the closed door, then she sank to her knees, falling face down on the carpet as she wept the most bitter tears of her life.

CHAPTER NINETEEN

"You cannot mean it?" Lady Patricia looked at Susanna in disbelief. "Lord Farringdon wanted to marry her and she refused him! Is the girl mad?"

"She is in love with someone else," Susanna began. "She does not want to marry for money . . ."

"Ridiculous!" Lady Patricia interrupted, giving way to anger. "I shall write to Lord Farringdon and ask him to stay myself. Beatrice must be brought to her senses. I shall make her see where her duty lies . . ."

"That you will not do." Sir William spoke sternly from the doorway. "If Beatrice doesn't want to marry Farringdon she will not. She will not be starved or browbeaten into submission as Susanna was. I shall not allow you to ruin her life, too."

"Bravo, Papa," Susanna cried, then as she turned to look at her mother's startled face, "I brought Beatrice home, but if you are unkind to her, I shall take her to Surrey when I leave."

"I'm sure I have no intention of being unkind to her," Lady Patricia said. "I have never done anything that was not in my children's best interests."

"That may be your opinion, ma'am," Sir William said. "It is not mine." He glanced at Susanna. "You may safely leave your sister here. I shall see that she is not made unhappy."

His wife glared at him angrily. In the old days he had never dared to flout her wishes. For a moment she wanted to rage at him, then her shoulders sagged. What did any of it matter any more? She'd wanted to improve the estate for Stephen's sake, but Stephen was dead.

"Pray don't concern yourselves," she said acidly. "I wash my hands of the whole affair."

She turned and walked from the room, leaving the father and daughter together. Sir William heaved a sigh of relief, then smiled at Susanna.

"She is misguided sometimes, my dear, but not a bad woman. It was my fault for allowing her to have her way. I believe she will not try to bully Beatrice, but if she does I shall let you know. I'm getting old, Susanna. My health isn't what it was."

"Oh don't say that, dearest Papa," Susanna said, a little sob in her throat. She rushed to embrace him. "I love you. I always have . . ."

"Even after what I've done to you?" He was full of concern. "If Digby is unkind to you, I could have a word with him . . ."

"He is not unkind . . . or only now and then." Susanna turned away with a blush. If her husband was unkind in the future she would only have herself to blame. "Please say nothing, Papa. I would rather you didn't."

"Very well. But if you change your mind, you have only to write to me, Susanna."

"I believe I know how to manage Digby now," Susanna said. "And now if you don't mind, Papa, I shall tell Beatrice that she may write to John and ask him to stay . . ."

As she walked upstairs, Susanna felt a warm glow inside. If nothing else, she had achieved happiness for her sister, so perhaps all was not lost. For a moment her thoughts turned to Adam . . . What was he doing? Who was he with? Then she dismissed them. She must learn to forget. Adam had his own life and she could never be a part of it.

Adam looked at the man sitting opposite him in the coffee house. Captain Bridges was searching for capital for his latest venture: a cargo of spices and silk from the East.

"So, Mr Blackwell," Captain Bridges asked, "can I count on your support? My last trip made a fair profit and I'm reasonably certain that I shall double it this time."

"Then why do you need to raise more capital?"

"I've a large family to feed, sir, and a debt to pay. My wife's brother had some personal trouble. I raised a loan to help him and he went off to America, leaving me to repay the debt. It will take me at least two more trips like the last to pay it off."

"That's a frank answer," Adam said. "I like you, Captain Bridges. You're an honest man."

"Then will you put up at least a quarter of the capital? I can raise a quarter myself and I have hopes of two others."

The idea appealed to Adam. His business was gradually expanding, but this was a way of earning several thousand pounds in one go. There was a risk of course. The ship could sink in mid-ocean or Captain Bridges could run off with his capital and never come back. This last was the least likely. The man was solid as British oak, he'd lay his life on that. The problem was that to invest the sum Captain Bridges was asking for would mean asking Jane, something he was loath to do. Adam needed money from another source, a few hundred pounds that he could invest without involving his wife . . .

Suddenly, Adam remembered the Marquis's ring. He had no idea of its exact value, but it should fetch a hundred or two at the very least, perhaps a great deal more. The blood pounded at his temples as he felt a rising excitement. He would not need to tell Jane anything about his new venture. If he were lucky and the gamble came off, it would give him the chance of making something for himself. He vowed then and there that if he made a profit he would instantly reinvest it.

"Nothing ventured, nothing gained," he said aloud. "I'm not sure how much I can raise yet, Captain Bridges, but I've made up my mind to come in with you. And here's my hand on it."

He would be taking a risk in selling the ring, of course, as there was always a possibility that someone would recognize it. But now that Lady Munford was dead, he doubted if anyone really cared what had happened to the Marquis of Brandon. It was just the work of footpads, another robbery. Besides, the risk added spice to the whole thing. His life had become dull and he needed a challenge. He would choose the pawnbroker with care and he would give a false name, perhaps even disguise himself. It would be like in the old days, when he'd pitted his strength against other men in the wrestling ring, but now it would be a battle of wits.

Adam felt a tingle of apprehension as he went into the dim interior of the pawnbroker's shop. He was dressed in his wedding suit and he had donned a pair of Robert's gold-framed spectacles. On the third finger of his right hand, he was wearing the Marquis's ruby ring. His blood raced as he waited for the man to come through from the back of the shop.

"Ah, there you are, my good man," he said, imitating the manner of one of his most haughty customers. "I am in town for a few days and I find myself embarrassed. Perhaps you would care to offer for this ring?" He took it off and laid it on the counter.

"Ah yes, sir." The pawnbroker peered at him, then, seeming satisfied, asked, "What did you want for the ring? Was it a loan you were thinking of – or a sale?"

Adam appeared to consider for a moment, then, "I believe I shall sell it. It is not a trinket I care for. A bequest from my uncle. As to its price, that is a matter for you . . . though I know it to be valuable . . ."

"Indeed it is, sir." The pawnbroker thought quickly. It was obvious to him that the gentleman had lost money at the gaming tables. Whenever the aristocracy came to him for money it was always after a reckless night. If he cheated him and paid too little, he would be caught out should the customer decide to buy the ring back. It was always best to be as fair as possible, at least with gentry.

344

"I could offer you five hundred pounds, sir," he said at last. "I know you would have to pay much more to replace it, but I must make a profit after all."

Adam could hardly believe his ears. His impulse was to accept at once, but that might arouse suspicion. He pretended to think about it. "Could you not make it six hundred?" he asked.

"Well . . . perhaps another fifty pounds, sir. I couldn't manage the six, I'm afraid."

"No . . . Then perhaps . . ." Adam turned away, stopped and appeared to hesitate. "Very well, I shall accept. You can pay in gold . . . now?"

"Of course, sir. If you would care to wait a few moments."

As the man disappeared into the back once more, it was all Adam could do to contain his excitement. Five hundred and fifty pounds! It was a small fortune! He would invest every penny of it with Captain Bridges. Just as long as the pawnbroker didn't change his mind!

A short while later, Adam was walking up the street, the gold safely inside his breast pocket. He decided that he would take it straight to his new business partner . . . a business that would have nothing to do with his wife.

Jane had told him that she was once again with child. He would not cheat her of her rights; she would receive every penny he earned from the workshop, but all his energy, all his ambition would go into building an empire of which she knew nothing. And one day . . . one day he was going to be a very rich man. He felt it with an inner certainty that needed no logical explanation. It was simply going to happen.

For a moment the glow faded as he remembered what it had cost him. A desperate longing for Susanna swept over him and he felt he would give up everything just to hold her in his arms once more. But then he crushed the thought as foolish sentiment. He was a man of business. From now on he would make work his life. He would not give himself time to remember . . .

* * *

Susanna stared into the furious eyes of her husband. He had walked into her bedroom when she was standing in her petticoat, and she had been unable to conceal her condition. For a moment he was struck dumb, then he dismissed her maid with a curt command that sent the girl scurrying.

"Well, madam," he said when they were alone. "What have you to say to me? I hope you do not mean to pretend that the brat you have in your belly is of my getting?"

Susanna took a deep breath. "I believe that would be to insult both you and me, Digby. I shall not sink to that level."

"I am relieved to hear it." His voice was glacier cold. "Well, am I to be told the name of your lover?"

"He was not my lover," Susanna said. She had prepared for this moment through many sleepless nights and her eyes were deceptively clear and innocent as she lied. "The Marquis raped me. It was the afternoon that Helen insisted I take tea with her. When I arrived she wasn't there, but Brandon was waiting. The blinds were drawn and I could see nothing when I went in. He locked the door and then sprang on me. Afterwards, he swore that he would tell you I was willing. He said that if I told you the truth, he would challenge you to a duel and kill you – that's when I promised to meet him."

Digby weighed up Susanna's story. She seemed to be telling the truth, but he could not be sure. Susanna had changed. She was no longer the young, innocent girl he had married, but a sophisticated woman who might be quite capable of lying.

"How can I be sure this is true?" he asked.

"Speak to Helen's servants about that afternoon," Susanna challenged. "They will confirm that she was out and Brandon was in her apartments. I believe she accepted money from the Marquis. She once told me that I should take Brandon as a lover. She thought that he could teach me how to behave with lovers. When I was shocked and rebuked her, she plotted with him against me."

346

Digby nodded, convinced now that she was speaking the truth. He knew his sister's vindictive nature too well. "Helen never made any secret of the fact that she resented me because I inherited the family fortune. She would have liked to be a man."

"She disliked me because I disapproved of her friends."

"I was wrong to force you to visit her. If she were still alive I would not permit it to go on. In future I shall listen when you complain of unwanted attentions, Susanna."

"In future, Digby?" She looked at him warily. "Am I to think that you will continue to accept me as your wife?"

Digby was silent for a moment, then, "I have a dislike of being made to look ridiculous, Susanna. If I were to accuse you of bearing a bastard it would soon become common knowledge. I should not enjoy that. It was my hope that we would have a child . . ."

"Perhaps one day."

Digby shook his head. "I think not, my dear. It would be better for both of us if all that nonsense were to stop . . . So since I cannot father my own child, I may as well accept yours as my heir."

"Digby . . . " Susanna started towards him. "You are so generous . . ."

He put out his hand to hold her off. "Be warned, Susanna. I have accepted your story. Brandon is dead and can do no more harm. But if you were to have another child I should not be so easily convinced of your innocence."

Susanna's cheeks grew warm. Guilt struck at her, but she could not tell Digby the truth. His pride would allow him to accept her story because the Marquis was dead and it could not be disproved, but he would never accept what really happened. She lifted her eyes to his as she said, "I promise you there will not be another child, Digby."

"Then we shall remain friends," he said. "And now, Susanna, I have business to attend. I shall see you this evening."

As he went out, Susanna sat down in front of her

mirror and began to brush her hair. She stared at her reflection, acknowledging her own beauty but without vanity. It would be easy to find lovers, she thought. She could find ways of deceiving her husband and she knew there were devices she might use to ensure that she did not have another child, but she had given her promise to Digby and she would keep it. He could have exacted a cruel payment for her betrayal, but he had chosen to believe her. He had behaved with great restraint and she was grateful. Besides, there was only one man she had ever wanted.

Sighing, she laid down her hairbrush. The years seemed to stretch endlessly in front of her. Empty, sterile years that would bring her little happiness. For a moment she was unbearably sad and then she felt the child kicking within her. A deep warmth began to spread through her. Her life would not be empty after all. She would have Adam's child . . .

CHAPTER TWENTY

Susanna was amused as she read her mother's letter. Lady Patricia had been invited to stay with Beatrice at the Earl and Countess of Grafton's country home.

"I cannot say that I approve of your sister's choice," she had written. "However, the connection with the Earl of Grafton cannot be denied. I believe a little informal dance is to be held for Beatrice and Mr. Browne . . ."

So Beatrice's engagement was soon to be announced and there would be a wedding late in the summer. Laying down the letter with a sigh of content, Susanna pressed a hand to her aching back. Her child was due to be born any day now. She had grown weary of late, her body heavy and awkward in the last stages of pregnancy. She thought she might lie down on her bed for a while. As she reached the stairs, the first pain struck. It left her gasping and a little fearful. The moment she had both longed for and dreaded was here at last: her child was about to be born. Taking a deep breath, she continued walking upstairs to her bedchamber and rang for her maid.

Digby was somewhere in the north of England on business. She was glad that he would not be in the house to hear her screams. She had worried that in her agony she might call Adam's name aloud. It would be better if Digby were not here to hear it.

She turned in relief as Dulcia came in.

"I should like you to help me undress," she said calmly. "Then I think you had better send for the midwife."

Adam stirred with excitement as he listened to Captain Bridges's tale of a long successful sea journey.

"You made good time, sir," he said. "I had not expected you back for a month at least."

"We had fair winds, Mr Blackwell," Captain Bridges said. "Fortune smiled on us this trip. I think you'll be satisfied with your share of the profits." He took a heavy bag of gold coins and laid it on the table in front of Adam. "Twelve hundred guineas, sir, and more to come when I've sold the last of the silk."

"So I've more than doubled my money." Adam nodded and laughed. "That was a profitable voyage, Captain Bridges. When do you plan to leave again?"

"Within the month. Will you invest with me again, sir?"

"Take this and whatever remains of my share," Adam said. "I'll put up half the capital this time."

"And I the other." They looked at each other in mutual appreciation across the table and raised their tankards. "To another fair wind . . . and a continuing partnership, Mr Blackwell."

Susanna looked at the child in her arms. She had a daughter, a beautiful little girl. The birth had caused her a great deal of pain, since she had been in labour for many hours, but the memory of that agony was fading as she watched the child. Her little girl . . . and Adam's. She wished with all her heart that she could tell him, but she knew it would not be wise. Digby was being very indulgent and kind to her. She knew that he would enjoy showing off the child to his friends. She must do nothing that would endanger the future of her little girl.

As the nurse took the baby to tuck her safely in her cot, Susanna lay back and closed her eyes, dreaming lazily. What should she call her child? A succession of names went through her mind, before she settled on one that appealed to her.

Lavinia. She would call the girl Lavinia . . .

The baby had hair of a slightly darker gold than her mother and beautiful wide grey eyes. Eyes that reminded

350

Susanna of Adam. She sighed and stretched. The pain was over now and she had her child to love, a child who would always remind her of the man she still loved. Would always love, no matter what happened in the years ahead.

Lying there, half sleeping, half waking, Susanna wondered where Adam was and what he was doing. Was his business prospering? She hoped he would fulfil all the ambitions she knew were a large part of his life and somehow she was sure he would. Already, his name had become well known and over the years he would no doubt become famous and rich. If only they could have met then . . .

Yet even as she admitted that their love had always been doomed to end in sorrow, Susanna knew that she did not regret one moment she had spent in her lover's arms. The years might sometimes be lonely, but she would not be too unhappy. Now that Digby had finally accepted the situation between them, she believed they could be comfortable together. He would divide his time between the estate and his mills, and she would live in London, entertaining her friends and loving her child. She would spend the spring in the country and perhaps invite her sister and family to stay. Life would not be so very bad after all.

It was the summer of 1774. Susanna bent to lay the lilies on her father's grave. Her mother's letter had arrived too late for her to attend the funeral but she had come as soon as she could. Tears stung her eyes as she murmured her private farewell.

"Sleep well, Papa," she said. "I love you. I always loved you."

She stood up and turned to leave. Then she saw him standing at another newly dug grave. It was strange that Jeanie Blackwell and William Warwick should die on almost the same day. An act of Fate perhaps. Adam was staring at her as she walked towards him.

"Adam," she said and smiled. "I was sorry to hear about your mother."

"And I about your father," he replied, more shocked than he was prepared to admit by his reaction at seeing her again. The sun was turning her hair to spun gold, dazzling him. She looked like a goddess of ancient times, freshly sprung from the earth, more beautiful in her new maturity than he had ever seen her. He felt a swift, urgent surge of desire. Would she always have this effect on him? Would he never be free of her? He fought the urge to take her in his arms, his face grim as he suppressed his emotion. "But I suppose it was to be expected in both cases."

"Yes." Susanna caught her breath. Her knees were trembling and she longed to be in his arms. Resolutely, she fought her desire, appearing calm and remote as she said, "Yes, I expect it was."

"How is your mother?"

"Relieved to be a widow, I think. She talks of taking a house in town when her period of strict mourning is over. Beatrice is having her second child. She seems very happy and she grows prettier every time I see her."

Adam inclined his head. Susanna's beauty still had the power to stir him, but he was wiser now and he had too much to lose. His first two sea ventures had paid handsomely and he was expecting a rich reward from his latest investments. His disappointments in business at the start of his career had stood him in good stead. Now he had a reputation for always driving a hard bargain. No one would make a fool of Adam Blackwell again. He was beginning to amass a large fortune and he had taken in three young craftsmen to work under him. He was well on the way to the wealth he had craved.

It would be ridiculous to throw all that away because this woman made him weak inside. Of late he had taken to visiting Mary-Ellen Watts again. She satisfied his carnal needs now that Jane was once again with child and growing ever more difficult to please. Child-bearing did not suit her. He had decided that the third would be their last.

"I hear you have a daughter, Susanna?" he said to break the awkward silence.

Susanna smiled, the familiar warmth spreading inside her as she thought of Lavinia. "Yes," she said, her mouth soft with love. "A beautiful daughter."

"I have two sons, neither of whom is very attractive, though Robert's hair is less ginger than it was when he was born. They do nothing but scream and drive Jane mad. I hope our third child will be a girl. Perhaps she will not scream as much."

Susanna's heart did a wild dance. Dare she tell him the truth?

"Would you like a daughter, Adam?"

"One child is much like another," he replied with a shrug.

"Yes, I suppose so." Susanna hid her disappointment. It would mean nothing to him. She would keep her secret. "The news from America is bad, is it not? I think that we may lose this war. The loss of the colonies will be a serious blow."

Adam frowned, wondering why she had changed the subject so suddenly. "I tend to agree with you," he said. "But it was inevitable. You cannot dictate to men who have carved civilization out of a wilderness. The King and his ministers were fools . . . " He hesitated, then, "Will you come back to the house? I know my father would like to see you."

Susanna considered the idea, but shook her head. It was too much of a risk. Every moment she spent with him was weakening her resolve. "Digby wants to leave in an hour. Perhaps another time." She smiled and turned away.

Watching as she walked gracefully through the church-yard, her skirts swaying seductively, Adam felt a wave of regret rush over him. For a moment he was tempted to run after her and sweep her up in his arms. He felt the loneliness swirl inside him, twisting and maiming him so that he almost cried his agony aloud. His senses stirred as he smelt the perfume of her warm flesh again, recalling the fulfilment that only she had ever given him. He was back in the dimly lit chamber of an inn, and his heart cried out to her. How could he bear the empty years without her? She was the only woman he would ever love. He wanted her so desperately. Nothing really mattered except Susanna, he was ready to throw caution to the winds. But then sanity returned as he remembered all the reasons why he could not sweep her up in his arms and run off with her.

She was not for him. His path was set, as was hers. They belonged to different worlds. Their love was a dream they had both shared for one brief moment in time. As bright, brief and glorious as a comet streaking across the sky. Now it was over. She had her daughter, he his ambition. It was enough. It had to be.

EPILOGUE

Lavinia was ten years old. It was her birthday and she had been given lots of presents by both Mama and Papa, but what she wanted most had been denied her: she could not ride her new pony, because it was raining. She wandered disconsolately into her mother's bedroom. Mama was entertaining friends downstairs. Lavinia could join them, in the sure knowledge that she would be petted and made a fuss of, but she wanted to go riding.

For a moment she watched the rain beat against the window. It was pouring now and she knew she had no hope of being allowed down to the stables. Her gaze moved round the room, then fell on her mother's travelling cabinet. How she loved that cabinet with its many drawers. She loved to open them one by one and examine the contents. But the best thing of all was the drawers themselves. They were so pretty.

Papa had a similar cabinet in his room, but that wasn't quite as attractive . . . and it didn't have the little broken heart in the corner of one drawer. Lavinia wondered about that, why the cabinet-maker had put it there. Once she had asked her mother, but Mama only smiled with that sad look she had sometimes and shook her head.

Lavinia was drawn towards the cabinet. Mama had had it made for her marriage to Papa. She knew that because her Aunt Bea had told her so. Aunt Bea was so much fun, always laughing and happy, not like poor Mama. Lavinia sometimes wondered why her mother wasn't really happy, not in the way Aunt Bea was. Mama had so many pretty dresses and her aunt's were all old-fashioned, but she didn't seem to mind in the least. Of course, Mama always gave her some of hers when she came to stay.

Lavinia wandered over to the cabinet, and took the drawers out one by one. She laid them all side by side on the floor, then bent her head to see what the inside of the cabinet was like. She had always been curious about the way things were made. She liked shapes.

Seeing a little knob at the top of one of the hollows now visible, she pushed it idly with her finger. As she did so something popped out from the back and she realized it was a secret drawer. She had never found it before, though she'd taken out the drawers many times. Now she saw that the drawer with the broken heart was narrower than all the others. Why hadn't she seen that before? Perhaps she hadn't had them all on the floor at the same time.

She drew out the hidden drawer, her heart hammering in her chest. What was inside? As her fingers thrust excitedly they encountered a tiny scrap of paper. She took it out and saw that it was yellow with age. It must have been in there a long time. Unfolding it, she stared at the writing. The ink had faded but she could just make out the words.

"Why did you betray me?" she read. "I loved you so much, Susanna. I was ready to go with you to the ends of the earth. Why did you break my heart?"

"What have you got there?"

Lavinia flushed guiltily as she heard her mother speak from behind her. She held out the note, saying, "I found it in a secret drawer. I'm sorry, Mama. I didn't mean to pry."

Susanna read the note. For a moment her heart stood still. If she had found this when the chests were delivered . . . Before both she and Adam were married . . . For a moment the world span out of control and she felt faint.

Lavinia was on her feet, staring anxiously at her mother's white face. "I'm sorry, Mama. Are you ill?"

As the world steadied, Susanna shook her head. "No, I'm not ill, darling," she said. "Will you put this back where you found it please, and show me how it works."

Lavinia obliged with a willing eagerness. "See how well

it was hidden," she said. "You have to press your finger very hard."

"What an observant girl you are," Susanna said. "I didn't know it was there."

Lavinia stared at her. "Then . . . who put the letter there, Mama?"

Susanna looked into the eyes that were so like Adam's and hesitated. The time might come one day when she could tell Lavinia the truth, but it was not yet.

"One day," she promised, "one day perhaps I shall tell you . . . And now, my love, our guests are waiting . . ."

Putting her arm about her daughter's waist, Susanna led her downstairs. Later, when she was alone, she would read Adam's letter again – the note that could have changed the course of her destiny, if she had been as inquisitive as her darling daughter.

The Hawthorne Heritage
Teresa Crane

'A finely crafted romantic novel.' *Yorkshire Evening Post*

Jessica Hawthorne grows up a strange, isolated child in the sumptuous beauty of her family's home, Melbury New Hall, in 19th-century Suffolk.

Robert Fitzbolton, a young aristocrat, is the companion of her lonely childhood, her comfort through family tragedy and the heartache of young love.

But is the support of Robert's friendship enough? Locked together in a disastrous marriage, they flee to Florence for freedom and fulfilment.

Robert finds what he is seeking, but Jessica is a true Hawthorne and is drawn – inevitably – back to Melbury, to her destiny . . .

ISBN 0 00 617671 2

Rhanna
Christine Marion Fraser

A rich, romantic, Scottish saga set
on the Hebridean island of Rhanna

Rhanna

The poignant story of life on the rugged and tranquil island of
Rhanna, and of the close-knit community for whom it is home.

Rhanna at War

Rhanna's lonely beauty is no protection against the horrors of war.
But Shona Mackenzie, home on leave, discovers that the fiercest
battles are those between lovers.

Children of Rhanna

The four island children, inseparable since childhood, find that
growing up also means growing apart.

Return to Rhanna

Shona and Niall Mackenzie come home to find Rhanna unspoilt by
the onslaught of tourism. But then tragedy strikes at the heart of
their marriage.

Song of Rhanna

Ruth is happily married to Lorn. But the return to Rhanna of her
now famous friend Rachel threatens Ruth's happiness.

Storm Over Rhanna

The 'islanders' popular minister, Mark James, mourns the tragic
loss of his family, and turns to Doctor Megan Jenkins for comfort.
But Megan has a post from which she cannot escape.

'Full blooded romance, a strong, authentic setting.' *Scotsman*

Philippa Carr

Her bestselling *Daughters of England* series

THE MIRACLE AT ST BRUNO'S
THE LION TRIUMPHANT
THE WITCH FROM THE SEA
SARABAND FOR TWO SISTERS
LAMENT FOR A LOST LOVER
THE LOVE CHILD
THE SONG OF THE SIREN
THE DROP OF THE DICE
THE ADULTERESS
KNAVE OF HEARTS
VOICES IN A HAUNTED ROOM
THE RETURN OF THE GYPSY
MIDSUMMER'S EVE
THE POOL OF ST BRANOK
THE CHANGELING
THE BLACK SWAN
A TIME FOR SILENCE

HarperCollins Paperbacks – Fiction

HarperCollins is a leading publisher of paperback fiction. Below are some recent titles.

- ☐ THE SEVENTH WAVE Emma Sinclair £4.99
- ☐ IN NAME ONLY Barbara Wilkins £4.99
- ☐ SILK Nicola Thorne £4.99
- ☐ SEVEN FOR A SECRET Victoria Holt £4.99
- ☐ GOOD TIME GIRL Kate O'Mara £4.99
- ☐ A WOMAN UNDER SUSPICION Naomi Ragen £4.99
- ☐ TRESPASSING HEARTS Julie Ellis £4.99
- ☐ THE MARRIAGE CHESTS Anne Herries £5.99
- ☐ FORGIVING LaVyrle Spencer £4.99
- ☐ IMAGE OF LAURA Joy Martin £4.99

You can buy HarperCollins Paperbacks at your local bookshops or newsagents. Or you can order them from HarperCollins Paperbacks, Cash Sales Department, Box 29, Douglas, Isle of Man. Please send a cheque, postal or money order (not currency) worth the price plus 24p per book for postage (maximum postage required is £3.00 for orders within the UK).

NAME (Block letters)_____

ADDRESS_____

_____